DIAGNOSIS:

Deadly Conflict

HARRY NORTON—as a medical student and intern he had learned the rules . . . and lived by them to reap rich rewards. Then he went out on a limb to save a patient. Now he was getting burned—by his best friend.

MOE MICHENER—as a young doctor he was too rebellious for the hospital bureaucracy. He'd been bounced out of the profession fast. Now he was a big-time lawyer in malpractice, seeking revenge against all doctors—even Harry Norton.

KAREN MICHENER—as Karen Marshall she had become a first-rate doctor. She had loved Harry but married Moe. Now she was a woman caught in the middle in the brutal final innings of . . .

The Doctor Game

"A sturdily crafted book."—*The Kirkus Reviews*
"Gutsy . . . entertaining."—*Variety*

The Doctor Game

by

HOWARD A. OLGIN, M.D.

A Dell Book

For Aviva Bette Olgin and Liliane
with special thanks
to Joseph and Miriam Olgin
who made it all possible

Published by
Dell Publishing Co., Inc.
1 Dag Hammarskjold Plaza
New York, New York 10017

For information address J. B. Lippincott Company,
Publishers, New York, New York.
Dell ® TM 681510, Dell Publishing Co., Inc.

ISBN: 0-440-12006-3

Printed in the United States of America
Reprinted by arrangement with
J. B. Lippincott Company, Publishers.
First Dell printing—August 1979

CONTENTS

The Physician's Oath

I swear by Apollo Physician, by Asclepius, by Health, by Panacea, and by all the gods and goddesses, making them my witnesses, that I will carry out, according to my ability and judgment, this oath and this indenture. To hold my teacher in this art equal to my own parents; to make him partner in my livelihood; when he is in need of money to share mine with him; to consider his family as my own brothers, and to teach them this art, if they want to learn it, without fee or indenture ... I will use treatment to help the sick according to my ability and judgment, but never with a view to injury and wrongdoing. .... I will keep pure and holy both my life and my art. .... In whatsoever houses I enter, I will enter to help the sick, and I will abstain from all intentional wrongdoing and harm, especially from abusing the bodies of man or woman, bond or free. And whatsoever I shall see or hear in the course of my profession in my intercourse with men, if it be what should not be published abroad, I will never divulge, holding such things to be holy secrets. Now if I carry out this oath, and break it not, may I gain forever reputation among all men for my life and for my art; but if I transgress it and forswear myself, may the opposite befall me.

—HIPPOCRATES (c. 460–400 B.C.)

PROLOGUE

"This will not be the usual bullshit speech of welcome, men. I want you to all know very clearly what lies ahead.

"From the minute you entered this medical school, from this very day on, through your internship and whatever specialty training you may take, and into private practice or research, nobody's going to give you anything free. . . .

"It's a battlefield out there. You'll need a suit of armor to survive in the doctor game. A suit of white armor. With it, you will hopefully become good physicians. Without it, God help all of you. . . ."

Harry Norton heard only part of the dean's thundering tones that greeted his medical school class on the first day. He thought he had entered the army recruiting station by mistake. The forms and paperwork alone were overwhelming. Did the dean want his last name first or his first name last on the admission forms? And what about his middle initial?

Harry looked over at the fellow next to him. He seemed to know what he was doing. He had even volunteered to hand out and collect all the papers for the dean. . . .

"Michener, Moe W., Yale University. Major: Bi-

ology . . ." his form said, and Harry had his answer.
It was last name first.

He looked down at his own set of credentials.
"Norton, Harold M., Princeton University. Major:
Philosophy. Senior thesis: 'The Existence of God as
Analyzed by David Hume.' Graduated cum laude;
junior varsity baseball. . . ."

Harry thought about that for a moment. Well, they
had scrimmaged with the varsity . . . and he *had* sat
on the bench for the Harvard game. He quickly
crossed out the word "junior" and read it again.
There. ". . . varsity baseball." It looked much better
now—in fact, just as good as Michener's papers. But
why did Michener look so sure of himself, and why
was he scared to death?

There were so many things he had to decide. Which
anatomy book to buy for the next day, Gray's or
Grant's. Grant's had more pictures, but somebody
said Gray's was deeper in detail. Maybe he should
get both. And which dissecting kit, the one with three
scalpels or two? Which microscope? Everything was
so damned expensive!

Harry glanced over at Michener's desk again.
Michener had already taken *Gray's Anatomy,* and the
large dissecting kit with three knives. He figured he
had better do the same.

He thought over the list of bills he was accumulating. Tuition, $1,500. Books and instruments, another
$500, even if he got them secondhand. And his apart-
ment, and some furniture, and food . . . it would all
cost. And he still hadn't paid off anything on his
Princeton loan.

Well, Harry knew where he could pick up a complete set of used books and a secondhand microscope
at a bargain. Morris would be glad to sell him his stuff

real cheap. Morris, who had also majored in philosophy . . . and had dropped out of medical school last year after only three months.

Morris's psychiatrist had called it a mild nervous breakdown brought on by the stress of dissecting out the groin of his cadaver in anatomy lab. Morris was enrolled in the graduate school of languages now. He seemed much happier.

Harry glanced at the girl on his other side. "Marshall, Karen A., UCLA. Major: Biology . . ." Another one! She was too gorgeous to have majored in biology, much less to be studying medicine. Yet even she seemed to know what she was doing.

Did he really want all of this? Harry wondered. Another four years of being a student? Of debts? Of skimping? Would he be selling his books to the incoming class a year from now?

Was it going to be any different for him? He and Morris both came from the same mold. They both knew a shitload of stuff about the Age of Reason and empiricism . . . and Plato . . . and pragmatism . . . and even God. And Morris had gone off his nut in three months here!

And what about Reality . . . and Truth . . . and Beauty? Harry looked around at Moe Michener. How was his four years of studying about those things helping him here today?

Harry remembered his final exam in Philosophy of Art. "The beauty in the above picture," his professor had written, "is (a) in your eyeballs, (b) in the work of art itself, or (c) somewhere in between." Harry had checked off (c), but (a) turned out to be the answer.

"Your eyeballs, Norton. Your eyeballs, boy!" the professor had pointed out, touching Harry's face admiringly. "You don't have much appreciation for the philosophy of art, but what a color in your face! What a suntan!"

Harry suddenly realized why Michener and Marshall and the others were so confident. Advanced biology! Anatomy! Biochemistry! Those bastards had all majored in science. They knew this stuff cold, even before classes began. He and Morris had been advised to take only the four minimum basic science courses. To be well rounded. Hell! His professors at Princeton had all lied. In theory, he and Morris didn't need to major in a science, they had said. In theory, he and Morris wouldn't wind up reading comic books at age fifty for relaxation. They would be the modern, well-rounded doctors of tomorrow, interesting to talk to at cocktail parties, leaders of their communities. Well rounded, hell! He and Morris had been unprepared! Why the hell hadn't he concentrated on a science? Why hadn't he been smart, like Michener?

The trouble was that even Harry's four basic premedical courses had been tough for him. He still remembered his burned fingertips in chemistry lab every Tuesday morning. And the swinging pendulum experiments in physics lab. The long endless afternoons measuring the arc, the amplitude, and the angle of that damned thing as it swung from the ceiling. The nights spent charting it out on graphs and papers.

And he remembered his struggles in biology. The hours of lectures and scribbled notes on life in a South American rain forest: how the trees and plants and animals lived there, how they struggled for sunshine and water, how the animals fucked and ate and killed each other, how their shit turned into nitrogens, which went back into the air and the earth, and nourished everything anyway. . . .

"Memorize these principles," the biology instructor had said, "and you'll all be better doctors someday."

Harry remembered asking his premedical adviser about it. What did it all have to do with becoming a doctor? Should he be concerned that he was only an average student in the lab? Should he go into philosophy, or business, or something else?

"An easy decision," the adviser had said. "It's simply a matter of economics. An average doctor eats very well. An average philosopher doesn't. Any further questions?"

At the time it had seemed to make sense. He had already suffered through the swinging pendulum and the South American rain forest. He had already burned his fingers in chemistry class. He deserved something in return.

As he sat listening to the dean's opening remarks, Harry was terrified. He knew he wasn't exactly plunging into medicine with a wild-eyed enthusiasm. He was sort of backing into it . . . cautiously . . . with one foot in the door, ready to turn and run.

He had to develop the assurance that Moe Michener seemed to have. That Karen Marshall seemed to have.

Harry put down his pen and looked at Karen. She gave him a cold, icy glance. At that, he started to turn away but then decided to break the ice some way.

He smiled his most ingratiating smile and spoke. "Who's the enemy?"

Karen Marshall was startled. "Pardon?"

"The old man says we're going into battle, but he hasn't told us who the enemy is."

Harry could see right off she didn't have much of a sense of humor. She didn't even smile at his remark, but said softly, "The enemy is disease; isn't that pretty obvious?"

But, once the ice was broken, Harry wasn't to be put off. "To hear the old man talk, the enemy is the patients—or the other doctors."

Karen Marshall scowled at him and put an index finger to her lips. Obviously, she thought the old man was worth listening to. Harry decided to pretend he was interested as well, but he was still shaking.

And what about tomorrow? Would he be able to stand it when he saw his first dead body? Would he throw up like the dean said someone did last year? Or pass out? Why was he so damned nervous anyway? Why wasn't he calm like Michener and Marshall?

Medical battleground? Suit of white armor? Doctor game? The dean's words buzzed through Harry's brain. At the time he didn't realize what was ahead, that the swinging pendulum and the South American rain forest were only the beginning. At the time, he was too confused and busy to understand what the dean was trying to say. . . .

PART ONE

Whipple

1 THOSE STUDENT DAYS

1964, Philadelphia

During the third year of medical school, when the students had their first glimpse of real patients during their emergency-room rotation, mistakes were difficult to hide.

In classes, Harry noticed, Moe Michener had always tried every trick he could to be noticed and praised. To emphasize how important he considered the professor's words in microbiology class, he'd tried to take down every sentence. Although Moe's notes were always four pages longer than everyone else's, his compulsive nature wasn't satisfied. He went out and bought a tape recorder, and taped every lecture from then on.

Whenever a volunteer was called for, Moe would always be the first on his feet, even though it usually ended in disaster for him.

It was Moe who offered to have a big rubber tube passed from his nose into his stomach to demonstrate the collection of acid in the clinical lab class. He had gagged and retched for twenty minutes, but finally swallowed the tube. After the test Moe had looked very pale. He was sent off to the hospital infirmary and given the day off.

And it was Moe again who had volunteered his body for a chest tap, to show a group of students in pulmonary medicine how to stick a needle into a lung cavity. This time the demonstrator happened to poke him on the wrong side of the rib, where the blood vessels lie. Moe coughed and moaned a lot while the teacher tried to put pressure on the large hematoma that appeared on Moe's chest. He had a swollen black-and-blue mark the size of a grapefruit for the next two months to remind him of that one.

Harry didn't know whether Moe was just aggressive by nature, whether he really had a burning desire to help out, or whether he just plain enjoyed suffering. Or maybe he was just scared, like the rest of the third-year students, green and anxious about their new world of needles and tubes and proctoscopes and patients. Harry concluded that Moe just wanted to be noticed, and that was his reason for stepping into the limelight so often.

Harry had suspected that at least some of Moe's showing off was for the benefit of Karen Marshall. Because of the alphabetical proximity of their names, the three of them—Karen Marshall, Moe Michener, and Harold Norton—had been thrown together almost constantly. From the first day of school, they had been seated together in classes; they had worked the emergency room together; and later they had made rounds in the same units. And from the very first day, it had been obvious that Moe had been more than just casually interested in Karen.

Harry had felt an attraction for Karen, too, and for a while the two young men had competed for her attention. She *was* beautiful—tall and leggy. But Harry seemed to find soft, defenseless women the most attractive, while Karen had always tried to play down her femininity.

This never seemed to bother Moe. To the contrary, it had seemed to make him try even harder to impress Karen with his own abilities, his own toughness.

However, his efforts had always seemed to come off—at least to Harry—as somewhat less than successful.

Harry still remembered Moe's first proctoscopy. The patient had been a middle-aged woman who had asthma and was slightly on the heavy side. She had been suffering from rectal bleeding for a year, and her decision to check in at the emergency room had been prompted by a large amount of bright red blood in her stool that day.

"I . . . I hope it isn't cancer," she had wheezed, as O'Hara, the intern, began to examine her. He had asked Harry and Moe to help him get the patient onto the table. (They had done so with some effort.)

"Don't worry," O'Hara assured her. "We've got to look up there with this little tube."

"Up there" was at least twelve inches into the patient's rectum. "This little tube" was a solid steel proctoscope with a light on the end. O'Hara was planning to ram it up her ass.

With the help of Harry and Moe, he got the woman into position, on her knees and elbows, leaning forward and facing the wall. Only her giant nude behind had peeked through at them from under a mountain of drapes.

As O'Hara was about to insert the proctoscope, a nurse on the other side of the draperies had screamed, "Two drug overdoses! Hurry, Dr. O'Hara!"

O'Hara had turned to Moe. "Just stick it in and I'll be right back." He handed Moe the metal tube and disappeared.

Moe stood there for a moment, not knowing what to do. Neither he nor Harry had ever done a proctoscopy.

The woman let out a grunt. Moe took a deep breath, told her to relax, and gently touched the metal instrument to her skin.

"Ouch!" she cried. "Oh, Doctor! I can't stand it!"

"It's not in yet," Moe reassured her.

The patient calmed down, and he continued, slowly sliding the proctoscope into the dark hole. At about four inches it ran into something solid. Moe had tried to push the scope past it, but it wouldn't budge. The patient was moaning, and Moe was afraid to force it farther, so he looked through to the lighted end. What he saw was a firm, smooth, pinkish mass.

He had turned to Harry and whispered, "I . . . I think it's a tumor."

Harry had taken a look into the scope, and he saw the same solid lump. "My God, it is a tumor. And it must be enormous."

While Harry rushed out to try to get O'Hara or another of the interns, the woman grunted again. "Doctor, is it finished yet? I'm getting nauseous."

"Only a few more minutes," Moe assured her. "We've got to get another doctor to have a look."

Harry came back without O'Hara, but Karen Marshall was with him.

While Karen looked into the proctoscope, Harry explained to Moe that the emergency room was overloaded and it would be a few minutes before O'Hara could get there.

Karen looked up from the proctoscope and grinned wryly at Moe. She moved away from the patient and Moe followed her, wondering what was so funny about cancer of the rectum.

"Wrong hole, guy," she murmured. "You put the proctoscope in her vagina. May I remind you that a female has two possibilities there."

Karen pulled the proctoscope out of the vagina and reinserted it properly. "Now for the second part of the procedure," she announced to the patient.

With one smooth motion, she slipped the scope to

the hilt, looked through it, and then took it out, announcing to a perplexed Moe, "Perfectly normal, as far as I can see, except for a few hemorrhoids."

That had been a harmless little mistake, compared to others. The thing that had really scared the shit out of Moe Michener and Harry had been the doctor heart stat. When O'Hara first mentioned it to the students, none of them had ever heard of the term.

"Many patients are going to come into the emergency room and drop dead," he had said. "And that means a 'doctor heart stat,' which is the code name for a cardiac arrest. If someone's heart stops beating anywhere in the hospital, just scream it out. The page operator will blast it into every area. It's the most serious of all emergencies. Only the doctors and nurses know the code. You have to hustle when you hear it, and when you get there, you can't stand around with your finger up your ass. . . . Excuse me, Miss Marshall, but we're all doctors here."

Karen had smiled at O'Hara to show that she was not offended.

"Now, let's go over what to do. First, establish an adequate airway. The patient must breathe. Next, closed-chest cardiac massage. Third, a good intravenous line. . . ."

They all busily jotted down O'Hara's points, all of them wondering how they could ever translate them into action.

"Now, remember, in pounding on the chest, you must be firm. A few cracked ribs are nothing to worry about."

The first of the students to be faced with a doctor heart stat was Moe. A nurse came hurrying up to him in the hall, explaining, "The ambulance brought a man in a minute ago. Found him on a curb. I don't know whether to call a doctor heart stat or label him dead on arrival. He's in Room One."

Both Moe and Karen hurried into Room One to see a large, sixtyish man with a very gray look to his face. Moe quickly checked for his pulse, listened at his chest, opened his eyelids, tried the EKG. The man certainly looked dead—cold and lifeless and staring. The EKG showed just a flat line. And there was no blood pressure.

Moe was tempted to pound on the chest—but he was scared. The nurse was watching. And Karen was watching. Finally, he shook his head at the nurse— "Dead on arrival"—and signed the death certificate.

"Wait." Karen moved decisively over to the man, raised her fist, and with half-closed eyes, punched the poor dead bastard in the center of the chest.

"What?" Both Moe and the nurse were astounded that Karen had so much strength in her. "What the hell?"

"Step two," she gasped, rubbing her sore knuckles. "Closed-chest massage."

Suddenly the nurse screamed. "Doctor, Doctor . . . he just moved. And the EKG isn't flat anymore!"

Indeed, the patient—still icy cold and a ghastly shade of gray—actually moved one arm and groaned. And the EKG did show blips and curves. He was alive. Karen had brought him back!

Moe wasn't quite as enthusiastic. "Oh, shit," he groaned, trying to hide his signed copy of the death certificate as the nurse rushed into the hall, shouting, "Doctor heart stat! Doctor heart stat!" Within seconds the room was a madhouse of activity. There were so many doctors and interns around the body, neither Moe nor Karen—nor Harry, who had come after the call—could get near enough to watch. They brought the patient's pressure back to normal and wheeled him off to the intensive care unit.

"Damn it," O'Hara chided, tearing up the paper Moe had been concealing behind his back. "A medical student can't sign a death certificate, anyway. But you should at least know whether a patient is alive."

"Don't be so quick to sign him off," Buxbaum, the chief surgeon, added. "Dead is dead. No movement. No nothing. If you're still not sure, read up on it at home. And by the way, good work, Marshall!"

For the next few weeks Moe looked at Karen with a certain sense of awe and anger. He walked around with a slight twinge of guilt that he had so easily written off a human life. And he couldn't help regarding Karen Marshall as the villain who had punched a dead man in the chest just to get him, Moe, into trouble.

Aside from the proctoscopies and the doctor heart stats, the third-year students were constantly faced with the formal ritual of the H and P, the history and physical exam.

In theory, this was supposed to be a smooth affair. First CC (Chief Complaint), or *why* the patient was being seen, followed in an orderly fashion by the HPI (History of Present Illness), ROS (Review of Systems), FH (Family History), and SH (Social History). In theory, this was to lead smoothly into the physical exam, then to the doctor's diagnosis and treatment. But it never seemed to work out quite that way—and Moe wasn't always the one to blame.

Mrs. Bartholemew, an obese black lady, came through the emergency-room doors screaming and dragging her nine-year-old boy, one Monday morning, and bumped directly into Karen Marshall.

"My boy! My boy!" she cried. "H—he's caught his gentiles in his zipper!"

Karen was caught slightly off guard.

"Y—you mean, his genitals?" she asked, as a nurse rushed Mrs. Bartholemew and her wailing son into a room.

"Yes! Yes!" screamed the woman over the hysterical sobbings of her son. "His gentiles! He's caught his gentiles!"

With the patient lying on the table in agony, Karen proceeded with her formal H and P, as she jotted down, "Chief Complaint: patient caught genitals in zipper." She was through the HPI and into Review of Systems when O'Hara came into the room.

"Did your son ever have measles?" Karen asked, as O'Hara stared in amazement at the sobbing mother and son.

"No, no, Doctor, no measles. . . . Please—"

"How about mumps or chicken pox?"

"Goddamn it!" O'Hara roared, grabbing scissors from the nurse. He hacked across the bottom of the zipper and pulled it apart, freeing the boy's pinched flesh.

"Just have him soak it in warm soap and water for two or three days," O'Hara told Mrs. Bartholemew. He was glaring at Karen. "We'll see him back in the clinic on Wednesday."

Turning to Karen in the hallway, O'Hara grumbled, "Be a little practical, Marshall! Damn! That kid's schlong is caught in a zipper, and you're asking him if he's ever had measles. Damn!"

O'Hara stormed on to the next disaster, leaving Karen Marshall to contemplate her unfinished H and P: "Chief Complaint: patient caught genitals in zipper. . . ."

* * *

Harry was not immune from the early student-day disasters, either.

One of Harry's unhappiest blunders had involved an emergency patient with the implausible name of Chester Lee Butterfield. On a particularly busy night in the emergency room, O'Hara announced to Harry, "There's a guy in Room Three with a knife up his ass."

Harry got Chester Lee Butterfield's history from a cop.

"Is he under arrest?" Harry asked.

"We need to question him," the cop returned, "but we'll wait till you people get through with him. He's a big pimp who likes flashy clothes. Stabbed by another pimp. One of Butterfield's girls called emergency."

When Harry entered Room Three to look at the patient, Butterfield was lying placidly on the table, face down. He was wearing a bright red vest with an even louder orange tie. He was stripped from the waist down, and protruding from his right buttock was the bright ivory handle of a knife.

"There's no telling how deep the knife goes," O'Hara mused aloud. "He'll need exploration to make sure the bowel's not cut." He went to the phone and called for Buxbaum, the chief surgeon.

Harry proceeded to take Butterfield's H and P. "What happened?" he began, trying to look the patient in the face. Chester Lee Butterfield was surprisingly cheerful for someone in his condition.

"Got cut a bit, is all."

Harry was puzzled, as he wrote down the chief complaint. "Just that, you got cut a bit. Who did it?"

"Dunno, Doc."

Harry rambled through a quick "H," and then asked the patient to turn over so he could begin the "P."

"Hunh?" Chester Lee looked at him in disbelief. "With a knife in my ass, Doc?"

Harry blushed and qualified his request. "Just turn over on your side and unbutton your shirt."

With some painful effort, the large patient managed to roll onto his side and unbutton his vest and shirt.

Examining the chest and stomach, Harry inquired, "What are these scars?"

Chester Lee smiled faintly, with a trace of pride. "Ain't the first time I was nicked. This scar here," he pointed out with a trace of pride, "San Francisco, 1968. A warehouse—you might say I got those duds wholesale! And this one, San Diego, 1972—a real mean set of loafers and three suits, two pairs of pants, and shirts . . . and . . ."

He grinned again, showing a gold tooth among the pearly whites. "You see, the trouble is, I like nice clothes. Best way to get 'em is to peddle ass. That c'n get to be rough."

Harry Norton noticed the chief surgeon arrive in the emergency room, so he decided to go in and observe the examination. From all appearances, Chester Lee wasn't injured too badly. There was some blood present on rectal examination; and on proctoscopy, the bowel looked frayed and bleeding.

To Harry and Moe, Dr. Buxbaum's examination of the patient was impressive—quick, efficient, and knowledgeable. Both wondered if they would ever possess the skill the chief surgeon evidenced. To compound their awe, Buxbaum *looked* like a doctor—tall and thin, with dark hair graying at the temples. Outside the hospital, he dressed in the most elegant and expensive clothes—Gucci shoes, a Cartier tank watch, tailor-made suits. He drove a Jaguar. He had been married and divorced three times and seemed to be headed toward the altar for a fourth.

Buxbaum acted and talked like Harry thought a surgeon ought to. He was always rubbing expensive creams and lotions on his hands. "Got to protect and lubricate those golden digits," he would say. "Like money in the bank, boy, like money in the bank."

Moe thought that all Buxbaum's emotional energy was wrapped up in his surgery. Cutting out cancer, sewing vessels together, removing blood clots—that was his life. A leaking bowel anastomosis was of greater concern to Buxbaum than an unhappy wife. It was a more personal thing.

Buxbaum's descriptions of the opposite sex were classics around the hospital. Harry heard two of them during a hernia operation and passed the news on to Moe.

"Can you imagine!" Harry gasped. "Dr. Buxbaum told everyone at the operating table that his third wife was a lousy lay. Right in the middle of a hernia repair. I mean, he was actually tying off the hernial sac when he said it. The scrub nurse almost turned purple. And then Buxbaum added, 'On a more *personal level,* her fried chicken wasn't very good either.' Before the scrub nurse could recover, Dr. Sims says, 'That new nurse I saw you with, Buxbaum, tough, real tough. Legs that never seemed to end.'

"'They ended,' Buxbaum said, and he and Sims roared their heads off while the scrub nurse nearly went catatonic."

"The wound doesn't seem to be serious," Buxbaum announced casually, over Chester Lee, "but there is the possibility that the knife might have cut through the bowel. I think we'd better take him up to the operating room for exploration."

He had obviously noted the effect he had on the two students, because he added, "And you two can come along to observe."

With some elation, the two students followed the chief surgeon upstairs. They were to witness their first major surgery. Excitedly they followed the chief surgeon into the locker room and changed into the regulation pants and shirts, covering their hair and shoes with the disposable paper covers. If their garments had not been a dull gray, and had not been so wrinkled, they might have felt they were children getting ready for a birthday party.

Buxbaum finished suiting up quickly and hurried out to scrub in. Both Harry and Moe had difficulty tying all the strings in place, so they had to hurry to catch up.

They tried to keep up with Buxbaum at the sinks but the surgeon was too fast for them; by the time their hands were in the water, Buxbaum had moved into the operating room.

They tried to follow his every move but found it impossible. Harry could not hear what was being said in the operating room, but he craned his head to see. What he saw was Chester Lee Butterfield, now divested of his finery, lying on the operating table, being connected to the intravenous by the anesthesiologist, while the scrub nurse gestured vaguely at the ivory-handled knife, still sticking from the large dark buttock.

With what seemed like a laugh, Buxbaum reached over and pulled the instrument out and surveyed the long bloodstained blade.

Harry felt an almost weightless sensation in his stomach and a feeling of light-headedness. Quickly he turned back to see Moe Michener all suited up and ready to go inside. He started to follow, but Moe quickly pointed out, "You've forgotten your mask."

Harry turned beet red. He hurriedly got one of the little plastic masks and adjusted it uncomfortably over his nose and mouth. Because of his mistake, he now had to scrub again.

By the time he finally arrived at the operating table, he could see a trace of annoyance in the dark eyes of Dr. Buxbaum. Chester Lee had been turned over and the scrub nurse had already finished shaving his body from ribs to groin. The patient was now completely under the anesthesia. When Harry had taken his history and physical, the black man had seemed so big and tough, more than a little intimidating. Now he lay on his back on a table, totally naked, totally relaxed, and totally helpless. Without the flashy personality, Chester Lee Butterfield might as well have been a sleeping dog or cat, or a specimen under a microscope.

"Look at the size of the prick," Moe whispered nervously to Harry. "The Foley catheter is sure going to smart when he wakes up."

"Enormous!" Harry echoed weakly. "And he's asleep, too. Imagine when he's excited! Somebody's missing a good friend tonight!"

"Goddamn it! Come on. Let's get ready and cut!" Buxbaum brought the two out of their fantasies and back to the room.

The operating room had a quality of unreality about it. It was mechanical and modern, with its bright lights and the organized clutter of various boxes and containers on shelves. And the human figures that moved about the room, hidden behind their gray masks and gowns, seemed mechanical, devoid of personality. The movements and actions of the anesthesiologist and the scrub nurse seemed particularly mechanical. The only thing that *looked* human to Harry was the large bare body lying on the table in the middle of the room, but that body seemed to have had all life drained from it, at least temporarily.

And that touch of humanity would soon disappear as well. Gradually, one sheet at a time, the nurses began to screen off everything that was visible of Chester Lee—except his belly. The most dramatic screen was the one that would shield his face from the view of everyone except the anesthesiologist.

Harry tried to stand well out of the way of the chief surgeon, but Buxbaum's eyes seemed to encompass everything in the room.

"No, boy, stand over here—close by the table—so you can see everything."

Reluctantly, Harry moved over to stand next to Moe Michener, looking straight down at the lower portion of Chester Lee's belly.

Taking the surgical knife in his gloved hand, Buxbaum announced, "Now, boys, we're going to have to go into the peritoneal cavity to have a look at the large intestine."

In one great sweeping movement, Dr. Buxbaum pulled the knife against the soft pliable skin, cutting a shallow incision from the rib cage down, around the navel, and to the groin. With another swift slash along the incision, he was completely through the skin and fatty tissue. In contrast to the monochrome of the surroundings, the layers of flesh were brilliant with color.

"Wow!" Moe exclaimed, elbowing Harry.

Buxbaum looked up, acknowledging the appreciative audience. "Big surgeons make big incisions," he announced proudly and returned his attention to the patient.

Harry wondered why they didn't install air conditioning in the operating room. Suddenly the place seemed awfully warm and stuffy. And the tight plastic mask wasn't helping the situation either. He had the urge to move his hand to lift the mask slightly, but checked it.

Buxbaum pulled back the skin and fascia to reveal Chester Lee's dull-colored guts. Beginning with his index and middle fingers, he shoved his entire hand into the belly.

The heat in the room was beginning to get to Harry. Beads of sweat were breaking out on his forehead, and he was finding it more and more difficult to breathe.

Harry could see slight bulges in the flesh, indicating that Buxbaum's fist was moving about inside—first in the vicinity of the ribs, then around the navel, and finally for a prolonged period around the groin.

Harry tried to check a slight twinge of nausea.

Buxbaum grunted. "Humph, there doesn't seem to be anything in the region to suggest that the knife wound went into the colon. No bleeding. No swelling. No spilling of fecal matter."

He looked up at Michener's eager eyes. "How would you like to have a feel, boy?"

Moe responded eagerly, stuffing his hand inside the belly much the way he had seen Buxbaum do it. After a few significant grunts and nods of his head, Moe suddenly piped up, "I think the bowel was perforated."

"Why?" Buxbaum asked curiously.

"I smell gas," Moe said.

"That was me, son," Buxbaum replied evenly.

Moe and the scrub nurse reddened while Buxbaum turned to Harry. "How about you?"

Harry took a deep breath and extended his hand into the opening. He felt around the organs, but everything felt the same to him, like the inside of a slosh bucket—wet, warm, and bulky. He desperately tried to remember his anatomy book, his cadaver, anything. Where the hell were the liver and the gallbladder? And the goddamn small intestine? And the cecum and the spleen?

And how the hell could he keep down the nausea when he couldn't breathe?

He removed his hand and tried to shrug nonchalantly. "Nothing," he said weakly.

Air. He needed air.

Swiftly, Harry reached his clean hand up to his mask and pulled it slightly away from his chin so he could gulp air. He was beginning to feel faint, sweaty, and nauseous, all at the same time.

Even with the mask removed a fraction from his face, Harry felt sick. He had to get air—but no matter how hard he heaved in and out, he couldn't fill his lungs. Through blurred eyes, he saw Dr. Buxbaum take a large fishhook needle with blue thread and begin to sew up the long incision.

Harry knew he was sick. He desperately tried not to think of what he was seeing. He tried to tell himself that Chester Lee Butterfield was just a fish—a very large fish—and that this whole experience had nothing at all to do with real, living, breathing people. But that was worse. He could not dismiss the image of a very large, naked black man, with an enormous penis, dangling from the end of a fishing line.

He felt it coming and tried to stuff his hand between his mask and his mouth. But it didn't help. He puked.

As he began to heave, he turned away, so that none of the vomit flowed into the patient's intestines, but it was so close, Buxbaum and Moe and the nurses stared at Harry in shock and amazement. Buxbaum stopped his sewing to snap at Harry.

"Thanks for turning away. A few inches closer and you would have all but killed the patient."

Harry was now able to speak. "I'm sorry, Dr. Buxbaum," he mumbled.

Chester Lee Butterfield had survived. Dr. Buxbaum no doubt had long ago forgotten the incident—though Harry had been clumsier about it than some, he was not unique; there were always a few third-year students with queasy stomachs. But Harry had blushed about it for a long time.

2 HERMAN WEXLER

November 15, 1975, Encino

Los Angeles was hidden in the morning haze, but Herman Wexler knew it was there; he could conjure up its skyline in his memory. He had been in Valley View Hospital for three weeks, and he had spent many hours looking out the window of the third-floor lounge, anxiously wondering when he would be able to move about again in the life that he could only observe now from the sidelines.

But that feeling of anxiety was a familiar one to him. For so many years—how many he couldn't count —he had realized that getting anywhere as a writer was just beyond his grasp. He had sacrificed his days and nights for well over thirty years on the butcher block of responsibility and obligation. He had postponed his own aspirations day by day to enable those he loved—his wife and his children—to have a better chance at their hopes and dreams. He had looked forward to the day when he could retire—at age sixty-five—with a pension. Then he would be able to try for what he had always wanted, an opportunity to prove that Eric Hoffer was not the only longshoreman who could attain distinction.

That day had arrived just five months ago. And, as if to confound him, he had had less than two weeks to himself before the pains had hit, before he had to give himself over into the hands of doctors for the endless tests and examinations.

Herman wasn't sure which had made his life more unbearable these past months—the constant, stabbing pain in his belly or the indecisive, swarmy, mealy-mouthed doctors who had hemmed and hawed over "being absolutely sure" and needed confirmation from lab reports, first one test and then another. Herman Wexler thought he knew what he had. His wife Miriam thought she knew what he had. It was the Big C—cancer. This new young generation of doctors was just too damned dependent on machines and microscopes. While they fussed and fidgeted around, playing their little games in the laboratories, their patients were allowed to suffer and even die.

But finally Herm had found a doctor who seemed to know what he was doing. Herm's first reaction had been that Dr. Norton was too young to know much; he seemed fresh out of college. Norton was exactly the kind of son Herm Wexler would have liked to have had—decisive, self-assured, confident, outgoing, sympathetic, understanding—totally unlike the sissified mama's boy who was Herm's son.

Although Dr. Norton had ordered tests, just like all the other doctors, he had admitted from the start that cancer was a possibility. He had laid everything right up front, and Herm respected that. When Norton had determined that the only way of being sure was an exploratory operation, he had been direct and honest about the chances of success or failure. The odds had been pretty high that Herm wouldn't even survive the operation.

But here he was—up on his feet and walking around the hospital. And, except for the pain and itching of the incision, Herm felt better than he had felt in almost a year. That is, he had until today, when he had felt another kind of pain in his stomach. But the doctor had looked him over and discovered he was only constipated, and an enema would solve that little problem.

In a way, Herm was proud of his operation, as he was proud of his young doctor. When he had come out of the fogginess of the anesthetic, Norton had given him a respectful grin and said, "You're a pretty tough old fellow; you've just survived one of the most radical operations a doctor can perform." The doc called it a "Whipple" and had explained to him that half his stomach and some of the other organs —including the pancreas, Herm thought—had been removed.

Just as Lyndon Johnson had shown off his scar to newsmen, Herm had proudly showed off Dr. Norton's handiwork to Miriam and the children. Unfortunately, their reactions were not what he expected. Sure, Miriam was her usual stoic self, but she had to set her jaws and look away to hold back the tears. But at least she hadn't cringed and exclaimed, "Oh, Papa, that's disgusting!" like that sissy Robert. Sarah, the older one, reacted in a way that was typical of her.

"What in God's name did he take out of you, Papa?" she said angrily. "Did he *leave* anything? That's the longest, ugliest, most mutilated mess I ever saw!"

"Sarah, hush!" said Miriam. "I told you what the doctor took out. Half his stomach, most of his pancreas and duodenum, and some lymph things. And now he thinks Papa's going to be all right."

"Dad," Sarah snapped, ignoring Miriam, "I don't want to upset you, but maybe this Dr. Norton is one of those knife-happy surgeons who cuts too much so he can get a fat fee."

Herm Wexler made an effort not to lose his temper.

"Sarah," he said, "if you feel this way, do yourself a favor and don't come again. You'll visit me at home."

"I can't help feeling that maybe you were butchered. Lord, the stories I hear about doctors!"

"I know," her father said. "I also heard those stories. But Norton is *good*. He cares about people."

"Maybe so," Sarah said. "I won't try to second-guess. But I've got some friends on the staff of the University—"

"Sarah, please!" Mrs. Wexler said. "You're upsetting your father. He needs his rest."

Sarah pulled her arm away. "Did the doctor definitely say what he found, Papa? Was it a cancer in the pancreas?"

Herman Wexler looked at the floor. "Well, he's not sure yet—he's still waiting—he said he was almost certain—the chances were so high—"

"The chances, Papa! This is your life we're talking about. I certainly think someone competent should look into this."

After they left, Herm Wexler thought that none of them had understood. Not one member of his family had realized that Dr. Norton had given him the chance to redeem his life, had provided him with a little more time in which to prove to himself that there was something in him of value. That his entire life had not been a waste.

Of course, Herm realized, they would never understand because they were a part of that waste. They were his great failure. He had devoted all his time and his energy to them, saving very little for himself, and what was the end result?

Herm did not regret having married Miriam—not really. He had truly loved her. He still loved her, but somehow they had never had the life together that he had envisioned. Economic necessity had been partly at fault. The times had been to blame. No woman could have been more understanding or more patient than Miriam had been. Her bitterness—that hard-bitten mean approach she now had to life—had stemmed from the same source that had caused Herman's anxious, resentful bursts of temper. It had been that economic barrier that they had faced together—day after day, month after month, year after year—that had walled off and sealed away their hopes of fulfillment.

He had been the youngest of eight children born of immigrant parents; she had been an only child, the grandchild of immigrants. His parents and her grandparents had come seeking a better way, and Herm often wondered if they had truly found it. He had no way of knowing, no means of comparison. He only knew his own life had been a desperate struggle for something that continually eluded him. He had been a bright student when the century was young; he had had so much potential. There had been prospects for college, and hopes for a career as a teacher, possibly even a chance to try his hand at writing. But after the stock-market crash brought on a depression that looked as though it would never end, he had to postpone his plans.

He realized he could have gone on after that first year of working his way through college. But it would have meant letting his family down. His older brothers and sisters had families of their own, and his parents needed his support.

The first few years, Miriam had understood and waited patiently for Herm to marry her. So, when times improved, it had been a choice between going back to college or marrying Miriam. They had had a fine wedding.

Then it had been the children. And then the war.

He supposed he should have been glad that, as the head of a family, he had not had to go into the military service. But he felt that the army might have been better. True, he might never have come back from the trenches, but would that have been any worse than getting stuck working on the docks for the rest of his life?

With the manpower shortage, he had been mobilized for the shipyards in Brooklyn for the duration. After the war was over, he had become a longshoreman, first in New York, then gradually working his way around the country's coast-line to California.

And for what?

Merely to keep his wife and children housed and fed. And to give Sarah and Robert the chance for the kind of education he had had to postpone.

And what good had it done?

Sarah had turned out to be a bitch. That was a crude term for him to use to describe his own daughter, but Herm was a crude man, and a fact was a fact. She was a bitch. She was tough, and she was mean. There was nothing soft or endearing about her. It was a wonder she had been able to produce three grandchildren for him, two boys and a girl, and he wondered how they would ever develop properly. Especially when she hardly ever saw them, because of that damned accounting job she had. Imagine! His daughter, an accountant—a CPA, no less, with a secretary! Liberated, she called it. Irresponsible, Herm thought.

But Herm loved those grandchildren; he delighted in watching them scamper about his backyard. And it made him feel all warm inside to hear the little one—little Daniel—call him "Pop-pop."

In a way, they made up for his disappointment in Sarah. His feeling of betrayal, really. When Sarah had been younger, she had dated a great many Jewish boys, but she never seemed to see any of them more than twice; usually only once. Herm realized that it was because no self-respecting Jewish boy would stand to let her cut off his balls. It was when Sarah was in college that she had taken to dating goyim.

And she had ended up marrying one—not only a goy, but a goy with a first name for a last name and a last name for a first. Maxwell Howard. Oh, Max was a nice boy, but he was almost as much of a namby-pamby as Herm's own Robert.

Herman had worked all his life with gentiles. Very few Jews ever became dock workers, and those who did stood out. Herm was called "the Hebe," but with undercurrents of respect. He was as tough as the toughest of them and could more than hold his own with a bottle as well as the hook.

Herm ate alone, and that was because Miriam prepared kosher food. It was not that they were so religious, but each believed in tradition, and their parents had been strict Orthodox. Herm respected gentiles for their beliefs, as he was respected for his. He did not believe in mixed marriages, and neither did most of the Catholics he worked with. Herman resented deeply that his daughter had no respect at all for his religion, and Robert hadn't the guts to defend *any* position.

Yes, Herm had to admit, Robert was his biggest disappointment. He had been delighted that his second child had been a boy. Although he hadn't had much time for Robert in the early years—with his war work at the shipyards and his service in the National Guard—he had spent as much time with him as he could, trying to teach him to play baseball and football, and buying him boxing gloves so he could learn self-defense—an important thing in their tough neighborhood.

But Robert had never taken to sports. When Herm would toss him the baseball, Robert would flinch and throw his arm up in front of his face. Although he would catch the football, Robert would never run with it, and—try as he might—Herm could never get him to even try to kick it. The boxing gloves had lasted one day. Robert had been intrigued with trying them on; but the first time Herm had hit him in the face, Robert had burst into hysterical crying. Miriam had made Herm put the gloves in the attic, and—when they had moved a couple of years later—he had given them away to one of the neighbor's boys.

Robert had always preferred to stay in his room alone painting pictures. When he went out to play, it was usually for some silliness with Sarah and the two girls next door. He was always getting beaten up by the tough boys in the neighborhood, and finally—when Robert was in his teens—Herm just gave up on his son, realizing they would never have anything in common.

Robert had gone on to take a college degree in art, and he had made a good career for himself as an interior decorator. But he was thirty-six years old now, still a bachelor, and Herm was pretty sure he would remain one. Herm didn't know much about his son's personal life, because they never talked much to each other.

The only love Herman Wexler had at this time of his life was Miriam's, and he knew it was faded like a rose pressed in Webster's dictionary. Herm didn't know when Miriam had begun to retreat into herself, hiding her thoughts and opinions, but he realized he was at fault. There had too often been times in his life when he couldn't contain all the rage and frustration he felt, times when he would let go, shouting at the top of his voice and smashing anything he could get his hands on.

He was always sorry when it was over, but that hadn't been much good to Miriam. He was sorry now.

It had been painful for Herm to see Miriam's frightened face when she had come to visit him last night. As usual, she brought him food, and she sat staring miserably into her lap while he ate. He hadn't minded eating the hospital food, but he knew it would make her feel less helpless to let her bring him homemade matzo-ball soup and gefilte fish. Dr. Norton had approved the diet, and Herman made a big show of enjoying it. But Miriam looked just as glum when she left with the clean plates.

The morning haze had lifted over the hills and mountains, and he could see Los Angeles in the bright sunlight. It was still the same as it had been yesterday. And the day before. He knew he would stand here in this very spot tomorrow. And Los Angeles would still be there and the same, unchanging—at least visibly. At least not changing the way a man changes, as he grows older day by day, watching his life run out of its alloted time.

Suddenly, from behind him, a voice broke into Herm's thoughts. "Oh, there you are, Mr. Wexler."

He turned from the window to see that plump, pretty little nurse with the blond hair.

She smiled affectionately at him, as if to say, It's all right; you can be anywhere you want to be.

But what she said was, "Will you come with me? It's time for that enema now."

3 HARRY NORTON

November 15, 1975, Los Angeles

"Hey, butcher! Think fast!"

Harry Norton turned just in time to catch the basketball aimed at him. It was typical of Moe Michener to arrive twenty minutes late and to avoid any apology by putting Harry on the defensive. It wasn't that Moe was always late; if he followed a distinct pattern, Harry could adjust his own schedule accordingly. But Moe seemed to like to maintain an air of unpredictability. Sometimes he would be twenty minutes late; sometimes, twenty minutes early. Once or twice, just to break the monotony, Moe had been precisely on time.

But whenever it was, Moe Michener always had to make a startling entrance, had to call attention to the fact that Moe Michener had *arrived*.

Harry was pretty much prepared by now for whatever Moe would try to throw his way—or at least he knew to keep on his guard. Except for the period when Harry had been in Sweden and Korea, while Moe had been in Florida and in law school, the two had played basketball together twice a week for the past fourteen years, beginning with medical school.

Harry remembered the sandlot a few blocks away from the anatomy lab, and the scrimmages he and Moe had had as they tried to unwind after eight hours of tediously dissecting the neck of their cadaver, after memorizing the courses of nerves and tendons and arteries through endless tunnels of fat and skin and bone. He remembered the rock pile behind the emergency room at City Hospital that had served them during their internship, when they had tried to sandwich their games in between ward rounds, scut work, patients, and trips to the operating room.

And it continued still. Now that Harry was a successful surgeon and Moe was establishing his reputation as a medical-malpractice attorney, now that they both belonged to the exclusive Los Angeles Athletic Club (Harry had sponsored Moe for membership just a few months before), their rivalry went on. Only the quality of the basketball court had changed.

Usually, in the middle of the afternoon, they would have the gym entirely to themselves. Occasionally there would be an observer or a couple of other players, but generally their victories and defeats were private matters, just between the two of them. Their shouts—taunts, threats, challenges, obscenities—were always empty echoes that faded quickly from the gym and from their memories.

That was why Harry paid little attention to the fact that Moe had called him "butcher." It was no different from any of the names Moe might give him—or that he might give to Moe. In medical school, it had been "klutz" or "butterfingers" after Moe had dropped the turtle's heart on the floor in physiology lab, or "golden blade" when Harry had stumbled through his first appendectomy in four hours. (He now did them routinely in twenty minutes.)

But, what mattered at the moment was the ball. And Harry had it. Without really aiming, he tossed it toward the far goal, sending Moe dashing after it. The ball bounced off the rim; Moe leaped, caught it, and began to dribble casually back toward him, his long legs and arms moving in their own distinctly disjointed rhythm.

Moe was grinning at him mischievously. "I didn't expect you to catch on to your new name so quickly. You responded to it pretty fast."

Harry wasn't going to admit that he didn't know what Moe was talking about. "Why shouldn't I? I know my job. What would you like to take home to Karen for dinner tonight—a stomach, some kidneys, maybe a gallbladder?"

Moe dribbled slowly and deliberately toward Harry now, threatening, his grin growing until he looked like the cat who had just dined on the proverbial canary.

The echo of the ball slamming against the smooth yellow floorboards filled Harry's ears as he carefully stalked Moe's advancing figure. Not too close. . . . Give him room. . . . Watch the drive. . . .

The years had changed Moe, but not as drastically as they might have. Despite the strands of gray in his dark hair and beard, and despite the strained lines around his eyes, Moe looked like the same brash, arrogant young student Harry had met that first day in med school. He still carried his six-foot-two frame like the clumsy kid next door. The gray sweat suit he wore might even be the same one he had worn fourteen years ago.

"How about Herman Wexler's pancreas?" Moe challenged.

Herman Wexler? Harry was so startled by the name he leaned backward and his legs crossed for a split second. That was all Moe needed. Seizing the opportunity, he darted toward the hoop with one swift dribble. Before Harry could recover, Moe's lay-up shot swished through the cords.

"Quick bucket," said Moe, smiling. "I didn't think you'd be so easy."

Harry pretended not to hear, but his next shot was far off the mark, missing the basket completely. How the hell did Moe know about Herman Wexler? The patient, now recuperating on the third floor of Valley View Hospital, had been worrying Harry all week, but he didn't recall talking about him to Moe. He rarely talked about his patients outside the office, especially with Moe. Had he mentioned the case to Karen?

Harry had performed a Whipple on Herman Wexler, and the radical operation appeared to have been a success. It had been almost ten days now, and the sixty-five-year-old man was up and walking about the hospital corridors and eating normally. But Harry had not yet received the final biopsy report that would confirm that the operation had been necessary. Gregorio, the hospital pathologist, had sent the slides to San Francisco for a second expert opinion.

The two biopsies Harry had obtained while Wexler lay on the operating table had been inconclusive. Not knowing whether the tumor in Wexler's pancreas had been malignant or benign, Harry had weighed the options, considered the odds, and decided to go ahead. It was not a small piece of surgery. He had cut out half his patient's stomach and most of the pancreas and duodenum, together with all the large and swollen lymph nodes in the area. Three separate anastomoses! Three suture lines to worry about! Seven hours in the operating room!

Harry realized then that most doctors would have closed and waited—waited for the results of the biopsy. They would have protected themselves. But if the biopsy did reveal a malignancy, the patient's chances of surviving a second operation would have been much less. Dr. Harold Norton had been so certain that Herman Wexler's tumor was malignant, he had decided to proceed in the hope of saving the man's life. He had decided to go for a cure.

Harry tossed the ball back to Moe now. "How'd you hear about Wexler?" he asked, trying to sound casual.

Moe made a beeline for the goal, again dribbling in great strides. Harry tried to keep up, but the two were not well matched for basketball. Harry was five-ten, and the weight he had gained in recent years had slowed him down considerably. Moe used his extra height and speed to maximum advantage as he leaped up and over Harry and sent the ball plunging through the goal again. His elbow caught Harry behind the left ear, as he came back to the floor.

Breathing heavily from the slight exertion, Harry stood under the basket, holding his throbbing ear. Sweat stains were beginning to darken the armpits of his gray sweat suit. His wavy brown hair was beginning to fall in limp strands over his forehead, and beads of perspiration were showing on his mustache.

"Why did you ask about Wexler?" he repeated.

Moe shrugged. "His daughter does my taxes—she's a CPA. She asked me if I'd look into her father's case. She didn't know I knew you."

Harry dropped the ball, allowing it to roll aimlessly to the side of the court. He looked as foolish as he felt at that moment. Already beginning to look more like the successful doctor than the athletic kid, he would have felt more at home facing this kind of confrontation in hospital whites than in a sweat suit that needed washing. Color drained from his tanned face and his blue eyes clouded, as he stared up at his friend.

Finally, he found the words that would seem the

least foolish. "*Case?* How can you use the word *case?* Where does *case* come in?"

"Hey, keep your shirt on. You're overreacting. The daughter has been hearing stories about knife-happy surgeons—her words—and she remembered about my law practice so she phoned me. That's all."

"What do you mean, that's all? Are you taking this so-called case?"

"Of course not. There *is* no case that I can see. But I told her I'd make some inquiries for her. If I hadn't, she'd just go to someone else. She was really steamed up."

"Does that mean you *are* planning to look into it then?" Harry asked angrily.

"Well, maybe I will—just to keep me honest, that is—or maybe I won't. Anyway, what difference does it make whether it's me or someone else?"

"It makes a lot of difference. It's a question of ethics."

"Ethics? Cut out the theatrics, Harry, this is no big deal. What can happen? As long as you've covered your ass, that is."

One of the first rules the two had learned as interns and medical students was: "Before you do anything else, cover your ass." That was what the doctor game was all about. Oath of Hippocrates? Devotion to duty? Care? Love? Whatever else one could think of that was good? Yes, that was part of it too, but primarily, he and Moe knew, it was: "Cover your ass." That was the number-one rule.

Moe had never approved of the rule, and it had cost him dearly—his future career as a doctor. He had refused to obey it and had been kicked out of his residency. Harry had never given the rule too much credence, but he had never openly flouted it the way Moe had. He never dared.

"When I was in the operating room"—Harry stared at his friend—"I was concerned about Herman Wexler's cancer, not about covering my ass. I was trying to save a man's life."

Moe strolled over to the side of the gym to retrieve the ball. "Harry, I'm reasonably sure what you did was right. I told the daughter you were *good*. Damn good. Maybe I'll unhinge some of her fixed notions. But she was determined to find someone to check the record. She accused you of butchering the bastard. Doesn't think you had the right to perform such a big operation—thinks it wasn't necessary."

"Goddamn it, I saved her father's life, and if she thinks she knows more than I do, then why didn't she—" The color was flowing back into Harry's cheeks as his anger grew, and his voice echoed harshly into the empty gym. "Wexler signed himself into my care! He knew what he was in for—I explained it all to him! And to Mrs. Wexler! And they both thanked me for pulling him through all right!"

Moe grinned back at him from the sidelines. "Here!" he called, tossing the basketball. "Let's play ball!"

Harry caught it, but immediately slammed it angrily to the polished floor, sending it flying foolishly into the air and back to the sidelines. "Screw the ball! Screw you! I don't like the idea of you looking into one of my cases like I'm some fucking quack!"

Moe laughed nervously. "Hey, come on, Harry, don't get so carried away. We're here to play ball."

"The hell we are!" He turned and started off toward the locker room, but stopped for a moment. "Have you seen Herman Wexler or talked to him yet?"

"Of course not. I haven't done a thing. Cool off, Harry."

"Well, I suggest you talk to the patient himself

before you go too far." Sweating profusely, Harry stalked off to the locker room to shower and change.

"It was benign." Joe Gregorio's voice over the phone cut as sharply as one of his autopsy knives. "The tumor in Wexler's pancreas was not cancer. It was just bad scarring and inflammation from a chronic pancreatitis, consistent with a long-standing intake of alcohol. Nothing more."

Harry Norton continued to hold the phone receiver to his ear, but he did not listen to the pathologist's high-pitched, coldly dissecting words. It had to be cancer; Gregorio must be wrong.

Joe Gregorio was a damned good pathologist—one of the best. He had to be right, but Harry wanted to lash out at him and protest. His reason for operating—that tumor in Wexler's pancreas, that thickened, yellow lump he had felt so carefully through his gloved hand at surgery, that he had fondled cautiously for several agonizing minutes, that he had biopsied twice for Gregorio to read on frozen section, and that he could have sworn was cancer—had to *be* cancer. But if Gregorio was right, Dr. Harold Norton had made a dangerous mistake.

Gregorio's high staccato continued. "It's a bitch of a situation, but everyone goes along with the final diagnosis. Even Derrington in San Francisco. I sent him a copy of the slides. Looks like your tit's in the wringer on this one, babe."

Norton did not say what was racing through his mind. He tried to be calm. He sat back and looked at his cluttered mahogany desk, scuffed his shoes on the thick shag carpet, and surveyed the cheerful yellow drapes that matched the custom-tailored paper on the walls. The expensive signs of success should have soothed his anger, but they didn't.

The flashing yellow lights on the master panel above his door indicated that six of the seven examining rooms were already filled. Knowing the patients were there waiting should have reassured him. But it didn't.

The dozen framed certificates and diplomas ostentatiously bearing the name Harold Norton, neatly arranged above his desk, should have helped. But they didn't.

At age thirty-six, Dr. Harold Norton was ahead in the doctor game. The years of struggling—through medical school, through internship and residency, through a year in Sweden and two years in Korea, and through establishing a practice in California—had paid off and paid off well. He was affiliated with two hospitals in the Valley and operated out of two offices there; he was in the process of establishing an office and a hospital affiliation in the mother lode of Beverly Hills. A serious mistake like this wasn't supposed to happen.

Harry's only comfort was the realization that Herman Wexler had survived the operation, that he would soon be out of the hospital and resuming a relatively normal life.

But the anxious face of Mrs. Wexler plagued him. He could not dismiss the way her eyes had looked up at him fearfully after the operation as she asked, "Was it cancer?"

He had replied as gently as he could, "We can't be sure, Mrs. Wexler. We can't be sure until we see the final slides and get the report."

And then those dark, careworn eyes had stared straight past him and focused on the door he had just walked through. "My brother died of cancer. He was two years in the hospital. They injected him with chemicals and poisons. They burned his skin with x-ray treatments. He lost all his hair and was in pain night and day. He looked like a skeleton, Doctor. No one should have to suffer like that."

Harry knew that Mrs. Wexler had taken his hesitation as proof her husband had cancer. She knew that doctors never came right out and said it straight. They hedged and twisted. They toyed with the words —"final sections," "pathology specimens," "special stains," "consultations"—all words to avoid coming right out and saying the awful truth.

But after fourteen years in medicine, with every modern advance available to him, Dr. Harold Norton couldn't give her a more definite reply. Was it cancer? He had thought so. He had bet Herman Wexler's life on it. And now he had to tell Mrs. Wexler—and tell Herman Wexler himself—that it had not been cancer at all. That the operation had not been necessary.

It would not be easy. Would they believe him when he explained that all the signs and symptoms had been there? The twenty-pound weight loss, the dark, bile-tinged urine, the blood in his bowel movements, the upper GI series with the widened duodenal loop on x-ray, the arteriogram: they had all meant one thing to Harry Norton—cancer.

But they were also the signs and symptoms of an old, scarred pancreas, burned out from too many years of hitting the bottle.

Joe Gregorio realized Harry hadn't been listening. "Harry, are you there?"

"I'm here," Harry responded briskly, "and I've got the picture. But I want you to know, Joe, if they've got me by the balls, you're not exactly smelling like a rose yourself." And he hung up.

Harry had at least some justification for being angry. Gregorio was cocky because he was safe—his ass was covered. While Herman Wexler had lain on the operating table, Harry had sent two specimens to pathology. But the two biopsies had been inconclusive. Gregorio had popped his head into the operating room door and announced, "I can't give you a definite. I've had everyone in the lab look at the frozen section. We'll have to wait for the final slides to be sure."

An inconclusive answer had been fine for Gregorio; he could give his opinion and vanish. But, based on that answer, Harry Norton had to make a decision—whether to go ahead with the radical operation or to wait.

Harry had weighed the chances—the mathematical odds—trying to make the judgment cold and objective. If the mass he had felt was cancer, and if he waited a week or two, Herman Wexler would be a dead man. The odds were almost entirely against him. If it was cancer, the only chance of his survival was the Whipple, even though there was a ten-percent chance of his dying from the radical procedure itself.

The surgeon could have played it safe. He could have followed the rules of the doctor game; he could have covered his ass by closing up the incision and waiting for nature's verdict. He could have compromised and done a lesser bypass procedure. But Harry Norton liked Herman Wexler—maybe it was that he reminded him of his own father—and he wanted the man to live.

Harry suddenly realized where he had made his mistake. He had let his feelings affect his decision. After Gregorio had left him to his own counsel, he had looked around the operating room for a long moment—at the scrub nurse, at his assistants, at the anesthesiologist, and finally around the screen at Herman Wexler's face, sleeping peacefully, trustingly. It had been a mistake to look at the man, to consider the human being that lay under his knife.

Looking at the man had made him lose his objectivity. He had wanted Herman Wexler to have a fighting chance, so he had made his decision to go ahead.

Damn it anyway! What if he *had* made the wrong decision? Herman Wexler was alive, and Harry Norton was still a good and a successful doctor. Even if Wexler's daughter did bring suit with the help of some lawyer or other (not Moe, surely?), Harry had pulled his patient through a very difficult operation.

And he had an excellent reputation among his colleagues. He was sure they would attest to his ability and judgment.

The affluent signs of success that surrounded him could not be dismissed easily. The new office building he had built was an impressive addition to the Valley. The architect had given it just the right blend of simplicity and modern flair to impress but not overwhelm. And the decorators had tastefully avoided the standard look of doctors' offices. The entire five floors of Medical Plaza West looked great. And it belonged to Dr. Harold Norton—mortgaged to the hilt, bank payments up the ass, but all his. And almost all the offices were rented out. Only Schwartz was hesitating; he hadn't signed his lease yet.

In a way, Harry was hoping Schwartz would decide against the space. He had a waiting list of at least six other doctors. Schwartz was ears-nose-and-throat. In terms of income, Harry would prefer a GP or a family-practice man in the suite who would refer surgical cases to him. But he had never placed income first, and Schwartz was welcome. Harry did want a decision now, though, either way. He dictated a quick memo into the little black recording machine on his desk. "Miss Hopkins, contact Dr. Schwartz about his lease today. It's due."

The combination of medicine and real estate often made Harry smile. He at all times liked to regard himself as "real." He had worked fourteen years to become a good doctor and a good surgeon. Now he was interested in the other aspects of the doctor game; that is, the political intrigues that go on and the malpractice fears. Also the real estate, the investments, and the managing of the money, the profits.

He picked up the brochure from his desk and looked it over for the third time that morning. The deal was tempting. "Pinewood Lakes invites you to seek out our competition . . ." He skipped down to the bottom of the page. ". . . because you will find we have none." Confidence. He liked that. "One thousand acres of pines in the mountains of northern Arizona, with protection from overdevelopment due to a national forest on one side. . . ."

The red button flashed on his desk phone. Harry picked up the receiver, anticipating the sweetly formal voice of Ellen Hopkins. "I'm sorry, Doctor, but Mrs. Warren has phoned three times. Her incision itches and she wants to know if she can take a shower." She hesitated a moment, then added, "And the patients are waiting."

Harry had removed Mrs. Warren's gallbladder ten days before. He had received her check for $1,000 in the mail that morning. She deserved special attention because she was the wife of the bank's vice-president— the bank that was holding his loans.

"Yes, of course. Put Mrs. Warren on the phone."

Harry assured Mrs. Warren that she could now take a shower, and then he returned to the papers on his desk. The Arizona deal looked better and better. Everyone liked it—his accountant, his banker, everyone. Two hundred thousand dollars' worth of land, with annual payments of just $22,000 interest—

a complete tax write-off, and it could only go up in value.

Harry had a record of making all the right decisions —well, almost all. It might have been a mistake not marrying Marianne and bringing her home from Sweden. No other woman since had quite measured up to Marianne. And a successful doctor really needed a wife.

The image of Ellen Hopkins flashed into his mind. She had all the right attributes for success—but Harry could not make up his mind whether those attributes were better applied to a secretary or to a helpmate. She was very attractive, with just the right combination of legs and figure to make her appealing in the reception room, at a cocktail party, or in the bedroom. Her softly styled auburn hair was in the best of taste, and her voice and manners cultivated and charming. The more Harry thought about her, the more he was tempted to drop his formal businesslike manner with her. But she was so damned efficient, he wasn't sure he could replace her in the office.

The intercom flashed again. "Mrs. Wexler on line one, Doctor," Ellen Hopkins announced.

Harry did not want to hear Mrs. Wexler's sweet, respectful, motherly voice right now. He did not want to give her the results of Gregorio's tests.

But he did want to find out if she and her husband approved of her daughter's calling in Moe Michener.

He took the call.

"Doctor, excuse me. Usually, I would never telephone on shabbat. I just came from the synagogue. But my Hermie . . ."

She had the kind of voice that offered caring and begged for kindness. She was easy to be kind to, a natural, gentle woman who had even tried to mother Dr. Harold Norton. When she had learned Harry was still unmarried, she had become concerned about his eating habits, about whether he got enough rest and relaxation. And she had hinted at the vast possibilities of Miss Hopkins even before the thought had occurred to Harry.

"Yes, Mrs. Wexler. Your husband is doing fine—out of bed, with a good appetite. Yes, I know he had some pains in his stomach this morning. He was a little constipated last night, but the enema I ordered will help. And I'll be looking in on him this afternoon."

He wasn't sure how he wanted to formulate the question, so he decided to state it as a fact and see how she responded. "Mrs. Wexler, I understand your daughter has asked someone to look into the operation I performed. Are you dissatisfied with what I've done?"

"Oh, no, Doctor. My Hermie couldn't be in better hands." She was obviously embarrassed. "It's our Sarah. She got so upset when she saw the wound. We tried to stop her, but . . . she's always had a mind of her own."

Harry felt somewhat more assured.

"Please don't let it bother you, Doctor. I'm sure she'll understand when she sees you've done the right thing for Hermie."

That statement echoed in Harry's mind long after he had hung up the phone. How, he wondered, would Sarah feel when she learned she had been right all along? How would Mrs. Wexler feel? And Herman Wexler?

And, damn it, how would Moe Michener feel? Did he already know? Harry—after he'd cooled off, as Moe suggested—could understand Moe's initial reasoning: if he'd turned her down, Sarah would have gone to someone else. Moe hadn't actually accused Harry of doing anything wrong; where cancer was involved, one couldn't be certain that any cutting was excessive. But it wasn't cancer, and now the daughter had more solid ground to stand on. Where would Moe stand?

Harry wondered how much Moe remembered, dwelled on, the past. If it hadn't been for Harry, Moe Michener might never have gotten anywhere at all. Except for Karen Marshall, who had eventually become Mrs. Michener, nobody but Harry had stuck by Moe throughout that long and difficult period when he had been kicked out of the hospital, gone heavily into drugs, and had himself committed to the mental institution. Harry and Karen had encouraged Moe to get back on his feet again, go to law school, and take advantage of his medical degree by specializing in medical malpractice.

But Moe had bounced back from that defeat a long time ago. He was now almost as successful at his profession as Harry was at his own. Harry couldn't recall the last time Moe had lost a case in court.

Just two weeks ago, he had won a negligence decision against a well-known plastic surgeon. The case had been reported prominently in the newspapers. Dr. Charles Raleigh had failed to advise his patient about possible complications from operating on a tendon in his hand. The patient had developed an infection after surgery, and now he could not move his wrist or three of his fingers. Dr. Raleigh had brought in four expert witnesses. All of them swore that the plastic surgeon had done nothing wrong.

But Moe had been brilliant in his cross-examination. He had used his knowledge of medicine and his authority as a doctor to good advantage. And, perhaps more important, he had used his looks and personality. Back in medical school, Moe had been insecure because of his looks—he was tall, thin, and gangly, with a large hooked nose and dark, deep-set eyes—but he had developed a suave and forceful manner to make up for his appearance. He continued to wear his hair in a crew cut, which accentuated his nose and ears, and he now purposefully used his clumsy arms and legs to give a jury or a judge an impression of a young, twentieth-century Abe Lincoln.

He had concluded his case against Raleigh by parading the poor, abused patient before the jury, emphasizing his client's inability to move his hand properly. He talked on and on about the handicap for hours, how the patient could no longer run the pumps in his gas station properly, how he could not handle the intricate maneuvers involved in repairing car engines, how he couldn't provide for his wife and family, and how he never would have consented to the operation had he been properly advised.

The jury had responded exactly the way Moe had wanted them to. In an extremely emotional decision, they had settled nearly $200,000 on the mechanic. And Moe had received a nice fat percentage of that amount as his fee—just about half.

As a result, Dr. Raleigh's career was finished in the Valley, and he would have difficulty continuing to practice at all. If he could get malpractice insurance after that case, it would be at least ten times as high as it had been before. Harry had no idea what Raleigh's rates would become, but his own were now up to $21,000 a year. And they could go to $30,000 or even $40,000, if the new malpractice increases were allowed. Harry knew what it was all leading to. Next the government would be stepping in, would pay everyone's malpractice, and the doctors would be on salary. Like in Sweden.

Harry remembered vividly that year the Professor had sent him to Sweden as a surgical fellow to practice medicine under a totally socialized system, where the doctors were employees of the state. That, to him, was the real horror show. Doctors had no incentive to come to work at all. And the patients . . . if they thought they were getting a bad deal now, in Sweden they at times had to wait six months to see any doctor at all, and often three years for an operation. And then they came through on an assembly line—one doctor worked them up, another did the operation, a third took out the stitches. The patients had no choice of doctor at all!

Goddamn the insurance companies anyway! And the lawyers with their contingency fees! And the unhappy patients who came to them! And goddamn Moe!

Harry wasn't sure which gave Moe greater pleasure, the enormous fees he collected or the satisfaction of driving other doctors out of business. There weren't many people around the Valley who knew what he knew about Moe Michener—that his law career had been built upon a desire for revenge. His record in medical school and during internship had been good, but he had been fired, kicked out, denied his residency in surgery for a peripheral reason. The medical system—the doctor game—had been unfair to Moe Michener. And Moe had found a way to fight back.

Was it possible that Moe would fight the system now by going after his old friend Harry? What *about* that friendship? Was it real on Moe's side? Harry, after all, had seen Moe at his worst during the bad period in Florida before he'd gotten himself together again. That, plus the fact that Harry had come to his rescue and helped him ever since, should have established a strong bond between them—yet there had always been an uneasiness underneath Moe's banter. Perhaps Moe had never forgiven him for precisely the things Harry had done for him.

Was it possible that Moe would be actually eager to face his old friend in court? Suddenly Harry realized it was entirely possible.

Today, with the benefit of hindsight, Harry Norton could see that Moe Michener had never been cut out to be a surgeon. Of course, Moe was a lot different now from the way he had been fourteen years ago— just as Harry was different—but still, Harry thought, the man has to be made up of all his past experiences.

But, Harry also wondered, how much of his understanding of Moe Michener was illusion? He had known Moe for many years, and yet the longer he had been friends with him, the less Harry had truly known him.

With a sigh, Harry told himself he had to dismiss such things from his mind. He was far behind schedule today, and he had to devote some attention to the patients who were waiting.

He buzzed Miss Hopkins to come in with the morning's schedule. She was there promptly and efficiently, with everything nicely organized, advising Harry that he was already half an hour late for the first appointment.

As she ticked off each patient and his or her problem, Harry gave her an appraising look. Despite the care she had taken in pinning back her auburn hair to look appropriately businesslike, no-nonsense, the light in the office gave luster to the reddish tone. She did not wear much makeup; her face had a healthy and well-scrubbed glow, suggesting subtly that makeup was not necessary and probably in poor taste anyway. Her legs were long and shapely, but she kept them crossed decorously beneath a skirt that was not a fraction of an inch too short.

When her green eyes looked up and met Harry's gaze, they immediately comprehended his look and quickly returned to the list of appointments. They were both saved from embarrassment by the light flashing on the phone.

Miss Hopkins promptly picked up the receiver and announced sweetly, "Doctor's office." There was a pause, and a slight flicker of emotion crossed her face. Then she spoke cautiously and softly. "Just a moment. I think you'd better speak to the doctor. He's right here."

Putting the phone on hold, she extended the receiver to Harry, saying, "It's the hospital; I think you'd better speak to them."

The look she was giving Harry was the look of sympathy she usually reserved for patients who had little reason to hope. Whatever the call might be about, Harry realized immediately it was serious. The nurse's voice from the third floor of Valley View Hospital confirmed his apprehension; she was hushed and confused as she blurted out, "Dr. Norton, it . . . it's Mr. Wexler. I just passed by his room and looked in on him."

Harry was abrupt, somewhat irritated by her confusion. "Yes, Miss Traylor. Well, what is the problem?"

Her answer was quick and succinct. "He's dead."

Harry hung up the receiver and sat for a moment looking down at a doodle he had made on the memo pad on his desk. It was a large, hostile circle, reinforced over and over again with one black swirl after another. It was a zero. Nothing. What he had accomplished with his radical operation. What was left of Herman Wexler. And what Dr. Harold Norton would probably have left after Sarah Wexler finished with him.

Ellen Hopkins interrupted his dazed reverie by asking, "Shall I dial Mrs. Wexler's number for you?"

Harry looked at her. She was more than officially

sympathetic. She realized at least some of the implications, and she was concerned. "No," he answered. "I have to think for a few minutes first."

Ellen Hopkins's businesslike attitude changed completely. When she asked, "Would it help to talk to me about it?" she was just one human being concerned about another.

He blurted out everything—the confrontation with Moe Michener, the call from Joe Gregorio, and now this. "It couldn't have happened," he said over and over again, "not at this stage. If he was going to die from the Whipple, it would have happened days ago—not now. He had fully recovered from the damned operation."

"Do you think you ought to call a lawyer?"

Her question was a perfectly reasonable one. But Harry felt that would be an admission that he was guilty of some criminal action. And he knew he was not. He was guilty only of making a mistake, and at this point he did not even have any idea what that mistake was. As far as he could see, he had done everything exactly as he should have.

But Herman Wexler was dead.

Harry did not have anyone else to talk the problem over with. It did not seem advisable to discuss the matter with one of his colleagues; any one of them could be called to the stand to testify. So he talked to Ellen Hopkins.

He told her the fears he had about the kind of techniques a lawyer (like Moe) might use against him. He told her the problems that might arise with his insurance as a result of a case like this. He explained how it might cut off his medical practice entirely.

And he told her about his fourteen-year friendship with Moe Michener. And how he would feel if he found that it had never been a friendship at all.

4 MIRIAM WEXLER

November 15, 1975, Fairfax Area

Miriam Wexler loved her grandchildren, but she wished that Sarah hadn't asked her to take care of them for the day. They were very good children, really. But they required constant attention. Although John was old enough to take care of himself, Heather and little Danny had to have some kind of adult supervision.

It wasn't that Miriam objected to the responsibility; any other time she would have delighted in their company. But, ever since Hermie had been in the hospital, she had had so many things on her mind.

Mostly she thought about Hermie and about the terrible operation he had had to undergo. Miriam recognized her husband's symptoms; she had seen them before in her brother Sidney. It was cancer, and she knew they hadn't yet found a cure for the terrible disease. She knew her Hermie didn't have long to live even if the operation had been successful. And what time he had left would be terribly painful.

Of course, she realized the doctors did their best with the knowledge and the technology they had, but she believed it was actually cruel of them to try to keep a patient alive, while in pain, as long as their technology would permit. If her Hermie was going to die of cancer, she prayed each day that it would be swift, that he would be spared the terrible months of lingering painfully on and on like Sidney had.

Miriam knew that Hermie had tried to keep her from knowing when he was in pain. He was a tough man, and he had had a hard life; he could endure a lot without complaining. But, when she had seen his wound, she had known: there was no way a human being could survive an operation that big and be as healthy and strong as Hermie pretended to be.

He had tried to make her and the children feel he was proud of that horrible incision. Miriam had tried to go along with his pretense, but it was obvious that Hermie could see through her efforts. And Sarah. Their daughter had made such a fuss, she had the whole hospital in an uproar.

But it wasn't Dr. Norton's fault that Hermie had cancer. It wasn't the hospital's fault.

Miriam had been puttering around her kitchen as long as she could. Now everything was about as clean and neat as she would be able to make it. Dinner was in the oven, and there was nothing more she could do while she stood at the back window that overlooked the yard where her grandchildren were playing.

There actually was plenty of work for Miriam to do —in the living room or in the bedrooms—but she wouldn't be able to watch after the little ones from that part of the house. Miriam knew she had to keep herself busy, or she might be tempted to give in to feeling sorry for herself. But, with the children there, it was now a choice between sitting in the kitchen or sitting out back in the yard.

She had no choice but to work on her afghan. She glanced outside to check on the children and then hurried into the living room to pick up the needles and the big pile of yellow and black that would eventually be an attractive comforter for chilly evenings.

The grandchildren were building a city out of odd pieces of wood and pipes they had found in Hermie's garage workshop, driving their little metal cars in the bare dirt of a flower garden Miriam had never gotten around to planting. When Miriam stepped outside with her handiwork, letting the screen door slam behind her, they all glanced up to look at her. Johnny and Heather went back to their construction work, but little Danny toddled over to her, extending his red fire truck and exclaiming, "Mom-mom."

Miriam wasn't sure if Danny was trying to say "Miriam" or "Grandma," or trying to make the sound of a fire engine, so she responded by asking, "Are you having a good time, Danny?"

Danny nodded his head affirmatively and toddled back to join his brother and sister, while Miriam moved the aluminum lawn chair into a shady spot where she could concentrate on her crocheting.

They were really very good children, a bit timid perhaps, but that was to be expected with parents like Sarah and Max. She wished Sarah wouldn't be so hard on them; children needed a soft, warm, affectionate mother, not someone who ran her family like it was a high-pressure business. The children—especially Johnny—would be silent and sullen when their mother was around. Max tried to make up for the situation by being overly attentive and understanding. But Miriam was sure that the children would be much better off if things were the other way around.

Miriam felt she herself was properly grandmotherly, and Hermie . . . if only Hermie were here. The grandchildren loved Hermie so much. He could keep them entertained for hours. If Hermie were here now, he would be right there in the middle of them, supervising the building of their make-believe city. They would all fight and argue over the best way to put up a building, and where the roads ought to go, but the children would love it. And they would tease Hermie, and Hermie would love it, teasing them back.

But Miriam realized painfully that those days were over for the little ones. Even if Hermie were able to come home from the hospital . . .

She didn't have a chance to dwell on that morbid thought. She and her grandchildren all heard the sound of a car pulling into the driveway by the side of the house. Miriam knew it was too early for this to be Max and Sarah, but the children had no sense of time, and they went dashing off around the house, assuming it was their parents.

With a vague sense of apprehension, Miriam got up, set her work down in the chair, and slowly followed after little Danny, who could run only a little faster than Miriam could walk. Her apprehension grew stronger when she was met by Heather and Johnny, slinking shyly back around the house, confirming that the visitor was a stranger. When Miriam saw the shiny little green sports car and recognized the man getting out as Dr. Norton, she knew. She did not have to look at the doctor's grave face or hear him speak to realize that her Hermie was dead.

Miriam did not cry. She did not even let herself think about grief. Her first thought was, It is so kind of the doctor to come to tell me in person, when it would have been easier for him to use the phone.

Ever since she had met him, Miriam had thought Dr. Norton was such a nice man. He was the kind of son she wished she had been able to give Hermie.

And she regretted that she hadn't been able to tidy up the living room; she wouldn't like to have the doctor think she was a sloppy housekeeper.

"Do you have time to come sit for a cup of coffee or a bottle of soda pop?" she asked graciously.

Dr. Norton smiled considerately, but his blue eyes had a sad gray look to them. "I'd like to stay for a few moments if you don't mind, Mrs. Wexler. But don't trouble yourself. I just want to talk to you."

"Oh, no trouble," she coaxed. "Just come into the kitchen with me." As she led him around the side of the white-frame house to the back door, she explained. "I'm sorry, but I have to stay where I can keep an eye on the grandchildren."

The three little ones had returned to their playing, but they eyed their grandmother and the stranger curiously as they went into the house.

Inside the kitchen, Miriam sat her guest down at her spotless Formica-topped table and put on a pot of fresh coffee. She was glad there was still a lot of the chocolate Uneeda-Biscuit cake left; the doctor was a bachelor, so she was sure he rarely got good home cooking. She set the table for two—not unaware that she would not often do so after this—and cut him a nice big piece of cake. He protested politely, but she could see by the look in his eyes that he liked chocolate.

When the coffee was poured, she sat down at the table to join him. "When did it happen?" she asked simply.

Dr. Norton answered nervously. Miriam knew people didn't know how to talk to someone who had just lost a loved one, but she thought the doctor ought to realize that the straight truth was the only way. "I wasn't there when it happened," he spoke, staring down at the cake and fork. "One of the nurses looked in on Mr. Wexler about one o'clock this afternoon and . . . and found him." He looked up at her, his eyes confused and glazed over. "Mrs. Wexler, I want you to know I'm sorry."

Miriam tried not to look at the doctor's eyes. If she permitted herself to think of tears, she knew they would flow and she wouldn't be able to stop them. So she asked, "Would you like some more coffee?"—and got the pot, and then realized he hadn't touched his first cup.

When she set down the pot, she looked at Dr. Norton. She was puzzled; he knew as well as she and Hermie had that he might die. Why, then, was he so upset? It wasn't doing her any good to see him that way. She set her jaw and took a deep breath to keep from falling in with his grief.

"Doctor"—she forced her strength—"I've been prepared for this ever since the operation. I knew it was cancer; I knew that Hermie wouldn't last too much longer."

But the doctor did not seem to be comforted. Something more than Hermie's death seemed to be bothering him. He frowned painfully as he pushed his fork around, stabbing at the cake, obviously not thinking of eating. "Mrs. Wexler," he said finally, "when I asked Mr. Wexler if he drank quite a bit, he told me that he sometimes had a beer when he got home from work."

"Yes." Miriam was puzzled.

He heaved a great sigh and finally managed to look at her directly. "I wish that one of you had told me that he drank quite a bit more than that."

What was the doctor trying to say? Images of Hermie's violent rages when he was drunk flashed through her mind. Those had been the part of their life together that neither she nor Hermie liked to think about. They were not the happy times. Blushing, Miriam groped for her voice: "It was his pride. . . ."

"Mrs. Wexler, Herman didn't have cancer," Dr. Norton blurted out suddenly. "What I thought was cancer of the pancreas was just heavy scarring caused by alcohol."

What he said hit Miriam too suddenly. She couldn't pick out all the implications fast enough to respond. She just sat there staring at the doctor, her mouth open, her eyebrows furrowed.

When she answered, it was little more than a whisper. "Hermie didn't have cancer?"

Dr. Norton shook his head gravely. "We don't yet know what caused his death. It could have been the operation; it could have been something else. All we really know for sure is that it wasn't cancer."

Miriam hadn't prepared herself for this. She couldn't hold back the tears. Despite her every effort to remain firm, the tears welled up in her eyes and began running down her cheeks. It wasn't possible; she had thought of every possibility, and she had prepared herself for each one. It simply couldn't be this way; she couldn't surrender control or she would be lost.

"I'm sorry," the doctor said again. "I know I didn't do you or your husband one bit of good." His hand reached out and took Miriam's. "I know it doesn't help to say 'I'm sorry,' but I was so sure the operation was right."

Miriam squeezed nervously at his hand. "I know, Doctor. I realize. . . ." She couldn't say any more. Her resistance was broken; the tears had given way to sobs.

"Can I call your son or your daughter for you?"

Miriam shook her head negatively.

"Can I get one of the neighbors to come stay with you?"

She continued to shake her head.

"Can I prescribe a sedative?"

Finally Miriam found her voice, but it came out as a hoarse whisper. "No, thank you, Doctor. I'm all right." She looked at him kindly. "I think I'd just like to be alone for a while."

"I understand," he responded hoarsely, finding it difficult to keep from crying himself. He got up slowly from the table and edged hesitantly toward the door. "But if there's anything I can do, please call me."

Miriam nodded affirmatively, and added, "Thank you, Doctor. And thank you for coming by to tell me."

When he had gone, Miriam put her arms and her head down on the table and cried without restraint. She had no idea how long she sat there, letting it all out in heavy sobs, and she only realized that she had forgotten the children when she felt the presence of little Danny at her side. She lifted her head to see his confused, frightened little face, and her tears left her immediately. She grabbed her youngest grandson and hugged him desperately.

Hermie wouldn't want her to carry on like this. He would want her to keep up with her duties and responsibilities. It was getting late now, and the little ones must be getting hungry.

5 MOE MICHENER

"I don't understand why you got into this Wexler business in the first place." Karen mixed herself a drink, took a sip, poured it down the drain, and then mixed herself another drink before continuing. "Of course, you'll have to back out now."

Sometimes it was difficult for Moe to figure out whether Karen was being Dr. Karen Marshall or Mrs. Moe Michener. Maybe it was because sometimes she seemed to be somebody else entirely, and he had never figured out who that third woman was.

Right now was one of those times.

"Why do I have to back out?" Moe realized he was responding more to his wife's enigmatic attitude than to what she was saying.

On the rare occasions when both Moe and Karen managed to make it home in time to have a "quiet little drink" together before dinner, they inevitably spent the time fighting—with each of them releasing on the other all the tension, anxiety, and hostility acquired during a day of work. The fights had never run the same way twice, mostly because there were so many variables: whether Moe had spent the day in the office or in court, whether Karen had been at the hospital or at the office, whether the traffic from downtown Los Angeles had been bad or they had both come home together from just across the Valley.

If there was any consistency to their fights it was that Moe always came out on top, or thought he did, or was led to believe that he had. What galled Moe most about that was that Karen never seemed to *have* to come out on top—which meant that Moe could never really feel that he had won.

Karen was always too goddamned cool and self-possessed and perfect—she always had been.

She finally sat down and crossed her long perfect legs and sighed a deep sigh. But then she opened her mouth again. "In the first place, it would be unfair to your clients to represent them against your best friend." She paused to take another sip of her collins. "And in the second place it would be unfair to Harry."

Since Karen had finished with the bar, Moe decided he would mix himself another drink. It was a good excuse to speak to her with his back turned. "What's more important, friendship or principles?"

"For God's sake"—Karen's voice rose an octave—"will you stop playing games like a college sophomore?"

Moe turned to look at her. "Now, I think that is a perfectly valid question."

Karen closed her eyes and leaned her head back against the chair cushion. "Maybe in a court of law, but not in real life."

That was one of Karen's pet lines, one that she knew would be guaranteed to infuriate Moe. It did. He cracked a cluster of ice cubes against the bar, sending several of them scurrying across the parquet floor to land on the edge of the oriental carpet.

"Don't your principles have anything to do with personal loyalties?" she continued. Her eyes seemed to be closed, but she was staring at him beneath her eyelids.

Moe stared back at Karen. "You seem to have quite a bit of loyalty to Harry yourself," he said sharply.

Karen held his gaze, then looked away. She said nothing.

After ten years of marriage, Karen still watched for signs of change in Moe. She still hoped that, with time, he might mellow just a bit. But he still had the same crusading passion for all humanity that she had seen in him as a student, a passion for humanity, she'd come to realize, that seemed to exclude simple caring for individual people. She kept hoping that one day his feelings for her might turn to love.

She knew he cared for her, but it was a selfish kind of caring. Intellectually, Moe accepted her as his equal. She could never accuse him of male chauvinism, because he would only hotly deny it and be offended. But, like so many things with Moe, there was a difference between what he said and what he did.

Taking Moe at his word, one would consider him a democrat with a little tin "d," almost a radical with a spray paint "r." But over the years, Karen had come to recognize him as more deeply chauvinistic than most men: he was indeed a chauvinist with a big platinum "c" and a hypocrite with a zircon "h." He had been an idealistic crusader for as long as she had known him. It had been his idealism that had caused him to clash head on with the hospital administrators and brought about the loss of his residency during his internship, turning his crusade into one of vengeance. She did not quite know what it was, but his posture of goodness and honesty and unselfishness was only a facade. There was, underlying it all, a very deep selfishness that she did not yet understand.

He would never recognize that this was the way it really was. Instead he would rationalize that he was out to remind doctors about their Hippocratic oath and to drive them out of office if they continued "to sacrifice their patients on their altar of greed."

Some might see Moe's actions as those of a heroic, unselfish figure, but Karen knew it was simply Moe's way of shouting "Me!"; of proving to himself that he was better than the next guy.

At times like this, Karen wanted to scream at him, to make him see how foolish she thought he was. Instead she said at last, evenly, coolly, "Harry Norton is not just another doctor, Moe."

After three drinks, Moe was beginning to feel the liquor, and the liquor was beginning to release his rage. "Don't you think I know that? If I didn't know that, I wouldn't have a problem!"

Karen resented the alcoholic slur of his words; it was the one thing that could break through her calm. "But you don't have a problem at all. I don't see that you have any choice but to drop the case. Let some other lawyer take it."

What good was a wife, he wondered, if she wouldn't listen? If she couldn't understand the terrible ache inside, the hurt and the confusion?

Karen had always been too sure of herself—had always known exactly what she wanted in life. She had followed the system. She had never wanted anything more than her work, a home, a husband, and children. He had given her everything she wanted, except the children. But Moe couldn't see that she had given him anything in return. Especially not any understanding of what it was he was trying to achieve.

Karen only wanted the ordinary things. Moe wanted to have more. Do more. Be more than ordinary. He had so much inside him that he considered special. She had once led him to believe she understood that. She had once made him think she was just as special.

Damn it, she *was* special. She was beautiful; she

was charming. She had overcome a lot of obstacles to carve out a medical career for herself. She was a damned good pediatrician, and she was what a doctor ought to be—capable, considerate, and caring. Yet something was missing. It was as if they too often marched to different drums.

Moe's own experience had shown him that the problem with doctors today started in their training. A special attitude was bred into them in medical school. Moe couldn't exactly put that attitude into words, but it involved indifference toward patients, along with selfishness.

A med student didn't study to learn medicine; he studied to pass tests. He didn't scrub in for operations and work the emergency room to learn how to care for patients; he did it to impress his superiors. But the major rule was: if you make a mistake, cover your ass. Don't admit it's your mistake, and if necessary lay the blame on somebody else.

Moe began to realize that Harry Norton had been the best example of the rotten system. There had been that mistake Harry had made in the third year of med school, when they had been working the emergency room. It had been at final-exam time, and it had been difficult to keep up the emergency-room work while doing all the necessary cramming.

Harry had put a lot of effort into learning what questions had been asked in previous years, and he had put most of his time into memorizing those answers. Harry had heard that one of the professor's favorite questions was: "List the thirteen main causes of *Lupus erythematosus multiform*." Called "lupus" for short, it was a very rare disease—affecting the kidneys, lungs, liver, skin, blood vessels, just about everything—and lupus became an obsession with Harry.

One night, while he was memorizing his lupus list, Harry got a call. "There's a drunk son of a bitch here with a big chunk of his lip gone. Get your ass down to the emergency room and start sewing!"

The patient was a Mr. Wesley Almond, and he was sixty-one years old. He was very drunk, and he was sitting with one hand over his mouth, humming softly to himself, and spitting blood on the floor.

When Harry entered the emergency room, the man called out, "Hey, Doc, I got bit by a dog."

Harry moved the man's hand away from the jaw and saw a gaping hole where the upper lip had been. Blood oozed from the ragged edges, and pieces of muscle and fat hung in strands and blobs all over the man's face. Through the hole, Harry could see three of Wesley Almond's gold-capped teeth.

"Where's the rest of the lip?" Harry asked.

"I guess my dog swallowed it." Wesley Almond didn't seem too concerned about the fact. "My old lady's home with him now, trying to get him to vomit it up so you can sew it back."

The thought of sewing on a lip that had been thrown up from a dog's stomach didn't particularly appeal to Harry. He was fresh out of two years of sitting in classes—anatomy, biochemistry, pathology, microbiology. He had peered into microscopes until his eyeballs hurt. He knew theory well enough, the basics of how things worked in the body and why. He had measured carefully the output of the giant turtle's heart. He had studied the zigzag lines that were made when the brain and spinal cord of the North American bullfrog were dipped in acid and then alcohol. He had heard the loud crunch of a long needle as it entered the brain of an Australian salamander. He had torn out rabbits' kidneys, cut off the heads of mice, and injected cancer cells and poison drugs into the stomachs of countless numbers of dogs and cats. It all seemed terribly cruel, but he was told that he was learning how to help people. . . . And now the time had come. His experience with surgery on humans was limited to one cadaver. The most inexperienced nurses were far more advanced than he was. Yet Mr. Almond was a sick person, son of a bitch or not, who was depending on him. The responsibility was terrifying.

He grabbed O'Hara's arm. "The guy with the missing lip," he stammered.

"Yes," O'Hara answered coldly and decisively, "a good case for you. Clean it up well, and it will come together easily. Most of it is muscle retraction. Plenty of give. We won't be needing the other piece. Keep an eye on him, though. He's a wild one. Already tried to bite one of the nurses. He probably bit the dog first."

To them, it was something to laugh about. O'Hara and the others never even bothered to talk about patients by name. Instead, they referred to them as "the Ulcer" or "the Appendix" or "the Leg." Wesley Almond was "the Lip."

Wishing he was back in his room studying his lupus list, Harry scrubbed and put on a pair of gloves while the nurses washed Wesley Almond's wound. Sweating, Harry thought wildly of his more pressing obligations. His upcoming exam was like a chain around him. He just couldn't think about anything else, and he knew he couldn't be free until he had passed. What good would it be if he were the world's best lip suturer and flunked out of medical school? He longed for the quiet of his room. He much preferred to memorize diseases rather than treat them. Signs and symptoms . . . statistics . . . their incidence in males versus females, young versus old. . . . He thought about his lupus list again. How much more attractive it now seemed to him than did Mr. Almond's terrible lip!

Harry approached the patient. Mr. Almond was not humming now. He had become almost unmanageable. He began to rage and scream in a shrill voice, "Dirty fuckers! White trashy fucks!"

The nurse tried to calm him down, and he spat directly into her face.

"Now see here, Mr. Almond—" Harry stepped in and put a hand on the patient's shoulder as he tried to get off the table. He was rewarded with a few "fucks" of his own, and a big wad of spit mixed with blood from Mr. Almond's lip.

Harry's fists clenched, and O'Hara grabbed his arm. "Take it easy," O'Hara said firmly. "He doesn't know what he's doing. Out of his head."

While Harry put on a new pair of gloves, O'Hara gave Mr. Almond ten milligrams of Valium intravenously to calm him down. Finally, Harry began sewing the lip. He placed the first stitch too high and the second one too low; and when he tied them in place, Wesley Almond's face became twisted into a sardonic grin.

It was then necessary for O'Hara to cut out the stitches and replace them himself. Harry finished the case by washing the wound with saline, putting on a clean dressing, and giving a shot of penicillin. With a final instruction to Wesley Almond—"Let's see you back here in a few days"—Harry was able to rush back to studying his lupus list.

That night Harry reviewed once again the causes of lupus for his exam. Bee stings. Mumps. Morphine injections. Aspirin. Tetanus toxoid injections. Tetanus! Harry wondered if Mr. Almond had received his tetanus shot in the emergency room. Figuring someone else had taken care of it, he dismissed it to go on studying.

But three days later, when he saw Wesley Almond again, the lip was swollen to three times its normal size. The thermometer registered 104 degrees, and the entire left side of his patient's neck and face had puffed up like a balloon. Still, Harry didn't mention the matter of the tetanus injection.

O'Hara instructed Harry to give his patient aspirin and antibiotics, admit him to the ward, cover him with a cooling blanket, and wheel him upstairs so that the pus could be drained.

The surgical team worked furiously on Mr. Almond. Sims, the surgeon, snipped out Harry's stitches, and a greenish mess spilled out onto the bed and the floor. A specimen was scraped up, and Harry ran it down to the laboratory for a gram stain and culture report.

Meanwhile, Mr. Almond complained about a pain in his jaw. He broke out in profuse sweating, and his heartbeat increased alarmingly to 180 beats per minute. His whole body appeared to tremble, and he was having difficulty opening his mouth.

The report came back from the lab thirty minutes later, and Wesley Almond was moved quickly to the operating room. The number of his attending doctors and nurses was doubled. The report read: *Clostridium tetani*. Tetanus! Mr. Wesley Almond had lockjaw!

For the next two days, Mr. Almond lay alone in a darkened and isolated room at the end of Ward One while the poisons of the *Clostridium tetani* bacteria invaded his spinal cord and brain. He hung between life and death, surrounded by doctors, nurses, assistants, and specialty teams, and he was treated with everything in the pharmacy.

When Harry learned the reports of the tests, he

became quite upset. Moe had to grant him that. He quickly forgot about studying his lupus list; instead, he boned up on tetanus in hopes of finding out the Lip's chances of survival. But he didn't admit his error to anyone except Moe and Karen; he told them everything, including the fact that the tetanus shot had occurred to him that first night.

Mr. Almond couldn't urinate on his own, so the surgeons placed a sterile Foley catheter in his bladder. They did a spinal tap. They took cultures of everything—his blood, his sputum, his skin—and Harry was kept busy running back and forth to the lab with small bottles and specimens teeming with the organisms.

He felt so badly that he found it difficult to go into Mr. Almond's room. He couldn't face him. It didn't matter that Buxbaum and Sims said it was a very rare case. It didn't matter much that even O'Hara said he shouldn't blame himself. Harry knew he had forgotten the tetanus shot.

Harry wondered if Mr. Almond knew it too. Would Mr. Almond's family try to kill him? (Only two weeks ago O'Hara had told him that the relatives of a severe diabetic who had died in the intensive care unit tried to stab his doctor in the parking lot! And that guy hadn't even made a mistake!) Or would he be kicked out of school and lose his medical license even before he got it?

Standing in the doorway of Mr. Almond's room, Harry watched the urine dripping from his catheter into the bag at the front of his bed. He listened intently to the clicking of the respirator and the *beep* . . . *beep* . . . *beep* of the cardiogram machine. Harry couldn't read the EKG machine, and he didn't really understand how the damn respirator worked either, but he knew as long as the beeping and the clicking continued, and the urine went into the bag, Mr. Almond was still alive.

Keep dripping, he prayed silently, as the hours drifted. If the dripping stopped, it would mean kidney failure and death. Please keep dripping. His exam was now less than twenty-four hours away. He knew he should be studying, memorizing, but he couldn't. He just couldn't. He had forgotten the tetanus shot.

Harry's entire world had narrowed to Mr. Almond and the urine going into his bag, the dripping and the clicking and the beeping. He had counted ten drops per minute when Sims briskly wheeled the patient into the operating room, took out his sutures, and drained the pus from Mr. Almond's lip and mouth and neck. He had counted eight per minute when Mr. Almond turned blue on the operating table and gasped for air during a prolonged muscle spasm while Sims put huge tubes and drains into his neck area. Sims instantly found the trachea. Grabbing onto it with a small silver hook, he had cut a hole in one of the tracheal rings. A gush of air and white frothy fluid burst out of the hole. Sims quickly pushed in an orange tracheostomy tube and blew up the balloon. The color returned to Mr. Almond's face almost immediately. He coughed and gasped.

Harry counted six drops per minute when the night shift nurse noisily closed Mr. Almond's window at three in the morning and the harsh sound sent all the muscles in his patient's body into severe spasm. He watched Mr. Almond clench his teeth vigorously, arch his neck and back, and extend his arms and legs in a rigid and fixed position. The nurse placed a padded tongue depressor to keep Mr. Almond from biting off his tongue, and sucked out the saliva which drooled forth in large amounts from the corner of his mouth. Fortunately, with an extra dose of muscle relaxant, Mr. Almond came out of the attack in ten or fifteen seconds. It had seemed like hours to Harry.

Throughout the night Harry's admiration for the surgeons, Buxbaum and Sims, kept increasing. Everything they did was so exciting to him. They moved with assurance. They cut out the pus, the germs, the death. It seemed so thrilling—so skilled, so precise, and so far beyond him. Harry made another small vow to himself that night, that if he ever got out of medical school, if he passed his exam, he, too, was going to become a surgeon.

During the second day of Harry's vigil, he was counting the urine drops again. They were down to four per minute, then three. He wondered if he should call someone. He decided against it.

Two minutes later, he wished to God he had. A sudden silence filled the room. The clickety-click of the respirator had stopped. The beeping of the cardiogram was silenced. Perhaps it was a short circuit? Perhaps the electricity was off? No, the lights were still on.

Harry looked up. No! It couldn't be! It couldn't happen! Mr. Almond was ashen white. He didn't seem to be breathing. And Harry was all alone!

Harry leaped to his feet. "Please, Mr. Almond," he begged. "Please, breathe for me. Please."

Harry's mind quickly raced over O'Hara's talk. "Get an adequate airway . . . closed chest massage . . . Adrenalin into the heart . . ."

"Please, Mr. Almond, please breathe!"

Harry forgot everything O'Hara said in that one moment.

He ran out of the room, colliding at the door with O'Hara, the intensive care nurse, Karen, and Moe Michener.

They stared at his distraught condition as he

blurted out, "He's dead! The Lip is dead! I killed him!"

Harry ran down the hall, up a flight of stairs to his room, and flung himself on his bed. Karen followed him there, trying to calm him down, while the others hurried into Mr. Almond's room to take over.

Harry heard the page in the distance. "Doctor heart stat, intensive care unit . . . doctor heart stat . . . doctor heart stat . . ." He shook off Karen's attempts to comfort him. He had killed Mr. Almond. He had killed him, and everyone knew it. He tried to put a pillow over his head, but the words continued to come through: "Doctor heart stat . . . doctor heart stat . . ." Then, suddenly, they stopped, and there was silence.

In that small room with only a bed and a sink and one dim light, Harry hid his head under a pillow and cried.

Harry Norton had caused Wesley Almond's death, and he had behaved like a fool. But, Moe mused sardonically, there must be someone who watches over fools like Harry. When the final exam had come, it had included no questions about lupus, but one very important one was about tetanus. And Harry Norton had passed with flying colors.

Harry had confessed to Moe his fear that Wesley Almond might be the end of his career; but, as it had turned out, Harry probably owed his career to that "drunk son of a bitch."

They had all had their fears and their uncertainties in those student years—the things that had made them want to give up, the things that had determined whether they would stay on course or drift away to teaching or research, or—as Moe had—to medical law.

Moe had seen enough horrors—perpetrated by the residents and surgeons, as well as by the students and interns—to create the biggest scandal in medical history. But he hadn't said anything much then; he had just protested about minor issues. He had stored away each piece of information for the day when it might be useful.

He had learned very early that the practice of medicine in this country was a disgrace—unsanitary conditions, irresponsible doctors, uncaring nurses, and abusive orderlies. Researchers experimenting on patients, operations that didn't have to be performed, patients who didn't have to die, illnesses that were misdiagnosed, physicians who weren't physically or mentally competent to practice: the list of faults seemed endless; there were as many faults as there were patients.

When Moe had decided to go into medical law, he had had to do a lot of rationalizing. He had achieved his degree, but he had failed as a doctor. It grated. Many less qualified doctors rose to prominence, often capitalizing on their mistakes. As a medical lawyer, he decided that those incompetent doctors had to pay for their sins. He had indeed set himself out on a crusade, outwardly designed to clean up American medicine.

Now, as he saw it, he could not make an exception for Harry Norton just because he and Harry had trained together.

Their "quiet evening at home" had finally gotten Moe and Karen to the dinner table. They had hardly spoken to each other for some time. Their housekeeper, Valentina Cortez, had nervously slipped in and out, serving each course, well aware of the tension in the air.

After Valentina had served the main course, it was Karen who spoke first, breaking the silence. "Did you see the article in the newspaper this morning about the new malpractice rates?"

"Ummm," Moe responded noncommittally, as he chewed on a piece of overdone roast beef.

"The insurance companies are insisting on a rate increase—possibly as much as seven hundred percent." She took a bite and eyed Moe carefully.

Moe remained silent, looking down at his plate.

"That would mean my rates would be about forty-two thousand dollars for a year. Even if the rates finally go up only four times, that's twenty-four thousand dollars." She paused, looking for a response she didn't get. "Unless I double my fees—which would be unfair to my patients—I may have to quit my practice."

Moe had finished his roast beef, but he continued to find something of interest in the empty plate.

"Some of the other doctors have been talking about organizing a statewide strike."

Finally she got a reaction from Moe. "That would accomplish a lot, wouldn't it?" he said meanly, through a clenched jaw. "What are the lives of patients compared to the doctors' pocketbooks?"

"So far it's only talk." Karen continued quietly and casually, ignoring Moe's reaction. "They're hoping the threat of a strike will prompt the legislature to act to place some limitations on the insurance companies."

Moe started to react loudly and violently, but at that moment Valentina came in with the dessert, and he had to restrain himself. "If doctors had been responsible in their practice, the situation would never have gotten this far in the first place."

"I don't think—thank you, Valentina." Karen

smiled at her housekeeper, then leveled her gaze at her husband. "I don't think doctors are any less responsible today than they were thirty years ago." She waited until Moe had been served, then continued. "It's the patients who have changed. They're like children now, placing the entire responsibility of their health in the hands of the doctors."

Moe smiled at her sardonically. "Pediatrics patients have always been children."

"But their parents haven't," she shot back.

Moe sighed heavily, setting down his work. "Look, I don't think you have to worry about any hike in malpractice rates. My income is high enough now that we can take care of your insurance no matter how much it costs."

Karen returned his steady gaze. "You have your work and I have mine. One has nothing to do with the other. I didn't marry you so you could support me while I practice medicine as a hobby."

"You supported me when things were rough on my side."

Karen blinked and dropped her gaze. There was no point in discussing obligations in marriage, what one owed the other, trying to figure out the tally on a balance sheet where some entries were tangible and some weren't. Not after ten years, anyway—ten years without annual accounting.

They had finished the dessert and the coffee and were simply sitting staring at each other by the time they returned to the real issue. Karen finally got around to making the point Moe knew she had been getting to.

"You know," she began defensively, "Harry Norton's rates are already twice what mine are." She took a bite to let this register with Moe. "After a court case, he may not even be able to *get* insurance."

Moe had prepared himself for this, and he gave it to her simply and without anger. "Whether I take the case or someone else does, Harry's going to have to go to court. He's made a mistake, a very serious one, and now he's got a lawsuit on his hands. I didn't bring this on him; he brought it on himself."

Karen looked at her husband pensively before she spoke. "You're telling me that you've decided to take the case, aren't you?"

Moe would not return her look; instead, he stared out at the lemon trees in the now-darkened garden. He suddenly thought of Karen following Harry into the on-call room after the Lip's heart had stopped beating. He thought of several other nights in the past few months when Harry and Karen had worked late at the hospital together. Harry was consulting on several of Karen's sick surgical patients, they had said. And the time they both came to him in Florida.

Karen had always been especially concerned about Harry. Even now. . . .

"Look, Karen, this all started off as a half-assed accusation made by a neurotic woman. I never really thought Harry could have made a mistake like this. I thought he knew what he was doing, that the Wexler woman was just overreacting. But she was right: he did butcher the bastard. And he's got to pay for that."

Moe did not tell Karen that Sarah Wexler, and her brother, too, had spoken with him on the phone a few hours earlier, late that afternoon. He had not given them a definite answer then. Now he would.

6 SARAH WEXLER HOWARD

November 15, 1975, Fairfax Area

Sometimes Sarah's mother could be absolutely exasperating. Old-fashioned religious customs were all right, as long as they were not inflicted on those who doubted. And right now, Sarah knew, it was more important to determine the cause of her father's death than it was to rush into an immediate funeral, just so they could go through seven days of sitting in a darkened house on stools in their bare feet, as their parents' parents had done.

Sarah had been trying to get her mother to sit down and discuss the matter seriously and reasonably, ever since she and Max had gotten home from their day at the beach cottage. But Miriam had already called the rabbi and made preparations for the services; and, only five minutes after Sarah and Max had walked through the door, Miriam had instructed them to look after the kids because she was going to the supermarket to get food for the week they would be stuck indoors.

And when she had gotten home from the supermarket, it had been one phone call after another.

Finally Sarah had to scream. "Mama, for God's sake, will you sit down and listen to me?"

Her mother had glowered at her, as if restraining the urge to slap her face, but she had sat down and listened.

"Mama"—Sarah sat down beside her mother—"you've got to postpone the funeral. At least for a few days. Robert and I have—"

"I can't postpone it."

"Will you listen to me?" Sarah grabbed her mother's hands and squeezed them too tightly. "Just for a few days, is all. We've got to let the hospital do an autopsy on Papa."

"No!" Miriam Wexler thrust her daughter's hands away. "There will be no autopsy!"

"Mama." Sarah tried to keep her voice from shrieking. "Robert and I have talked to a Dr. Michener. He's a doctor, but he's also a medical-malpractice attorney. And he thinks we have a good case."

"What do you mean, a good case?" Mrs. Wexler drew her shoulders up, tilted her head back, and looked defiantly in her daughter's eyes. "A good case of what?"

Sarah fidgeted at her mother's knee. "Mama, will you just listen? Dr. Michener feels we have grounds for a malpractice case against the doctor who operated on Papa."

"Dr. Norton?" Miriam got up from the sofa. "You want to sue Dr. Norton?"

Sarah rose to follow her mother. "Mama, he killed Papa; you know he did. That operation he performed wasn't necessary. It wasn't necessary at all."

"No." The older woman made a gesture toward moving away. "There will be no autopsy! And there will be no suing that nice Dr. Norton!"

Sarah pursued her mother like a dog stalking a bird. "Mama, I think Robert and I have as much right to a voice in this decision as you do."

"If Robert wants this, why isn't he here?"

Miriam knew as well as Sarah did why Robert had

chosen to wander off to look after his niece and nephews. He did not have a great liking for this sort of family confrontation. Sarah had wheedled and badgered him into going along with her to see Michener; Miriam knew, when it came to wheedling and badgering, Sarah could have a strong effect on Robert.

Sarah stamped to the hall door. "Max!" she shouted. "Will you and Robert come in here? Mama wants to have a talk!"

Miriam cast her eyes heavenward as if to ask, Lord, why did you burden me with a daughter like this? and returned to her place on the sofa. Sarah remained standing in the doorway waiting to see if the two men would respond. Mrs. Wexler eyed her daughter suspiciously. Sarah was dressed in her usual manner—a slacks outfit that might have been purchased in a men's department, designed to show off her flat, inadequate little butt; and a brightly colored shirt of some limp synthetic fabric, which showed off her equally flat, inadequate chest.

How Miriam and Herman had come up with a daughter like Sarah, Miriam had no idea. She was at least a foot taller than either of her parents, and twice as skinny. But both of their children were tall and thin, and both had Hermie's prominent nose and full mouth.

Miriam's son-in-law could not have been more different from her son and daughter. Max was not only blond and blue-eyed, he was also soft-spoken and respectful toward her, too respectful. Neither Miriam nor Sarah could ever be quite sure which side he would be on in a dispute, or precisely what he was thinking. Although Hermie had always felt some disappointment that Sarah had married outside her religion, Hermie had liked Max, perhaps more than he had liked his own son. Max was a writer, and Hermie had always had dreams of writing, though he had never quite managed to get beyond a feeble start or two.

Both Max and Robert entered the living room cautiously, aware that they were about to enter a family squabble. Sarah returned to her place on the well-worn sofa by her mother. Max and Robert edged their way to armchairs well in view of the two women, both avoiding the big, ugly, green Naugahyde chair that had always been considered Hermie's.

Sarah hurried to explain. "Mama and I have been discussing—"

But Miriam restrained her daughter with a firm hand on the shoulder. "Robert, why do you want to sue Dr. Norton?"

Robert turned red and then green, as he blustered, "I never . . . it wasn't . . . Sarah and I simply phoned Dr. Michener to get a second opinion. I didn't know . . ."

As Robert's long narrow hands fumbled nervously for the words, Sarah realized it was a mistake for her ever to depend upon her brother. Anxiously, she interjected, "Robert and I discussed this after we talked with Dr. Michener, and we agreed—"

"Shhh." Her mother again pressed her hand on Sarah's shoulder and, eyeing her admonishingly, said, "I want to hear what Robert thinks."

Realizing he wasn't going to escape, Robert heaved a sigh and sank back into the chair. "Well, Mama . . ." He groped for words, stammering slightly. "There's really no harm in giving the okay for an autopsy, is there? And then, when we know the results, if . . ."

"Do you know what that would mean to your father's religion?" Miriam's tone of voice was firm and direct, surprisingly self-controlled for a woman whose husband of forty years had been dead only a few hours. "It would mean cutting up his body like a butcher would cut up an animal—do you know what that would mean?"

Sarah leaned forward to obstruct her mother's line of vision. "But Dr. Norton has already done that. Didn't you see that incision? And Papa was still alive then."

But Miriam remained firm, her voice calm against her daughter's shrillness. "According to our religion, your Papa's not dead until his body is buried in the ground." Her eyes narrowed at her daughter. "And it would not be respectful to him to let someone do something like that to him."

Sarah could not hold herself still. "But, Mama, we're in the twentieth century now! We can be reasonable people! We don't have to—"

Sarah was interrupted by Max. His words were soft, almost inaudible, but the very fact that he spoke startled his wife into listening. "Mrs. Wexler, I didn't know about the religious objection to an autopsy when I told Sarah I thought it would be a good idea to see Dr. Michener. I can see how that would be something very difficult for you to approve of, but—"

"Max," Sarah started to protest, "it's just an ingrained, outmoded superstition, like not eating pork."

Maxwell raised his voice slightly to override his wife. "But I'm sure there must be situations where your religion would permit exceptions. If you spoke to your rabbi . . ."

"Oh, she doesn't have to speak to a rabbi," Sarah said, scowling. "These days, any rabbi would tell her to do whatever she wanted."

Max did his best to ignore Sarah and to proceed

in a gentle, understanding manner. "I don't know if Dr. Norton was responsible for Mr. Wexler's death. None of us do. There's no way of knowing unless they carry out an autopsy. I think you might agree, if you would just postpone the funeral and go in to see Dr. Michener on Monday morning."

They could all see that Miriam was listening seriously to her son-in-law's words. She sat, thinking quietly, before answering. "I know you mean well, but you don't know much about our religion. Hermie has to be buried quickly—first thing Monday morning."

Sarah recognized her opening, and she leaped to it. "We could call Dr. Michener. I'm sure he'd be glad to talk to you tonight. We could drive over—"

"I'm not going anywhere." Miriam's tone changed noticeably when speaking to her daughter. "I'll talk to him on the phone, but I'm not leaving this house tonight."

With a look of exasperation on her face, Sarah rose and headed toward the phone. "I'll see if he is willing to come over here."

Even Sarah was somewhat shy about calling a man of Michener's importance at home on a Saturday night. But she was surprised to find him extremely cordial toward her request, a fact that was doubly surprising when she sensed she had called as he was just finishing his dinner. But he had answered, "No problem. I understand. I should be able to get there in about an hour, perhaps a little less." And he had taken down the address.

Sarah was both pleased and irritated at her mother's response; if Dr. Michener was stopping by, they had to clean the house—and Sarah had to help. Sarah thought it would hardly matter if Michener thought her mother a poor housekeeper, but she accepted the dustcloth, hoping it would help change her mother's mind about the autopsy.

Miriam set about picking up the odds and ends that manage to get scattered about a living room in the process of living an ordinary life—a stack of newspapers neatly folded to the daily crossword puzzle, a pile of crochet work, a small stack of paperback books, a collection of mail. She also removed the slightly soiled antimacassars from the sofa and chairs and put the furniture back into the right position. And then she began to vacuum, thereby ending any possibility of further discussion with her daughter.

The modest little living room practically glistened by the time the doorbell rang.

Sarah was a little startled by the appearance of Moe Michener, partly because he was dressed casually in slacks and a brightly colored sports shirt and partly because he seemed to be slightly intoxicated. That, Sarah feared, might prove to be unfortunate. Although her father had been a fairly heavy drinker, she knew that her mother had never approved.

It was obvious that Miriam noticed the guest's condition, but it did not prevent her from showing her respect or her hospitality. As soon as they had been introduced, she offered him coffee, which he accepted. While she went to the kitchen to prepare it, Sarah sat Michener down to explain the situation more fully.

When Miriam returned, the lawyer was prepared to turn on the charm. The older woman was having some difficulty balancing the tray with the coffee and so many cups, so Michener rose ostentatiously and took the tray from her, flashing a sympathetic smile.

After the ritual of cream and sugar, they settled uncomfortably around the little living room—Sarah and Miriam back in their places on the sofa, Max and Robert returned to their respective chairs. No one told Michener the green reclining chair he was perched on had always been exclusively the property of the deceased.

"Mrs. Wexler," Moe began smoothly, "I want to offer you my condolences. I only met your husband once, and for a very short time, but I had the impression he was a fine man."

"Thank you." Miriam was gracious but not morbidly self-pitying. "Dr. Michener, I'm sorry you have to be faced with this problem, but my daughter and my son approached you without my permission."

"I know they did, Mrs. Wexler." Moe was careful to be understanding. "And the reason they did was that they were concerned about you and your welfare. They called because they wanted my opinion and my advice."

"According to my daughter, your advice is to sue Dr. Norton." Miriam tried to restrain her tone so as not to be ungracious toward her guest.

"No, ma'am." Moe smiled sympathetically.

"But—" Sarah started to protest, but Moe ignored her.

"I said that—depending on the results of examinations and tests—you might decide to sue Dr. Norton." Moe set down his cup. "I am not anxious to take Dr. Norton to court, because he is a very good friend of mine. I know that you like Dr. Norton, and so do I. However, I'm afraid that he's made a mistake, and I'm afraid that his mistake has cost your husband his life. If that's true—mind you, I'm not saying it is—but if it is true, I don't see how you—or any of your family—could defend Dr. Norton."

There were traces of tears in Miriam's eyes. She took a sip of coffee and thought silently for a moment before responding. "Hermie liked Dr. Norton. I think he would have forgiven him. If Dr. Norton made a mistake, it was a mistake made in good conscience. I'm doing what I think Hermie would have wanted."

Around the dimly lit room there was a long silence, unbroken except for the sound of cups and saucers. Finally Moe spoke, softly, respectfully.

"Mrs. Wexler, I don't think I could even venture to say what your husband would have wanted. I don't think anyone could, especially since. we don't yet know the actual cause of death. I know it's a difficult decision for you to make, but I think it would be a mistake for you not to allow the autopsy. Once the body is buried, no one will ever be able to know for sure why your husband died."

When Moe looked up from his coffee, he saw that Mrs. Wexler was not looking at him. He wondered if she had been listening. She was looking at her son, Robert. Suddenly she rose to her feet and walked over to a table that had a number of framed family pictures. She took her time, looking from one to the other—a picture of Hermie alone, a picture of him with Sarah as a baby, one of the four of them with Miriam holding baby Robert, with Sarah standing stiffly by her father, successive school pictures of each of the children, showing them gradually growing older and more mature. After a few silent moments, she turned and walked over beside Robert.

"I guess I've been more upset today than I thought I was," she said sadly. "I guess I didn't realize that Hermie was actually gone." The tears that she had been trying to hold back all day began to slip slowly down her cheeks. "My son is the man of the house now. Whatever decision there is to be made, Robert has to make it."

Sarah stiffened noticeably, but she did not speak;

she knew—according to her mother's faith—she was right. Sarah knew that her brother was weak and indecisive and ill equipped to be the family leader, but she could reason with Robert. She could influence him much more than she could influence her mother.

Robert was too stunned to know what to say; he was not accustomed to being the center of attention as far as the family was concerned. In his own world —among his business associates and friends—he could do anything; but he had always shrunk from involvement in family affairs.

Miriam sat down on the arm of Robert's chair and took his hand in hers. Robert blushed uncomfortably, trying to keep himself from crying as he looked at his mother's tears.

"Mama," he began hoarsely. "Mama, you know as well as I do that I have no idea of what Papa would want us to do in the situation. I don't have any idea of whether we should sue the doctor or not. But I do think we should okay the autopsy. I do think we ought to find out why Papa died."

Mrs. Wexler's tears seemed to stop as her son's decision registered in her mind. She took a crumpled handkerchief out of her apron pocket and dabbed at her face. She rose to her feet slowly and returned to her place on the sofa. The matter had been decided; it was out of her hands. Lost now, she had to ask for favors. "Dr. Michener, is there any possibility that they could perform the autopsy tomorrow so we could still have the funeral on Monday morning?"

Michener smiled at her kindly. "I'm sure that can be arranged without any difficulty at all."

PART TWO

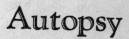

7 HARRY NORTON

November 16, 1975, Encino

The Los Angeles skyline was a dull red haze in the distance as Dr. Harry Norton entered Valley View Hospital at six in the morning. He hadn't slept well at all. The anxiety of what Moe Michener would do about the Wexler case—or what Moe might dredge up from the past—had occupied much of his thoughts.

But equally upsetting was his concern about what Joe Gregorio's autopsy might turn up.

The new Valley View Hospital was an expensive structure, and it looked it. Of brick and green glass, with beautifully landscaped grounds, it appeared to be a first-quality hotel or a luxury apartment building rather than a hospital. The interior had been decorated in elegant shades of blue and gold, with modern paintings in complementary colors adorning the walls. The floors and many of the hallways were covered in a thick pile carpeting. The lighting was subtle and indirect. On the patients' and visitors' elevators, soft music played.

Open only six months now, it was already three-fourths filled. George Mason, the hospital administrator, had predicted only a few days ago that it would be filled to capacity and ready to expand within a year.

As a limited partner in the hospital, Harry had taken that as good news indeed. But he was not quite as optimistic as George Mason. Talks between the management and the hospital-workers' union seemed to have broken down, and there was a pretty good chance of a strike. There was also the new problem with malpractice insurance. If there was a rate hike, it seemed a number of doctors also might strike, along with the nurses and orderlies. Most of the beds in the hospital were devoted to surgical patients. With a strike, there would be no surgery—and with no surgery, there would be no filled beds.

The hospital management might have to give in completely to the demands of the hospital workers, and that would certainly cut heavily into any projected profit. To keep the doctors working even with the enormous hike in insurance rates, there had been some discussion of the hospital paying for the insurance of its surgeons. That too would cut heavily into the hospital's income.

But, despite these financial worries, it was a great comfort to Harry to be a part of this elegant complex with its modern equipment and cheerful, competent staff. It was nothing like City Hospital, where he had interned. In fact, Valley View had been set up largely by doctors from City who were simply fed up with the miserable conditions of the publicly funded hospital. Here they all felt they could give their patients better care in better surroundings with better equipment.

Harry realized he had time for a cup of coffee before Gregorio's autopsy, so he went directly to the hospital coffee shop, a cheerful room with a small snack bar and cafeteria setup and about fifteen tables and modern paintings on the walls. The paintings were changed every month by a local artists' group, and they could be purchased by staff members.

Harry needed to wake up and be as alert as possible

for the meeting with Joe Gregorio, so he ordered two cups of black coffee. And he chose a table in a quiet corner to be alone to think.

Gregorio had given himself the title of "Hospital Prick." In some ways it was deserved, but in others it was not. Gregorio had practiced internal medicine in Vienna for ten years before the war, treating diabetes, heart failure, and strokes. He had come to America as a refugee and had wound up going back to medical school and taking a residency in the specialty he now practiced. He had been a pathologist in the Valley for twenty years.

He was an older man now, past the normal age for retirement. But, despite his own disclaimers, he liked his work. He generally avoided reminiscing about his practice before and during the war, but occasionally there would be references to the effect that national socialism had on the practice of medicine. They were not positive references.

But Gregorio was always quick to point out that the war had not been the only reason for his giving up his practice. "I honestly did not believe that I helped anyone as an internist for ten years," he was often heard to say, "so I became a pathologist. At least I cannot harm anyone here."

However, Gregorio's favorite lecture was: "The surgeons, they can do everything but don't know anything. The internists, they read all the journals and know everything, but they're clumsy. They can't do anything. The pathologist, now he is the one who knows everything, and can do everything. But too late—always too late."

Despite the title he had given himself, an aura of likability surrounded Gregorio, with his twinkling gray eyes and his sixty-odd years of living. He looked like he had been put together by some person in a terrible hurry, working with a minimum of materials. Wisps of gray silky hair drifted carelessly from both sides of his receding hairline. His sharp nose was set prominently between thin high cheeks, which would quiver when he became excited. His mouth always appeared to be smiling. And he sported an enormous white mustache.

Gregorio had the responsibility for making the final diagnosis; he was the supreme judge, the highest court. The surgeons might reason and bicker and argue; the internists might obtain biochemical tests, blood tests, x-rays, and then debate further. But in the end, Gregorio always had the last and most accurate say.

Sometimes Gregorio had worn his authority too well and deserved the title he had given himself. Harry had heard the story several times of a Grand Rounds mortality meeting at the amphitheater before the combined medical-surgical staff. The patient had died of a pulmonary embolus, a blood clot to the lung, after a fracture of the hip. The hip had not been fixed for a few days because of the patient's shock condition and fluid imbalance.

Gregorio, standing under the bright lights of the podium, had revealed his autopsy findings, showing his colored slides of the inflamed veins next to the fractured bone. And he had piped out, "The clot that finally lodged in the patient's lungs causing death was formed in the veins adjacent to the fractured hip. We know statistically, gentlemen, that there is a *decreased* incidence of clot formation in veins when a fractured hip is reduced and pinned early. But nothing was done for this man for three days!"

He had paused for a moment to scan the room dramatically, and then he had thundered, "Gentlemen, who killed this man?"

As Harry sat sipping his strong hot coffee, he wondered if there would be a similar indictment of him. He tried to imagine how the other doctors on the staff would react. He had known some of them almost as long as he had known Moe. In his years as an intern and resident, his work had been subjected to the approval or disapproval of O'Hara and Buxbaum. When Valley View had been built, they had eagerly joined the staff of the new facility; Harry realized wryly that he would again be subjected to their judgment.

O'Hara was sitting at a table nearby with two other doctors, Kramer and Minton, gulping down a rather large breakfast. They were talking about what everybody seemed to be talking about today—the possibility of a doctors' strike.

O'Hara's early tendency toward a potbelly had by now taken over completely, making it very difficult for him to get close enough to the table to scoop in the food. And much of his wiry red hair was now gone, leaving him only a bright fringe around the sides and back. His earlier abruptness was now closer to bluster; when O'Hara spoke, everyone around heard him.

"The hospital administration will simply have to understand that the strike is not aimed at them; it's aimed at the state legislature." He paused for a mouthful of pancakes. "Some kind of control has to be placed on those fucking insurance companies."

Minton spoke quietly, but Harry could hear his words clearly. "I don't know. . . . I just don't know that we should all go out entirely. There has to be some kind of medical care available—at least for emergency cases."

Kramer broke in. "I admit we can't just let people die in the streets. But going on a strike is better than all of us having to give up our practices. And that's what we'll be forced to do if the insurance companies have their way."

"It's not just the insurance companies who are at fault, though," O'Hara bellowed. "Those poor patients who may be dying in the streets—they're the ones who are really to blame. They come into the hospital begging, 'Doctor, Doctor, please help me'; and when they're all right and out of the hospital, they head straight for their asshole lawyers!"

Moe Michener walked into the cafeteria just in time to catch the last two words of O'Hara's comment. He glanced at the table but pretended not to have heard. He also noticed Harry Norton, sitting alone, and then quickly looked down at the selection of pastries in the display case.

As Harry watched, Moe continued to stand there, clearly unsure about his next move. It confirmed what Harry had guessed to be true: the battle between them was on. Moe would not, as he often did, join Harry at his table—yet he would have to sit with someone because all the tables were occupied.

Harry quickly gulped down the last of his coffee and made a quick exit from the cafeteria. He would go up and look in on a few patients before the autopsy began. The patients and nurses might be a bit surprised at seeing him on his rounds so early, but that would be better than sitting still listening to today's problems and facing the memories they dredged up.

It had been so strange sitting there hearing the other doctors talking about striking, hearing them blame their problems on lawyers like Moe, and then to remember that first strike he and Moe had been through together during their internship.

*   *   *

They had called that first strike a "heal-in," and the object had been to try to improve the conditions for both doctors and patients at City Hospital. Hospital Workers' Union 408 had been striking then too. Only they hadn't been concerned about conditions—they had wanted more money. Many of the doctors had supported the union in its demands, hoping an increase in wages would give the hospital workers more incentive to perform their duties adequately. Unfortunately, the opposite eventually turned out to be true: the union got its demands and discovered it had considerable power; therefore its members didn't have to work quite so hard, and conditions for both patients and doctors deteriorated.

The trouble had begun on the day they operated on Mrs. Goldstein. Both Moe and Harry had gotten beyond their early difficulties in the operating room. They were competent doctors, and the day when they might also be surgeons seemed to be in sight. They had already been permitted to perform a few operations with Buxbaum's guidance—hernias, breast biopsies, a couple of hot appendix removals—though their success had been somewhat limited. They both had realized that taking care of patients was one thing; taking up the *knife,* tying knots, cutting and sewing, and clamping blood vessels was quite another.

Buxbaum had helped Harry with his first hemorrhoid operation the week before. He hadn't exactly filled Harry with confidence as the case began. "Try not to cut yourself," he had said.

From that point on, things had gotten progressively worse. Nothing Harry did seemed to please Buxbaum. Harry cut in the wrong places. His knots were either too tight or too loose. Most of them broke and had to be tied again. And he couldn't get the hemorrhoid out. Everything he touched seemed to bleed. Harry had finally wound up with his hands crossed, off balance, with a small pumping artery just out of view. The entire field was a bloody mess.

Buxbaum finally took over the case, "Look," he had said, as they stopped, panting and sweating during the disaster, just to catch their breath, "it doesn't matter what you do in the operating room, but, for Christ's sake, at least look good doing it."

Harry hadn't looked very good on that one. He later told Moe that he suspected Buxbaum had led him into many of the mistakes on purpose—just to get the case. "You learn to fix one asshole right, and you can learn to fix them all," Buxbaum had said at the end of the operation. Buxbaum was one asshole Harry and Moe wanted to fix—but good.

Mrs. Goldstein would have been Moe's big chance. He would have assisted in, rather than performed, the operation, which was a very unusual one, with only a few similar cases actually on record. The operation was to be written up in great detail, and Moe would be right there in the action.

It had been an opportunity for Harry, too, because Buxbaum had ordered him to be in the OR to scrub in if necessary, for "an extra pair of hands." And to make sure the hospital camera, the special lenses for close-ups, and other equipment for photographing the operation were available.

Mrs. Goldstein had had an aneurysm, a large dilation of the superior mesenteric artery in her abdomen. Through this blood vessel raced all the blood to her liver, stomach, and intestines.

Moe cared about Mrs. Goldstein. He had been the first one to see her in the clinic, with her two children and small, anxious husband. He had taken her history of increasing diarrhea and weight loss and pains in the stomach. And he had ordered her first x-rays, which showed the calcified tumor mass, about four centimeters in diameter, sitting in the middle of her gut.

Moe had wheeled her to x-ray himself for her arteriogram. He had held her hand when the radiologist injected the burning solution through the femoral artery in her groin. She had screamed out in agony, and Moe was a little terrified himself.

Moe had seen the faces of Sims and Buxbaum light up when they saw their suspicions confirmed—the mass was indeed an aneurysm.

"It sure explains her diarrhea," said Sims. "Ischemia of the bowel. A great case. A guy would be lucky to do one of these during his entire residency."

"Only a handful of them in the literature," Buxbaum added.

Moe knew that Sims, as the chief resident, would get to do the case, with Buxbaum assisting. Moe would be second assistant.

Sims had been accepted as the first black surgical house officer at City Hospital four years before. He was a technical artist. He had the best pair of hands of any surgeon in the hospital.

Sims was almost through his training now. He could see the light at the end of the tunnel. He was hesitating between private practice and a career in research. Moe knew a paper written up on Mrs. Goldstein's case would help both Sims and Buxbaum on the road toward an associate professorship.

"But what are the chances the aneurysm will burst if nothing is done?" Moe had asked. "Does she really need an operation?"

"The chances? Why . . . er . . ." Buxbaum hesitated. "Well, it is difficult to say. There are so few cases.

But it has to come out. There's no question about that. Besides, Sims and I have already practiced a half-dozen times on these grafts in the dog lab. It was easy. No technical problem."

Moe remembered wanting to ask Buxbaum if he expected Mrs. Goldstein to bark at the end of the operation, like one of the dogs in the experimental lab. He remembered his first proctoscopy patient, and Harry's patient, the Lip. Were the doctors being trained to help people? he wondered. Or was it all some gross extension from the animal laboratory? Were they dealing with people? Human beings? Or just *things?* Moe said nothing.

In the operating room, Moe stared out past his glasses, which hung loosely on his nose, and into the belly of Mrs. Marvin Goldstein. A pulsating bubble, red and glistening and smooth, about the size of a golf ball, rose and fell with the patient's heartbeat.

Moe knew this bubble was the aneurysm. He knew also that if it burst on its own at this moment, or was nicked by Sims's scissors, or was brushed by Buxbaum's fat little fingers, they could all kiss the patient good-bye. Mrs. Goldstein would never wake up again.

Moe strained and grunted as he shifted his body for a better view around the crowded operating-room table. The two metal retractors cut deep, painful notches into his hands as he tried to provide the exposure for the others. As usual, no one was satisfied.

Sims had complained, "Goddamn it! I can't see a thing." And Buxbaum had chided him. "Careful, easy, easy. You're digging into the pancreas. Careful, boy."

Moe had pulled a little more, trying to ignore the steamy fog that had begun to creep into the corners of his glasses. With each breath he had taken under the paper mask, the cloud in front of his eyes had increased. He had tried breathing through his mouth to lessen the haze, but it hadn't worked.

Outside the operating-room window, where people were not attached to metal retractors, where they were free to move and clear their throats and defog their glasses, there could be heard the sounds of the strike. There had been low rumbles, with an occasional high-pitched shout or curse as the police had pushed back one of the more unruly demonstrators. Intermittently there had been the chanting of "We shall overcome! We shall overcome!"

But inside, Moe had felt glued to the two pieces of metal in his cramped fingers. He had not been interested in Mrs. Goldstein. He had not been interested in her aneurysm. He had certainly not been interested in how similar or dissimilar this had been to the operations Buxbaum and Sims had performed on the dogs.

He had simply stood there, holding the retractors hour after hour, occasionally looking up at the clock on the wall.

At three in the afternoon, he had realized he had been there for five hours, and the case had been only half over. With his glasses completely fogged, through one corner of the lens, he had gotten a glimpse of the bubble again, just as Sims had cut the vein.

"No! No! Goddamn it! I told you not to . . ." Buxbaum had shouted fiercely. "Snaps! Suck! Suck!"

Buxbaum and Sims had managed to get a few ties around the bleeder, and the operating field had dried up again. But Moe's nose had not. It had begun running into his mask, slowly at first and then, to his dismay, faster and faster. He had sniffed in loudly, but a stern look from Buxbaum had made him stop.

"Not while we're cutting, boy. We're trying to concentrate here."

With the mucus in his nasal passages and mouth, he had gagged and choked, resisting the natural urge to sniff again.

Then he had felt an inch in his groin. He had tried to lean against the table to scratch it without being noticed, but he had bumped into Sims's leg instead.

"What the shit are you doing?" Sims had demanded.

Standing frozen in place, Moe had found that the itch grew unbearable. He had desperately wanted to rip off his mask, blow his nose, scratch his balls, and clean his glasses—all the things normal people do. He wanted to yell, "Fuck it! Fuck Buxbaum! Fuck Sims! Fuck Mrs. Goldstein! Fuck the operating room!"

He had tried to think of ways he might get away. He could pretend to faint. Not too obviously, of course, a few subtle complaints and whines about the heat or not feeling well. Well spaced, about twenty minutes apart, and then a slight slip and stumble away from the table.

No, he needed a better idea. Perhaps he could announce that he had to go to the bathroom. No, he had used that one already. It wasn't enough of a reason.

Moe had tried to relax and let his mind wander to the lines of pickets and people crowding the entrances to City Hospital. He imagined them parading past the main entrance with their large signs and placards: STRIKE AGAINST CITY! UNFAIR TO LABOR UNION 408! DOCTORS AND WORKERS UNITE FOR LIVING WAGES. The signs that Moe and his committee had worked so carefully to prepare.

It had been a clever idea, to combine the doctors' strike with the demands of Union 408, Moe thought. As head of the House Officers' Association, he had presented the idea eloquently to a receptive group of young City Hospital interns and residents only a week before.

"These bastards have been using us for years," Moe had shouted to the packed group. "We get paid less than the administrators who sit on their fat asses in the plush offices up front. And we run our cans off here every night, in thirty-six-hour shifts. We have less to say around here than the porters and elevator operators."

He had paused to give the other doctors time to digest his message. All heads had nodded in agreement.

"I'm tired of working for less than a living wage," Moe had continued. "I'm tired of sleeping in an on-call room that looks like a shithouse every night, with paint falling off the walls, and dirty linen, and no hot water. I want action, and if we don't get it immediately, I'm calling for a unanimous show on the part of the doctors—a strike, a 'heal-in.' "

The doctors had all listened intently. And nodded again.

Moe's plan had been so simple and so good. A "heal-in." It had worked at Los Angeles County Hospital the year before. The doctors would not discharge any patients from the hospital. Or sign any insurance forms. They'd create the biggest damn bottleneck the hospital had ever seen! People waiting for routine admissions would get backed up for hours—even days and weeks.

"In Los Angeles, they kept the patients an extra few days," Moe had said. "There were always reasons. A low blood count. A little protein in the urine. A repeat chest x-ray. And it worked! The angry patients and citizens and insurance companies complained—to the administrators, to the newspapers, even to the mayor himself. The press and TV ran daily coverage. No one wanted bad publicity. The doctors finally got their demands—in less than three days."

The doctors had all been in agreement . . . then. Moe was their leader. Moe, who had changed a great deal since his early days as a medical student, was more secure and outgoing now. He was the most popular young doctor on the staff, and the spokesman for the group. He was also responsible for "Moe's Moat," the small wooden bridge that ran over a large puddle of water in the corridor by x-ray.

For years the leaky pipes in the tunnels underneath the hospital had been defective. Large volumes of water collected in the most dependent portion of the tunnels, halfway between the emergency room and x-ray. Moe had headed a committee that demanded that the pipes be fixed immediately. Nothing had been done.

"No funds have been allowed for that in the hospital budget this year," the hospital director stated.

Things had come to a head one night during a heavy thunderstorm. The corridor became flooded with three feet of water at that point. A patient being wheeled to x-ray fell off a stretcher and almost drowned.

That very night Moe had cultured out the gully. The reports on the water grew out *E. coli, Streptococcus faecalis,* and several other bacteria that inhabit the bowels of human beings. A porter finally admitted taking a crap there on the early morning shift just before the storm broke. A copy of the culture report and the story reached the desks of the hospital director and the mayor.

Owing largely to Moe's efforts, and his threat of leaking the whole thing to the newspapers, a compromise had been reached. There was still no money to fix the pipes, but a small wooden bridge was constructed over the area in question. This was named

"Moe's Moat," in honor of the intern who had cultured out the gully. It was looked upon as a triumph, however small, of the house officers over the administration, and a reason to continue striving for new gains. The porter involved in the case was reprimanded and transferred to another part of the hospital. . . .

"Come on, boy. Wake up." Buxbaum had brought Moe's thoughts back to the operation.

The aneurysm was out of Mrs. Goldstein's body. It lay in a large pan on the scrub nurse's table, surrounded by fresh green sheets.

Inside the patient, two heavy vascular clamps grasped the ends of the vessels that supplied the blood to her liver, stomach, and intestines. The final step of the operation was still ahead for them—to reestablish flow to these organs using a vein graft that had been dissected out of Mrs. Goldstein's right groin at the beginning of the case.

At the moment, no blood was flowing to the patient's guts—no nourishment at all. No one seemed very concerned.

"Let's get a few good pictures of the specimen in the pan," Buxbaum barked, as the circulating nurse and the hospital photographer moved in with a camera and several lenses. "We want a good one of the aneurysm in the bucket. Green-towel background."

Flashbulbs popped again and again as Buxbaum ordered the golf ball photographed from every possible angle. He wanted only the best slides when he reported this case.

Moe used the few minutes to unclench his hands and restore circulation to his painful palms and knuckles. They were white from the retractors. He looked inside the patient again. Mrs. Goldstein's bowels were beginning to look pale and swollen. They were turning a light purple, and the peristalsis, or natural motor function of the intestines, was actually slowing down before his eyes. He pictured the tens of thousands of cells dying every minute. How long could they survive without blood supply?

Buxbaum next ordered clean blue towels to be draped around Mrs. Goldstein's wound. "Good contrast," he said, beaming. "Green for the aneurysm, and blue for the vessels inside the patient. It will look great on the screen. Right, Sims?"

And Sims nodded.

The pictures continued for another ten minutes. At one point Buxbaum even had the anesthesiologist stop breathing for the patient for a precious few seconds, so the film wouldn't be blurred.

Finally, Moe had to speak up. "What about the bowels and the liver?" he asked. They looked more purple and swollen than ever.

"Relax, relax," Sims said. "It's been shown in the literature that they can live for over one hour. We'll put in the graft in a minute. These shots are a once-in-a-lifetime chance."

They were talking about Mrs. Goldstein's lifetime. It was not only the liver and gut that were in danger here. By prolonging the surgery time, the patient had a much greater chance of getting a pneumonia and a wound infection later on.

After the final series of pictures was taken, Moe moved back to his retractors. Buxbaum and Sims began to sew in the graft. Moe kept further opinions to himself. He was low man at the table. The other intern, Harry, hadn't bothered to speak up at all.

Moe took one final glimpse at the bowel. Mrs. Goldstein would be lucky if she woke up barking, damn lucky! Only once before had he seen the intestines looking so purple and swollen and sick. It was at the end of the experiment on a North American bullfrog, years before in medical school.

"Come on, boy, hold back there." Buxbaum prodded him again, none too gently, replacing the retractor in his hand, and giving it a tug.

The clumsy son of a bitch trapped Moe's finger rudely against the metal, and Moe squirmed, then lunged forward to get a better look at what he was holding.

Suddenly, he found he could see nothing but a blur. His glasses had fallen off his nose!

There was a long silence in which no one seemed to move. Moe blinked stupidly, trying to see where the glasses had landed. Slightly out of focus, he perceived them lying in the wound.

Deftly, Buxbaum reached in with a forceps and retrieved the heavy frames. "You know you have just dropped two million bacteria into Mrs. Goldstein. You may have just killed the patient." And then Buxbaum heaved a sigh and said, smiling, "Well, I guess you guys are improving. At least this time it wasn't a milk shake and two undigested Big Macs."

Then the surgeon turned to Harry. "Norton, are you scrubbed?"

Moe had been relieved when Harry had taken over the retractors. He had won his little victory, though not intentionally. He had gotten away from that table and out of the operating room, after standing there for six hours.

Moe returned to the wards. He made rounds on the twenty-five patients he hadn't had time to see that morning. He was preparing to join the crowd and the strikers in front of City Hospital, when he got paged to the emergency room for a stat call.

The patient, a highly irate Alvin Wasserman, was a little more difficult to handle.

"What's the matter?" Moe asked.

"My wife's pregnant!" came the sudden reply.

"Well, congratulations," Moe offered. "Wonderful news! Mazel tov!"

Wasserman wasn't quite so enthused.

"Mazel tov, my ass!" he snorted.

Moe had forgotten to take a very important part of his patient's history: Wasserman had undergone a vasectomy several months before. Moe tried to soothe his patient's feelings by suggesting that perhaps Wasserman was not the baby's father. The patient became enraged. He swore that his wife had been faithful to him.

Indeed, on reviewing the slides, it turned out that no vas specimen could be seen on the right side, only strands of scrotal sac and some nerve bundles. Moe took a repeat sperm count on Wasserman to settle things. It should have read zero. It came back an all-time hospital high, in the millions! Moe admitted the patient to urology for a complete vasectomy in the morning.

Moe got Wasserman ready for surgery. He drew his routine blood tests and steered him through x-ray.

"Have them shave off the hair around his groin," he said to the black orderly. "Abdominal prep, nipple to knees."

The orderly smiled. "Who is this *them* you're talking about, Doc?" he asked. "You know we're extra short today. Union 408's out on strike. There's only me and Smith and Jonesy here. Smitty's on coffee break now. Jonesy's taking a patient to x-ray, and I'm all tied up down the hall. If you want it done real quick, Doc, you'd better do it yourself."

Moe knew the orderly was right. "How about a

razor, then?" he asked. "Or is that too much trouble?"
But the orderly was already gone.

Moe was furious. The lazy bastard! The dirty fuck!
All the same! Every last one of them! The porters,
the orderlies, and the elevator operators at City Hospital ranked high among the lowest human beings he
had ever met. Alcoholics, men down on their luck,
perverts. They did next to nothing, but hung around
the emergency room and the corridors, smoking and
drinking coffee and laughing among themselves.

It seemed as if the porters had all the higher-up
connections that Moe had been missing. "I got in here
as a black and a hardship case," the same orderly had
told Moe, when Moe had demanded that he wheel a
patient to x-ray two months ago, "and I ain't working
my ass off for nobody. Besides, Doc, my cousin knows
the mayor's secretary . . ." and he added with a wide
smile, "personally."

The orderly had only one arm. The other had
been taken off at the elbow during a street fight years
before. The orderly did drive a big yellow Cadillac,
though, and parked every day in the main lot right
next to the hospital. Moe and the other doctors had
to park in a rock-filled area three blocks away.

Moe began to shave the hair from Wasserman's
groin. He thought of the years of study, four in the
university and four in medical school, which had led
to this one divine moment. God, maybe he should
have gone into something else, something a little
easier. Maybe surgery wasn't for him. Maybe he didn't
have the hands of a Sims, the confidence of a Buxbaum, or the persistence of an O'Hara. Could he
stand it for another five years? Was he such a maso-
chist? His friends from the university were all getting
married now—comfortable homes, normal hours—and
here he was shaving some guy's groin for peanuts!

And peanuts it was! Moe quickly thought back to his take-home pay. Three hundred and sixty dollars per month. Ninety dollars per week. And he had to pay for the shit food in the cafeteria himself. It all came to less than a dollar an hour!

Moe knew he was right in championing the cause of the house staff. Overworked and underpaid. They were slave labor for those bastards. Eight years of education, and just a bunch of slaves!

Moe felt the strike and heal-in would be ending soon in favor of the doctors.

As the weeks had gone by, the news in the papers and on television had created a momentum that the mayor's office and the negotiators had had to meet head on. The news reports had created sympathy for the downtrodden members of Union 408. But the reporters had chastised the doctors for hindering the care of patients. The news media had seemed to know which side their bread was buttered on.

The hospital finally had had to capitulate to the union. The mayor and the profit-and-loss statement demanded it. But nobody had forced anything in the doctors' heal-in. Nobody had seemed to care about the filth and the crowded conditions at City Hospital. No one had been concerned that doctors were having to stay awake on drugs, so they could continue to perform operations on patients thirty-six hours at a stretch.

So the doctors had just simply given up, releasing their patients and going back to following the rules of the doctor game. And because the heal-in had been Moe's idea, he had been left holding the bag.

While the negotiations were being concluded in the mayor's office, a large crowd gathered on the steps of City Hospital. Almost a thousand people paraded slowly in front of the building in celebration, while inside the doctors were releasing patients by the score and scheduling operations for those who had been waiting weeks to be admitted.

The other doctors had had very little to say to Moe. The failure had been his alone. Harry had done his best to try to cheer up his friend. Although he had not put his energy into the heal-in as other doctors had, he had stood by his friend when he felt that loyalty called for it.

Moe had been determined to go out front to see the enormous demonstration. Harry had considered that unwise; but, when Moe insisted, Harry had decided to go along with him.

The two of them stepped out of the hospital to see the biggest crowd the union had ever managed to attract, with newsmen, photographers, and television cameras everywhere. The crudely painted picket signs seemed to extend forever. And the noise of the chanting and catcalls was deafening.

As they walked into the crowd, they heard one of the union leaders telling a television newscaster, "There's every indication that we've won a total victory. The thing that really did it for us was the fact that those doctor boys scheduled their heal-in at the same time."

The newsman spotted Moe and turned to him suddenly. "Dr. Michener, Dr. Michener. We understand that the heal-in is over, that the doctors have given up their demands completely. Do you have anything to say?"

"No." Moe stepped aside. "No comment."

"Is it true that all the patients have been released from the wards?" another reporter asked.

"No comment."

At that moment, one of the demonstrators grabbed Moe and shouted, "Hey, Doc, what are you doing out here? Get back inside and move those stretchers!"

Moe pulled himself away and tried to move off through the crowd, but the demonstrator followed and grabbed his arm again. Harry recognized the man as the one-armed porter with the connections in the mayor's office.

His jeering voice resounded over the crowd, "What'sa matter, Doc, afraid to admit that Whitey ain't got what it takes?"

Again Moe tried to pull away, but this time he found himself pinned in one place by a number of demonstrators. The one-armed porter held Moe's arm as if he wanted to twist it off. And the photographers and the television cameras converged on the spot, further blocking his escape.

The one-armed porter was in his glory. With the cameras aimed on him, he had the eyes and ears of the world, and he was determined to take advantage of it. "You doctors supposed to be big men! Heroes! The white knights! Well, you don't look so big no more! Things is the other way around now, baby! Whitey is going to have to learn to kiss some black ass!"

That had been more than Moe could take. Pinned in, unable to move, suddenly the whole situation had become a race war. A vendetta. If that was what they wanted . . .

"Up your ass, nigger!" Moe lashed out. "Up your dirty black ass!"

Harry Norton was more stunned than the demonstrators and newsmen. He knew Moe Michener. Moe was the biggest bleeding heart of any bleeding-heart liberal, and Harry was sure this was the first time in his life Moe had ever used such words.

But the demonstrators were elated. They had suddenly found someone to loose their pent-up anger on. Their rage had suddenly found a way to unleash itself in violence.

"Kill him!" a voice cried out. "Kill Whitey!"

Someone locked an arm around Moe's neck, while demonstrators thrust their picket signs at his head and others plunged their fists into his groin and tore at his clothes.

Several of them lunged at Harry, knocking him to the ground. He struggled to get up, but a hand pulled at his tie, almost strangling him in the noose. Someone else kicked him over and over again in the belly.

The police who had been supervising the demonstration used their clubs to try to break up the disorder, swinging them indiscriminately at anyone who might be in the way.

The newsmen were being jostled and shoved, but they managed to keep the flashbulbs popping and the TV cameras rolling.

The sound of sirens brought more men in blue into the battleground, but it took at least half an hour for them to restore order. When it was over, Moe's face was a bloody pulp, his clothes were ripped and torn, and he had a broken arm and a fractured rib.

Harry had gotten away with a large gash over his left eye, some bruises in the lower regions of his body, and a ripped coat. A policeman helped him to the emergency room for treatment, but Harry noticed that Moe was being helped into a police car, one of eight being arrested and taken to jail. Harry also noticed that the one-armed porter was not one of the eight.

Mrs. Marvin Goldstein died the night after her operation. Her heart just stopped beating and never started again. Sims got permission for an autopsy from the family.

The post-mortem showed her intestines were gangrenous and dead. The grafted anastomosis was intact. No leaks, but full of clots. No blood flow to the intestines at all. Moe was very upset. But Harry had assured him that it hadn't been his glasses that had killed the patient.

Buxbaum's presentation of the case a few weeks later at Grand Rounds was impressive. He reviewed all the statistics from the world's literature: incidence of such aneurysms, percentage of spontaneous rupture, signs and symptoms, x-ray and lab tests, types of operations, and results.

The slides turned out to be terrific too. The green background had showed up the aneurysm in the bucket very well. The blue towels surrounding the blood vessels and the anastomosis looked just fine. Buxbaum had even taken a few extra pictures of Mrs. Goldstein at autopsy, using a white background. He threw these in at the end of his talk, just before they turned on the lights.

To Harry Norton, hospitals like Valley View were the real hope for the future of American medicine. Since they were privately owned, their continued success depended upon providing the best that medical science had to offer. People who could pay the high cost of up-to-date techniques and equipment would choose a hospital like Valley View. Patients wanted to be treated like human beings when they were ill; they wanted consideration and care. They did not want the kind of treatment they received at places like City Hospital.

And Valley View also had provision to give equal care to those who could not pay. The emergency room received all patients who came or were brought to it. Medicare and MediCal paid for many of them. But even when they had no means of payment, patients were not turned away. "Z" numbers, patients who were acutely ill, unconscious, or in danger of losing life or limb, with no money and no insurance at all, were admitted to Valley View's intensive care unit and assigned emergency MediCal numbers later on.

All of Harry Norton's patients were doing well at the moment, even those in intensive care. He wondered how many of them would be alive and doing this well if they had been treated at City Hospital.

Before he left intensive care to go downstairs for the autopsy, he took one last look at the line of television screens by the nurses' station. Each screen monitored the important life functions of one patient; if any one of them registered a change, the nurse could be there even before the patient rang for help.

Dr. Harold Norton wouldn't admit it to just anybody, but he was proud of being a doctor; he was proud that he could give his patients the best care available. It was true that he also liked financial security; he liked the things that money could buy. He would be the first to admit that he was not the perfect image of the old-fashioned noble and selfless physician. But he simply did not see that his own interests and the interests of his patients had to be mutually exclusive.

As he waited for the elevator, he anxiously wondered just how much longer he would have his life the way he wanted it. How long would he be able to care for his patients the way he wanted? How long would he be financially secure? How long could he even practice in the state of California?

If Moe Michener had his way . . .

When Harry stepped into the elevator, he found himself face to face with Joe Gregorio.

If Gregorio had been Irish, he would have grown up to be a leprechaun. His eyes twinkled when he saw Harry.

"Good morning, Norton," he chirped. "Are you ready to be dissected?"

Harry didn't laugh. "I know it won't be the first time you've done a post-mortem on a live doctor," he needled. "But it's the first time for me, and I'm a little bit scared, frankly."

The two men were approximately the same height, but there was more than a thirty-year difference in their ages. The difference between their backgrounds was so great it could not be measured.

"Harry," Gregorio began, looking down at the floor nervously as the elevator stopped and the door opened. When no one got on, he continued. "Harry, I want you to know I'm sorry my first tests were not more conclusive."

"You did what you could," Harry replied, smiling weakly. "I'm sorry I lost my temper yesterday."

It was difficult for Joe Gregorio to praise or console another doctor, but he tried. "If it had been my decision, I don't know what I would have done." He paused, waiting for the door to open, then followed Harry out of the elevator. "There was every reason to believe it was cancer. But still, to be safe . . ."

"I know," Harry said as he stood in the hallway, grateful to talk to the man who would be his judge. "To be safe, I should have closed and waited for a more definite answer."

"If it had been cancer, the family would look at you as a hero right now."

"I wasn't trying to be a hero." Harry sighed. "I was simply trying to save the man's life."

"You know"—Gregorio tried to lighten the conversation—"you're a good surgeon. From what I've seen, if I had cancer of the pancreas, the man I would want to operate on me would be Dr. Harry Norton."

"After today," Harry asked seriously, "do you think the state of California would permit Dr. Harry Norton to operate on you?"

"I don't know," Gregorio said simply. "I don't know."

8 ROBERT WEXLER

November 16, 1975, Beverly Hills

"Bobby." The voice that wakened him was soft and gentle, but Robert's sleep had been restless and his dreams confused, so he awoke in fright. "Wake up, Bobby. I've brought you some coffee."

Robert Wexler had had only three hours of sleep, but he had asked to be waked up at eight o'clock, because there were so many things he would have to do that day. He rubbed his eyes, sat up in bed, and tried to focus on his roommate.

Carl set a tray containing a pot of coffee, two coffee cups, and a plate of Danish on the table by Robert's bed. Carl had had almost as little sleep as Robert had, but he managed to look fresh and beautiful in his crisp white-silk caftan. Robert made room in the big double bed, and Carl perched himself Indian-style between the coffee and his roommate. After flashing a sympathetic smile and giving Robert a soft kiss on the forehead, Carl served the coffee and cake without speaking.

Robert was grateful for the silence. Somehow Carl had known exactly what to do and precisely what to say to be a comfort to him. Robert wished that his roommate could be with him through the funeral and throughout the ordeal of the mourning period, but both of them realized that this would be frowned upon.

His father's death had upset Robert Wexler very much, and for reasons he could not easily discuss with his mother or sister, neither of whom would understand. Only Carl could understand. For Carl was more family to him than his own family had been.

He and Robert had been business partners as well as roommates for the past eight years. "Wexart"—a combination of their last names, Wexler and Arthur—had achieved a position of distinction among Beverly Hills interior designers. With Carl's understanding of traditional design, and with Robert's flair for the modern, they had established a reputation as *the* most flexible and adaptable of stylish decorators, able to work individually or in concert.

And their personal relationship had proved equally successful.

Carl was somewhat older and more even-tempered than Robert. Both of them were aware that there was more than just a little of the father-son to their relationship, and that was why there had been more than a little strain between them since Robert's father's operation. And that was also why Robert was more than a little grateful for Carl's patience and understanding.

Robert had not been able to leave his mother's house until well after midnight, and he had not arrived home at the apartment in Beverly Hills until around one. Carl was sitting up waiting for him, concerned to know if Robert was okay. And then the two of them had sat up and talked into the early morning hours.

Carl had experienced the death of his own father some years before, and he knew that what Robert would be feeling most right now would not be grief, which is what most normal children feel at the loss of a parent, but guilt. And he had been right. Robert had been overwhelmed by the realization that suddenly there was no time left to get to know the father whose gestures of friendship had always been rejected by the son.

Robert was perceptive enough to know that his father had never really been happy, and he now felt perhaps he had been at least part of the cause, telling himself and his friend, "If only I had tried harder to get to know him—perhaps we might have grown to like each other."

But there had been other things he and Carl had talked about, things that were of more immediate concern. Robert had had very little to do with his family these past few years, seeing them only on holidays and special occasions; and even then the time he spent with them was more an ordeal than anything else. Now, suddenly, he found himself being looked upon as "the man of the house," and he didn't like the idea at all.

And Robert did not like the idea any better after having slept on it. As he sat up in bed, sipping his strong black coffee, his conscious and unconscious minds struggled with each other for full control. He knew he had to wake up, but he really wanted to go back to sleep. Often in such a state, one part of him would look upon the actions or reactions of the other part as childish or foolish. But this morning they were in complete agreement—taking on responsibility for his mother and sister would be a terrible mistake.

Objectively, he could see how impossible it was for anyone to attempt to be "the man" in his family. His father had certainly failed miserably, caught as he was between two women whose emotional machinations were beyond comprehension and seemingly always at cross-purposes. He realized that his own lack of participation in the family had contributed to his father's sense of futility; he had withdrawn as much as possible into his own world in the hope of staying out of the line of fire.

But now, his mother was using "tradition" to try to draw him in, and he knew he had to find some way to avoid it. His father had been a strong man, and yet he had literally been destroyed by responsibility. What, Robert wondered, could he himself expect?

Intuitively, he had only a vague feeling that he ought to attend to his own life and concerns and to steer clear of anything to do with his sister. He had been apprehensive about going with Sarah to see that lawyer, and now that his mother was objecting, his apprehensions were confirmed.

As far as Robert was concerned, there was no point in suing Dr. Norton. Papa had wanted this doctor to operate; he had gone from one physician to another until he had found one who agreed with his own judgment. This whole new movement of suing doctors for any little error, Robert felt, was indicative of the greed that pervaded too many levels of society.

He looked pensively at the kind face of his roommate. "Carl," he said softly, his voice still husky with sleep, "do you feel that your body is your own, and that you alone are responsible for it?"

Startled at so serious a question so early in the morning, Carl responded with a laugh and an incredulous "What?"

"I'm serious," Robert continued. "If you had something wrong with you, and if you went to see a number of doctors about it, then picked the one you agreed with, wouldn't the treatment you received be as much your responsibility as the doctor's?"

"I suppose so," Carl answered cautiously, "but then, I think I keep myself more aware of my body than most people do today. Most people never bother to learn anything about the way their bodies function. They'd rather leave it all to the doctor."

Robert set down his coffee cup and leaned back against the pillow. "But that's so stupid, isn't it? I mean, they're placing their lives in the hands of another human being who's supposed to know everything but can't possibly."

Carl smiled sympathetically, his dark eyes softening. "You're still upset about your sister and that lawsuit, aren't you?"

Robert nodded. "I wish she'd just leave everything alone. Papa's dead, and no matter what kind of a fuss she makes, it won't bring him back to life. But there was something Papa used to say about Sarah all the time. 'You can't reason with that girl,' he'd say to my mother, 'when she's got a broomstick up her ass.'"

They both laughed mildly at the image that conjured up.

"She is a witch, she really is, with a capital 'B.'" Robert sighed as he heaved himself out of bed and stumbled toward the bathroom. Carl got up to open the drapes and blinds to let in the morning sun, and then returned to the bed to pour more coffee.

He wasn't sure if Robert could hear over the sound of running water, and he wasn't sure he wanted him to hear, but he suggested, "You know you can very easily handle your sister, don't you? As long as she's got a broomstick up her ass, all you have to do is give it a shove and a twist."

Robert heard him. He came bursting out of the bathroom drying his face and hands in a big brown towel. When he dropped the towel to wrap it around his waist, his face had an obviously pained expression on it. "The problem is"—he plopped himself down on the bed beside Carl—"the problem is, if I do that, I've taken on the family responsibility that Mama wants to push on me."

"Love"—Carl took hold of his hand and looked straight into Robert's eyes—"I don't actually think you're going to be able to avoid it. It is your family, whether you like it or not."

"No," Robert said, closing his eyes and clenching his teeth. "No, no, no. You are my family. My only responsibility is to you. If they accepted you, and gave you your rightful place, that would be one thing. But as it is, whatever I give to them, I have to take away from you. It's just too unfair. You'd have to listen to all my grousing and complaining, and what would you get out of it? Nothing."

"If you don't know by now"—Carl grinned—"you're a dumber cunt than your sister."

Robert continued to look pained. "No, I'm serious. I don't want to harm our relationship by getting my mother and my sister on my back."

"Look, have I ever complained?"

Robert shook his head. "No, but you haven't met my sister."

"No," Carl agreed, "and I don't want to, after what you've told me. But"—he grinned impishly—"after looking at those family pictures of yours, I wouldn't mind meeting her husband."

In mock rage, Robert grabbed a pillow and hurled it at his roommate.

"Hey, watch it." Carl laughed. "You'll spill my coffee."

When their laughter had subsided, they both fell into the pensive silence that, years ago, had ceased to be uncomfortable for them. Neither of them had to worry excessively over what the other might be thinking.

Carl's assurances should have helped Robert to

make up his mind, but he was more confused than ever now. Actually, he had rather liked having Carl as an excuse to salve his conscience. He didn't want to get caught in the middle of a fight between his mother and his sister. He would prefer to sit quietly by on the sidelines, watching them slug it out.

But now it was his decision to make, and his alone. And he did feel a gnawing kind of obligation to his mother. Sure, she would be taken care of financially by Papa's pension, but she was alone—except, of course, when Sarah forced the kids on her, which was pretty often. She had only Robert and Sarah to rely on, and Sarah was incapable of thinking of anyone but herself.

And, after all, his mother was his mother, and he supposed he did owe her something, though he wasn't sure what it was. If it made her happy to think he was the man of the house, maybe he should go along.

Perhaps most important were the feelings he had been experiencing since his father's death. It was too late for him to offer his father anything now; he did not want to face the same feelings when his mother should die.

Lying back against his pillow, Robert extended his hand and gently squeezed Carl's knee. "Will you promise to tell me if it gets to be too much for you?"

Carl lay down on his stomach beside his friend, so their eyes would meet intimately when he answered. "Don't worry about it, babe. We'll survive."

9 MOE MICHENER

November 16, 1975, Van Nuys

Moe was sure that his political activism had been the chief cause for his dismissal from the hospital. A secondary reason had been his inability to gain people's confidence. He had tried to be so smooth, so self-assured, but somehow the patients had seen through that pose to the real insecurity beneath. And, he feared, so had the doctors and the professors.

A week after the heal-in ended in disaster and riot, Moe Michener had been called into the Professor's office. He had guessed he'd be fired when the Professor's secretary called him and told him in very grave tones, "Dr. Michener, the Professor and the hospital director would like to see you in their office. Right away."

Moe had had a week to recover from the brawl outside the hospital, but he still looked more like a patient than a doctor. He had taken a quick look in the mirror to see if there might be some way to disguise the large gash on his forehead, the black eye that was now lurid shades of purple and green, and the pavement burn on his jaw. But there had been no way, short of swathing his head in bandages and hanging a coat over his cast-covered arm, that he could hide the evidence of his fight.

When he entered the Professor's office, the doctors and administrators were sitting in a great semicircle, with the Professor in the middle behind his desk. None of them smiled at him, through Buxbaum gave him a nod. Moe hadn't realized he would be confronted by the entire Residency Committee.

The Professor gestured him to a chair that was a sufficiently uncomfortable distance from the desk. A thin, prune-faced man with a shock of white hair, the Professor had the annoying habit of never looking directly at you but at a location just over your left shoulder, making you constantly want to turn to see what he was looking at.

Moe knew the Professor was a prick. In the past, one of the Professor's favorite tricks in interviewing applicants for internship at City Hospital had been to nail down the window in his office. He would then complain about stuffy air and ask the intern candidate to open the window for him. The poor bastard would pull and tug at it, trying to please the Professor and yet not appear ill at ease. The old man felt he could better judge in this way how a young doctor would react under the stresses of internship. Some just gave up. Others banged and hammered and sweated. O'Hara, in his anxiety, had actually smashed the glass by mistake. The Professor had been pleased.

"You've got yourself a job," he'd told O'Hara, as he himself had sewed up the small lacerations in O'Hara's palm. "We need an aggressive type here at City."

Apparently the board of directors had advised the Professor to change his interviewing tactics, because Moe hadn't had to go through that initiation to obtain his internship. He had guessed there wasn't enough money in the budget for fixing glass windows or sewing up applicants.

Flanked by the full committee now, the Professor began to drone, "You may or may not be aware that

...a year to review the records
...nd residents. It's always a diffi-
... for us. Many good applicants
...cent years, more than any hospital
... Of course those who are already
...spital program are always given pref-

... hell was he waiting for? Moe would have
... that the Professor just tell him he was out
... him leave.
. . . unless there are factors in the record that
...not be ignored."

There it was, Moe decided, the strike, the complaints over conditions in the hospital.

"We have to consider a great many factors in making our decisions—the doctor's record in surgery and
emergency room, his attitude toward the patients, his
ability to get along with the other doctors, his incentive for learning and working, and even his attitude
toward the hospital itself."

Moe had been scarcely able to contain himself
while the Professor had wandered evasively around
the subject. Finally, he blurted out, "Why don't you
just come out and say it? I'm out because I've been
trying to rock the boat—to change things around here."

The Professor smiled smugly. "That is only one of
our concerns, but, yes, we have considered—"

Moe's anger was beyond control. He interrupted
loudly, "I wish to hell you would just say it. Stop your
fucking hedging. It was the heal-in, wasn't it?"

The Professor continued to look vague and sheep-
ish. "Not just the heal-in. You must realize that it has
not been extremely favorable publicity for the hospital to have one of our doctors arrested for brawling
in the street, to have it appear on the front pages of
all the newspapers and shown on television that one

of our doctors instigated the riot. It simply i
thing the hospital cannot afford to have repea

"And now, one of our porters, a black fellov
only one arm, claims he was severely attacked by
And he is pressing charges."

"One of *our* porters!" Moe leaped to his feet. "W
the hell am I? I'm not one of *our* doctors? Am I
somebody else's team?"

"These things are out of my hands," said the Pro
fessor, trying to ignore Moe's outburst. "You are a
good doctor, and you should do very well somewhere
else."

"Somewhere else!" Moe shouted. "Where else can
I go when I've been fired from this hospital? This is
the bottom of the barrel. There's no place else that
would take me!"

"I'm sorry." The Professor stared down at his desk,
making it quite clear that this was the last word on
the subject.

Before Moe walked out of the room, however, he
had flown into an uncontrollable rage, hurling every
epithet that had come into his mind. When he realized
that they hadn't even been listening, that they were
simply smiling smugly, hoping he would leave, he
stamped out, slamming the door behind him.

Almost ten years later, it still made Moe furious to
think about that damned committee. He still hoped
that one day he would be able to put each one of
them in as painful and as difficult a situation as the
one in which they had placed him.

Moe's memory was not too clear on the weeks and
months that had followed the end of his internship at
City Hospital. He remembered that he had spent a
lot of time in his room. He knew, though he did not
actually recall, that much of the time he had been

high from booze or spaced out on drugs. He did remember that Harry Norton and Karen Marshall had come to see him a couple of times. They had both started their residencies, in surgery and pediatrics, respectively, by that time. And Karen had even moved into his apartment for about a week, trying to break him out of his depression.

Finally, the two of them had convinced Moe to try to find a job. He could work as a GP. He wouldn't be able to perform major surgery, but he could at least practice medicine. And in many parts of the country GPs were still doing operations.

They had kept their eyes out for the want ads in the medical journals, and they had made Moe write letters of inquiry, make phone calls, and go on interviews.

At last Moe had followed up on an advertisement for a job in Tampa, Florida. He had regrets at leaving Karen behind, but the move to Florida seemed the only way he could go ahead with his career. And Dr. Groton had seemed so enthusiastic on the phone.

Moe had entered a gray, flat, one-story building in Tampa, Florida, with more than a little apprehension. The bronze letters on the top of the building read SOUTHEAST MEDICAL CENTER AND HOSPITAL.

On the cornerstone of the small hospital was carved in old English script:

. . . For I will restore health unto thee . . .
JEREMIAH XXX-17

He noticed that two of the Xs after *Jeremiah* had been either chipped away or stolen, and the words, scrawled in vivid red crayon directly above *Jeremiah*— "Dr. Groton is a dirty fucking bastard"—took away just a little from the original meaning.

The large waiting room was packed mostly with black and Spanish-speaking patients. The air was heavy and moist, in apparent defiance of two small air conditioners that whirred and gurgled but didn't succeed in sucking up the stench of medicine and sweating bodies from the room.

Two small reception windows opened and snapped shut every few minutes in the middle of the room. The sign over the first window said: MEDICAID PATIENTS REGISTER HERE. PLEASE HAVE YOUR CARDS AND NUMBERS READY. Over the second: MEDICARE, CASH AND COMMERCIAL INSURANCE HERE.

Two placards sitting on a nearby brown wooden table surrounded a group of wilted yellow flowers. They reminded the public that "Cash patients *must* have a $15 deposit *before* being seen by the doctor" and "Admission to the hospital requires $400 deposit *beforehand*."

Moe approached the window. A heavy woman with a sharp jutting chin and a sagging face gave him a quick "I'm sorry, sir, but there are twenty-two people ahead of you. Take a medical form and fill out the front sheet. The doctor will be with you as soon as he can."

"I'm Dr. Michener," he offered just before the window slammed. "I'm here to see Dr. Groton."

"Oh, I'm sorry." Her tone changed slightly but not very much. "Have a seat and Doctor will be with you in a few minutes."

Moe found a vacant chair in a corner of the room. Now he could see only the receptionist's chin moving up and down methodically as she spoke on the phone. "Hello, Medicaid? Yes, this is Dr. Groton's office. We are confirming the Medicaid number on a Dorothy Camilo. . . . Two-four-seven-five-nine. Thank you."

And then: "Oh, yes, that is interesting. Thank you again."

Turning to the young Spanish girl who fidgeted and shifted from foot to foot in front of the window, she said, "I'm sorry, Miss Camilo, but you have used up your Medicaid for the month. You'll have to pay cash for the doctor to see you today."

"But all I want is my stitches out. He put them in last Friday. And I got another discharge too. But I ain't got no cash today."

"I'm sorry. Medicaid won't cover this. Fifteen dollars is required for the visit."

There followed a brief, awkward moment of indecision, and then the girl walked slowly away, grumbling. The window closed again.

A black pregnant mother, already blessed with four children but unfortunately only two hands, was desperately trying to corral her herd as she sauntered up to the window from her chair. Moe noted that two of the kids had runny noses, the third had a rash, and the fourth was scratching his head savagely. The "rash" and the "scratcher" were screaming and whining as they clung to their mother.

"I'm Lucy Jenkins," she said, pleadingly. "How much longer must I wait for Dr. Groton?"

And the answer: "You're still thirteenth on line, Mrs. Jenkins. Doctor will see you as soon as he's free."

In the opposite corner of the room, Moe saw a partially balding man in a white coat bending down and emptying the candy machine. The man had his back to him, but Moe could see gray strands of hair shooting wildly out from his shiny dome in all directions. He could hear the muffled tones as the fellow counted, ". . . Eighty-five . . . ninety-five . . . goddamn it! I knew it! Goddamn. . . . There *is* a quarter missing. . . ."

Seemed like quite a devoted worker, Moe thought. Real upset over losing a quarter.

"What's an arthritis, man?" a patient filling out one of the extensive medical forms next to Moe was saying to his friend. "It says here, did I ever have an arthritis?"

"Does your bones hurt, you dumb ass?" the more experienced one advised. He had been to the medical center before. "That means, Does your bones hurt?"

"Oh, I get it." He smiled, checking the appropriate box. "Yes, sir. My bones is hurting all the time."

Moe sat back and closed his eyes for a moment. Since he had left Karen and Harry at City Hospital, he had seen many situations like this. Too many.

The advertisements had all said about the same thing:

> Excellent opportunity for a young ambitious doctor. Good location, schools, recreation. Unlimited earning potential. . . . Salary first year plus incentive, 50% of gross above this level, 40% of net below that level. . . .

The truth was that most of the numbers confused Moe, but he didn't dare to admit it. He left most places not really knowing what the hell the doctor had offered.

The plush spots in the big cities were full, certainly for specialists and even for GPs. Yet the old-timers were all waiting, waiting like vultures with their various deals.

Moe recalled one fellow in Los Angeles. The man had been going strong in practice for thirty years.

Now the doctor, the office, and the neighborhood seemed to be fading at the same time.

"I've put in my years," the older man had said. "Quite frankly, I'm tired. I don't need the money anymore. And I've got land investments to look after. What I want is the time."

The doctor had then stood up and put an arm on Moe's shoulder. "If you'd take over, I'd go to Europe with my wife and family tomorrow. I'd leave you the office, my records, my secretary, nurses, everything. And I'd even be willing to give you, shall we say, forty percent of everything you made!"

Only 40 percent! Moe couldn't believe it. "But you'd be making sixty percent on my work, even though you weren't here."

The old man's voice had softened then. "Look, son," he said—and Moe felt that he had used the words many times before—"I don't want to make money on you. I'm an honest man. . . ." A pause, and then: "But neither do I want to give anything away. I built my practice up from nothing before you were even born. You wouldn't want to take anything from my pockets, I'm sure. Think it over. I'll be glad to stay around for a few weeks or even months, and introduce you . . ."

Moe did think it over. It wasn't a good deal. The doctor had been cutting back on his practice for the past few years. His worn and musty records did not forecast a thriving business for a new man. What patients were left had been seeing "the doctor" for many years. There was no guarantee they would come to Moe. And finally, he found out that a travel agency and two clothing stores were moving from the same street, "relocating uptown" at a more desirable location. The doctor hadn't bothered to mention these things.

Then there was Dr. Lipschitz. "You've got good credentials, son," he said, after the usual tour of his office and rooms. "But nothing counts like experience. You're an unknown quantity in private practice. No telling how much money you'll make. And naturally I don't want to lose money on you."

Dr. Lipschitz had agreed to supply Moe with office space, patients, and equipment, plus malpractice insurance, hospitalization, a salary of $1,500 per month, and a bonus at the end of the year. "And after two years, if we're compatible, son, like I know we're going to be, you can buy in and become my partner."

Moe was tempted on that one. Fifteen hundred dollars per month sounded like an awful lot of money. And a partnership in two years! Then he discovered that the last three doctors who worked for Dr. Lipschitz had, for one reason or another, not been compatible when it came time for partnership; the good doctor exercised his option to fire his employee each time. He never seemed to have much difficulty in getting another scut boy to do his dirty work for a year or two. In the twenty-five years he had been in practice, Dr. Lipschitz had *never* had a partner.

The smaller towns and the newer, growing areas, of course, were more wide-open. But there, too, even the younger doctors were waiting. In a small town in southern California, Moe spoke with a Chinese physician who had been just four years ahead of him in medical school.

"Four years ago when I came to this town, I was just a Chinese," he said proudly. "Now I am a very rich man."

Moe found out his friend was not only very rich but had learned his lessons well. He offered to set Moe up with everything, in exchange for 60 percent of his earnings the first year.

"I also control emergency rooms at two small hospitals in area," he said. "If you sign with me, I will see that you get all the patients you need from these sources. I will not let you starve."

Moe knew the emergency room was an invaluable asset for a new doctor beginning in practice. This was where he could get most of his new patients.

"And what if I set up my own office?" Moe asked. "Can I still get rotating time on the emergency-room panel?"

The Chinese doctor stiffened. "Ah, that is another situation. Then I couldn't guarantee anything. At all. So sorry."

Moe's thoughts had been suddenly interrupted by a big coarse hand stuck in front of him.

"Hello, there! I'm Dr. Groton," the man began, with an excessive show of energy.

Moe shook the hand firmly.

As he walked into the office, Dr. Groton continued, "Welcome to my hospital. I own everything you see, and, contrary to the etchings on the front of my building this morning, I am not a dirty bastard."

Moe took a seat in the office. "I am an honest man," Dr. Groton said. "I want you to know that from the start. I do not want to make money off you."

Moe didn't even hear the last remark. He couldn't believe his eyes. Suddenly he recognized the wild strands of gray hair shooting out from Dr. Groton's partially balding head.

It was the same man who had been emptying the candy machine.

Dr. Groton sat behind an enormous desk in a heavy black-satin chair and talked downhill to Moe, who slouched into a small collapsible sofa and gazed up.

"The name of the game here is making bucks,"

Groton began. "M-O-N-E-Y." Dr. Groton spelled out the word slowly, almost savoring the letters, as if he were a little reluctant to let them go. To emphasize the point, he drew a large dollar sign on the blackboard. "That is what it's all about. It's a jungle out there, and you'll need a suit of armor to survive."

The same words the dean of the medical school had used so long ago, Moe thought.

Dr. Groton paused for a moment. "I figure you ought to make at least one hundred thousand dollars your first year out. If you don't, you're doing something wrong. But here you'll have to do both surgery and general practice, whatever comes through the door. Later on, when you're more established, you can concentrate on surgery alone."

Dr. Groton talked on, but Moe heard little more. One hundred thousand dollars. After all those years of studying and skimping. He didn't hear that he'd be paying his own malpractice insurance, which would come to about $4,000, his own hospitalization and disability. He didn't really hear that he'd be getting only 50 percent of the net amount collected from his efforts. One hundred thousand dollars. He signed a one-year contract.

"You've made a smart move," Dr. Groton said, as Moe was leaving. Seeing his apprehension on passing by the waiting room again, Groton added, "These type of people appreciate more what you do for them—much more than the rich pricks over on the beach. You've made a smart move, son. It'll be a gold mine."

The next day Moe stood in the operating room and watched Dr. Groton perform the first of four scheduled TOPs—abortions. He knew that since becoming legalized in Florida and many other states, the termination of pregnancy procedure had become popular among private doctors, GPs and specialists alike.

"A real money-maker," Dr. Groton said, as he scrubbed his hands before putting on a gown and gloves. "I charge two hundred and twenty-five dollars a scrape. Medicaid insurance, which most of these people have, allows about a hundred and sixty, and then pays only sixty percent of that, so I wind up with about a hundred and ten per operation. It only takes me five minutes, however, and there's little chance of a complication. Yes, sir, if I knock off four or five in a morning, I'm five hundred dollars ahead right there."

Moe watched Lucy Jenkins, the patient, being put to sleep, and her pelvic area prepped and draped for the upcoming procedure. Lucy was thirty-two years old and three months pregnant, according to the dates on the chart. She had four babies already and didn't need or want a fifth. There had been no father at the Jenkins household for many years, but a plethora of uncles, aunts, and cousins.

Moe recognized Mrs. Jenkins as the same woman who was trying to gather in "the scratcher" and "the rash" in the waiting room the day before. He didn't know why, but he suddenly recalled that she had been thirteenth on line.

The patient's legs were placed in stirrups, and Dr. Groton sat down on a stool at the foot of the table. He had put a small metal catheter in the urethra to draw off the urine in Lucy's bladder, and Lucy had bucked a little on the table.

"Give her some more gas, goddamn it," Dr. Groton had barked. "She's paying for it. And send this urine for culture and sensitivity." Turning to Moe, he had winked, saying, "It's an extra thirty-five-dollar charge."

Dr. Groton had placed a heavy retractor in the bottom of the vaginal cavity and grasped the cervix with a clamp. Again the patient had fidgeted and groaned.

"Goddamn it! Someone miscalculated. She's at least five months pregnant. I can feel the baby's skull and some other small bones. And I don't want to perforate the uterus!"

Moe knew that this was one of the complications that a GP could get into during the operation. If the curette passed through the back or side of the uterus, it could wind up in the abdominal cavity, sticking in a piece of bowel. This was a bad complication, usually making the patient very ill and requiring a second operation. If undetected, it might cause an infection of the abdomen or even death. This danger was one of the main arguments used by Ob/Gyn specialists to prohibit other doctors from performing the procedure.

Moe had watched Dr. Groton place a sound in the uterine cavity. Then he had passed a series of seven metal tubes into the uterus, each one a little larger than the last. "Now we're ready to scrape," he had announced.

Then Dr. Groton had inserted a thin-edged curette into the uterus, moving it over the four walls with a smooth motion. A spurt of blood and grayish-red tissue had gushed out of the vagina into a rubber glove that Groton kept near his lap. This had been a part of the baby, but it obviously hadn't been the main part. Dr. Groton scraped again. "I still feel the skull and bones," he had muttered. "And I've got to get them out."

Moe had felt a bit sick as Dr. Groton had reached inside the uterus with a clamp and pulled out a miniature leg bone and an arm, complete with hands and fingers. He had continued to pull, fetching next another arm, then the torso and the lower part of the fetus's body; finally, with a giant wrench, the head of the embryo had appeared in his grasp, complete with tiny eyes, nose, and mouth.

Dr. Groton had placed all the fetal parts on the sterile table next to him, displaying them like trophies. "There we are. I think we've got everything. Not bad."

While Moe had been feeling increasingly sicker, Dr. Groton had actually been enjoying it.

"Put the patient on a Pitocin drip and get my next case ready," he had told the nurse. Tearing off his gloves with a great air of accomplishment, he had left the room, explaining to Moe, "I write my orders now. And I send the patient home in the morning if there's no further complication."

That day Moe had watched Dr. Groton whip through three more cases. And, by the time Moe had gone home from his first day of work at Groton's Medicaid Factory, he had found it necessary to raid the drug supply room for something that would help him forget. By paying regular daily visits to the supply room, Moe had managed to spend the next few weeks at Groton's, fascinated by the machinations of the man himself, as well as simply repulsed and offended. He considered it a vital part of the overall learning process.

Even the paper work involved in insurance forms had fascinated Moe—when he had the help of the drugs. Dr. Groton had a staff of five women who worked in this area alone. Very few people paid cash. Each doctor had a number registered with the state Medicaid office. So did each patient. When someone presented insurance credentials at the front window, the woman had to call Medicaid, announce both the doctor's number and the patient's transaction number, and make sure the patient was eligible for treatment.

Medicaid forms were orange; workman's compensation cases were blue; no-fault automobile insurance, green; Medicare, blue and white; and the various commercial insurances were yellow. The fees for initial office visits, laboratory tests, x-rays, penicillin injections, and other treatments were all coded on cards. The doctor had only to circle what he had done, and a computer handled all the rest.

When Moe had examined his first patient, a nine-year-old boy named Marvin Jones, Dr. Groton had shown him how to fill out the forms. Marvin Jones had a simple sore throat.

"This one is Medicaid," Dr. Groton had informed Moe, seeing the orange slip. He ordered a throat culture and sensitivity ($25), a chest x-ray ($16 for the picture and $6 for interpretation), a urinalysis ($6), and a blood hematocrit ($3). For treatment, he ordered a shot of penicillin ($5) and a cough medicine, along with another antibiotic, which were to be filled at the pharmacy for $9.

He had put down two diagnoses—acute tonsillitis and pneumonia—on the Medicaid form, neither of which Marvin Jones actually had.

"It's simple mathematics," Dr. Groton had explained. "If you don't put down a diagnosis, the bastards won't pay you at all. If you write down *acute tonsillitis*, they will pay only for a throat culture and not the chest x-ray. They cover that only if the diagnosis is pneumonia."

The total bill for Marvin Jones's visit had come to $85. "You may think I've padded things a little," Dr. Groton had said, "but remember, those bastards at Medicaid only pay sixty percent of what I put down. If the government can try to screw me out of money,

I've got an equal right to screw them back. That's democracy."

It had been at Dr. Groton's that Moe had learned the real deep-seated greed of doctors. He had hated the committee at City Hospital for making it necessary for him to have to go to a place like that; but, at the same time, he had been grateful to them for allowing him to prove his point about the medical profession.

10 HARRY NORTON

November 16, 1975, Encino

City Hospital had seemed a very dull place without
Moe. While Moe was down in Florida, Harry had
seen a great deal of Karen, but he had realized that
he was just a substitute, someone she could spend
her time with until she would see Moe again. In the
first few weeks after Moe had left, Harry had hoped
for something more than a friendship with Karen.
But the two lovers had kept in constant touch by letter
and by telephone.

After a few months of having Moe all the way
across the country, the strain had begun to show on
Karen Marshall. And there had seemed to be something more that she wasn't talking about. Harry had
asked her several times what was bothering her, but
she had shrugged it off. She had managed to keep it
all bottled up inside until one afternoon on the
wards.

Karen had been supposed to administer a hypo-
dermic to a young boy who was in severe pain after
an automobile accident. But her hand had shaken,
and she hadn't been able to find the vein. Finally, she
had burst into tears and asked the nurse to take over.
Harry had stopped her in the hall on her way into
the ladies' room.

She had not wanted to talk then, but agreed to

meet Harry for drinks and dinner when they were off duty. After a couple of stingers, Karen had come out with it. "Moe's on drugs; he has been for some time, but now—" She had groped shakily for a sip. "Now he's lost his job."

"How did it happen?" Harry had asked.

"I don't know exactly," Karen had responded vaguely, focusing somewhere inside. "But apparently the head of the clinic found out about it. Anyway, Moe's down there without a dime, just sitting stoned in his apartment, day after day. And when I try to talk to him—" She had fought to hold back the tears. "When I try to talk to him, he doesn't make any sense."

Harry had known immediately that the only thing to do was to arrange for him and Karen to fly to Florida to do whatever they could to help Moe get on his feet again. He had talked to Buxbaum, who had agreed to let him and Karen both leave for three days. It wasn't much time, but they would at least be able to talk to Moe.

Harry had made plane reservations and arranged for rooms at a motel that he had thought might be near Moe's apartment. After the six-hour trip, with a layover in Atlanta, they had both been exhausted and more than a little tipsy from too many in-flight drinks, but Karen had insisted that they go straight to Moe's place.

He had been living in a two-story pink-brick complex that surrounded an unimpressive pool. Moe's apartment had been on the second floor on the long west wing of the crisp, clean, sterile structure. As they rang the bell and knocked, the sun was just beginning to come up, and lights were gradually being switched on in apartments. But there was no answer from behind Moe's door. They had stood there ringing and knocking for almost five minutes, before Karen had decided to see if the door was unlocked.

It had opened.

They had been hit by the smell before they saw Moe lying nude on the sofa surrounded by garbage, soiled clothes, and feces. His eyes were open, staring at the intruders, but Harry had the feeling Moe was unable to see them. His first impression was that his friend was dead, but then Moe's eyes blinked, and Harry realized that he was just spaced out.

While Karen picked her way through the garbage to Moe's side, Harry set about raising the venetian blinds and opening a few windows to let in some fresh air. It was probably the morning light streaming in the window more than their presence that at last roused Moe to a half-awakened stupor. He rolled over and muttered incoherently into the pillow.

Karen placed her hand gently on Moe's shoulder, seating herself on the edge of the couch. "Moe," she said softly, "it's Karen. Karen and Harry."

"Go away," Moe answered into the pillow.

Karen tensed, her spine going rigid, her chin set. Her voice became stern, almost cold. "Goddamn it, Moe, we've just flown three thousand miles to see you! The least you can do is talk to us!"

Slowly Moe turned over, drawing a soiled shirt over his privates, and stared at Karen. "What do you want?" he asked coldly.

"I want you to stop pretending to be a fool."

Moe's dark eyes glowered at Karen, then stared for a moment at Harry, before coming back to her. "What's *he* doing here?"

"He came for the same reason I came," Karen answered simply. "He's your friend; he wants to help."

"I don't want any help." Moe started to roll over

again to shut them out, but Karen reached out and stopped him rudely.

"Stop acting like a child!" Her voice turned shrill. "We're here, and you're going to sit up and talk to us!"

Moe stared at her for a moment before answering. "I'll talk to you, but he has to go away."

Karen started to protest, "He's not going to—" but Harry interrupted quietly.

"I'll be outside in the car if you need me."

After an hour and a half of sitting in the car, Harry curled up on the seat and went to sleep. When Karen finally came out and awakened him, she looked a complete wreck. Her eyes were great red smudges in an otherwise gray complexion; her hair was damp and matted; her clothes were soiled, wrinkled, and sweat-stained. Her voice was hoarse, and all she said was, "I need some sleep."

Their motel had turned out to be on the other side of town from Moe's apartment, and it seemed that they would never get there driving in the midday traffic. There was little conversation. The sun was bright, and the sky was postcard blue. The strange surroundings gave them a feeling of unreality.

After he helped Karen settle into her room, Harry asked, "Do you want to sleep or do you want to talk?"

Karen sat down wearily on the double bed. "I've got to get some sleep, but I don't know if I can. Would you stay for a few minutes?"

"Sure." Harry smiled reassuringly. "How about ordering up some lunch?"

They had eaten their sandwiches silently, and the basic animal function of chewing, swallowing, and digesting had given them both a slight hold on reality again. After sipping a second cup of coffee, Karen had lain back on the bed and stared at the ceiling.

Finally, she spoke. "I don't think he's going to be able to get himself out of this mess."

Harry got up from his chair and moved over to sit beside Karen on the bed, taking her hand and holding it gently. "He doesn't have to do it alone."

Karen looked up at him, her face expressionless. "We don't have enough time." Then she paused, her eyes returning to the ceiling. "Unless I forget about going back to City Hospital."

"Maybe Moe would come back with us," Harry suggested, realizing as he said it that it was a foolish thought.

"Harry"—Karen lifted herself up on her elbows— "Moe's suicidal. Oh, he hasn't threatened anything, but I can tell from what he says that it's been in the back of his mind. You see, the reason he lost his job wasn't just the drugs. It was because he killed a patient, or thinks he killed him."

Harry was more shocked at this than he wanted to show. His initial urge was to shout, How could he be such a stupid ass? Instead, he said simply, "I'd like to know what he did."

"Even if he'd be allowed to practice medicine, I don't think he'd let himself do it." She sat up and massaged her face with her hands, trying to awaken her tired brain. "I don't know precisely what happened, but apparently he had been on drugs for some time, managing to time his injections according to the length of time he'd be in the operating room. It seems that this one operation ran much longer than he'd expected; the drug wore off, and he got the D.T.'s."

As she sat staring at their reflections in the motel-room mirror, her eyes began to fill with tears, and she trembled slightly as she tried to fight them back.

"He should have known the chances he'd be taking."

Harry reached out and put his arm around Karen to comfort her. The gesture took all resistance from her, and she finally broke into helpless tears, her head on Harry's shoulder, her arms automatically embracing him. He held her snugly in his arms for a long time, allowing her tears and sobs to run their full course.

Finally he kissed her, a gentle affectionate kiss on the cheek. Karen responded by lifting her lips to brush Harry's cheek, but he turned slightly so that her lips met his.

It probably never would have happened if Karen hadn't been totally defenseless, hadn't felt Moe's situation was completely hopeless. But she had needed someone else's strength that night. She had needed love. It hadn't mattered that night that the love she had always felt for Harry had been more a sisterly kind of love; it was still love, and it seemed to be all she had.

She welcomed Harry's kiss, and she returned it. And she gave in completely as his lips found their way down her neck to her breasts, and as his hands explored her body.

To Harry, sex was giving pleasure as well as receiving it. He cared deeply about Karen, and he gained passion from knowing he was exciting her. Because of the fatigue, the tension, and the strange surroundings, their lovemaking had a desperate, frantic quality about it. Their excitement was heightened to frantic animal sounds; their pleasure had traces of ecstatic pain.

It was inevitable that they would both have regrets when they had climaxed and lay silently in each other's arms. Their regrets were simply that they had somehow betrayed Moe. But their feelings for each other had not changed, and each knew why they had made love. It had been a necessary and a natural thing. And it had brought both of them back down to reality again.

They fell asleep locked in an embrace and slept for several hours. When they awoke, at least partly rested, they were able to achieve some perspective. They realized that neither of them could stay in Florida to take care of Moe, and that it would be unwise for Moe to come home with them. They had to persuade him to seek help here, to find his way out of his troubles himself.

When they went back to see Moe that evening, there were obvious signs of improvement. He had showered and shaved, though his hand had not been very steady, judging from the numerous nicks and cuts on his neck and chin. His apartment was not clean, but at least most of the garbage was gone.

This time Moe did not throw Harry out, but he continued to treat him with a distinct coolness. Harry passed this off as a part of Moe's drug-assisted self-control. Exactly what Moe was on at the time, Harry didn't know, but he was sure that it was some kind of a down.

Karen's first object was to cook Moe a good, well-balanced dinner. She and Harry had stopped off at a grocery store and picked up a few supplies, and she settled into the kitchen as soon as they arrived—leaving Harry and Moe alone together.

Moe was uncomfortable but obviously prepared. "Hey, Harry," he mumbled self-consciously. "I'm sorry about this morning."

Harry gave him a cuff on the shoulder. "No need to apologize. I can tell when three's a crowd."

"Would you like something to drink?" Moe offered,

a little too formally. "I don't have much, but I'm pretty sure there's some beer in the refrigerator."

"No, thanks." Harry laughed. "After that plane ride, I've had enough drinks to last me three months."

They were both ill at ease as they sat down facing each other in the living room. Despite their long and close acquaintance, the unspoken embarrassment had created a barrier. Their discomfort was greater than it would have been if they had been strangers.

Finally, Moe broke the silence. "I guess I don't have to tell you I've got a problem."

Harry had no intention of sounding like a Pollyanna, but it came out that way. "Look, before you start, I want you to know I'm your friend, and I'm here to be of whatever help I can."

"Thanks"—Moe sighed—"but there's not much anybody can do at this point. I know it's pretty much up to me. That is, if there's any point in doing anything in the first place."

"Now, that's no way to—" Harry began, but Moe cut him short.

"Don't try to give me any platitudes. I'm a doctor. Medicine's been my life. And I'm never going to be able to practice again. I don't feel sorry for myself. I know I got myself into this mess. It's my own fault. I was aware of what I was doing when I started on the drugs, and I know I can get off them if I want to. But what's the point? My medical career has gone down the drain."

Harry was stunned, not by the words that Moe had spoken, but by the way he had spoken them—totally dispassionately. There was no trace of self-pity; there was no despair; there was no fear or anxiety. He had spoken with the objectivity of a professor giving a lecture about plants.

The fact was, Moe had seen his own situation more clearly than Harry had; there seemed to be nothing he could say, no way he could help.

It was Karen who came up with the suggestion. Neither of them realized she was standing in the doorway throughout Moe's little speech, until she herself spoke. "How old are you?" she asked simply.

Caught off guard, Moe showed traces of feeling when he answered, "Twenty-nine. One year short of the Establishment."

"By the time you're thirty-four, you could be practicing law," she suggested, as she walked into the room and perched herself on the arm of the couch. "Maybe thirty-two. How many lawyers are there who also have medical degrees?"

Moe tried to pass it off as a crazy idea at first, but after they had finished Karen's family-style meal, it was Moe himself who came back to the idea.

That, apparently, had been the beginning of Moe Michener's crusade, begun innocently, genuinely, as a means of atoning for his own mistakes. Or had it been a straw he had grasped desperately that he would later turn into a crutch to give his life some meaning? Harry had never really been sure about Moe Michener's motivation.

The next day, Karen was as mystified as Harry was to learn that Moe had decided to sign himself into a state mental hospital rather than into a private sanitorium. He had admitted that he was broke, and Karen and Harry had offered him a loan in case he needed it, but he implied that it had something to do with his "atonement."

"There's no point in paying money to try to make it easier for me," he explained breezily. "The harder it is on me to come off the drugs, the less tempted I'll be to go back to them."

Neither Harry nor Karen liked the looks of the place. As they drove into the grounds with him, they tried to persuade him to change his mind. No place on earth could have done better justice to the words "state institution" than this hospital. There were treeless acres of one-story yellow stucco buildings, set in orderly rows and separated from the street by a steel-woven hurricane fence, twelve feet high, topped with strands of barbed wire.

Since visitors were never permitted beyond the administration building, there were some efforts at glamorizing that one structure. Unsuccessful efforts. It too was made of yellow stucco, and it rose two floors with a decorative tower third. Its approach was lined with palm trees and benches where visitors could stroll and sit with their unfortunate disturbed friends and relatives.

Inside, the walls were all painted a depressing babyshit green, and the floors were a yellow asphalt tile. There were no pictures on the walls, no rugs, no draperies—no objects that could be thrown, pulled, shoved, or swung from. For seating in the big main hall, there were benches bolted to the floor.

They were greeted by a gray-haired matron with gray eyes and a gray face, wearing a gray uniform and gray crepe-soled shoes. When Moe explained his presence and his purpose, the matron eyed Harry and Karen suspiciously, asking, "And who are they?"

"My friends," Moe explained simply.

"Ah, well"—she was far too abrupt for comfort—"they'll have to leave you now. We'll take it from here." And she picked up Moe's bag and ushered him through a door without any opportunity for good-byes.

Harry and Karen flew back to Los Angeles with an anxious feeling that somehow they had not quite achieved their purpose. Or maybe it was the feeling that they had not been needed in the first place. Moe seemed to need other people more as an audience than for mutual sustenance. Even when he was down—with his life in shambles—he was not able to allow his friends the full satisfaction of knowing that they had helped him.

This was particularly frustrating for Karen, who loved Moe in spite of himself. Karen had not confided everything to Harry, but enough for him to realize that the relationship she had with Moe had not been easy for some time.

11 MOE MICHENER

November 16, 1975, Encino

It gave Moe Michener a feeling of satisfaction to see Harry Norton gulp down his coffee and hurry out of the cafeteria to avoid speaking to him. That meant Norton was scared. It meant Michener was on top, which was where he wanted to be. Moe liked to start out on top, and he liked to finish on top. Keep them running scared; that was his motto.

Scared and uncertain. Moe had discovered that an opponent's imagination could terrify much more than anything he might actually threaten to do. And so his greatest weapon was silence. If Moe maintained an air of strength, self-assurance, and silence, his opponents would often do his job for him—offer themselves meekly like some patient too drugged to resist.

It also gave Moe pleasure to see O'Hara and Minton and Kramer sweating over the new increase in malpractice insurance rates. Let them see what it's like to suffer and struggle like ordinary people for a change, he thought to himself. Let them blame it on the patients and the lawyers now. They'll have to face up to it eventually—the goddamned doctors have created this situation themselves.

Moe ordered coffee, a prune Danish, and orange juice from the motherly woman behind the counter, paid the skinny girl at the cash register, and decided to join O'Hara's group at the table. There was a table left empty by Harry Norton's hurried departure, but Moe wanted to join the discussion about the malpractice rates—just to rub it in.

Without asking, he set his tray down at their table and pulled up a chair.

"You don't mind?" he asked, after the fact.

The doctors all nodded and murmured "Of course not" and "Sit down."

"Have you boys decided how you're going to vote yet?" he asked bluntly, basking in their discomfort.

O'Hara stopped his fork halfway to his mouth, allowing a strand of syrup to drop to his tie.

"You mean about the strike," Kramer said, returning Moe's straightforward gaze. "I, for one, plan to vote for it."

Kramer had guts, Moe decided.

O'Hara finished shoveling the large bite of pancake into his mouth, ignoring the syrup on his tie. When Moe turned his gaze on him, he muttered between chews, "We don't really have any other choice."

O'Hara had always been the best ass-kisser in the business. As an intern, he had learned how to follow his leader on rounds, bowing and acting humble and gratefully scribbling down any tidbit of information thrown his way, however trivial and worthless it seemed to be.

In the operating room, O'Hara had been even more fully indoctrinated into the system. He had learned how to scrub his hands just twenty seconds longer than the staff man and then file into the room at a respectful distance (usually, two or three feet) behind him. If he scrubbed with the Professor, who washed his hands for a full ten minutes, O'Hara scrubbed for ten minutes and twenty seconds. If he had a case with Buxbaum, who barely rinsed his hands at all, O'Hara washed for only half a minute (ten seconds for Buxbaum's time, plus twenty of his own). That way, he was always twenty seconds cleaner than his boss, and he didn't lag too far behind to piss anybody off. It was really quite an art.

During the operation itself, O'Hara had learned how to hold the retractors and keep his mouth shut when the staff man was in a bad mood; how to joke and flatter at the right times; how to praise a deft move (even though he knew he could probably do it better himself) ; how to apologize and make excuses when his boss fucked up a simple procedure or obviously cut the wrong thing.

When a bleeder got away on one of the Professor's private hernias and needed two units' transfusion, O'Hara had said delicately, "A tough dissection, Professor. I don't know how you even saw the blood vessels at all. Terrible tissue to work with. Yes, sir. A real toughie."

And the Professor had smiled at O'Hara's bowing figure and nodded silently.

O'Hara had learned the lessons of survival well. Kiss ass. Flatter and fawn. Kiss ass some more. And he had done it well, so well that Moe thought he must have been sick of it all, the chief resident, the staff surgeons, the Professor, and probably most of all, himself.

One thing was certain to Moe Michener. O'Hara's self-image hadn't improved over the past years. In fact, it was hard to recognize the young, enthusiastic intern now. In the years since, O'Hara had progressed from kissing ass to eating shit. And it seemed to go down pretty well—not too much gagging or choking. At least not on the outside where it showed.

Moe decided O'Hara would make an ideal witness

for him to call against Norton. He would be able to bend him any way he wanted to, make him say anything.

Minton broke into Moe's thoughts quietly. "It's a very serious problem this country is facing. The public has simply assumed that, as long as they have money to pay, they'll have the finest medical care in the world. They look at us as somehow different from ordinary human beings, more secure, more wise. To them, we can't possibly have problems. What bothers me is that—if we do strike—the public will never believe that we have a legitimate complaint."

Michener, Kramer, and O'Hara simply stared at Minton in silence. Minton was the sort of person that people hardly ever know is there; the sort of person who keeps his mouth shut and listens, who never speaks in strident tones, whose ego never screams for attention.

Minton was the kind of doctor Moe Michener was somewhat in awe of, the kind of doctor—like Karen Marshall—who simply goes about his work competently and efficiently, but with a very sincere attitude of caring for his patients. Moe had always believed that that's what a doctor should be like, but he had never been able to understand any doctor who actually lived up to that ideal.

It was almost time for the autopsy, and Moe did not want to be late. Properly speaking, he had no right to be present, since he was not on the hospital staff. He knew this, and simply saw the impropriety of his presence there as another lapse in a series of many which he could exploit.

One of Moe's beefs was that, regardless of how much mayhem a doctor might have committed, his license to practice medicine was virtually safe from being revoked. Moe himself remained an M.D., although his living came from being a malpractice lawyer, and this fact served him well. He was a familiar figure at the hospital, as a former practitioner who had become a good malpractice man; he was sometimes even called upon to help doctors in their malpractice cases, assuming he was not involved on the plaintiff's side. When he wanted to come into an autopsy, or if he hung around the corridors, no one tried to stop him. Some thought it unwise to step on his toes. They hoped he would be on their side if a case against them ever developed, because his medical training added to his value as an expert.

Now he was eager for ammunition he could use in the Wexler case—which he preferred to think of as the Norton case. In medicine it was simply "Wexler," but in law it was *Wexler* v. *Norton*. And in Moe's logbook, it was "Norton."

He waited at the elevators with a pair of black women wearing blue uniforms labeled "Maintenance." They each carried several small glass bottles and some linen.

One of them reminded him a lot of Lucy Jenkins, but this one's name tag read "Myrtle." Moe wondered if Myrtle had ever had a barbaric abortion like the one he had witnessed. Like some of those he had found himself performing.

"I just hate to go down there," Myrtle whispered to her companion, whose tag said "Claudessa."

"Yeah, I know," Claudessa responded. "They're doing an autopsy on that nice little man in Three-oh-four. Herman Wexler, you know him?"

"I remember, because his wife was always bringing him all that Jewish food to eat—gefilte fish and matzo balls."

Claudessa tried to whisper so Moe wouldn't hear.

"They're gonna use these jars to put his insides in."

"Yeah," Myrtle answered. "It always gives me the creeps."

The elevator came, and the two women allowed Moe to get on first, but he held the door for them so they could get on with their clumsy burdens.

"He died yesterday, around ten in the morning. Willie Mae was telling me. She was there at the time. Said it was real quick and kind of peculiar. The nurses were all screaming and running around."

Claudessa obviously didn't like talking about death, because she quickly tried to change the subject. "I hear the doctors may be going on strike."

"I hope that don't mean no layoff for us," Myrtle rejoined. "I need the money."

"Yeah, doctors shouldn't be doing things like that. The work they does is necessary."

The elevator stopped at the subbasement, right in front of the door marked MORGUE, KEEP OUT.

As she got off, Myrtle said, "I think I'll just leave the bottles by the door." She stooped over to deposit her load, and Claudessa followed suit.

"Sam can pick the stuff up here," she agreed. She knocked gingerly on the door and then moved back toward the elevator.

Sam Carter, assistant to Joe Gregorio, opened the door. As he bent down to pick up the supplies, Moe Michener stepped by him into the morgue.

Most of those who were to observe the post-mortem examination were already assembled. There was a sickly otherworldly appearance to the room. The walls were a pale green, and the room itself was dark except for a single light over the inert naked body of Herman Wexler lying on the autopsy table.

The table was constructed with gutters so that the fluids might pass off easily. It looked like a small pool table. In fact, the entire room resembled some sort of a macabre billiard parlor. But the game to be played here, Moe decided, gave one very little chance for a return match.

Harry Norton stood quietly at one end, not speaking to anyone. Buxbaum and O'Hara were off in a corner, probably discussing Buxbaum's latest amorous conquests. Their laughter and good spirits seemed to ignore the dead man on the table.

It would be very easy to dismiss the cadaver of Herman Wexler as something not quite human. Lying there pale and stiff and naked, he bore more resemblance to a wax figure, with his dark eyes staring straight up into that bright light.

But it was impossible for Moe to ignore the fact that the room smelled of death. The odor of chemicals cut smartingly at his nose and lungs.

Joe Gregorio approached the autopsy table with the matter-of-fact efficiency of a man who knew what he was doing. A post-mortem required intricate details and exactness to establish a final diagnosis.

Sam Carter had set up two large bottles of fluid. The first contained orange Zenker's solution, into which the tissue sections would be placed. After that, they would be mounted and stained by the lab to provide small slides that could be studied under a microscope.

The second bottle, which contained Formaolin, would preserve tissue sections in case further slides would be needed later.

Six pieces of string had been placed at one end of the table, to be used for tying the small and large bowels before removing them from the body.

Gregorio began the post-mortem by taking a yardstick from the end of the table and measuring the total body length of Herman Wexler. "One hundred and eighty centimeters," he mumbled, jotting the figure down on the sheet of paper beside him.

Harry Norton drew closer to the table, looking almost as pale and white as the cadaver.

As the others gathered around, Gregorio announced, "We will begin by looking for external marks on the body."

He surveyed Wexler's head and neck—the fixed, dilated pupils—and then observed the stiffness of the joints.

"Rigor mortis present," he informed.

A purplish patch was present on Wexler's back. "Lividity," Gregorio said. "Collection of fluid and venous blood in the dependent portions of the body."

The abdominal scar from Wexler's operation, three weeks old, was the only unnatural mark on the body.

Well, Moe thought to himself, that's only on the outside of the body. Harry Norton did his work inside of Herman Wexler. That's where we'll find his mistakes.

12 HARRY NORTON

November 16, 1975, Encino

To Harry Norton, the autopsy room seemed like a
scene out of Dante; whether it was purgatory or hell,
he couldn't be quite sure. But it was definitely not in
the same order of time and space as the one in which
he ate and slept and worked. He sensed that it was
cold in the room, but he also experienced a strange
absence of sensation—as if he could not truly feel the
cold. He certainly had no feelings like love and
hate. He looked at Moe Michener across the body of
Herman Wexler, and the inexpressible rage and
frustration he had previously felt at the appearance
of his former friend was absent.

Looking at Moe dispassionately, Harry suddenly
saw him as an adult would see a child—innocent, perhaps a bit foolish, and certainly unable to comprehend
the full implications of his actions. Gregorio and the
others were about to take apart the body of a human
being. They were not going to try to repair that body,
and they were not going to look for anything earth-
shattering, like a soul; they were simply going to look
for a mistake that might have been made by another
human being.

Harry had never really thought that it would come
to this. Herman Wexler ought to be up walking
around the hospital wards, feasting on the foods his
wife brought him each day. But Harry was perhaps

too much of an optimist. The cold gray body that lay helplessly on the table was distinctly the body of the man who had placed himself trustingly in Harry's care.

"Feel this," said Joe Gregorio, taking Harry's hand and placing it on Herman Wexler's abdomen. The skin was cold and clammy.

"Distended," Gregorio grunted. "The abdomen is swollen. Also there is a dark pigment under the fingernails, and the skin of the palm is slightly thickened."

Anxiously, Harry offered an explanation. "The patient had a normal postoperative ileus. No bowel movement for the past three days. He was impacted on rectal exam. We gave him a light enema on the day of his demise."

Harry could feel Moe Michener staring darkly, mentally taking note of everything he said, watching for any slipup that could be used against him.

Gregorio nodded at the information Harry had offered, but he did not look up from his work. Instead, he promptly picked up a Number Eighteen needle that was attached to an underwater apparatus by a thin wire tubing. "We'll have to be sure that the enema you ordered didn't kill the patient. Enema fluid entering the rectum can cause a perforation. If air escaped from the bowel into the abdominal cavity, that might have done it."

At that, Michener drew closer to the table, his eyes zeroing in with his body, eagerly watching Gregorio insert the needle into the midline of Herman Wexler's belly. But Harry's gaze turned anxiously to the underwater bath, where the results of the test would appear. If free air were present in the abdominal cavity, it would bubble into this apparatus.

There were no bubbles.

"Obviously, it was not the enema that killed him. We'll have to look inside," Gregorio announced brusquely.

As Harry Norton relaxed a bit, he noticed a trace of disappointment on Moe Michener's face. It pleased Harry to think that Moe would have to wait for his answer. The longer it took Moe to get the "evidence" he needed, the happier—and possibly the safer—Harry thought he would be.

Gregorio picked up a large scalpel from the autopsy table and routinely turned on two water hoses, one attached at each end of the marble slab containing the cadaver, sending a soft wash of water around it.

The pathologist spoke as if he were addressing students. "We'll use the standard Y incision."

Harry Norton had cut open more bodies than he could count, but he felt a mixture of terror and anxiety as Joe Gregorio smoothly and confidently cut into the skin and yellow fatty tissue beneath. His mind raced with thoughts of what might be found inside—a sponge they had missed in the count, a scalpel or two, a massive ugly tumor he had overlooked, a slush of blood and pus.

The first two incisions were from each shoulder to the middle of the chest. Gregorio joined them neatly, then proceeded with a third incision, straight down the stomach to the pelvic bones. As he began roughly peeling the thin red muscles of the chest back on either side, revealing the rib cage, Harry wanted to protest: Wait, that's a human being you're ripping apart. That's a man who's dreamed all of his life of being a writer, a man who, like all human beings, was his own heaven and hell, as Omar Khayyám had once put it.

Wexler had had to abort college and had suffered from a negative self-image ever since. He had told himself that he was not a common laborer but a longshoreman, a member of a powerful union; in effect, it added up to the same thing. Anyone with muscle could do what he did. He was self-conscious about his writing, though he was aware that one did not need a formal education to write with insight and color about people. But he feared that he was not starting new paragraphs at the right places.

Wexler had his family obligations, and worked overtime and on Sundays and holidays to give two ungrateful kids more than they deserved. In short, Wexler had been a *man,* with all the joys, blessings, fears, frustrations, and contradictions a man experiences.

These were thoughts and feelings that rarely, if ever, occurred to Dr. Norton during his professional work. They did now. Did Gregorio "hear" Harry's thoughts? Certainly he interrupted his explorations and stopped his audience dead by saying, "Damned instruments are too dull. We used to have a good collection, but most have been sent to the cemetery with the patients' bodies." And he gave Sam Carter a dirty look. Carter looked sheepishly at the floor. "If only half our patients went to heaven, Saint Peter would still be able to do his own autopsies—with some of the best instruments available."

Moe Michener laughed a little too knowingly, a little too coldly. Did he perceive some way the deceased could sue a pathologist for making them carry extra weight to their graves?

Gregorio grabbed the rib-cutter and sliced easily through each of the twelve ribs as if he were carving up a Thanksgiving turkey. When each had been severed at its softest point, he removed the entire rib cage with his hands, revealing all the organs of Herman Wexler's chest—his heart, lungs, and great vessels.

Harry Norton broke out in a clammy sweat. In the

end, this was what it all came down to—a collection of assorted organs, completely still. No steady pumping from the heart. No blood moving through veins. No air filling and evacuating the bellows of the lungs. No heartfelt devotion to a wife who could be extremely loving—and so carping Herman often had to yell, "Shut up, damn you!" Now there was no tension and anxiety over how far he could stretch a paycheck. No concern over the fact that his daughter had not only married outside her religion, but picked a man with whom he simply could not communicate. No more frustration that his son had no balls. No eager delight at observing his wife opening little parcels of gefilte fish, potato salad, and kosher pickles.

Just the unbelievable stillness of a cold body lying on a cold piece of marble, not feeling the cold water gurgling quietly and steadily all around.

"Did Wexler have any complaints for the few hours before his death?" Gregorio asked.

Yes, Harry thought, he complained that his daughter had married a goy, that his son hadn't grown up to be a man, and that the hospital food was shit.

But Harry answered, "He said he had a fullness in his belly the day before. And a little constipation. But that was all."

Gregorio nodded to acknowledge that this piece of information had registered, while he proceeded to open the pericardial cavity, the fatty encasement that houses the heart. When a small amount of yellow clear fluid oozed out, Moe Michener asked, a bit too anxiously, "What's that?"

"Normal." Gregorio marked down "100 cc's fluid" on his notes. Methodically, he returned to the cadaver, lifted the heart gently, and injected a needle into the inferior vena cava, withdrawing a tube full of dark red blood.

"For blood culture," he muttered by way of explanation. "Once in a while I pick up an infection in the bloodstream that was missed on the wards."

At that, Michener quickly took a notepad from his pocket and made a penciled memo to himself. Gregorio gave the notepad a disdainful glance and then proceeded to sever the main pulmonary artery, checking it for blood clots or obstructions by manipulating his finger into it.

The pathologist frowned in contemplation. "It's not likely that he died from a pulmonary embolus." He extracted his finger from the vessel and turned to the heart itself. As Gregorio roughly cut Wexler's heart out of the body, Harry's eyes finally met Moe's —both of them nervous, anxious, aware that the heart was the crucial test.

Picking the severed organ up in his hands, Gregorio squinted at it, examining its surface before cutting open the valves and chambers.

Within minutes, there was nothing left of Herman Wexler's heart. Drops of blood fell quietly into the swirling water and disappeared down the drain.

"No pathology here," Joe Gregorio muttered. "The heart valves are all normal. The chambers are not enlarged. Coronary vessels are all open." And then he added, with a slight note of puzzlement, "There are a few small areas of hemorrhage under the endocardium."

Moe Michener leaped at the statement with his notepad. "Would that be an indication of excessive stress brought on by—"

"I don't know what it indicates as yet, young man." Gregorio cut him short. "If you'll just be patient, you'll get a copy of my report along with everybody else."

That seemed to quiet Moe for a while, at least throughout the inspection of Herman Wexler's lungs. But when they arrived at the belly, at the area of the operation, the lawyer simply could not restrain himself. When Gregorio opened the abdominal cavity with one long smooth cut, Moe shoved himself in front of Buxbaum to look.

To Harry Norton, the abdominal cavity looked just the way he had left it. All the vessels seemed to be intact; all the stitches had held. There was no blood, no pus, no abscess pockets under the diaphragm or liver.

"It looks pretty clean," Gregorio acknowledged. "It doesn't appear you made any mistakes with the operation itself."

But Michener wasn't about to be satisfied with that answer. A little too eagerly, and a little too offensively, he pushed. "Doesn't that look like a leak under the pancreas, where it's sewed to the duodenum?"

Gregorio picked up a silver probe and lifted the organs. "No"—he shook his head patiently—"there's no leak. The anastomosis seems intact."

But Moe pursued his point. "What about a collection of pus under the diaphragm or under the liver?"

Gregorio probed again, inserting his left hand, sweeping beneath the diaphragm and liver. "No," he concluded, "no evidence of any leakage whatsoever. No pus."

Irritably, Moe persisted. "There has to be. Shouldn't you look more carefully?"

Gregorio slowly set the probe down on the table and looked Michener in the eye. "Young man," he began slowly and evenly, "I know what I'm doing. There is no great hurry to come to a conclusion here. We don't have to worry that our patient may die on us. He's already dead. I have a suspicion about what may have killed him. But we must not be hasty. We must be thorough and accurate."

"Yes, sir." Moe looked sheepishly at the floor. "I beg your pardon."

"It will take at least a week to get the final slides back on this case, even after the gross specimens are examined," Gregorio continued. "And I'm sending all the slides to Dr. Derrington in San Francisco. This case is important enough to be reviewed by the best in the field. And the chemistry tests, the special analysis may take even longer. Two things we are sure of *here*—Mr. Wexler is dead—and we will have our answer eventually. But please—a little patience!"

As Gregorio returned to his work, roughly ripping out the neat threads that Harry had taken hours to sew into place, Harry was thinking that Moe really hadn't changed very much since his student days. All the troubles and difficulties he had lived through had taught him nothing—or at least very little. Standing over what was left of Herman Wexler, Moe demonstrated about the same concern for the man as a vulture tearing at a cadaver's entrails. Moe, it struck Harry, was such an unaccountable mixture of sensitivity and callousness, intelligence and foolhardiness, passion and cold detachment, that Harry would never understand him completely. It was obvious that Moe, in clear conscience, was his enemy. He cared no more for Harry and Harry's past help to him than he cared for the body on the table. Moe had not asked for that help. They owed each other nothing, and never had.

Strangely, this realization was a comfort to Harry. Understanding the truth lessened some of the anxiety. He still had to face doubts about his judgment, but there was no longer a need to question his life and his approach to his fellow man.

There was, after all, no reason to stop caring.

He had not been wrong to care about Moe Michener; he had not been wrong to care about Herman Wexler. But his judgment? Had his caring for Wexler—the vague resemblance to Harry's father—interfered with his ability to judge what was truly best for him? Despite his certain belief that the man had cancer, should he have closed and waited and let nature take its course?

Standing there, in the strange green glow of the autopsy room, staring at the eviscerated organs of what had once been a kind and complex and gutsy man, Harry was totally unable to judge himself. Caring had not been a part of his training. He had been trained in distinctly categorical knowledge and with precise, if not infallible, skills. But had the training of his judgment been somehow lacking?

He had done his work on a human being who had pulsing blood vessels that carried oxygen to a functioning brain. He had operated on someone who would wake up and walk and talk and think. And be alive. Someone who would be a comfort to his wife and family—a husband, a father, a grandfather. Someone who was loved and needed and wanted. Someone whose heart beat just a bit faster when he heard a small child call him "Pop-pop."

And now, what was left of that man? Only a collection of guts and fat and bone. Was this the result of all of Harry's training? Of all the years in school and internship and residency? To start with a live human being and wind up with a disemboweled cadaver?

Harry realized that this was the most inevitable rule of the doctor game: in the end, the doctors always lost, and death was the final big winner. The doctors might prolong life a few months or a few years, but death always crossed the finish line first, and Gregorio always took care of their patients sooner or later.

"Liver, two thousand grams, heavy," Gregorio was noting aloud. "A sure sign of cirrhosis, of course. But there's something. . . ." He cut a slice through the glistening purple capsule of the liver and pointed to a mottled yellow pattern scattered on the surface. "Fatty infiltration and early death of thousands of liver cells here." He frowned pensively as he cut at the tissue with his scalpel.

"In your estimation"—Moe broke in—"what would that indicate?"

"I'm not sure," Gregorio muttered, his mind elsewhere. "Yet. It could be any one of several things."

The neuropathologist had joined them and had been working away at Wexler's skull, while Gregorio concentrated on the abdominal cavity. He had removed Wexler's skull plate and had taken the brain out in his hands to slice methodically into its many sections. Now he was able to report the brain exam as normal. Herman Wexler had not died of a blood clot there. Nor had he succumbed to a stroke.

Gregorio moved on to his examination of Wexler's pancreas—or, at least, what had been left of the pancreas after the operation. There was a trace of admiration or approval in his voice as he announced, "What is left of the pancreas in the patient is not as severely damaged as the specimen I received from his Whipple operation. But it is filled with chronic end-stage inflammation. And look at this: the aorta and the other major vessels are smooth as a baby's ass. No plaques or cholesterol deposits at all. The results of years of alcohol."

Harry had seen the same combination many times before—a battered liver and a pancreas torn to shit, yet the blood vessels were clean. Why had Wexler's years of boozing attacked certain organs, yet somehow left others untouched? The arteries in his belly, just like his coronaries, had been completely protected.

Cautiously, Moe asked, "Was his death a direct result of the alcohol?"

Gregorio laughed. "Direct result? Probably not, though I can't be sure as yet. But poetically one could say 'It was the alcohol that got him.' " He pointed to the slices he had made in the gritty liver and pancreas specimens. "All I can tell you right now is that these are not the organs of a happy man."

When Gregorio went on to remove and examine the kidneys, he muttered cautiously to himself, "Very interesting," and again, "Very interesting."

"What is it?" Michener asked anxiously.

"These small areas of bleeding under the swollen areas," the pathologist responded vaguely.

"What do they mean?"

Gregorio smiled patiently at Moe. "We'll have to do some tests to find out."

As the autopsy moved on slowly, anxiously, through the normal ureters, bladder, spleen, adrenal glands, and the intestines, Moe Michener became less and less patient for an answer. When Gregorio nodded his head knowingly upon discovering the intestines swollen and puckered and lined with red streaks, Moe's irritability became more evident.

"Obviously you know what the cause of death is," he grumbled, "but you prefer to keep it to yourself."

Gregorio looked up at Moe pointedly. "Young man, there is no urgency to come to a conclusion. The patient is already dead. And you might live a little longer yourself if you would learn to relax." And he turned to make a few notes on his forms.

Finally, after a lengthy silence, he announced, "Gentlemen, I am going to have to reserve judgment on the cause of death here until after we have performed a number of tests. Even under normal circumstances, I would have to state that the physical evidence with this patient is inconclusive. However, I am aware that there has been talk of a malpractice lawsuit in this case, so I must be absolutely certain before I make a judgment that might affect a doctor's career or might bring further grief to an already grieving family."

Gregorio paused for a moment, staring down at the cadaver as if he expected it to reply; then he continued. "It is obvious to me, though, that Dr. Norton made no errors in the surgery itself. It is also obvious that his operation did not help the patient. But as for the question of whether the operation might actually have been the cause of death or might have contributed to the death, I must reserve judgment until I can see the results of the slides and chemical tests. I will notify each of you when those results are in. That's all for now."

Harry was dumbfounded. The autopsy was over, and all his feelings of dread and apprehension had come to this. To nothing. He had no more idea now of his future in medicine than he had had when he had come into the room. He was almost as impatient as Moe was to know the verdict.

As the others filed out of the room, Gregorio and his assistant remained behind, stuffing the remains of Herman Wexler back into the body so they could sew him up with thick running catgut. Harry remained in the shadows for a moment, staring silently at the body. Something flitted through his mind as elusively as déjà vu. And something in the back of his head toyed foolishly with the last line of a T. S. Eliot poem: "Not with a bang but a whimper."

Hoping all the others had caught the elevator already and had dispersed, going about their business, he slowly walked out the door into the hall.

The bright light of the hallway hit his eyes suddenly and harshly, making the experience of the autopsy fade like shadows in a blackout. This was the reality he had to deal with; this was now. Herman Wexler was already a part of the past.

He was relieved to see that the others had already gone. There was no one in the hall except Ellen Hopkins, waiting patiently by the elevators. Suddenly, he felt very good; his spirits lifted brightly and vibrantly.

"I thought you might need a big, alcoholic lunch," she announced, "and I wouldn't want you to have it alone."

"That's a very good idea," he said, smiling warmly and taking her arm, "but it's going to be my treat, and it's going to be as far away from Valley View Hospital as we can get before starvation sets in."

The two of them talked very little as they sped along the freeway into Beverly Hills. Ellen had asked the important question while they were in the elevator—"What was the verdict?"—and Harry had told her, "No answer yet."

The freeway was open at this time of day, and Harry was able to take the opportunity to release some of the tension on his powerful little Mercedes, English racing green just for kicks. He was pleased to note that Ellen Hopkins suffered no excessive awe at the car nor any loss of composure as a result of his driving well over the speed limit. Noblesse oblige, he thought, but where did she pick it up?

Just for size, he decided he would try her out on Pips, the ultimate in Beverly Hills nouveau chic. He wouldn't need a reservation because very few of the members had caught on to the fact that the place had recently started serving lunch as well as dinner.

Ellen Hopkins wasn't impressed. Or, if she was, she didn't make a display of it. She settled into the snug booth and asked for a Bloody Mary as if she owned the place, or at least as if it were no better than the corner drugstore. When the waiter had served their drinks and taken their orders, Ellen announced decisively, "I've found a lawyer for you, and I'd like you to talk to him."

Harry was more amused than surprised. "Oh, you have, have you?"

"Yes." She ignored the slight note of sarcasm. "His name is Dick Darwin, and his office is here in Beverly Hills. But don't be put off by that; I understand he's one of the best lawyers around."

Harry was speechless. He knew Darwin's reputation, but he had absolutely no idea of how Ellen Hopkins had gotten to know him. Her efficiency seemed to know no bounds.

"Why should I be put off? I have nothing against Darwin or Beverly Hills."

"Well, some people, when they meet him, think they've gotten into a carnival by mistake." She brushed a strand of hair into place. "But he really knows what he's doing, and I've already told him about your case."

"How did he react?"

"He's very interested. But of course I couldn't speak with any real understanding or authority."

This side of Ellen Hopkins was entirely new to Harry. In the office, she was always sedate and businesslike. But here, she was bubbling with emotion and enthusiasm. And a surprisingly strong self-assurance. What was even more startling to Harry was that—while he found her attractive in the office—outside the office he found her so beautiful he thought of lavish images.

Harry was so intent on looking at Ellen that he wasn't sure if he really asked the question. "How do you know Dick Darwin?"

Ellen shrugged. "I don't know him very well. It's just that his parents and my parents used to have summer cabins in the same area."

Harry heaved a deep sigh, finished off his drink, and signaled to the waiter that he'd like another round. Then, staring at his empty glass, he said morosely, "I suppose if anybody can help me out of this mess, he can. But I'm afraid it may be impossible —even for him. It's pretty obvious by now that I've made a very serious error in judgment. And that's fatal for a doctor."

Neither of them spoke while the waiter served the second round of drinks, but as soon as he had moved away, Ellen asked simply, "What would be the worst that could happen to you?"

"The worst?" Harry thought for a moment. "You know, I haven't really thought of it that way. Financially, I suppose a court could award the family as much as half a million dollars in damage. Because of that, I could be relieved of my duties with the hospital—dismissed, fired. And I would probably not be able to get medical insurance again—or at least I'd have to pay more for insurance than I could ever hope to cover. In terms of reputation, I honestly don't know. But I'm sure the damage would be enough to prevent me from ever working in California again."

"Could you practice medicine at all—anywhere?" Ellen asked her questions in seeming innocence, but with a strange sort of confidence that suggested she was leading Harry somewhere.

"I guess there might be ways. If I gave up surgery and went into general practice in another state. Or a foreign country. But there's hardly much future in that. The best I could hope for with that would be minimal subsistence. Even if I could get insurance for general practice, the rates would be so high—with the new increases—that I might actually lose more than I would make."

Ellen listened very seriously, frowning contemplatively into her drink. "Then what it all comes down to in the final analysis is money?"

Harry stared at her in bemusement. "Isn't that what everything comes down to really—in the final analysis?" He realized they were playing a game, one where words were a ball and their snug banquette table a court. They would go on tossing the ball back and forth across the court until one of them slipped and missed. Or at least until one of them called out "Foul." And finally, when one of them had won and one had lost, it would mean very little. It would change very little.

Ellen must have realized this, because she laughed and tossed her hair back from her forehead. "You know, most of us ordinary folks have the impression that doctors are better than the rest of us. More noble. Selfless. Or at least we think that's the way they ought to be."

They had to call time out at that point, because the waiter arrived to serve their food. But Ellen was obviously still thinking very seriously, because, as soon as he had gone, she immediately leaped back into the discussion.

"Before all this came up, what sort of goals had you set for your life? What had you set out to accomplish in your work?"

"In twenty-five words or less?" Harry asked, grinning.

"Give or take a few."

Harry stabbed aimlessly at his salad with his fork. "I can give it to you in one word: success. There must be a dozen aspects of that word—everything from being respected for doing my work well, and for helping people, to accumulating a sizable bank account, a nice home, and a swanky office in Beverly Hills. But they all boil down to success. Ego gratification. The feeling of accomplishment."

Ellen looked skeptical. "Money and Beverly Hills? Are they a real measure of success? They strike me as rather hollow symbols compared to the knowledge that you're helping people and that you've earned their gratitude."

"Gratitude?" Harry frowned. "Patients very rarely say thank you to their doctors. And when they do, it's a pretty good sign that they don't intend to pay their bills. No, money in the bank says thank you a whole lot better."

Ellen got very coy, smirking almost, as she asked, "Then you don't believe in that old maxim, 'Money can't buy happiness'?"

Harry sat back and thought for a long time before he replied. "I suppose I know it's true. But most people use that maxim to imply that money actually buys unhappiness, and I honestly don't believe that's true. Nor do I believe that poverty guarantees·happiness. It's much more likely that poverty breeds misery. I've been poor, and I can say confidently that it wasn't much fun. In a way, I think that's why I wanted so much to give Herman Wexler a few more years of life. He was like my father in a lot of ways. He worked hard all his life, and he was unhappy at throwing away his years just to make life easier for his wife and his children. Now that his children had grown and he could retire, he finally could have thought about himself and what he wanted to do with his life. Whatever years I might have given him, he could have used to try to be happy. He wanted to write. He had always thought that would make him happy."

"But that's not you," Ellen persisted, "that's Herman Wexler. Will money and a nice home and an office in Beverly Hills make you happy?"

"Not by themselves, no," Harry answered honestly. "But they'll buy off a couple of the ways that I might have otherwise been unhappy."

He paused for a moment, staring into his drink with more melancholy than he wanted to show to Ellen Hopkins. He took a drink, made an effort at smiling, and added, "Or at least they might have— before Herman Wexler came along."

13 MAXWELL HOWARD

November 17, 1975, Fairfax Area

A funeral was a strange place to contemplate the meaning of prejudice, but that is what Maxwell Howard found himself doing. He had been apprehensive about what would be expected of him at the gathering of friends and family who would be paying their last respects to his father-in-law, but nothing Sarah could have told him could have quite prepared him for the experience of being the only gentile at a Jewish service.

He would have to have been totally insensitive not to realize there was a barrier between him and everyone else who had gathered at the funeral parlor. But who had set up the barrier, he wondered? Had he, or had they? Was it inherent in his own awareness of being the outsider, or were the others—either intentionally or unintentionally—seeking to make him feel uncomfortable?

Ever since he had first learned what prejudice was and what it did to people, he had striven to avoid any feelings in himself that might possibly be construed as anti-Semitic or anti-black or anti-Spanish. But he could not easily set aside the resentment he felt at not being accepted at this gathering. He was certain that this resentment was not, in itself, a sign of prejudice—but it made him think things that, he felt, he ought not to think.

When it had first begun to surface, he had thought, We're all of us human beings—whatever our differences—and we're united here in our common caring for Herman and Miriam Wexler. But after he had been consistently shunned or stared down by one guest after another, he had begun to think, Well, they're not really any different from anybody else; they can be just as susceptible to prejudice as gentiles. In quick progression the thoughts finally arrived at: They want me to be anti-Semitic; they thrive on it the way a blind man finds an identity in being blind, and then extends it into the be-all and end-all of his existence.

And that thought—or the idea that he was capable of thinking such a thing—upset him and made him angry at himself and at his adopted family.

Of course, Max realized that his feeling of separation was accentuated by the fact that the Jewish religion separated him from the mourners because he was an in-law, and not of the immediate family. In his own church, he would be with his wife and not sitting among a group of strangers. He wished now that he had agreed to bring the children with him. It would have been difficult keeping them quiet, but at least he would have felt he belonged.

The ceremony was mercifully brief and simple. There were no flowers, and there was no painful viewing of the remains, which rested in a plain coffin beneath a black drape, lighted with two candles at each end. The rabbi gave a brief eulogy and recited a traditional prayer. As Sarah and her mother and brother filed out of the little chapel, Max could see that their grief had not been heightened by the service they had just gone through.

What gave him the ultimate sense of separation, however, was that his wife did not even look his way when she passed. She too considered him an outsider;

she seemed to have no need for his strength or his comfort in her time of grief. Despite her intellectual rejection of her Jewish heritage, Sarah was first a Jew and second a human being. There was, Max now suspected, something deep down inside of Jews that made them different from other people. It was something that he and Sarah would never be able to share, no matter how many children they might have together and no matter how much their cultural and social interests were alike.

Max felt a sudden chill, and a terrible panic inside.

Since Sarah would be riding in the mourners' car, Max drove to the cemetery alone, his car far back in the procession. At each corner, he had the urge to turn suddenly and leave the uncomfortable ceremony to those who belonged there. But he did not. He would never be able to explain his feelings to his wife. Or to her family.

As he followed the line of cars through peaceful streets, his windows rolled up and the air conditioner on, the sun shot arrows of light off the chrome of the other cars, irritating his eyes. He prayed silently that these thoughts and feelings would leave him once the funeral was over, and life could get back to normal. To distract himself, he turned on the car radio to loud, fast, happy music.

Although Max had gotten along very well with his father-in-law, Herman Wexler had objected to the marriage from the very first. Had he possessed more wisdom than either Max or Sarah had given him credit for? Was the reality of human existence more complex than human reason and rationality tried to make it? Max felt very small and very inadequate, and very close to despair.

Max and Sarah had believed strongly in closing up

the differences between people. They had been convinced by the philosophy and history and sociology they had studied in college that—underneath the differences of heritage and tradition and religion—everybody in the world was basically the same. Max was now beginning to suspect that they were not. And he had a vague feeling that somehow they should not be, that the great beauty of humanity existed in the differences.

He knew that he loved Sarah, but alone right now in his car, he did not really know why he loved her. Was it because she was so much like him or because she was so different from him? At times, he felt confident and affirmed, because her ideas and her beliefs were so much like his own. But at other times he could be challenged and excited by the vast differences between them.

Of course they fought like any other married couple, but their fights were never of any serious consequence. In the end they always fell back on their love, on their deep caring for each other. In all of his confusion right now, that was the one belief that he could not be shaken from. That was what it was all about—caring. Caring for each other because you were human beings and alive, whether you were alike or different, and life was short.

By the time Max had parked his car and followed the crowd of people to the grave site, the coffin containing the body of Herman Wexler was already in place above the grave, and Sarah and Robert and Mrs. Wexler were seated in folding chairs alongside, waiting dry-eyed. As soon as all the guests were assembled, the coffin was lowered unceremoniously into the grave, and the soil was shoveled in on top of it.

Once the grave was filled, according to Jewish belief, Herman Wexler was officially dead. Promptly, the rabbi stepped forward for the prayers.

As he listened to the strange sounds of the mourners' kaddish, Max looked at his wife. Briefly, Sarah's eyes met his, but she quickly looked away. She was not crying, but she seemed perplexed, confused. She did not belong in this group either; she looked and felt out of place, perhaps not as out of place as Max, but nevertheless an outsider. Was it, Max wondered, a difference of generations? Certainly most of the people present were neighbors, and most were of the same age as Herman and Miriam Wexler. They dressed the same, they looked the same, and their lives were more or less the same. Their dress was simple if not downright dowdy, and their lives looked backward rather than forward. Sarah was dressed stylishly, her makeup and hair artistically done, and she and Max had dreams and plans for the future.

And certainly her brother, seated on the other side of their mother, was different. If anybody was out of place at this ceremony, it was Robert Wexler. Perhaps others present might not be aware of it, but Sarah and Max had long ago realized her brother was a homosexual. No one had ever said anything, but his mannerisms and his dress and his voice were unmistakable.

Strangely, Robert Wexler was the only member of the family who was crying. The incongruity struck Max as somewhat ridiculous. There had never been any love lost between Robert and Herman Wexler. As far as Max knew, the old man's greatest despair was that he had never been able to communicate with his own son. Was Robert Wexler crying because he, too, felt the differences? Because he did not belong, had never belonged in his own family? Had the barrier that had existed between him and his father not really been of his own making?

Were there, despite the apparent homogeneity of the crowd, barriers that existed between them all? Had there been barriers for Herman Wexler himself? Max seemed to have nothing but questions. He longed for the familiar surroundings of his home. Maybe there wouldn't actually be any answers there, but he could find refuge from questions.

But Max knew his home would not be a refuge for some time to come. Sarah's time and energy would be devoted to this malpractice lawsuit against Mr. Wexler's doctor. They still did not know the cause of death, even after the autopsy, but the lawyer seemed to think they had a good case. Max knew that contacting the lawyer had been the right thing to do, but he dreaded the long-drawn-out period of tension and anxiety that would be involved.

And, when it got right down to it, Max really didn't like to fight. He liked to settle differences peaceably and amicably. There was that word again—differences. Sarah had differences with her father's doctor over the medical care. The same word that described the natural barriers between people was used for barriers that were created by the social, economic, and legal structure of society. One was taught to ignore (or to try to ignore) the first kind of difference, but the second kind, paradoxically, was encouraged and fostered.

That realization presented Max with another whole set of questions. And he was not happy with a single one of them.

With the prayers spoken, the funeral service was at an end. As the family rose from their chairs, the guests formed two long lines facing each other, and Sarah, her mother, and Robert passed through, acknowledging their presence.

As they passed by Max, each of them glanced at him briefly, and Mrs. Wexler gave him a faint, sad smile. Max smiled back. He felt a great heavy rush of grief overcoming him, as he watched the three black-clad figures moving on down the line, and tears welled up in his eyes. Max knew that he was not grieving for his father-in-law; he was grieving for his wife or for himself. Max did not know who or what it was he was crying for. But he stood there, among the Jews, with tears streaming down his face.

PART THREE

Mortality and Morbidity

14 MOE MICHENER

Karen glanced at her watch and immediately set down her coffee cup. "Oh, I'm going to have to run." She tossed her napkin onto her tray. "I want to look in on a patient before the meeting, and it's getting late."

Moe was startled by his wife's abrupt announcement. "I thought you were going to go up to the meeting with me," he said casually, but he looked at her guardedly, even suspiciously.

Since their Saturday evening confrontation on the subject, they had both studiously avoided any serious discussion of the Harry Norton (or Herman Wexler) situation. The subject was one of those embarrassing reminders that the two individuals who made up this marriage were not always one. Of course, they had both been aware that each of them was going to be attending the Mortality and Morbidity Conference at the hospital this afternoon, and Moe had simply assumed that they would go together.

In fact, he had been hoping that his presence at the meeting would not be quite so noticeable if he came in on the arm of his wife. Although he was used to attending meetings, Moe knew that he was tolerated more than welcomed, and for that reason he did not attend too many.

Now, as Karen collected her things and got up from

the table, Moe realized his wife saw through him completely, and he suspected she had invented this "patient" in order to circumvent him.

"I'll see you upstairs," she announced, flashing him an enigmatic smile.

As she hurried out the door, Moe had difficulty hiding his feeling of irritation. There was still a piece of inedible, chemically produced lemon-meringue pie on his tray, and he used his fork to vent his wrath on it, jabbing at it until the crust had crumbled and mixed into a goo with the lemon and the meringue.

This was her territory he was on. Although he had his M.D. title, staff privileges did not extend fully to him. When his wife was at the hospital, she was Dr. Karen Marshall, and Moe felt it was an area from which he was excluded. She was in the inner circle here, and he was somewhere outside the circumference —maybe close enough to be on the line, but still outside.

He wouldn't want to admit it to her, but he felt he needed her right now. He saw himself as not unlike the hero of a Frank Capra movie, an idealist standing alone against the world, and he needed his woman by his side to give him courage.

Moe looked at his watch. He had twenty-five minutes to waste. He had already skimmed over everything that was of interest in the newspaper. But, as long as he was going to be here idle, he figured he might as well skim it again.

The headline that had interested Moe the most had been DOCTORS MEETING TO DISCUSS STRIKE. Moe was pleased; that meant the fat cats were sweating. He decided to read the article again, because it gave him a certain pride to know that he had played at least a small part in backing them up against the wall. He was accomplishing something with his crusade. Up to now, it had been relatively little, but before long the hospitals and the medical schools were going to have to realize reforms were necessary. Doctors were going to have to learn their science a helluva lot better.

He permitted himself to dream. Someday . . . someday the medical profession would be returned to the Dr. Welbys and the Dr. Kildares. The medical schools would stop teaching ethics with all sorts of gray areas and realize that—when it came to human life—there was only black or white. If doctors would not live up to the ideals of the medical profession, there would have to be laws that would force them to. That would be the day that Moe Michener would know the sweet taste of total victory.

When it came time for the Mortality and Morbidity Conference, Moe was feeling the euphoria of selfless righteousness. He had had to reinforce his belief in what he was doing without the help of his wife, and he had done a splendid job. As he took the elevator upstairs to the conference room, he was champing at the bit, ready to fight any and all doctors who might stand in the way of progress.

He no longer felt the need to slip into the meeting on the arm of his wife.

When he stepped off the elevator, he saw the enemy scattered about the hallway, talking in friendly clusters. Many of them he knew well. Some he had known from his days as an intern. O'Hara was the most conspicuous of them all, with his loud, boisterous manner. And the man he was talking to—Moe almost took him for a stranger—was Sims, the black doctor who, like himself, had dropped out of the doctor game, though Sims had gone into research. Minton and Kramer were near the conference-room door talking to the one doctor Moe despised above all others, Buxbaum, the chief surgeon.

The dapper, often-married, rich Dr. Buxbaum represented everything that Moe thought a doctor should not be. And Buxbaum was standing right beside the door through which Michener would have to pass. One of these days, Moe would like to confront that man in a courtroom, but right now he wanted to avoid any words with him.

Moe couldn't very well turn and walk the other way; that would be too obvious an admission of insecurity. So he decided to stop and say hello to O'Hara and Sims. He wasn't particularly eager to be bored by O'Hara, but it had been many years since he had spoken to Sims. He wasn't even sure which university or research foundation Sims was with now.

As Moe approached, O'Hara was saying, ". . . no way any doctor is ever gonna go out on a limb for a patient—"

"Sims," Moe said, extending his hand. "It's been a long time." Seeing Sims's puzzled look, Moe added, "Moe Michener. City Hospital, a great many years ago." And then Moe nodded respectfully to O'Hara. "O'Hara."

"Well, I'll be!" exclaimed the research doctor, breaking into a grin.

"Excuse me," O'Hara muttered, eyeing Michener. "I see George Mason down the hall. I have to talk to him." And, as he darted off, he added over his shoulder, "Good seeing you, Sims."

It didn't bother Moe at all that O'Hara had just made a point of snubbing him. It was Sims who was startled by the abrupt departure.

"Michener. Moe Michener, where the hell have you been hiding yourself?" Sims seemed truly pleased to see him. "It's been at least ten years, hasn't it?"

"Just about." Moe avoided filling in the gap. "Where are you now?"

"Cancer Research Institute," Sims responded. "Still one of the Professor's boys. Are you with Valley View?"

"Associated with it." Moe decided to remain at least somewhat ambiguous. "I'm in law—legal medicine."

"Oh, yeah." Sims grinned broadly. "That's where the real money is now. Either you were pretty lucky or damned smart."

Moe decided to ignore the implication that he was just as greedy as almost everybody who studied medicine. He liked Sims; Sims had had it rough, maybe just as rough as Moe had. Medicine had been relatively open to blacks since the fifties, but there were still some problems that were bound to crop up because of prejudice.

Sims had had the misfortune to face one of those problems, and he hadn't been strong enough to survive it. Back at City Hospital, a young white woman had come into the emergency room with a burst appendix. Sims had been the resident on duty, so it had been his case. By the time he had reached the operating room, she was already under the anesthetic, and he had set to work, getting to her just in time.

When the woman had come out from under, Sims had been introduced to her as "the man who saved your life."

She had become hysterical, screaming, "No!" and "He had his black hands inside of me!"—over and over again, emphasizing "black hands."

That had so shaken Sims that he had gone into a deep depression that had lasted for weeks. When he had come out of it, he had decided to give up surgery. He had first tried to set up general practice in the Watts area of Los Angeles, but found it too unprofitable. Buxbaum had gotten him a job in research on a grant from the University.

After a few minutes of reminiscing, Sims said, "It looks like everybody's going inside," and started for the door. "Are you here for the meeting?"

Moe nodded affirmatively and started to follow Sims inside. But he was halted by a hand on his arm.

"Sorry, Michener," Buxbaum announced, "but this is a private conference."

Moe was so startled he was speechless at first, but he quickly got control. "What do you mean 'private'? I'm not on the staff, but I enjoy a doctor's privileges."

Buxbaum stepped smoothly in front of him, barring his entrance into the room. "Not today, you don't. You're representing the Wexler family in a malpractice suit. This isn't a courtroom, and some of the doctors have expressed a desire to give their opinions freely without fear of being quoted." Buxbaum's voice was soft and even, his manner mild. He smiled a gentlemanly smile. "You understand."

Michener was not about to remain a gentleman in the face of this kind of insult.

"Like hell I understand," he spat out angrily. "I have a right to attend this meeting! My clients have a right to know what happened to Herman Wexler!"

Buxbaum kept his calm manner. "You will be provided with a copy of the autopsy report." He smiled condescendingly. "When it's available. The hospital respects the rights of the Wexler family. But the members of this committee also have rights, and one of those is the right of privacy." Again he smiled.

"You all stick together, don't you?" said Moe, managing to keep his tones even and threatening. "Well, when I get through with your hospital, it'll be a parking lot! And none of you will ever be able to practice medicine again! I'll sue Norton! I'll sue you! I'll sue your whole goddamn hospital!"

And he turned and stalked off to the elevator. One of the doors was opening, and, still raging, he stormed in without looking, colliding with someone getting out.

It was Karen. Before the doors could close, he stepped back out, grabbing her arm to speak to her.

"Baby, you've got to help me," he said softly but urgently. "They won't let me into that meeting. I've got my tape recorder in my briefcase. You've got to take it into the meeting for me and record everything."

Karen pulled away and stared at him, dumbfounded. After an incredulous moment, she shook her head.

At first her rejection didn't register with Moe. "You've got to," he urged. "I have to know which of those doctors I can get on the stand to testify against Norton."

"No, Moe," said Karen when she found her voice. "I'm sorry, but I won't do it."

Suddenly, he understood: Karen was one of them. She was a doctor, and doctors would stick together. When it got right down to it, being Mrs. Moe Michener meant very little to her. The only thing that was important to his wife was being Dr. Karen Marshall. Her membership in the medical fraternity superseded any obligation she might have to her husband.

His eyes smoldered from the rage he felt inside, but his words were cold and even. "I see. If that's the way you want it, that's the way it will be. But I promise you, if you get in my way, I'm going to make it just as hard for you as I will for the rest of them."

Still raging, Moe stalked off down the hall to the stairs. The way he was feeling right now, he didn't have the patience to wait for the elevator. He wanted to get the hell out of this hospital as fast as he could. He had a lot to decide and a lot to do.

Moe had suspected that there had been something more than just friendship betwen Karen and Harry ever since they had come together to see him in Florida. Florida! Shit! That was what it always seemed to come back to for Moe. That was when he had seen what doctors were really all about. What people were all about. Everybody had been out for themselves—doctors, patients, even friends. He had found that the old-fashioned ideals of goodness and kindness and caring were just that—old-fashioned ideals.

After he had been working at Dr. Groton's Medicaid Factory for only a few weeks, Moe had discovered what the man and the place were all about. He remembered Dr. Groton introducing him at the first meeting to the other doctors who worked there.

These men, Melman, Horowitz, and Tracy, were all GPs like Dr. Groton. They were in their late fifties and had left thriving practices in the north and come to Florida to sort of semi-retire. They played golf and sailed their boats and still made enormous amounts of money at Dr. Groton's, working fifteen to twenty hours per week. They all gave Groton 50 percent of their take.

Moe knew these doctors were experts at ordering large numbers of blood tests from the laboratory and x-raying the patients to death. They gave injections of vitamins and estrogens to nervous old women, a handful of Valiums and a tender pat on the ass to nervous young women, and penicillin to almost everybody else. To Moe the most impressive thing about them was their suntans.

"Dr. Michener is new with us," Dr. Groton began. "He is a partially trained surgeon. He is qualified to do certain procedures in the operating room. I've listed them on the board and also the simpler ones that he will be splitting with us."

Moe scanned the list. The dollar sign that Dr. Groton had drawn on the board several weeks before was still visible.

> Breast biopsy
> Excision of skin masses
> Hernia
> Appendix
> D and C
> TOP
> Vasectomy

"As I said, we will be using a system of splits in these cases," Dr. Groton continued. "Dr. Michener will give fifty percent of his fee to each doctor who refers him the case. This will stimulate interest in the other GPs for finding him patients to operate upon. Everyone will be fairly paid."

Moe was stunned. That was totally unfair. It was more than unfair. It was illegal!

Moe had heard enough. They were talking about him and dividing up his surgical fees as if he weren't even there!

"Wait a minute!" he shouted. "Isn't this fee-splitting? I don't believe you're suggesting that I give half my fee for these surgical procedures to the referring GP. Why, I already give half of everything I make to Dr. Groton. That would mean I'd be doing the operations for one fourth!"

Dr. Groton turned a light crimson.

"Well, we don't like to label it with a name, son," he began. "Fee-splitting isn't a nice word. Remember, you're new here. The fellows don't know you yet. They could refer their cases to you, or to me, or to someone else on the outside. This way, you're getting all their referrals, and one fourth is certainly better than nothing! It will be a gold mine in the long run."

"But . . . but . . ." Moe was confused. "I'm paying malpractice from my own pocket to do surgery. Why don't these good doctors split that cost?"

"Trust me." Dr. Groton spread his palms across the desk in a final motion designed to soothe all. "May I remind you that you are not a fully licensed surgeon. I've overlooked some of your past record at City Hospital. I have made some inquiries too. But I have trusted you. Now, trust me."

The knot in Moe's stomach tightened. He was tempted to quit on the spot. The thought of giving three fourths to these bastards enraged him. But he held back. After all, there was the hundred thousand dollars. And they could hold his record at City Hospital against him. They all knew. They could blackmail him. He had to think things through.

The meeting ended, and Dr. Groton stormed out of the office. Moe knew he was very upset over the way the meeting had gone. Over the next hour Dr. Groton's behavior became more bizarre. He roamed up and down the halls of the hospital looking for mistakes. He fired two nurses and a nurses' aide for not knowing a patient's temperature. He kicked out a laboratory tech and dictated a note to himself to can the emergency-room nurse who worked the night shift.

With a continually growing group of trembling nurses and nurses' aides, two Cuban resident doctors, and the night x-ray man for an audience, Dr. Groton stood there raving in the hallway, beads of sweat on his forehead, hair flying in every direction.

At the height of his speech, Moe saw Dr. Groton drop his pencil into the crowd. Moe was sure he had done it on purpose. Two nurses and one aide scrambled to pick it up for him, almost colliding on the floor, but one of the Cuban residents won the prize by grabbing it. Moe saw Dr. Groton beam. He looked more excited than he had been during the TOPs. Moe saw him smile for the first time that night.

He was a dirty fucking bastard, Moe thought. The writing on the front of the building had been correct.

As the weeks went by, Moe realized he had been trapped. Groton had him, and there seemed to be nothing else to do but submit. Unable to compromise his actions with his beliefs, Moe had sunk deeper and deeper into despair. And, in the despair, he began to turn increasingly to drugs.

Before each operation, Moe gave himself a shot of morphine sulfate, and as a result he was able to operate coolly and methodically, like a machine. His operations were fast and efficient, so successful that he began to perceive himself as a kind of super surgeon, unable to make a mistake. That is, until Juan Gonzales.

The Gonzales case had been his undoing. Sometimes, Moe thought wryly of that case as the watershed of his career.

Gonzales was a Cuban immigrant who had met an attractive girl, Tina Olea, at the University nine months before. The two had become quite close, but Juan Gonzales looked like he didn't have a friend in the world the night he came into Dr. Groton's emergency room with an umbrella lodged deeply within his stomach.

Shortly after 1:00 A.M., the umbrella, its tip very sharp, had been jabbed into his middle, opened with a sudden thrust, and then roughly manipulated so that it caught Gonzales's stomach and liver edge and then ended up in his right chest.

Tina Olea arrived by cab five minutes later. She was a pale blond girl of twenty, and she seemed quite upset. She was carrying the greater portion of her right thumb in her hand. A large towel, now a sparkling red in color, was failing to absorb the blood that oozed from her right hand and dropped steadily on her white-lace dress. Her thumb had been removed from its normal position at about ten minutes past one with a large kitchen knife.

Gonzales was ashen white when Moe first saw him, and a cold clammy sweat had broken out over his entire body.

"Blood pressure ninety over fifty. Pulse one fifteen and weak," reported the nurse.

"Oh, God, Doc," Gonzales cried. "Help me! The pain! I can't stand it. I'm going to die."

"Call Dr. Albright for the hand," Moe ordered. "And get a second OR crew stat."

Moe inserted two large needles into the veins of Gonzales's forearm. He ordered saline to run wide open in both. He typed Gonzales for six pints of blood. The orderlies shaved Gonzales's belly the best they could around the umbrella.

Thanks to Moe's prodding, at 1:50 A.M., thirty minutes after arriving at Southeast Medical Center, Juan Gonzales entered the operating room, with IVs running full blast and the umbrella still firmly in place in his stomach.

Dr. Albright, the hand surgeon, arrived several

minutes later. He worked fast, also, and soon had Tina Olea's thumb in a sterile solution of saline and penicillin. Tina was rushed into the second operating room, where her thumb was sewn into place.

Moe was certain the operation on Juan Gonzales would not be an easy one. He wasn't sure he was up to it. The operation might require more skill, more experience. Maybe he should consult another surgeon. . . .

He called in Dr. Juaristi, a local surgeon, who wasn't very busy and was happy to be called in any time by Dr. Groton or the staff, for the first assistant's fee.

While the patient was being prepped, Moe headed for the drug supply room. He wasn't sure how long the operation would take or how much he would need, but he was scared. He filled the syringe with as much morphine as he thought his system could take. It wasn't long before he felt cool and confident. His hand was steady as he opened the door of the supply room and stepped out into the hall in the direction of the operating room.

The operation on Juan Gonzales had gone well at first. Moe opened Gonzales's belly with a midline incision around the umbrella. He had seen Buxbaum do it many times before.

Moe found a large hole in the stomach along the lesser curvature. The stomach was full of sardines! Many were only partially digested and still recognizable, representing Gonzales's last meal.

"Sardines," Moe said, shaking his head. "Can you beat that? Sardines!" Dr. Juaristi nodded in amazement but said nothing.

As Moe continued to manipulate the contents of the abdominal cavity, he found the tip of the umbrella lying against the liver. He removed the um-

brella cautiously. He found a tear in the right lobe
of the liver, and a hole in the diaphragm, which di-
vided the stomach cavity from the chest. Fortunately,
the tip of the umbrella had just missed Gonzales's
right lung.

Even with all that damage, Moe felt confident that
he could save the patient. But he was troubled that
the drug didn't give him quite the self-confidence he
had expected. Moe plowed ahead, trying to ignore
the fact that his hand shook slightly. And his head
began to ache painfully, just behind the eyes, blurring
his vision slightly.

Despite these handicaps, Moe, with the increasing
help of Dr. Juaristi, managed to oversew the stomach
in two layers, to suture the diaphragm tightly, and to
close the bleeding liver edge with several deep,
chromic catgut stitches.

But it had taken a painfully long time.

Strangely, time seemed to be Moe's greatest ob-
stacle. In contrast to the other operations he had performed with the help of drugs, in this procedure his
hands seemed to move much more slowly than before.
He noticed the odd glances from Dr. Juaristi and the
others around the operating table, and he knew they
were wondering what was wrong. He didn't blame
them. He wondered himself.

Moe's mind was racing far ahead of his slow,
plodding hands. The longer the operation took, the
higher the risk for his patient. His hands felt stiff
and heavy as lead. And there seemed to be a weight
on his shoulders that increased with each stitch. But
it was his eyes that slowed him down the most; it became harder and harder to keep them focused on
the work.

Finally, it was done. The scrub nurse helped him
drain the belly with eight or nine liters of saline.

He put a chest tube into the pleural cavity and closed.

For the first few days after the operation, Juan Gonzales seemed to be doing okay. On the sixth day, however, his temperature spiked to 102 degrees, and he complained about fullness in his stomach. His white blood count rose to twenty-four thousand, and x-rays showed a giant pocket of pus pushing the stomach to one side. Juan Gonzales had developed an abscess in his belly!

Gonzales's temperature was 104 degrees the next night. The nurses sponged him hourly with ice and alcohol, but his bed was still drenched with perspiration.

"Am I going to die, Doc?" The boy looked up at Moe, frightened.

"No, no." Moe knew the abscess would have to be drained with a second operation in the morning. "You're going to be fine," he said, with a confidence he surely didn't feel.

· "I didn't mean to do anything," Gonzales moaned. "I just lost my head. The knife . . . the umbrella . . . everything happened so fast. . . ."

Moe nodded. He was making preparations for Gonzales's second operation when he received a call from Dr. Groton.

"Look, that Spanish boy you have in recovery room. His insurance ran out two days ago. My girls just informed me. Besides, he's a sick cookie. We wouldn't want to get the hospital in any trouble. I think it would be best to transfer him over to County Hospital. It's what we do with all our patients when their insurance can't cover their hospital stay."

"But . . . but . . . he's sick as hell. He needs to have his abscess drained. The trip over to County might kill him."

"Well, they can drain the abscess over there. And if the kid has to die somewhere, let's see that it is not at Southeast Medical Center. Have him out first thing in the morning."

Before Moe could reply, Groton slammed down the phone.

Moe arrived at Juan Gonzales's room early the next morning. The ward clerk was waiting for him with transfer papers. "Mr. Gonzales's insurance policy only covered one week in the recovery room in addition to the operation," he stated. "Dr. Groton asks that you transfer the patient immediately to County Hospital."

Moe glanced down at his patient. The boy looked up at him with saddened eyes. He apparently understood. The ward clerk handed Moe the transfer papers. Moe tore them neatly in half.

"Tell Dr. Groton," he said, "that the patient is going nowhere. He is scheduled for surgery here today."

The ward clerk hesitated.

"Go. Now!" Moe screamed, and she scurried from the room. "And tell him that Dr. Michener said so!"

The operating-room team came to get Juan Gonzales. The litter arrived for wheeling Gonzales to surgery at the same time the ominous shadow of Dr. Groton filled the door.

Dr. Groton placed his hands on his hips in front of the litter. "I gave very firm orders," he began, "that the patient was to be transferred to County this morning."

His tone was threatening. A dead silence filled the room.

"What is the meaning of this?" Dr. Groton demanded.

Moe swallowed hard. "In my opinion," he began,

ceive your checks on a monthly basis as they are collected. Kindly leave your forwarding address with my secretary.

A. Groton, M.D.

As he walked down the corridors for the last time, Moe saw a young man and his wife coming out of Dr. Groton's office.

"I can't believe it," the young doctor was saying. "One hundred thousand dollars. We're going to make a hundred thou, honey! We're rich!"

Dr. Groton smiled as he accompanied the new doctor toward the wards, past the candy machines.

He hires them and he fires them, Moe thought.

Moe blamed Dr. Groton for Juan Gonzales's death. He also blamed himself. He was out of a job now, and he was sure he would never be able to get another one practicing medicine. The system was lined up against him: City Hospital, the Professor, the committee, Groton; he would never get a reference.

Moe made one final trip to the drug supply room. If his life and his career were over, he might as well make the end as pleasant as possible.

He walked out past the sweating bodies in the waiting room, and into the warm sunshine. The last sound he heard was the voice of Dr. Groton, loud and shrill, saying, "It's a gold mine, son, an absolute gold mine"—and then the soft, soft patter of a pencil dropping to the floor.

When Karen had shown up at his apartment with Harry Norton, Moe realized he must have called her on the phone. But he had not remembered talking to her about his situation. In a way, he had been glad to see Karen, but he had been furious at her for thinking she needed Harry. He had realized he had to have help, but he didn't want Harry's help. He wasn't looking for humiliation on top of everything else.

It had been his pride that had prompted him to agree to signing himself into the mental hospital. Given a little time to himself he could have taken care of things alone. But, caught in an embarrassingly weak position, he had realized he had to make some sort of gesture that would assure Karen and Harry that he knew he wasn't himself.

Looking back on it now, Moe reasoned he had them to blame for that miserable experience. He may have had a few problems because of the drugs and the confused state, but he hadn't belonged in that filthy place with all the crazies.

It was odd that, being a doctor, he had never seen the inside of a state mental hospital until that time. He had made assumptions about what it would be like, that it would be a very human institution. But his assumptions had been totally wrong.

From the point when he had been taken into the admissions office by the attendant, he had been steamrollered so fast he had not known fully what he was doing. And from the moment he had entered the Quonset hut with the barred windows, and the door had slammed shut behind him, he had possessed no rights (not even the right of privacy) and no credibility in the eyes of others. In a place like that, self-respect was the first thing a man had to relinquish.

The next thing a man had to give up was his clothes. Under the watchful eyes of about a hundred other inmates who had crowded around to inspect the new member, Moe had been escorted to the shower room by the gum-chewing male attendant who had taken over after Moe had signed the papers. When he had given up his clothes, and they had been put into a brown paper bag and labeled, he had been told to shower, being careful to scrub all private parts.

When he had dried himself, he had been escorted to the middle of the room where three male attendants had inspected his body, in full view of all the other inmates. His mouth, his armpits, his pubic region, and his asshole—all had been inspected for foreign objects, live or otherwise. Just for good measure, while he was still bending over (with at least two hundred eyes gazing up his ass), he had been sprayed.

That first night, he hadn't been permitted to sleep with the other inmates, which would have been fine with Moe, except that his solitary-confinement cell had contained nothing but a bare mattress. He had been permitted neither a sheet nor clothes, and there had been a little peephole in his door where eyes constantly peered in. Sometimes they had been blue, sometimes gray, sometimes green, sometimes brown. He had had the impression that the patients had all been lined up outside his door throughout the night, surveying their new companion from head to toe.

After the first night, he had slept in the dormitory with most of the others, those who hadn't been violent, at least not generally. The beds had been set in five long rows, about eighteen inches apart, side to side, and about two feet apart, toe to head. Showers had been permitted twice a week, but somehow the big room had smelled continuously.

Neither patients nor attendants had believed him when he had said he was a doctor. They had all simply looked at him with eyes that said, Sure, and I'll bet you were Napoleon's doctor, too.

Although he had signed himself in for only a two-week period, he had been there fully five days before he saw a doctor or a psychiatrist. And, once they had him, they hadn't wanted to let him go. He had had to argue fiercely with the psychiatrist to get out after three weeks.

But Moe had to admit that the period of incarceration had done one thing for him. It had convinced him to fight like hell to keep from ever having to wind up in a place like that again. Even if he were to spend his life digging ditches or waiting tables, he would be determined to survive with his life in his own control. Spending his days staring out through the cross-barred windows, he had come to realize that feelings such as self-pity and hate and caring were simply indulgences. What was truly important was survival.

Once he had been let out, he had had to start over again with his life, planning for a new career. He had had to go back to school to study law, and he had been years behind his peers when he had finally set out into the world.

He and Karen had been married the summer before his second year in law school. He had been lucky to have her with him, patiently putting up with his schooling, working to support the two of them—paying the rent, the tuition, the food.

But now Karen had turned against him, Moe felt. He regretted it, but he would have to leave her.

By the time he had reached the parking lot of Valley View Hospital, he had decided that that was the first thing he had to do—go home, pack a bag, and move into a hotel. There was, it seemed, a conspiracy at work against him. Even his own wife was attempting to shelter Harry Norton. That meant there was definitely something they had to hide—Karen,

Norton, Gregorio, Buxbaum, the whole damned hospital.

Well, if that was the way they wanted to play the game, that's the way he would play it. While they were having their little Mortality and Morbidity Conference, he would file suit in Los Angeles Superior Court.

But first he wanted to get the hell out of the San Fernando Valley, away from Dr. Karen Marshall. His wife. Big joke. She was like all the rest of them.

Valentina was at home, preparing dinner. He could tell from the way she peered through the hall into the living room, holding a butcher knife in her hand, that she suspected he might be a prowler. When she saw it was Moe, she looked relieved but puzzled. He announced, "I'm just here to pick up a few things," and she nodded and returned to the kitchen.

As he packed, Moe began to feel sorry for himself. Karen and Harry had probably been carrying on behind his back for years, making a fool of him. Well, this was it; he wouldn't be a fool anymore. He threw things into the suitcase blindly, more out of anger and resentment than need. It was out of anger that he took the bathrobe that was his but that Karen always wore; it was out of resentment that he left behind the shirts and ties that Karen had bought him. If he had been thinking clearly, he would have remembered to pack underwear.

When he had crammed as much as he could get into the two-suiter, he practically flew down the stairs. He paused briefly in the hall to shout in to Valentina, "You can tell Mrs. Michener—no, tell Dr. Marshall—I won't be home for dinner."

And he left.

He had already decided not to check into one of the hotels in the Valley but to go to the Ambassador in Los Angeles, where he would be near the court-house. But that would have to be later. First he would have to stop off at his office to pick up the forms and fill them out. Usually he would have a messenger take the forms down to the court to file them. But in this case he wanted the joy of doing that himself.

As he breezed into his office, he was feeling a kind of euphoria. Maggie, his secretary, was transcribing from a Dictaphone. As he passed her, he called out curtly, "Get me some forms. I'm going to file the Wexler case."

Maggie was used to Moe's moods; one moment he would be up and the next moment down. She had been through a rough menopause, and so she had developed a sort of stoicism that enabled her to take her boss's extremes with a level head.

Depending upon his mood, Moe found his secretary either comforting or annoying. At the moment he found her leisurely pace annoying. As she ambled into his office, he anxiously grabbed the forms out of her hand and sat down at his desk.

This moment was going to give him great pleasure. He smiled with an inward joy. He would sue Harry Norton and the Valley View Hospital for a nice round one million dollars. His smile broadened into a self-satisfied grin as he pictured what it would be like at the courthouse. There were usually a number of re-porters hanging around the place, just to keep an eye on who was suing whom, and for what. He would find a way to strike up a conversation with a couple of them so he could make the Wexler case sound like a really big one. Unless somebody was bombing some-body else in the Middle East, maybe it would get front-page attention.

15 HARRY NORTON

Harry Norton decided his fellow doctors could be very irritating people. He was so nervous about this damned Mortality and Morbidity Conference (commonly called an "M and M") that he was having stomach cramps. But his associates were standing around laughing and talking about the usual bullshit as if a doctor's career were at stake every day of the week. Buxbaum, with his patent-leather Gucci shoes looking particularly shiny, and wearing an unusually loud sports jacket, was boasting in graphic detail of his exploits with a blonde he had picked up last night at Pip's. And O'Hara was still on the same soapbox he had been on ever since the subject of the doctors' strike had come up.

Harry was a little puzzled by the appearance of Sims at the meeting. Of course, it could be that the Whipple operation was simply in the line of Sims's current research, but Harry was well aware that Sims was Buxbaum's flunky. He would parrot anything Buxbaum wanted, and he would give it the impeccable voice of authority because it came from "Research." But Harry did not have the great awesome respect for research that many of his associates had. Research was cold and clinical and scientific—devoid of the human complications of practicing medicine.

Joe Gregorio and Karen Marshall seemed to be the

only ones who were approaching the meeting with any real seriousness. Gregorio had continued to be sympathetic toward Harry, but the most comfort he could offer was: "Still inconclusive. We have to wait for results of further tests."

Harry had been concerned about how he would talk to Karen, or even if he would be able to. But she had remained friendly, though rather nervous and possibly upset. He had taken it as a good sign that— for the meeting—she had chosen to sit beside him.

Her husband, much to Harry's relief, was not to be permitted in the meeting. But Moe's absence, Harry knew, would not ensure him an easy time of it. These M and M conferences could be hell. Harry had never been on the hot seat before, though he had seen other doctors undergo the fire of their peers. And he had never seen a single one of them get off light.

Harry looked nervously at his watch. The meeting was already ten minutes behind schedule. Gradually, the other doctors were beginning to take their places around the big conference table.

Characteristic of Valley View Hospital, the conference room had been designed to avoid the classroom or lecture-hall atmosphere of such rooms at other hospitals. The approach at Valley View was that of a plush corporation board room, with its thick velvety carpet, its big polished conference table surrounded by comfortable upholstered chairs, and its additional folding chairs (also upholstered) for larger meetings. The two longer walls were decorated with inoffensive modern paintings. The walls at each end were wood-paneled. At the chairman's end of the table, the panels could be opened to reveal a screen for showing slides, a closed-circuit television set for viewing surgery, and a blackboard for lecture use. The other end panels concealed a bar, refrigerator, sink, coffee maker, and all the implements necessary for refreshment. It was, in short, the perfect place for conducting the business of medicine.

Buxbaum made a flashy if not impressive chairman. When he took his seat, it was the sign for the meeting to begin. O'Hara was the last one left standing, leaning over Kramer's shoulder, continuing his proselytizing for the strike; but, as soon as he saw Buxbaum move toward the head of the table, he darted clumsily for his seat.

"Gentlemen"—Buxbaum adopted his most stentorian tones—"and ladies, the meeting is in order." His confident gaze made an acknowledging round of the faces at the table. "You are probably all aware that we have a very serious matter to discuss at today's meeting. Mr. Herman Wexler, a patient of Dr. Norton's, died on Saturday, after surviving a Whipple operation three weeks ago."

Harry self-consciously looked at the faces across the table. O'Hara and Minton glanced nervously in his direction; Sims was reading his agenda; Kramer kept his attentive gaze on the chairman. Harry looked down at his agenda. There it was in black and white:

Herman Wexler, Hosp. No. B-304589: 65-year-old white male, operated 10/23/75. Procedure. Whipple. Complication: Deceased. Diagnosis: Chronic pancreatitis, rule out carcinoma.

Buxbaum continued, "You will find the particulars of the case on the agenda that Miss Cranston has set before you. Dr. Norton, if you are ready to present the case. . . ."

Harry had the feeling he had just taken the first big dip on the roller coaster; his heart was in his throat. He tried to clear it, while fingering the paper shakily.

"The patient was a sixty-five-year-old white male, who apparently had a long history of alcoholism, though he did not offer this information during examination. When I saw him in my office, he complained of a twenty-pound weight loss over the past three months, with pains in his abdomen which radiated to the back."

O'Hara rattled his paper. "Was there any history of jaundice? Any suggestion of obstruction to the biliary tract?"

The interruption added to Harry's nervousness. But Buxbaum rescued him from having to answer the question. "No interruptions, please. There will be time for questions later."

Harry cleared his throat again and tried to continue by detailing the results of the physical examination—emphasizing that the patient's heart was strong and that the only abnormal finding was the presence of the mass in the upper abdomen. He explained all of the various tests that had been performed before he had decided to operate, and, as he spoke, he surveyed the faces around him, looking to gauge how they would judge him. It might have been his imagination, but it appeared that each face revealed negative signs.

It was with some relief that he turned the meeting over to Minton to show the x-rays. Minton fumbled a bit in trying to assemble the x-rays on the lighted view boxes at the front of the room. When it was done, he quickly surveyed them to make sure they were in order, and then he began, using a pointer to indicate the areas he was describing.

"As you can see here, the gallbladder was normal. And the upper GI series showed no evidence of varices or hiatal hernia. And no ulcer."

Minton was a very fastidious man. When he gave his presentations at these conferences, however, he came off as prim and self-serving. His quiet, precise manner always seemed to irritate the loud, blustering O'Hara, who had a habit of baiting Minton. Harry could see that O'Hara was already fidgeting in his chair, working up to something.

Minton continued. "The esophagus and stomach were clean. There was a suggestion of a widened duodenal loop, however, as it swung around the head of the pancreas."

O'Hara lunged forward with a bellow. "A suggestion, Dr. Minton? Can you be more specific?"

Minton was not put off by the question from O'Hara; it was expected. If anything, he became more prim and precise. "No. That's all I can say. I do not like to overread films or intrude a diagnosis into them. I can only report what I see."

Before proceeding, he glanced at the chairman for assurance. Buxbaum nodded and asked, "Were there any other pertinent x-rays?"

Minton proceeded to describe the arteriogram. "Again, gentlemen, you can see the vessels for yourselves. Smooth and clean up until the head of the pancreas. And then, a little ratty-looking, and they seem to be pushed aside by something. It was certainly suggestive to me of a mass lesion in the head of the—"

O'Hara burst in again, cutting Minton off. "Seem? Suggestive? Goddamn it, Minton, this is an expensive and a dangerous test you're talking about! Can't you be any more specific?"

This time O'Hara had managed to rankle Minton. His face became flushed, and his voice rose in pitch. "I'm sorry. I can only interpret what the study shows.

Some cases are more obvious. I do not make the patients' blood vessels. I only inject dye into them and take pictures. I can't say any more."

Decisively, Minton set down his pointer and returned to his chair. But O'Hara wasn't through. "You can't say any more? You're damned sure going to have to say more before this is all over with! It looks like this fucking case is going to court, and it's going to put the whole hospital—all of us here—on the spot. The insurance companies are already breathing down our necks. And all your 'seems' and 'suggestions' sure aren't helping matters!"

Chairman Buxbaum interceded as peacemaker. "Dr. O'Hara, I understand your concern. We're all concerned about the same thing. However, I don't think it's the time to discuss the matter. If we can proceed with the case?"

O'Hara sulked and glowered, but he did not answer.

"Dr. Kramer," said Buxbaum, turning smoothly to the amiable physician, "what were your findings?"

Kramer had a way of smiling blandly to try to hide the fact that everything he said was just a bit cagey. He smiled now, as everyone looked his way, and shrugged ingenuously. "I'm sorry, but I can't be any more helpful than Dr. Minton. My scope went into the stomach easily, and I confirmed that there was no ulceration or other lesion in the esophagus or stomach, but I was unable to get into the duodenum. I mean, the mucosa of the bowel was so—"

O'Hara interrupted. "Then what the hell good are you? Good God, can't anybody at this hospital do his job?"

Kramer smiled, but he did not look at O'Hara; instead, he looked down at the polished table. "It may appear that way sometimes." He paused dramatically and looked up at O'Hara. "But we're all of us human; and medical technology has not yet progressed to the point where we can be infallible."

Harry had been glad to be out of the line of fire. It may have been cowardly to let Minton and Kramer take the brunt of the criticism, but it was criticism Harry agreed with. However, now O'Hara turned on him.

"My God, Norton," he bellowed, "I can't believe you went into an operation as big as this without having any idea of what was wrong with the patient!"

It had been a sneak attack, and Harry was caught speechless.

"I . . . it was . . ." he stammered, "there were symptoms that made a very strong case for my diagnosis."

"Dr. O'Hara," said Buxbaum, coming to the rescue, "we haven't yet heard the pathology report. Perhaps . . . Dr. Gregorio?"

Harry realized it wouldn't be a rescue for long. Gregorio had been as uncertain as the others.

But Gregorio had a way of intimidating his listeners into silence. It may have been his age, it may have been his position as final arbiter, or it may have been as simple as the fact that he knew the power of silence. He did not respond immediately, and thereby he managed to have everyone around the table sitting attentively on the edges of their chairs, with their eyes in his direction.

While he sat silently, his own eyes were fixed somewhere beyond everyone at the table. Finally he spoke. "Before I make any comment about my tests, I want to remind you all that this meeting is somewhat premature. Although I have performed the autopsy, the results of all tests are not yet in, and I am not prepared to file my report."

He gave O'Hara an acknowledging but cold glance and then gazed again into the distance. "Dr. O'Hara may wish to attack me as he has the others here, because the tests I performed during the operation itself were inconclusive. However"—he paused, making O'Hara fidget—"however, I would like to remind Dr. O'Hara that if anyone has good reason to chastise Drs. Minton and Kramer and myself, it is Dr. Norton."

Again, his eyes focused in, but this time they made a survey of everyone at the table. "Yes, the biopsies I took were inconclusive. Dr. Kramer made the comment that we are all fallible human beings here. That is true. Medicine tries to be a perfect science, but it isn't. We are doctors. We ought to acknowledge openly something we all know privately, that there are times when a patient comes looking for help that we can't be absolutely sure of what is the best—or even the right—solution."

O'Hara had managed to keep silent as long as he could stand it. He spoke, but he kept his tones respectful. "I think that's the point, Dr. Gregorio. Faced with these inconclusive reports, did Dr. Norton make the right decision for this patient? Wouldn't it have been wiser, under the circumstances, to close and not to perform the Whipple?"

There it was. After all this time, the committee had come around to the question that Harry had started with. The committee! This meeting was typical of medicine by committee. Nobody going out on a limb. Nobody taking a chance. Nobody giving a shit about the patient's life. Just as it had been in Sweden.

One of the great advantages of the internship and residency at City Hospital had been its exchange program with Sweden. Each year one of the residents spent twelve months there, in exchange for a Swedish surgeon who did research in the lab with the Professor.

Harry had been selected between his second and third year of residency. He remembered how excited he had been to work under a socialized system of medicine for the first time, where the doctors were employees of the state.

"Totally different show over there," the Professor had told him. "Government runs medicine. The doctors are merely numbers. They get paid the same salary if they see one patient or a hundred. No incentive at all. But the system is coming to the United States in some form, so you might as well get used to it."

Harry Norton's enthusiasm for the one-year project had been high. Realizing that the American doctor had to oblige the Swedes by speaking only Swedish in the hospital wards, emergency rooms, and operating rooms, Harry had plunged into a four-month course at a foreign-language school in central Philadelphia. He had listened to Swedish records. He had read Swedish books.

Harry remembered how wonderful it had all seemed on that first day when he arrived in Sweden. The first line of his Swedish study book had begun, *Alla svenskar tycker om blommor* ("All Swedes like flowers"), and this was no more evident than around the grounds of Malmö General Hospital, his new "home." The place was a veritable flower garden, with quaint red-brick buildings sprinkled among the bushes and trees. The smell of roses, violets, and zinnias permeated every department.

Harry felt, like Ernest Hemingway, that he had finally found "a clean, well-lighted place." The town of Malmö, the streets, the rows of red-brick houses and new gray high-rises—the entire country, in fact— seemed spotlessly clean.

Harry had remembered what his Swedish teacher told him before he left Philadelphia: "Sweden is a totally socialized country. No one is very rich, and no one is very poor. The country shines like polished chromium. The state takes care of everyone, and everyone is happy."

Harry had felt himself to be in the forefront of a revolution—a medical revolution. An entire year working under socialized medicine! On paper, the Swedish system had seemed impressive; on paper, Sweden seemed to be one of the healthiest countries in the world. Under the influence of the Social Democratic party, all citizens were guaranteed free medical care from the cradle to the grave. And Sweden had the highest life expectancy and the highest infant-survival rates in the world. On paper. . . .

But what Harry had seen during his year in Sweden had not been quite so impressive. In fact, it had terrified him.

The biggest single problem he found with the Swedish medical system was that the patients waited . . . waited . . . and waited.

They waited hours and hours in the clinics. They waited years and years for elective surgery. Once they got into the hospital, things worked very smoothly, but until then, the bottlenecks were unbelievable.

Harry Norton saw patients sitting in the clinics when he went for breakfast in the morning. At noon the same people were still there, staring straight ahead. He knew they hadn't talked to their neighbors (or even moved very much) during his absence. They had simply waited.

Hospital life revolved around the concept of the

väntelista, or waiting list. In the Swedish system, impersonal treatment was an understatement!

The patients were initially evaluated at the emergency room *(akut intagning)* by one doctor. After many hours of telephone appointments and sitting in hospital lobbies, a second doctor saw them in the outpatient clinic, where a series of tests and x-rays continued. A third physician performed surgery. The patients had no choice in the selection of this man. A fourth, the anesthesiologist, took care of their postoperative problems. And a fifth took out their stitches in the clinic one week later.

The Swedish patients stoically passed through all this, accepting with little question the diagnoses and treatments proposed by the state. Good Swedes didn't ask too many questions, and certainly not from their government-appointed collection of doctors!

When Harry had arrived in Sweden, the *väntelista* for *gallblåsa* (gallbladder) was fifteen hundred people. In other words, there were fifteen hundred patients, all worked up from the clinics, complete with x-rays, cardiograms, and blood tests, waiting for their gallbladder operations.

On the first day of each week the Sister from each *gallblåsa* ward would call the top six names on the list to have their surgery the next day. With four such wards working, twenty-four Swedes were separated from their *gallblåsa* each day.

In his six weeks on the gallbladder wards, Harry had operated on about one hundred and fifty, probably more than most surgeons in America did in ten years. When he left, the *väntelista* for *gallblåsa* was still fifteen hundred. During his rotation, several hundred more had been discovered to have gallstones and had been shuffled through the conveyor belt. Harry was told that the gallbladder waiting list hadn't been less than one thousand for the past twenty-five years!

The *väntelista* on the other wards was in a similar condition. There were a thousand patients with stomach ulcers awaiting surgery, a thousand tumors of the breast, five hundred colon cases, two hundred and fifty thyroids, and even two hundred hemorrhoids.

Harry had been more than curious about the *väntelista*. The waiting period for elective gallbladder surgery was several years! When he had asked what happened to a patient who had become acutely ill while waiting for his *gallblåsa* to be removed, he had been told that "one attack jumped a patient several hundred spots on the list; two attacks, or a bout with bright yellow jaundice, and the patient went over the top and was done immediately."

And Harry had found out that a "King's Committee," a group of "experts" acting in the name of the king, dictated to the surgeons which type of operation to perform in each specific situation.

There had been two major operations for ulcers of the stomach—a V and P (vagotomy and pyloroplasty), in which the main nerves to the stomach were cut, and a *resektion*, in which up to three fourths of the stomach was removed and the remainder sewed to the small intestine. In the United States, surgeons chose one or the other, depending upon the location of the ulcer, the symptoms, and the age of the patient, on an individual basis. In Sweden, the operation a patient got depended upon one's birthday! The King's Committee had set up a ten-year study to try to determine which was the better operation. Patients with an even birthdate (like May 10, 1930) received a *resektion;* those with an odd birthdate had to receive a V and P.

"It's a scientific study," the *överläkare*, or senior physician, had informed Harry. "Random and double blind. A beautiful piece of work. By choosing the patients at random like this we can follow them for ten or twenty years in the clinics. Then perhaps we'll know which operation is really better for stomach ulcers."

Nils Wenkert had been a man of about sixty who had had the unfortunate luck to be born on May 11. He had lived on a farm just outside Malmö with his wife, his daughter, his son-in-law, four grandchildren, and six dogs. He had been treated for a "channel ulcer" for many years with antacids, Maalox, and a special diet. One night, his ulcer had begun bleeding and hadn't stopped.

When Wenkert had been admitted, he had become the patient of Dr. Dagerman.

Dr. Dagerman was a good Swedish surgeon. Noting the odd-numbered birth date, he had begun the V and P. He kept regular hours, eight thirty to five. When the five-o'clock whistle blew, like all good workers for the state, he was off duty.

This was brought home to Harry dramatically that day. Dagerman opened up Nils Wenkert with a midline incision at 4:30 P.M. He found the bleeding ulcer at 4:45 P.M. He oversewed it with silk sutures at 4:58 P.M. to stop the bleeding.

"The patient will need a V and P," he said at 4:59. "An odd number. Call Dr. Norton."

At 5:01, Harry had scrubbed in on the case. He was coming on duty, and Dagerman was going off.

"You're late," Dagerman muttered, looking at the clock, and was gone. Harry had said nothing, but proceeded to complete the V and P.

Harry had recognized immediately that Nils Wenkert had needed to have a *resektion*—to have the ulcer and two thirds of his stomach removed. Otherwise, the danger of the patient rebleeding would be too great. But Wenkert had been an odd number, and the King's Committee was firm about its study. A V and P was what Harry had to finish.

He had done the best he could for the patient, the best that the King's Committee would permit. But the whole thing had rankled. Something inside him had resented taking over an operation begun by another doctor, and something else had made him want to scrap what Dagerman had done and give the patient what he truly needed. Most important, it had wounded his self-respect, not to follow his own judgment but to have to submit to the cold orders of the king and his committee.

Nils Wenkert had continued to ooze slowly from his ulcer during the next shift. By the next evening, the patient was found in shock. His abdomen was grossly distended and his hemoglobin had dropped to seven.

The eight-o'clock shift: Dagerman was going off duty again, and Gustafsen was coming on. "You're late," Dagerman had said again, as he left for home.

In the operating room, Gustafsen had found what he had suspected—Nils Wenkert's stomach was full of blood from a big artery that was pumping briskly in the middle of the ulcer bed!

Gustafsen had resected the stomach, but the overall stress was too much. Nils Wenkert had died that evening in the intensive care unit.

Neither Dagerman nor Harry had been informed. Dr. Gustafsen had the duty now.

The death was probably a preventable one. If Nils Wenkert had had the *resektion* in the first place, he would have had many more years of life on his farm outside Malmö, enjoying his grandchildren and his dogs.

Harry had thought he would have liked Nils Wenkert. At first, he had felt guilty about the death;

but then he had realized it had been the committee's fault. He had decided then that a committee should never have control over life and death. There was truth in that old joke about a camel being a horse put together by a committee.

And he had decided then that he could not stay in Sweden and submit his own judgment to the whims of a medical committee.

But now here Harry was, back in the United States, submitting himself to just such a medical committee. And strangely, it all had to do with a patient who reminded him very much of Nils Wenkert. Harry had cared very much about his Swedish patient, and he had cared very much about Herman Wexler. But Nils Wenkert had died because a doctor had not been permitted to use his own judgment, while Herman Wexler had died because he had.

Harry Norton was confused and perplexed. He felt lost; there seemed to be no perfect solution. The Swedish system was not the answer. Doctors were human beings. They had to think, to judge for themselves; it was part of their responsibility. Yet where was the line? Doctors were not gods or saints, but merely people. Doctors could make mistakes too. And he, Harry Norton, had made a mistake with Herman Wexler.

Beyond his own involvement in this particular case, there was something Harry didn't like, but he couldn't quite put his finger on it. Somehow, in a group, something happened to the human conscience. Individual responsibility seemed to disappear in the safety of numbers. If the M and M committee voted to request Harry's resignation, there was no way Harry could blame any one member. It would be the group that would decide.

If Harry's fate lay in the hands of any one person, it was with Dr. Gregorio, the unimpeachable scientist, the man who practiced the only branch of medicine that could escape the weaknesses of human judgment. And yet Gregorio seemed to want to defend Harry. He was meeting O'Hara's strident criticism with gentle patience.

"Dr. O'Hara," he said kindly, looking up from beneath his bushy eyebrows, "I can understand your anxiety about absolving the hospital in this situation. However, I urge you—and the others here—not to be too hasty. It is true that the Whipple operation did not help the patient. But—"

O'Hara broke in. "That's the only question we can consider. Given the circumstances, I think it was a grave mistake for Dr. Norton to perform that particular operation."

"But," Gregorio persisted, "while I do not have all the results of my tests, I feel it is safe to say at this point that it was not the Whipple that caused the patient's death."

There was an uncomfortable shifting of bodies around the table, accompanied by a few coughs and grunts.

Buxbaum tried to interrupt politely, but he could not help evincing doubt. "How can you say that, if you do not yet have the results of your tests?"

Gregorio stared down at the table and sighed. "I'm sorry, but I can't answer that at this time."

O'Hara turned red in the face. "Damn it, you're asking us to take your word for a helluva lot, Gregorio."

"I realize that," he answered evenly, "but I must remind you that the autopsy had to be a rush job. Mrs. Wexler wanted to hold the funeral on Monday to conform with the Jewish custom of quick burial.

Consequently there wasn't much time for a thorough investigation. If you notice, each organ was sliced and sent to be frozen, mounted, so that they all could be turned into slides. That is why I asked that this meeting be postponed so that I might give a full report."

O'Hara slammed his hand onto the table. "Goddamn it, I'm fucking tired of you acting like God Almighty around here! We know that Norton made a mistake in performing a Whipple operation, and that's all we need to know. If we don't act now to save face for the hospital, his mistake is going to reflect on the rest of us, and we've got trouble enough with the insurance companies already. I move that we censure or suspend Dr. Norton here and now and cut out all the rest of this shit."

"You can't do that," Minton said softly, in barely more than a whisper.

"Dr. O'Hara," Buxbaum chided gently, "the chair is willing to entertain a motion, but it can only be one motion. You have to decide which you want—censure or suspension."

"I don't care." O'Hara shrugged. "Whichever will get us off the hook."

There it was, Harry realized; at least O'Hara was being honest about his intentions. That wasn't a great consolation, but it was something. It was an admission that the real issue was not whether a doctor had made a mistake; it was whether a doctor's mistake was going to cost other doctors a bit of money.

"Gentlemen"—Gregorio raised his voice for the first time—"I beg you not to be hasty. You may be making a very serious mistake."

"I don't think we're making a mistake by protecting ourselves," O'Hara persisted, "but if it will make Dr. Gregorio happier, I will move that we suspend Dr. Norton temporarily, pending further consideration of the matter at a meeting to be held two weeks from today. Would that be acceptable?"

Dr. Harris, one of the members with whom Norton barely had a speaking acquaintance, seconded the motion. Harry could feel the rage beginning to build inside him. All right, so he had made a mistake, but it was no worse than any of the mistakes that all of them had made at one time or another. The only difference was that they had managed to hide their errors or to hush them up. And their errors had all been that they had not done enough for their patients, not that they had done too much. That was the rule here: when in doubt, don't do enough.

Harry wanted to yell at them, but he knew it would do him little good. After the group had debated no more than ten minutes, Harry could see which way the wind was blowing. It was against him, and whenever it would stray, O'Hara would guide it neatly back.

A few of the surgeons were reluctant to condemn him without the full evidence of an autopsy report, but O'Hara reminded them that the question was not cause of death but whether the Whipple was a mistake. Under the circumstances, would any of them have performed a Whipple? No; it was unanimous.

A few, Karen Marshall and Minton among them, tried to defend him. If Norton's diagnosis had been correct, wouldn't a Whipple have been in order? Of course it would, but his diagnosis had *not* been correct. If he had closed and waited for the results of the tests, wasn't it likely that the patient then would have been unable to survive a second operation? Of course, but . . .

Harry grew tired of the arguments. He had carried them all on his head for days now; he knew both sides of the issue. But he did not actually lose control of his temper until Sims entered the discussion to present statistics. The research man presented percentages of success and failure of the operation in dogs and monkeys, explained what the laws of chance were, and tried to show academically how Norton's decision would have been wrong under any analysis.

"Goddamn it," Harry burst out, "this is not a game, Sims! We're not playing around in a laboratory with dogs and monkeys! This was a real case of surgery, and a real, living human being was at stake."

Harry soon realized he should have kept his mouth shut. His loss of control could be used as an argument against him; if he was so emotional, it might seem obvious to the others that his emotions could cloud his objective clinical judgment.

When O'Hara was certain he had more than a simple majority, he called for a vote. But Gregorio, who had remained silent for some time, interrupted.

"Gentlemen," he said wearily, "I don't think anyone needs to remind you that you are men of science judging a fellow man of science. However, you may not remember that you are also human beings judging a fellow human. This may seem to be a very strange plea coming from me. All of you who know me well know that I do not like to be at the mercy of human error. I left the practice of surgery and took up my present occupation precisely because there was too much room for error in surgical practice. I feel very comfortable with the certainty of science; I am secure when I am able to point to physical proof."

Gregorio was the oldest man in the room, and he had assumed the posture of a father advising his children. There were not many in the room who felt comfortable with that approach, though everyone listened quietly.

"I must remind you," he continued, "that you are

not behaving like scientists in taking this vote. You are making a decision without physical proof. You are opening yourselves up to human error in precisely the same way Dr. Norton did when he decided to perform the Whipple operation. I ask you all to search your own consciences, if you have any, before you take this vote."

The vote was a very lopsided one, nineteen to three in favor of suspending Harry Norton from the hospital for a period of two weeks. It would not have made a great difference, but Harry was not permitted to vote for himself. The only votes he had carried had been Gregorio's, Karen Marshall's, and Minton's. Kramer and Buxbaum had abstained.

As Harry walked out of the room with Gregorio and Karen, the pathologist shrugged and said simply, "I'm sorry." Harry smiled and tried to be cheerful. "Well, I guess I finally get a much needed vacation."

When Harry arrived in the parking lot where he had left his car, he found Ellen Hopkins waiting for him. Again. He wondered if she considered his welfare a part of her office duty, or if possibly she was getting more than just a little bit personally involved with him.

"Hi," she announced brightly. "I've decided to fix you a good home-cooked dinner tonight. That is, if you have no objection to slumming in my apartment in Brentwood."

Harry decided she was getting involved. He also realized he was too.

16 SARAH WEXLER HOWARD

November 17, 1975, Fairfax Area

"They're children." Sarah realized her voice was shrill. "What the hell do you expect them to do? They don't understand what's going on!"

"Don't use profanity." Sarah's mother was stern, but she did not raise her voice. "You are in your father's house, and here you obey tradition."

"They're too young to understand what tradition is." Sarah stalked across the room, her long arms flapping at her side. "Ouch!" She lifted her stockinged foot. "Damn it, I've gotten a splinter. See how smart your tradition is." She sat in a stuffed chair and tried to dig the splinter out with a fingernail.

Since her father's illness, Sarah had noticed a distinct change in her mother. Miriam had always deferred to her husband or to her children; now she had become stern and demanding and even contrary. Sarah was more than perplexed by this turn of events—she was annoyed. Particularly at all this religious nonsense her mother was throwing at them. Her parents had never been *that* religious before. Sure, she and Robert had gone through the motions of learning what it meant to be Jewish, but it was mostly in deference, it was generally assumed, to Herman's and Miriam's parents. But all this crap about sitting shiva. "You could at least let the kids watch television," Sarah launched in again.

"No," Miriam persisted, quietly. "My own children never learned about respect. But maybe my grandchildren will."

"Do you call that respect?" Sarah gestured at Johnny and Heather, who were sitting uncomfortably on the couch, surreptitiously trying to poke and kick each other and hide their giggles. "They're bored. And they're going to drive us all up the walls! If you'd only let them watch television, they'd at least be out of our hair." She paused for a moment, looking around the room. "God," she exclaimed in exasperation, "I don't even know where Danny is!"

She began searching about the darkened room, unable to see in the corners because of the candlelight. "Daniel!" she called. Finally, she found him in the dim hallway, sitting on the cedar chest with his grandmother's purse emptied out around him and with lipstick smeared all over his face. This was the last straw.

Sarah grabbed her younger son and gave him a series of slaps on the bottom. His insulted screams echoed throughout the house. The noise was made all the more grating by Sarah's routine, predictable screams of "You know better than that!" and "You've got to learn that some things aren't to play with!"

She took Danny into the bathroom and scrubbed his face until the skin was as red as the lipstick. When she returned to the living room, she found that Robert had taken Johnny and Heather into the kitchen for milk and cookies. And he lovingly took the insulted Danny from her arms and into the kitchen as well, whispering something in his ear that made him giggle secretively.

Sarah was sure he was saying something vicious about her. But she said nothing; she simply sat in a stuffed chair and sulked.

The whole scene grated on her nerves. This formal mourning struck her somehow as false; it was as if tradition dictated that she had to be told to grieve for her father. She knew he was dead, she felt the loss, and she resented the implication that she could not truly mourn his passing without following the rules prescribed by her parents' religion. That was an authoritarian way of life, and she resented authority.

She was also finding that she resented the way her brother was trying to throw his weight around. There had been an indefinable change in Robert since their father's death, and she didn't like it at all. Especially when it touched her children.

There was something perplexing about death—or about the death of someone as close as a father. It seemed to change the living; the personality of each member of the family seemed to be changing, shifting slightly to compensate for the absence of the personality of the departed. It was as if each of them were grabbing for specific characteristics or roles that her father had played. This was particularly unsettling to Sarah, because she had always considered herself to be more like her father than anyone else, and she considered his characteristics and roles entirely her property.

When Robert returned to the living room, uncharacteristically trying hard to look sober and masculine, Sarah felt the resentment swell up inside. Of course, he had been doing the only reasonable thing, mediating between her and her mother, but it galled her to feel he had bested her, that he could be stronger than she was.

Robert sat down on a wooden barstool as if what he had done had been nothing. He turned casually to their mother and remarked, "I was surprised to see the Feinbergs at the ceremony. It must have been ten years since they moved out of the neighborhood."

Sarah, determined to be as cool as her brother, offered, "Yes, and didn't Marsha look terrible? She's aged an awful lot, but I suppose that's what sitting at home raising six children will do to a woman."

Sarah could see that her mother objected to what she considered vicious gossip, but Miriam permitted her children to continue discussing the various old friends they had seen at the funeral. She sat quietly on her stool, staring at the flame of a candle, lost in her own thoughts. Occasionally Max would ask for an explanation of which guest had been which, but mostly the talk was between brother and sister.

It was ordinary conversation, incongruous with the external show of mourning. The initial tears for Herman Wexler's passing had already been shed; the full loss would not be felt for days or weeks.

Except by Miriam Wexler. None of the younger members of the family knew what was going through her head, but all were aware that she was thinking and feeling much that she was not saying. While Sarah and Robert continued their aimless conversation, Max got up quietly and moved over to sit beside his mother-in-law. Sarah could not hear what her husband said, but he talked in whispers and offered a comforting hand to Miriam.

At this point, Sarah wasn't sure how much of the conversation she wanted to hear. Sitting shiva, my ass! she thought. She was beginning to miss her office, her accounting firm.

Max hugged his mother-in-law comfortably. "I understand, Mrs. Wexler, but I think you're very tired and worn out. Why don't you go upstairs and lie down, and we'll clean up this mess."

Miriam nodded. "Yes, it *has* been a very tiring day." She padded off toward the hall slowly. "I guess my nerves just aren't what they used to be."

17 MOE MICHENER

November 18, 1975, Los Angeles

Awakening in a hotel room gave Moe the feeling he was on vacation in a strange city. It was only with effort that he managed to convince himself that he was actually in Los Angeles and that he had to get up and set off to work. It was odd, the sort of feeling one got from a modern hotel room. It was as if modern hotels were a culture unto themselves, so standardized that one could be in just about any one in the world and have the same familiar surroundings.

He managed to focus his eyes and fix his bearings sufficiently to dial the phone for room service and order coffee and breakfast and a newspaper. Then he stumbled toward the bathroom to perform his morning transformation.

Modern hotel bathrooms were beautifully constructed and extremely efficient; however, this morning, as most mornings, Moe could do without so damned many mirrors. He didn't like to have a full view of himself until he was quite certain he looked like a human being. When he saw himself naked in a full-length mirror, before he had had his shower and shave, he always saw himself as overweight, ugly, and hairy. But, somehow, once he was dressed, clean and shaven, it seemed to him he shaped up into an extremely attractive man, trim and muscular and dynamic.

In this bathroom there were mirrors and lights everywhere. Moe groaned and tried to keep his eyes closed while he stood at the toilet. In a way, it was rather nice to be able to get up and go about the morning alone. In another way, he already missed Karen.

Moe wondered how she had enjoyed spending last night alone in the big house.

But he didn't want to think about Karen right now; he knew he would only become enraged again. And he had to think clearly today so that he could find out exactly what had gone on at that meeting. He already had a plan, and he was pretty sure it would work.

He had just gotten out of the shower when there was a knock at the door. He quickly wrapped a towel around him and opened the door a crack at first, to make sure it was the bellboy with his breakfast. As soon as the tray was inside and set up, and the bellboy was tipped and had gone, Moe made a leap for the newspaper.

There it was, on the front page as he had hoped: FAMILY SUES DOC, HOSPITAL FOR $1 MIL OVER PATIENT'S DEATH. He felt a thrill of triumph run through him. But alongside it was a second headline: DOCTORS' STRIKE SEEMS CERTAIN.

Moe had not really considered how the strike might affect the Wexler case. It had never occurred to him that the two might be linked together in the newspapers. He wasn't sure he liked that idea: it could work for him, or it could work against him; it was something he couldn't control. But, whatever occurred with the strike, the legislature, and the insurance companies, Moe knew his cause was right.

As he ate his breakfast and sipped his coffee, he read over both stories a couple of times. The more he thought about it, the more he thought he could use the threatened strike to his own advantage. The doctors were not being entirely reasonable. And he suspected that the insurance companies also might be fearful of prolonged adverse publicity.

The fears and insecurities that existed on both sides might work out very well with his plans right now. Despite the fact that he had a hard time finding a tie in the suitcase that would match his suit and shirt, Moe felt very good as he left the hotel. It was a beautiful morning, and he felt as if he had the world in his hands.

When Moe arrived in his office, he asked Maggie to get Charlie O'Hara on the phone while he looked through the mail. When she buzzed the intercom to let him know O'Hara was on, Moe replied, "Okay, and while I'm on the phone, I think we have two accident cases pending—Rothman and Hodges. Would you pull those files?"

He switched the phone buttons, and immediately dressed himself in his hail-fellow-well-met voice. "Hello, Charlie, how are things going?"

O'Hara didn't answer the question. Instead, he shrilled through the phone, "You son of a bitch, what are you trying to do? Put every doctor and hospital in the country out of business?"

Moe laughed good-naturedly. "You flatter me. I don't think I'm quite important enough to be able to do that."

"The whole hospital out here is in an uproar after that article in the paper." It was obvious that O'Hara's temper would not be cooled very easily. "I've already had to cancel two operations. The patients wanted 'to think about it.' "

Moe decided he'd better adopt a soothing approach. "Well, I'm sorry if it's caused trouble for you. But if you want to get angry at somebody, maybe you ought to remember the doctor who started all the trouble in the first place." Before O'Hara had too much time to think about that, Moe figured he'd better get the bait on the line. "But that's not why I'm calling you. I'm calling because I've got a proposition for you."

There was a distinct pause before O'Hara replied, and his tone was both cautious and curious. "What kind of a proposition?"

"Often I get accident cases, and I have to refer my clients to doctors for consultation." He paused for a moment to let this register with O'Hara. "In the past, I've usually recommended Harry Norton. But now . . ." He paused, then added smoothly, "Well, you understand."

"What's the proposition?" O'Hara asked bluntly.

Moe struggled with himself to keep from being thrown off by the direct question. "Well . . ." He hesitated. "It would be a big help to me to know what went on at the M and M yesterday, and—"

"Your wife was there, wasn't she?" O'Hara asked confidently, knowing he now had the upper hand.

Moe was glad that O'Hara could not see him blush. "Unfortunately," he began sheepishly, "my wife and I are having a few marital problems right now, and I can't ask her." It galled him to have to place himself in a subservient role, but it was the only way he would be able to get anything out of O'Hara. He tried to tell himself that, beneath it all, he still controlled the situation. He knew enough about O'Hara to be certain that the doctor would discern a way of saving his own skin, even if the entire Valley View Hospital fell down around him.

He was right.

"On the average," O'Hara began cautiously, "how many referrals could I expect a month?"

"It varies," Moe responded eagerly, "but I would guess that there would never be fewer than one a month. It could be as many as five."

"And would you expect me to testify for you in court?"

Moe marveled at O'Hara's lack of subtlety, and tried to keep his grin from showing in his voice. "That would depend entirely on your own conscience. What I'm interested in right now is learning the opinions expressed by each member of the Valley View staff."

"Well," O'Hara offered generously, "I think I could help you out on that." He paused significantly. "You do know, don't you, that Norton has been suspended temporarily?"

This, Moe thought, is going to be easier than I expected. He turned on his tape recorder, so that he would have an accurate record of O'Hara's assessment of the situation. Then he sat back in his chair and listened appreciatively, letting his eyes roam about his office.

While his business quarters were certainly nothing he should be ashamed of, he realized they were not quite as grand and elegant as they ought to be for someone of his importance. Delightedly, it occurred to Moe that he could spend the entire fee he would get from the Wexler-Norton case to hire a decorator to refurbish his office from floor to ceiling. That would be justice. It had always been Harry Norton who had striven for the superficial signs of success.

He tried to envision the windows with nice bright-colored drapes, perhaps an oriental carpet on the floor, with sharp, sleek modern furniture. And, by all means, an enormous plant occupying the corner of the room. Moe didn't know anything about plants, but a decorator could surely come up with the right one.

He remembered that Robert Wexler was a decorator. That would be another bit of justice, to hire Herman Wexler's son for the job.

The more O'Hara told him about the views of the other doctors, the easier Moe believed his job would be. With the scheduled hike in malpractice rates, he knew he had them all by the balls, and all he had to do was to squeeze.

By the time he hung up the receiver, he was in such a state of elation that he let out a loud, shrill war whoop. But he was brought back to reality by the intercom buzzer. Embarrassed, thinking Maggie was going to ask him what was going on in his office, he responded meekly, "Yes?"

"It's your wife," Maggie offered hesitantly, still unsure about whether to call her "Dr. Marshall" or "Mrs. Michener." "She's been waiting here in the office to see you."

Quelling the urge to ask Maggie to tell her to fuck off, Moe answered resignedly, "All right, tell her to come in."

Moe didn't relish the idea of a confrontation with Karen right now. Things were going so well, he wanted to enjoy himself. He didn't want to think about personal problems. He certainly didn't want one of their bitter fights.

Karen had obviously come prepared. She stalked into the office wearing a very masculine pants outfit, complete with striped tie.

"I'm sorry to barge in unannounced like this," she began crisply, "but I thought we ought to get this over with quickly." She sat down and looked him straight in the eye. "What kind of a divorce do you want?"

Moe was taken off guard by the directness, but he kept himself from responding with a slack-jawed, Hunh? Instead, he managed a smug and cultivated, "What kind am I offered?"

"Take your pick," Karen answered, "from whatever's available. You can have anything that's offered in the western hemisphere. It can be long and bloody, or it can be short and sweet. I can get a Mexican quickie if you want, or we can slug it out according to California law. It all depends on you."

"It takes two to tangle," Moe replied, grinning, and then regretted his trite attempt at humor.

"Don't be cute. I'm quite serious." Karen's gaze was unwavering; her lips were tightly clenched. She sat across the desk from Moe, looking like a cold, unfeeling store-window mannequin, her back stiff, her legs crossed defiantly.

Moe was feeling too good to be irritated by her anger. Things had worked out so well with O'Hara that he regretted having lost his temper at the hospital. Certainly his moving into a hotel had been a childish act. Now he would just as soon forget the whole thing—kiss and make up.

"I'm serious too," he pursued gently. "If there's to be a divorce, it's not just my divorce. It's yours too. You'll have to give me some idea of what you want."

"I just want out as peacefully and as quickly as possible." Her voice began to falter, her chin to tremble slightly. She turned her gaze to the floor. "I can't take any more fighting. You can set the terms, as long as we don't have to fight."

Moe wanted her to give in, to plead with him to come back. He wanted an apology, and he wasn't getting it. Karen seemed to be serious—the realization began to gnaw at him. "How much?" he asked coldly.

"What?" Karen asked vaguely.

"What kind of financial settlement do you want?"

Karen shrugged. "It doesn't matter." Her determination was beginning to break. Moe could see her eyes filling up with tears. "I would like to be able to keep the house and the furniture, but if there's going to be a fight about it, you can have that, too."

This was too easy; Moe was getting suspicious. He turned his back to his wife to stare out the window as he asked, "Who's the man?"

"The man?"

He could not turn to face her. "Obviously you're having an affair with someone. Who is it? Harry Norton?"

Moe waited for the answer, trying not to turn around to face Karen. But there was no answer, only silence. He waited as long as he could before his curiosity got the best of him and he turned.

The question had definitely stopped his wife's tears. Her face was crimson with rage, and her eyes were narrowed so that they were almost closed. "You're sick!" she spat out softly but vehemently. "You need help, you really do. For you to say that to me, you have to be paranoid."

"You didn't answer my question."

"I didn't answer it because it doesn't deserve an answer." Karen tried to keep her voice from becoming shrill. "But, if you have to have an answer, it's 'No, there is no one else.' I simply cannot live with you any longer."

That was an answer that Moe's vanity could not take. It was impossible for him to conceive of any woman not wanting to live with him. And for Karen—who had done so much for him—to say that . . . no, there had to be something more to it. But he could not guess what it might be. He asked hesitantly, "You won't reconsider?"

Karen gazed steadily at him. "Only if you will agree to see a psychiatrist."

Moe knew that he could not hold his temper much longer. "Get your divorce, then."

Karen stood up and started toward the door. "Is Reno okay with you? Incompatibility?"

Moe turned to stare out the window. "Whatever you want."

Karen extended her hand to the doorknob, then paused. "Let me know when you want to pick up the rest of your things."

Moe did not respond, so Karen opened the door and left hurriedly.

Damn. She had to get in her licks, didn't she? She knew Moe would be flying high today, and she had to do whatever she could to get back at him for packing and leaving last night. By tomorrow, Moe thought, she would be all sweetness and light; she would never go through with getting a divorce. She just wanted to save her pride, show him she could be just as tough as he could be.

Well, Moe decided, this time she had gone too far. There wouldn't be any turning back now. If she didn't go through with the divorce, then he would. And she could just wait and see if she got the house and furniture.

Moe was lost in his thoughts, and the buzzing of his intercom took him by surprise. When he responded, Maggie's voice said uncertainly, "There's a Mr. Rothweiler on the line." She paused momentarily to read her memo. "He's from Pathfinder Insurance."

18   CHARLIE ROTHWEILER

November 18, 1975, Los Angeles

If he could only learn to fry eggs properly, Charlie Rothweiler would be pretty content with his life. Breakfast was his favorite meal of the day, and, if he had a pleasant breakfast, Charlie knew the rest of the day would be a good one. But often as not, having his coffee and eggs and bacon in a restaurant, Charlie would start his days uncomfortably. If he ate at one of the restaurants where he was known, invariably the waitress or the other customers would be too talkative; if he chose a strange restaurant, he always felt a little out of place.

Charlie had tried fixing his own breakfast a number of times, but that had always turned out to be absolute disaster. He figured it was because he started his day over a hot stove rather than over a nice plate that had been served to him by someone else. It probably stemmed from his childhood, when his beautiful mother had served him delicious breakfasts every morning. Those days had been the happiest of Charlie's life.

Occasionally he had thought of getting married, just so he would have a wife as beautiful as his mother to serve him breakfasts. But he knew that would be a foolish reason for getting himself tied down to a family.

Not that he couldn't afford a family. Charlie was

doing very well for himself. Very well indeed. The insurance business was booming. And the medical-insurance business, which was the branch Charlie was in, was never dull or routine. Despite the fact that there was considerable and questionable attention given to his business in the press these days, he was confident that his income was going to go up and up with no ceiling.

Sure, his company complained to the legislature that the increase in malpractice lawsuits, combined with the increase in settlements, meant that the insurance rates had to go up. But Charlie knew that higher rates inevitably meant a higher possible income for him. When you were dealing on the inside with big sums of money, you could demand and get big sums for yourself.

He realized he had been lucky. He had set out initially to go into corporation law and had gotten into the malpractice-insurance line by accident. It had proved to be a happy accident. At age forty-five, he figured he could retire if he wanted to and spend the rest of his life just fishing and be happy. If he could solve the problem of breakfast.

This morning, he decided to try a new restaurant. He pulled his silver Porsche into the half-empty lot of a place named Jack's. It appeared to be clean and bright and—most important—quiet.

As he entered Jack's, he spotted a stool at the counter a good three seats away from the other patrons, and he was pleased to see that the waitress was a gray-haired matron, a nice motherly type who would leave you alone if you wanted. In the mornings, he had no desire for the kind of flirtatious talk that the young ones always forced on you.

He decided immediately that it was going to be a good day. His impression was confirmed when the matronly waitress smiled, said, "Good morning," handed him a menu, and asked, "Coffee?"

Charlie smiled a closed-mouthed smile, to avoid showing the gold inlay in his teeth, which he believed looked too garish, and nodded affirmatively. "Black," he added, just to make sure they didn't serve it with the cream already in it the way they did in New York.

He didn't even bother to look at the menu. He knew what he wanted: the works—eggs over easy, crisp bacon, hashbrowns, orange juice, and toast. While the waitress delivered his order to the cook, Charlie went to the machine by the door and got a morning paper to read while he drank his coffee.

If the coffee was any indication, it was going to be a terrific day. A quick glance at the day's headlines confirmed it. His heart leaped with anticipation as his eye caught the words: FAMILY SUES DOC, HOSPITAL FOR $1 MIL OVER PATIENT'S DEATH. As he read the article, something inside him told him he would get the case. And he felt sure it would mean a big fee for him. A very big fee.

Charlie Rothweiler had one of the best breakfasts of recent memory. He even ordered a plate of pancakes to top the meal off, and they turned out to be as good as the eggs and bacon.

Charlie didn't particularly like reading about his cases in the newspaper before he was officially informed of them, but today he didn't mind. In fact, he figured it gave him some extra time to think about the case before he was faced with the particulars.

It seemed pretty obvious to Charlie that the story had been given out to the papers by the Wexler lawyer in order to create public sympathy. He had figured this because the article had contained much about the plaintiff, and almost nothing about the doctor.

Dr. Harold Norton. The name sounded vaguely familiar to Charlie Rothweiler, but he couldn't place it immediately. He knew that Valley View Hospital was a new one and that it had a good record with the insurance company; in fact, he didn't think there had ever been a judgment against it, at least not a big one.

By the time Charlie had arrived at the Pathfinder building, he had come to the conclusion that this case might not be as cut and dried as his breakfast had led him to believe. He had forgotten about this threatened doctors' strike, and about the scheduled insurance-rate increases. The board of Pathfinder Insurance would be concerned about keeping any publicity good. Charlie might not be able to push this case as far as he would like.

The company had a damned good lobby with the legislature, but if the public became aroused by the doctors, their lobby might not be quite so effective at determining the state-controlled insurance rates. Under the present circumstances, Charlie might have two jobs rather than one—not only to save Pathfinder some money, but also to save the company some face.

Charlie parked his car and hurried up to his office on the top floor. He would stop there briefly to put Carolyn, his secretary, onto obtaining the Wexler autopsy report and whatever other information was available, and then he would head straight for Ted Harrow's office. Ted, he was sure, would already have decided what course the company would want to follow.

Again Charlie had judged rightly. There was already a message from Harrow on his desk, asking him to report to the president's office. Charlie gave Carolyn her assignments and strode purposefully down the hall to the gleaming corner office.

Ted Harrow had hired a decorator to design his suite, and the result was impressive. It was starkly modern with white lacquered furniture, set off by a beige carpet and beige walls. The only bright colors in the office were in the Picasso lithographs and in the suits Ted Harrow wore. The effect was crisp, efficient, and businesslike—except to outsiders, strangers. To them, the effect was one of intimidation. With outsiders, Ted Harrow always had the upper hand because of the design of his office. With employees of the company, Ted Harrow always had the upper hand because he was Ted Harrow.

"You've seen the morning paper?" Harrow asked as Charlie entered. Today Harrow was wearing a dark blue suit, which gave a sober, formal look to the office.

Charlie nodded. "I saw it at breakfast. I've got my secretary calling for the particulars—"

"I don't want a prolonged case in the courts right now," Harrow cut in. "I don't care what the particulars are, the less news coverage, the better for the company. I want you to settle the claim and settle it fast. Out of court, and settle it high. When those damned doctors go on strike, we can point to this case and say, 'See what your malpractice is costing us.' "

Something bothered Charlie as he walked back to his office. He had guessed that Harrow would be concerned about the bad press, but not this worried. It was the first time he had seen Harrow make a decision that was not completely rational. Charlie didn't like it. Sure, Charlie was confident that he could get the case over and done with before the papers could drain it for every ounce of human interest. But settling it fast didn't have to mean settling high.

After all, Charlie Rothweiler was damned good at his work, and he did have some sense of what was right or wrong in a case. He had always shown good judgment; there was no reason he should stop now. There was also no reason for Ted Harrow to panic, or for him to pressure Charlie. The malpractice insurers had the doctors over a barrel, just as the doctors had their patients trapped. The system worked just fine, and it would keep on working that way.

Charlie felt even more unsettled when Carolyn gave him the results of her morning's work. "There is no autopsy report as yet; there won't be one for about two weeks. Some tests they're still waiting for. However, the hospital has temporarily suspended the doctor involved, pending the outcome."

Damn, Charlie thought to himself, this was going to be a good day. I was so sure.

His own judgment told him to sit tight and wait for the autopsy report, but Charlie had been given his orders by Ted Harrow, and he had to make a gesture toward obeying them. He reached resignedly for the intercom button. "Carolyn," he said reluctantly, "what was the name of that doctor? Norton? Get him on the phone for me." He paused briefly. "And find out the number of a lawyer named Michener. I'd like to speak to him, too."

19 HARRY NORTON

November 18, 1975, Brentwood

Harry Norton awoke in strange surroundings. It took him a few half-wakened moments to figure out where he was, and why. He was in Ellen Hopkins's apartment; she had invited him for dinner. And he was in Ellen's comfortable double bed, where the two of them had finished up after the meal. But where was Ellen? Harry felt around on the other side of the bed.

When he recognized distinct kitchen sounds, he realized she was preparing breakfast. Harry sat up in bed, looked around the clean, cheerfully decorated room, and tried to remember last night, tried to distinguish between what had really happened and what might have been a dream.

Yes, he was sure that the seemingly unbelievable part had been *real*. Ellen Hopkins was even better in the bedroom than she was in the office, and that had to be the best there was. Everything about Ellen Hopkins felt absolutely right, comfortable and exciting at the same time. Did that mean he was in love? Harry wasn't sure he knew what love was exactly, but he did know he had never felt quite this way before, not even with Marianne in Sweden.

Before this, with women, Harry had always felt he was either giving or taking. With Ellen, he felt as if he was giving *and* taking, both at the same time. And that was a fantastic way to feel. There was a natural equality between them; neither one was a winner or a loser. Each did what was done because it was right; neither had to demand and neither found it necessary to submit. They were two people who found it completely easy and natural to act as one.

Harry decided that was what a man and a woman were all about. This male superiority and women's liberation shit were for people who didn't know who or what they were. A man was never better than a woman, as long as it was the right woman. And a woman could never truly be liberated, because it was impossible for human beings to be free from themselves.

Ellen Hopkins had done something for Harry that no other human being—man or woman—had ever done: she had given totally of herself, without asking or demanding anything in return. And Harry had given everything he could, and he ached inside to be able to give more. He ached because he didn't know what he could give. He had so little to offer, especially right now.

That ache, he decided, was what people called love.

It might relieve that ache to go into the kitchen and tell Ellen that she was beautiful. Harry got out of bed and slipped on the shirt that he had crumpled and discarded in a chair. He padded barefoot and bare-assed into the apartment kitchenette. Ellen's back was to him. She was standing at the stove in a brightly colored quilted robe, her hair long and loose over her shoulders. She *was* beautiful.

Harry slipped up behind her, put his arms about her waist, and kissed her neck gently. "Good morning," he murmured.

Ellen turned from the stove, joined the embrace,

and kissed him just as softly on the lips. "I hope you like your eggs scrambled."

He grinned sheepishly. "Baby, you can scramble my eggs for me any time." His tongue reached for her open mouth. Their long embrace echoed and confirmed what they had both known last night.

Of course, the eggs turned out to be a little over-done, but neither of them really cared. Their thoughts were not on food. Harry knew he had a lot he would have to do that day, but he wanted to forget about work and just concentrate on Ellen, run off to Mexico with her or just spend the day in a little cabin by the shore.

When they had finished their breakfast, Ellen got up to remove the plates. But Harry took her arm gently and pulled her onto his lap. As he nuzzled her ear, he whispered, "Hey, baby, how'd you like me to take you away from all this?"

Ellen smiled. "You know you don't mean that."

"Yeah, I guess I don't." He grinned. "But I *would* like to spend the day in bed."

"Maybe tomorrow," she said and kissed him on the nose. "Today we've got something very important to take care of. We've got to see Dick Darwin."

Harry stared at her in puzzlement. In reply, she got up from his lap, went to the dry sink, and opened a drawer. She took out a neatly folded newspaper and set it down in front of him. Immediately, his eye caught the headline: FAMILY SUES DOC, HOSPITAL FOR $1 MIL OVER PATIENT'S DEATH.

There, in the story, was his name in black and white. And Moe was asking for a nice round one million dollars. He had no idea of how he should have reacted, but he certainly did not expect to laugh. However, that is what he did—he laughed nervously and uncomfortably.

And all he could say was, "Well, there ain't no flies on Moe Michener."

But Ellen had everything efficiently in hand. "I'll call Dick before we leave and see what time he can see us. Then we'll go into the office to cancel your appointments for the day."

Harry had to adjust his thinking to consider work. He added pensively, "We'll also have to cancel my surgery for the next two weeks—postpone what we can, and transfer all the emergency surgery to another doctor." He thought for a moment. "Buxbaum should be able to handle most of it—if he'll do it."

Harry had heard a great deal about Dick Darwin, but he still had no idea of what to expect. Darwin's offices were about the size of a tennis court and occupied the entire floor of one of the tallest buildings in Beverly Hills, so that he had a breathtaking view of the city and the mountains. In contrast to the modern efficiency of the building, his offices had been decorated in expensive antiques and old paintings.

Ellen explained to him later that the guiding spirit behind the furnishing of the offices—and the guiding spirit behind Dick Darwin himself—was Dick's secretary, Madge. In Darwin's office, appearances turned out never to be what they seemed. Madge, who greeted them in the outer office to usher them into Dick's presence, apparently hid a brilliant mind behind two of the biggest boobs Harry had ever seen on a living, breathing woman. When she spoke, which was rarely, she was gracious and charming; but Dick Darwin never conferred with anyone without Madge being present. At these conferences, Madge would sit quietly in a corner, taking notes.

This permitted Darwin to appear capricious and even flighty. But this, too, was merely one of the illusions that Darwin created. The soft languor of his manners was ingratiating to his guests. He could catch them off guard; he could gain their confidence.

He wore an elegantly tailored, three-piece suit, with a great many gold bracelets and rings. His hair was dark, long, and soft, and his speech was cultivated to the point of affectation.

But his dark eyes were shrewd; he never missed anything that was said or anything that happened in his presence, even the slightest gesture. He noticed everything, and Madge took everything down on her notepad.

Dick Darwin was trying single-handedly to maintain the grandeur and the illusion that had been Hollywood. And he was doing a pretty good job of it. He was still young and relatively new on the scene, yet legends had already grown up around him. His parties at his beach house were famous, and literally hundreds of beautiful girls had achieved instant notice or notoriety simply by being associated with him briefly.

Every Friday night he held court in his office, and anyone and everyone was invited. People came by with business propositions—rock stars seeking sponsorship, producers needing money, would-be writers wanting work, and beautiful girls looking for fame or a bit part in the movies. Darwin invested in some of them; he seemed to have a knack for recognizing which ones had something worthwhile and which were hustlers, con artists, or untalented dreamers. His investments always seemed to pay off.

His hobby was collecting people, and, despite outward appearances, he cared about them deeply. When he recognized potential talent but could not help, he would try to make the introductions that would be of benefit.

This reputation created the biggest illusion of all—
that Dick Darwin's life was that of a playboy. In truth,
he was a hard worker and one of the best lawyers in
town, with one of the most successful records in court.
Together, he and Madge were an unbeatable team, and
those who really got to know him well realized that
Dick Darwin was deeply and passionately in love with
his beautiful secretary. But that was a little-known fact
that no one would betray, so the illusion persisted
that Darwin would not take any woman seriously
enough for a lasting relationship.

When Harry entered Dick Darwin's inner office for
the first time, he was stunned by the opulence. Darwin
was sitting at the far end of the enormous room behind
a French eighteenth-century desk, inlaid with various
colored woods and trimmed in gold. The side walls
were lined with equally dazzling furniture of the same
period. And the wall behind the desk was all glass,
revealing the panorama of Los Angeles and the hills
and mountains in the distance.

Immediately Darwin rose from his desk, embraced
Ellen, and kissed her on each cheek. "Ellie, how are
you?" He beamed. "And how's the family?"

"Fine," Ellen responded, and then turned to introduce Harry.

Darwin smiled mischievously. "After this morning's
paper, you need no introduction."

Harry returned the smile. "Well, at least my problem doesn't need one. It looks like I'm going to be
dragged into court whether I like it or not, and I
need a lawyer. That's why we're here."

They sat down in the soft elegant chairs, and
Harry explained what had happened with Herman
Wexler, from operation to autopsy. He also explained
that the lawyer who was representing the Wexlers was

an old friend. Dick Darwin remained attentive and thoughtful throughout the recounting.

Finally he glanced at Madge, who nodded imperceptibly at him, and said, "It's a difficult problem, and of course it's even harder to judge before we actually know what the cause of death was, but I would say you have a good case. This is not a case of negligence —or at least it doesn't appear to be. You do admit making an error of judgment, but you made your original decision conscientiously and—as you saw it— wisely." Darwin paused, nodding at his desk. "Yes, I would say you have a pretty good chance. And I would be willing to represent you. But it will be expensive. Costly."

Harry smiled feebly. "It will be even more expensive if I'm never able to practice medicine again."

They continued to talk for a while, with Darwin and Ellen drifting into reminiscences of summer days at the lake and who was doing what now. It was the conversation of those who had grown up through a privileged childhood, never realizing they were privileged, the kind of conversation that made Harry Norton feel uncomfortable and terribly lonely. Life had always been a struggle for his family, and he himself had never known summers at a lake or winters in the Colorado mountains.

Ellen Hopkins and Dick Darwin had kept in touch with their childhood friends, because most of them had moved on into adult positions of responsibility or importance. Harry Norton had no idea of what had happened to any of the kids he had known growing up. Most had continued to struggle the way their parents had. Some were probably in jail.

Harry had to smile at the thought that he might yet run into one of them again, and he tried to envision the conversation passing between them as like the one that Ellen and Darwin were having. It was an incongruous thought.

Madge noticed Harry's smile and joined in with it, commenting, "There's nothing more boring than old-home week, is there?"

Harry shook his head, but he thought to himself, This is the world I've always wanted to be a member of, this is what I've worked toward—being accepted among the wealthy and the socially prominent of Beverly Hills—but that's not what's really important. What's important is my work, and now I may not have that.

As the friendly conversation wound down, and as Ellen and Harry made motions toward leaving, Harry mentally went through his list of present concerns. "Oh, yes," he interjected, "there is one other thing. There was a message on my answering service this morning to call someone from the insurance company. What should I say to him?"

Darwin smiled. "Just give him my name and phone number and tell him to contact me."

20 MIRIAM WEXLER

November 19, 1975, Encino

Driving on the freeway was always a harrowing experience for Miriam. She was much too old and nervous to keep up with the traffic that went whizzing by at unbelievable speeds. She longed to have Hermie back, so he could do the driving. He had always been able to keep up with the younger drivers in their newer cars, even driving the Wexler's ten-year-old Dodge Dart, which—for Miriam—coughed and sputtered in climbing the hills.

From the very moment she had known she would outlive her husband, she had realized that she would be unable to cope with a life alone. There were just too many things in this modern world that were totally beyond an old woman. As far as Miriam could see, her life had ended when Hermie's had. And all this nonsense from Sarah about suing Dr. Norton in her name had to stop. Miriam simply would not go along with it, and she intended to tell Dr. Norton that.

If she could just manage to get through the traffic to his office.

The article in yesterday's paper about the lawsuit had upset Miriam more than anyone could know. She had tried to continue sitting shiva respectfully, but she had been unable to stay still; and she had been totally unable to sleep last night. She had to stop this thing before it went too far. Now she was break-

ing shiva completely by driving a car. But Hermie
would understand; he would not have wanted her
mourning to prevent her from helping Dr. Norton.

Hermie had liked Dr. Norton so much. Hermie
had opened up and talked to the doctor the way he
had always wanted to be able to talk to Robert but
had never been able to. Hermie had been so proud
telling the doctor what he intended to do with his retirement. He had been so excited talking about finally
turning seriously to that box full of odd-sized sheets
of paper, mostly handwritten, that Hermie had worked
over in what few moments he had managed to get to
himself over the years.

Dear, sad Hermie. He had wanted to be a writer
so bad. He had worked so hard at being an educated
man. He had almost had his chance at some form of
recognition. He had written a story about racketeering
on the waterfront, which he had sent to a nationally
known magazine. It came back unread, with a printed
form that said the magazine considered submissions
only from literary agents. Included was a listing of
agents, both in Los Angeles and New York. Herm
began to send out letters. Most agents did not want to
bother with a new, inexperienced author. But one
New York agent did bother with Herm. It was this
agent who had sent the story to that radio program,
"Grand Central Station," and they had liked it and
asked for a rewrite. But Hermie never could get the
special slant the program needed. As week after
week had passed by, Hermie's chance had eventually
passed as well.

While Hermie had been lying in the hospital, he
had asked Miriam to dig out that old story to bring
in so he could show it to Dr. Norton. The pages were
smudged and yellow and torn from the years they
had spent on the closet shelf, but Hermie had been

proud to show it to his doctor. And he had been pleased when the doctor had praised it.

Miriam had suspected that Dr. Norton was just trying to be nice, but he had seemed interested. And later on, he had brought up the subject of the writing himself, asking Hermie to let him see the story after he rewrote it. It had seemed to Miriam that Dr. Norton had truly cared about her Hermie.

Partly for that reason and partly because she had liked the doctor herself, Miriam knew she could not allow her daughter to do this thing.

She had not called the doctor for an appointment; she was not even sure he would see her. Nor was she quite clear on what she would say to him. But if she talked to him, perhaps together they might come up with some way of stopping this vindictiveness. She knew that Dr. Norton was not a criminal; she knew that he had not killed her Hermie. Whatever the results of those tests had shown, she knew that Hermie had had cancer, and cancer always killed sooner or later. And usually it was later, after long slow months of pain and agony.

It was better that he had died quickly.

There were only two cars in the lot by Dr. Norton's office. Miriam's heart skipped a beat as she realized that he was indeed in his office, and he was probably not busy. Of course, she realized, after that article in the paper, who would want to come to see him? She heaved a great sigh of regret. It was all so cold-blooded.

She was frightened as she plodded slowly up the little path to the door. She hesitated before entering, fighting off the temptation to turn right around and drive back home. But she did open the door, and she did enter, and there was no one in the waiting room except that nice Miss Hopkins.

Miss Hopkins was such a sweet, pleasant girl that

Miriam had liked her instantly. Every time she had called, Miss Hopkins had inquired after her health and had given her assurances not to worry about Hermie. And it had been clear to Miriam immediately that, if Dr. Norton would ever slow down enough to think about it, he would recognize that Miss Hopkins would make him an ideal wife. But knowing the way doctors were, Miriam figured he would never slow down, and therefore never realize it.

As soon as she saw Miriam, Ellen Hopkins beamed brightly. "Well, good morning, Mrs. Wexler. How are you feeling?" But Miriam could see that there was doubt and hesitancy beneath the receptionist's cheerful greeting.

"Thank you for asking, Miss Hopkins, but I've been as miserable as I can be since the newspaper story yesterday." Miriam spoke softly and agonizingly. "I'm so sorry for all this trouble; I didn't want any of it to happen. And that's why I'm here. I'd like very much to talk to Dr. Norton to see if we can stop it before it gets any further."

"I'm sure he would like that too." Ellen smiled kindly. "Why don't you sit down for a moment, and I'll see if he can see you now."

Miriam was so anxious that she could not sit down, but wandered aimlessly around the empty waiting room while Ellen Hopkins disappeared behind the door to the inner office. When Miriam was finally confronted by Dr. Norton in his office, her anxiety had reached a point where she could not speak. She opened her mouth to say something, but nothing came out. Instead she burst into tears.

Harry Norton stepped out from behind his desk and hurried across the room to embrace her. His object had been to comfort her, but it seemed only to make things worse.

"Dr. Norton"—she managed to force out the words
—"I didn't want this to happen. And Hermie wouldn't
have wanted it either. It's just that . . . Sarah . . ."

"I understand," he replied softly. "Why don't you
sit down and take your time, and when you're feeling
better we can talk."

Miriam followed his direction and found a place in
the stuffed chair by the side of his desk. Immediately
she felt better. Dr. Norton had such a confident, comforting air, the kind of manner a doctor ought to have.
But—Miriam was confused. He ought not to be comforting *her;* he ought to hate her, to shout at her. Her
mind was incapable of taking everything in and com-
prehending it now; so much had happened so fast.

The words that came out were the words that passed
slowly through her mind. "I just don't know where
all the time has gone." Her brow furrowed in hope-
lessness. "Hermie and I, we had so many plans. But
the time, it just went by without our knowing it, and
now there's no more time."

"Mrs. Wexler"—Dr. Norton seemed uncomfortable
suddenly—"I think you ought to go home and go to
bed; I can prescribe a sedative. When you're not so
disturbed, when you've rested, there'll be plenty of
time—"

"No," Miriam interrupted, "there is no more time.
I've got to explain it to you now. This lawsuit has got
to be stopped. You've got to tell me what to do. Sarah
just won't listen to me anymore. She never would listen to me, all her life. Oh, Dr. Norton, it's all my
fault, and I just don't know what to do. You've got
to tell me. I don't want to hurt you. You're a good
doctor, you did your best; but Hermie had cancer,
and there's nothing anybody can do about that."

Miriam was uncontrollable, and the doctor grew
more and more stern. "Mrs. Wexler, please," he urged,

"I know that you and Mr. Wexler trusted me. I know that you had no intention of starting this lawsuit. But I can't try to change your daughter's mind; she'd just turn around in court and use my efforts against me."

Miriam stared at him through her tears. He was so sensible, so good. He smiled kindly at her and moved near her, perching himself on the corner of his desk so he could take her hand gently.

When he spoke, his voice was soothing. "The best thing you can do for me right now is to take care of yourself. You're not going to do me or yourself any good as long as you're in this condition. I'm going to give you a prescription for a sedative, which you're to take every four hours. I want you to rest and eat and take good care of yourself. And when this case gets to court, my lawyer will call you to the stand, and you can testify for me. That's the best way you can help. Do you understand?"

Miriam nodded and blew her nose in her handkerchief, but she didn't think *he* understood. It was just like Dr. Norton to be thinking of her instead of himself. She watched him as he wrote out the prescription, thinking, I don't deserve this kind of consideration from him.

As Dr. Norton handed her the prescription, he asked, "Can you get home okay by yourself? Would you like Miss Hopkins to go with you to make sure you get there all right?"

"No," Miriam protested, "no, I can get home by myself. Thank you."

Dr. Norton helped her to the door. Wait, she wanted to say, wait, I haven't said everything yet. This all has to stop. "Dr. Norton," she began.

He stopped and looked at her kindly.

But she couldn't find the words. Instead she asked,

"Do you remember when Hermie showed you the picture of himself on the beach?"

Dr. Norton nodded.

"He was such a handsome man, wasn't he? So strong then, and he could have made so much of his life. If only . . ."

21 HARRY NORTON

Human actions ought to be clear and obvious. They certainly shouldn't be mixed and jumbled this way. It made Harry Norton feel bedeviled. It bothered him that he had not known how to respond to Miriam Wexler. She was a sweet, gentle woman who obviously wished him no harm. But, because of circumstances, he had to try to look upon her as "the enemy." He must not treat her with natural human warmth.

He felt the way he remembered feeling as a child, when he had found it necessary to adjust his own inner feelings to the way the world said things ought to be. He felt confused.

He hadn't felt quite this way since he had been a child. He had consistently endeavored to live the way society had told him he ought to live, like a responsible adult. Sensibly, objectively, respecting science and knowledge and fact. And dismissing human sentiment.

This childish confusion had all begun with Herman Wexler, at that moment in surgery when Harry had looked over at the screen, at Wexler's sleeping face. In that instant he had given up his treasured scientific objectivity; he had given in to feelings, and he had opened up a Pandora's box. Now it was too late to stop the emotions that confronted him at every turning. The feelings he had about Miriam Wexler, the feelings about his own parents, the feelings about Ellen.

He supposed he ought to be grateful for all the developments because they had given him Ellen. But the deep fear within him was that he was now less of a surgeon than he had been, that he could no longer coldly cut into the body of another human being and mechanically perform the acts that were necessary to save lives. He had become sensitive to human life, and that was disaster for a doctor.

After Miriam Wexler left his office, Harry sat down quietly at his desk and tried to sort everything out so he could understand.

There was one thing that he was sure of—that he had cared deeply about Herman Wexler because Wexler had reminded him of his own father. And both of them represented what Harry Norton knew he had to avoid in his own life, letting love and responsibility interfere with his goals and ambitions. Herman Wexler's life had been one of frustration and failure, and so had Joseph Norton's. Both had given so totally of what they had that there had been little left for themselves.

Like Herman Wexler, Harry's father had been born of a poor family, and he had had to struggle and work hard to rise up out of the poverty. There were two things that always came immediately to his mind when Harry thought of his father—drink and basketball. The great love in Joseph Norton's life had been basketball, and because he had never been able to make a career as a professional basketball player, Joseph Norton had made a career of drinking.

There had never been any doubt in his father's mind that he had the ability to be a pro but that circumstances had interfered. Harry Norton could divide the moments he had spent with his father into two distinct kinds: when his father was sober, he spent all his time playing basketball with Harry; when he was drunk, he would pour out all the sorrows of his life for Harry to hear.

Harry had heard the stories so many times he could still remember all the little details.

From his earliest years, Joseph Norton had been put to work. His father's sash and door company had never been profitable, so Joseph had been looked upon more as an unpaid employee than as a member of the family. As soon as he would get home from school, he had to join his father in the shop, knocking together the frames and puttying the sash for the next day's deliveries. Often they would have to work far into the night.

In the beginning, Joseph had not resented the burden. In the beginning, his brother Phil had truly been too young to contribute a share of the work. But, as years had passed, Phil had continued to remain too young, spending his time playing with the dog or going out on dates with the neighborhood girls.

When Joseph had begun to steal time from work to play basketball, he had not felt guilty about it. After all, his father was being unfair in demanding of him what was not demanded of his brother.

But then had come the matter of the horse. A part of Joseph's job had been to deliver the doors, sash, and trim with a scrawny, ill-fed horse. The horse had been permitted more of a mind of his own than Joseph had; whether the sash and doors were delivered or not, when the six-o'clock whistle blew, the horse would turn around and head for home, and nothing Joseph could do would keep him working. Back at home, the horse would get fed, and Joseph would get hell.

One day, Joseph had gotten the deliveries finished

early, and on the way home he had stopped off to play
some basketball, leaving the horse tied loosely to a
fence. When the six-o'clock whistle had blown, the
horse had pulled himself free and started home. Without Joseph to restrain him, the horse had taken off
downhill at a gallop, pulling the makeshift wagon
after him. When Joseph had realized what was happening, he had chased after the horse and wagon, but
he had been too late. The horse had stumbled and
fallen, rolling chaotically—still attached to the wagon
—the rest of the way down the hill.

The horse had still been alive when Joseph had put
him into the stable for the night, but he was dead
when Joseph's father had found him the next morning.
Joseph had been beaten within an inch of his own
life and had been told, "From now on, you're the
horse." From that time on, until he had graduated
from high school and had broken away from home,
Joseph had been forced to deliver sash and doors by
carrying them on his own back.

The resentment he had felt at that injustice had
assuaged any guilt that Joseph might have felt about
setting out on his own life. He had been determined
to go to college, and he had been determined to play
basketball. He had been able to get into semipro ball,
being paid twenty-five dollars a game in the minor
leagues. Sometimes he had managed as much as two
and three hundred a week. But most important, he
had been good at it and he had enjoyed it. He had
looked forward to the time when he could move
up and really get onto an important pro team.

But then there had been the accident. Semipro ball
was a rough-and-tumble game; you had to be pretty
tough to take the blows. When Joseph had gotten
the elbow in the eye, he had thought nothing of it,
at least not until the next day, when he had awakened

to see a great black cloud floating in his line of vision. The doctor's verdict had been grim: he had suffered a hemorrhage. At best he would have twenty-percent vision in that eye. If he continued to play ball and suffered another blow, he might lose his eyesight completely.

That had put an end to his basketball career. Joseph had instead gone into teaching, taking a job as a high-school gym teacher, showing other boys what he knew about the sport.

At least that was what he had done when he was sober. His true career had been drinking. When he had been unable to handle the early morning classes, the school janitor had substituted for him while he had slept it off on the cot in the boiler room. Joseph Norton had managed to go on this way for most of his adult life. He had been an alcoholic; he had known it, and Harry Norton had known it.

That was the thing that plagued Harry Norton about Herman Wexler: how was it—if he had seen the other similarities between his father and Wexler—that he had missed the similarity in the heavy drinking? Sure, Wexler had denied his drinking, but Harry should have pressed him to admit it. Knowing the truth, Harry would have considered the possibility that the lump in the pancreas might not be cancer.

There had been other clues for Harry. Herman Wexler had been deeply disappointed in his children, and Joseph Norton had been disappointed in Harry. But Harry tried to tell himself that there was a difference. He had at least tried to please his old man, going along with the basketball as far as he could. It had not been Harry's fault that he did not have the build or the stamina to make himself a pro.

That was the difference: Herman Wexler would have been proud if his son had become a doctor; Joseph Norton could not have been proud of anyone but a professional basketball player. It was not until now that Harry saw that this difference was in fact a similarity, just one more disappointment for each.

But Harry tried to tell himself that neither man would have been disappointed in his son if he had made a success of his own life. And that was why Harry came back to his original belief. He must not make the same mistake; he had to satisfy himself before he could ever hope to satisfy anybody else. Sacrificing his own needs just wouldn't be living.

All of this thinking had gotten him nowhere. He was right back where he had started, with the same problem. What was he going to do with the rest of his life? What *could* he do? Even if he came out of this lawsuit okay, even if Miriam Wexler managed to persuade her daughter to drop it, would he ever dare to operate on another patient again? Would he be able to dismiss the fears that came with human caring?

He had learned a lot these past few days, and he did not think he could unlearn it. He realized now that the whole numbing process of med school had been a process of unlearning certain natural human responses. But the most important thing was—if he should manage to toughen his responses again—would he not have to give up what he had found with Ellen? (He balked at calling it love, though he now knew that was what it was.)

It all might be easier if he could only *do* something. But since he had been suspended from the hospital, he had felt it necessary to suspend his office work as well. And he had simply sat there thinking, hour after hour, going in circles, growing more and more anxious. The problem was, he didn't know what he could do. The circumstances all seemed beyond his control.

That was why he thought about Herman Wexler,

and about his own father. Their lives had been hemmed in by circumstances, increasingly so with the passage of time. Harry feared that, if he gave in only once to circumstances, he would find himself on the same kind of spiraling continuum, releasing more and more of his control over life and events.

Right now, everything was in the hands of Dick Darwin. Harry had finally spoken to the insurance agent, Charlie Rothweiler, and—as instructed—had referred him to Darwin. Of course, the lawyer had reported to Harry on his conversation with Rothweiler. He had told Harry that the insurance company wanted to settle the case out of court.

Harry had rejected that alternative immediately—and that had been before Miriam Wexler had come to him to deny her involvement in the case. Even if Harry had been sure he had been guilty of malpractice, he would not have relished settling without a fight, because that would have been an admission of guilt.

The only thing that Harry was willing to concede at this point was that he had made an emotional decision rather than an objective one.

The insurance agent had been unable to give Darwin any assurance that Harry would be able to get malpractice coverage after the settlement, even at exorbitant rates. Without that assurance, Harry felt he had nothing to lose by fighting. Whatever the outcome—of a settlement or a trial—the financial obligation was the insurance company's. But curiously, to Harry, the financial question was not as important as his ability to continue his career.

Harry was relieved when the telephone interrupted his reverie. Ellen buzzed him to tell him that Dr. Marshall was calling.

He was glad that Ellen had given him that information, because he did not recognize the thin, nervous voice at the other end, saying, "Harry, I need a friend."

The greatest solace to someone in trouble is to think about someone else's problems. Not that Harry was not truly concerned about Karen, but it made him feel good to sit back and listen to her. He did not feel particularly happy about the fact that the Wexler case had brought about the split between Karen and Moe, but Karen assured him, "It would have happened eventually, anyway."

"Besides," Karen announced miserably, "I can't sit home alone another night, brooding about it all."

"Ellen and I are having dinner tonight at Pip's," Harry offered. "How about joining us?"

22 MOE MICHENER

November 19, 1975, Beverly Hills

Moe realized he was drinking a bit more than he should have. But Charlie Rothweiler was late, and Moe had gotten to Pip's early for the appointment, wanting to start out the conference on his best foot. Now his best foot was looking a little blurred, as he stood at the bar sipping one Manhattan after another.

He had chosen Pip's because he had thought it would impress Rothweiler, but the insurance adjuster had never even heard of the place. Moe wondered foggily if Rothweiler were lost. He certainly shouldn't be; Moe had given him explicit directions on how to get there.

The club had been calculatedly planned to fill a wide variety of needs. The bar was functional, and it was situated as a convenient stopping-off place for anyone going from any one room in the place to another. The dining room was small and intimate, appropriate for a cozy romantic meal or quiet business dining. The backgammon room was tastefully elegant, with just enough of the atmosphere of the old-fashioned pool hall to lend an air of excitement. And the disco room? Well, it had been designed small, with mirrored walls, to be vaguely like a seductive vertical bedroom— for vertical orgies.

The disco room had long been an attraction for

Moe, because it was always filled with unattached women looking for men, but Moe had always been attached. He thought joyfully that perhaps tonight, after his conference with Rothweiler, he might just spend some time in the disco room, let himself go. Prove to himself that he didn't need Karen.

Charlie Rothweiler was actually only fifteen minutes late, but it had seemed like an hour. Luckily Moe was still able to appraise the man with some accuracy. As they shook hands, Moe registered several important facts: Rothweiler had terrible taste in clothes, obviously not having known the difference between a conservative gray suit and a shiny synthetic gray, he had a nervous habit of keeping his mouth tightly closed while chewing on the inside of the lower lip, and he was still a "wet head" when the dry look had been in for a good ten years. Moe knew immediately that (a) Rothweiler was a self-made man, (b) that he was insecure outside of his own social milieu, and (c) that it would be relatively easy to manipulate him.

Not wanting to risk another drink at the bar, Moe signaled the headwaiter that he was ready for his table, and they were quickly seated on the central banquette, where they could talk quietly.

Moe decided to allow Rothweiler to lead into the Wexler case, so he could determine just how eager the insurance company would be to settle it. Suavely, Moe talked about the menu, about the club, about the weather, about everything except the matter at hand.

"I hate to bring up unpleasant subjects," Rothweiler said at last, "but this Norton case—"

"Wexler," Moe interrupted. *"Wexler* versus *Norton."*

Rothweiler blushed. "I guess it depends upon your

viewpoint, doesn't it?" He had to shift himself in his seat to get back on the track. "As I expressed to you on the phone, my company does not feel that there is a great justification for the Wexlers' lawsuit, but because of the timing we would like to see the matter settled as quickly and as quietly as possible."

"I don't know about that—the justification," Moe interjected. "Your company probably does not yet have the complete facts. Once those are available to you, you're going to see that we have a clear-cut case of malpractice. If you're suggesting an out-of-court settlement, I'll have to refuse."

Rothweiler stammered, then got his bearings. "I will admit that this is a bit early since there's no autopsy report. But I have had a talk with the pathologist, and his opinion is that the final report will *not* show a clear-cut case of malpractice. Our reason for wanting to settle the case now, with no big news stories, is—"

"I know your reason," Moe snapped. He leaned casually back against the banquette. "But the fact that the doctors plan to strike to protest your company's rate hikes should not interfere with my client's rights. You mustn't forget that the Wexler family has suffered greatly because of Dr. Norton's mistakes. They're looking for justice, and my job is to see that justice is done."

Charlie Rothweiler smiled, trying to appear conciliatory, but—since he smiled with his lips closed—it came off as smug. "I think you're assuming too much about the motives of Pathfinder Insurance." He leaned forward ingratiatingly. "We are willing to be more than fair to your client."

"What about Norton?" Moe asked abruptly, throwing the insurance rep off guard.

"What about him?"

Moe smiled. "Has *he* agreed to settle?"

Rothweiler cleared his throat. "As far as we're concerned, it doesn't matter what he wants to do. Pathfinder Insurance pays the claim, not Dr. Norton."

Moe couldn't restrain his appreciative grin. "In other words, he wants to fight it out."

They both fell silent while the waiter served their dinner, but, as soon as the waiter had left, Moe continued. "Let me hypothesize for a moment. Suppose my client agreed to settle out of court. That would be an admission on the part of your company that Dr. Norton was guilty of malpractice. How lenient does Pathfinder Insurance intend to be with him?"

Charlie Rothweiler was obviously astounded by the question. "I honestly can't say," he blustered. "I suppose that would depend upon the ultimate facts in the case."

Moe decided to let his side of the issue rest for a moment. He didn't want to give his guest indigestion. He would give him three good mouthfuls of beef bourguignon before he resumed his questioning.

But, once his companion's third bite had been fully chewed, Moe had his question ready. "Would Pathfinder be willing to incorporate into a settlement a stipulation that Dr. Harold Norton would not be reinsured by the company?"

Rothweiler stopped his fork midway between plate and mouth, and his face turned pale. "I've never . . ." he stammered. "I wouldn't have the authority to say yes or no to that, but I'm sure something could be worked out."

Now that he had the insurance man completely baffled, Moe asked, "You're aware that my clients are seeking one million dollars in damages?" He smiled. "What kind of offer is Pathfinder prepared to make?"

Rothweiler blinked and bit his lip nervously. "I am authorized to offer up to one hundred thousand dollars."

"I don't think that amount would be satisfactory to my clients," Moe answered smoothly and offhandedly, "but naturally I will have to convey it to them." He relaxed against the banquette and smiled. "And, of course, I hope you will express the concern about Norton's reinsurance to your company."

As Rothweiler nodded, Moe glanced up to see a group of people entering the dining room. At first, he merely registered that the faces were familiar; but— as recognition hit him—he turned ashen. He did not know the other woman. But he saw his wife, and the man with her was Harry Norton.

All of Moe's deepest fears were confirmed in an instant. Karen *was* having an affair with Harry, and that was the reason she wanted the divorce. Harry, for all his pretense, had never been a true friend. Taking on the Wexler case had been the smartest thing he, Moe, had ever done, because now the truth had been forced into the open. At the moment, he was caught between his outrage and his confusion, not sure exactly how to deal with the embarrassing situation so that he might come out on top.

If they hadn't seen him, he might have had time to think about what he would do or say. But, as the headwaiter led them to their table only a short distance away, Karen caught sigh of him. She touched Harry on the arm and nodded in Moe's direction. Karen had had a pained expression on her face when she saw Moe, whereas Harry turned red and became agitated, stopping to stare.

It was a ludicrous tableau: the headwaiter held a chair for the other woman in the party, but she did not sit. She stared at Harry with a frightened expression. Harry, in turn, was staring at Karen, and Karen was staring at Moe. After a long frozen moment, Moe decided it was up to him to break the tension.

Since he was pinned behind the table on the banquette, he could not rise, but he gave a mock bow and announced loudly to his guest, "Charlie, here are some people I think you should meet," so that Rothweiler rose expectantly to his feet.

The insurance man's gesture was an expansive and a gracious one, and since he was a stranger to Harry and Karen, the two doctors could not be so rude as to ignore him. With obvious trepidation, they moved toward Moe's table.

Moe timed his introduction perfectly. "Charlie," he said, with a somewhat snide ring to his voice, "I'd like you to meet Dr. Karen Marshall and Dr. Harry Norton." Because he was extending his hand to Karen, Rothweiler did not hear Harry's name. But, as the two men clasped hands, Moe announced, "This is Charlie Rothweiler—of Pathfinder Insurance."

Harry dropped the hand as if he had been burned. Rothweiler appeared perplexed, and he muttered, "I'm sorry, I didn't catch the name."

"Harry Norton," Moe prompted, grinning. "Dr. Harry Norton."

Harry's voice was not entirely polite as he acknowledged the introduction. "I believe we've spoken on the telephone."

Rothweiler was obviously the most discomfited by the situation. He stammered, "Yes . . . we have," and then added foolishly, "It's nice meeting you."

Anxiously, Harry and Karen excused themselves and hurried to their table. Rothweiler sat down again and glared painfully at Moe, as if to say, You could have given me some warning. But the words he uttered were, "Well, it's getting late; I'm going to have to be getting on home."

Faced with the prospect of spending the rest of the evening alone, Moe almost regretted what he had done, but he did not press Rothweiler to stay. He signed the dinner check and accompanied his guest to the door, summarizing in a businesslike manner the status of their talk before saying good night.

All things considered, it had been a profitable evening so far, and there was no reason for him to stop now. The disco would just now be getting lively, and Moe felt like letting it all hang out. A few drinks, maybe some dancing, and—who knows?—perhaps he would find the right girl to take back to his hotel room.

It had been some time since Moe Michener had played the bachelor, so he chose to sit and observe the action for a couple of drinks before making a move. Indeed, the place was jumping, and there was plenty to observe. A new dance known as the "Hustle" was beginning to catch on, and its movements revealed much about what lay beneath the flimsy garments the girls were wearing.

The ringside couch that Moe sat on, sipping his drink, was so low that he found it necessary, because of his long legs, to sit in a semireclining position, looking upward at the bodies writhing on the dance floor. There was a good variety of girls to choose from, but Moe would have to follow each of them for a while to see which were definitely attached and which were available.

The first one to catch his eye was a tall redhead with green eyes and a creamy complexion. She was wearing a clinging, two-piece white lounging outfit, which showed she had very prominent nipples. He

could tell by her eyes and her expressions as she
danced that she had intelligence and spirit, which
were qualities that really turned Moe on. But after
following her with his eyes for a while, he determined
that she was a one-man woman, and she already
had her man.

His eyes next picked out a brunette, but, before
he could analyze her various qualities, his thoughts
were interrupted by someone sitting down on the
sofa beside him and placing a firm hand on his knee.

"You're exactly what I'm looking for," she said
sexily.

Moe turned to look at a girl who, he suspected,
was not yet old enough to buy her own drinks. She had
mousy brown hair, teeth that had been well worked
over by an orthodontist, and a nose that had been
botched by a plastic surgeon. She was also a little
too strong in the hips for Moe's taste.

"Oh?" he asked coolly. "What's that?"

"Tall, dark, and handsome," she said, fluttering
her heavy fake eyelashes.

"Sorry," he said, as he turned away to look for the
brunette on the dance floor. "You're not my type."

She continued to babble meaninglessly into his ear,
but he paid no attention, concentrating on choosing what he wanted. Eventually she went away.

Finally, after much searching, Moe located the
brunette in the crowd that was milling about on the
edge of the dance floor. The problem was, she now had
a man on either side of her. He decided she wasn't
worth fighting for; maybe she would turn up free
later on.

He continued to consider one possibility and then
another until he settled on a tall but buxom blonde
who was obviously getting bored with her short hairy

companion. When he saw her leave him and head for the disco bar, he decided to follow.

"Buy you a drink?" he asked, as he stepped up beside her.

She glanced at him coyly, hoping to disguise the fact that she was assessing him from head to toe. "Sure," she said. "I'd like a Bugs Bunny."

"Hunh?" Moe stared at her stupidly.

"The bartender will know," she said, grinning.

While waiting for the drinks, the blonde, whose name was Sherry, explained that a Bugs Bunny was like a Bloody Mary, but with carrot juice. Moe couldn't decide if she was dumb or only trying to appear dumb. The fact that he couldn't tell was enough to interest him. Besides, she was decidedly beautiful. He figured she was trying to get into pictures, because she had adopted the curls of Shirley Temple, but the pout of Marilyn Monroe, and the fashion sense of Jayne Mansfield. Hers was one of several standard formulas for pretty girls who came to Hollywood from small towns, and it was one that got them into more beds than movies.

As they sat sipping their drinks and chatting superficially, Moe came to the conclusion that she would be good for a one-night lay, but she could never be interesting over a long period as Karen was. He cursed himself for comparing her to Karen, for wanting Karen even now. His mind was growing fuzzy with the drink, but he could still think clearly enough to know that this blonde—whats-her-name, Sherry —was exactly what he needed. She was a hell of a lot sexier than Karen could ever be. And Moe wanted to make sure that Karen saw him with her before the evening was over.

"Do you play backgammon?" Moe slurred, looking deeply into her sharp blue eyes.

"No." She shrugged. "Nobody's ever had the patience to teach me."

"Would"—he restrained a belch—"would you like me to teach you?"

The disco was so crowded they had a difficult time squeezing their way through, especially since Moe had trouble keeping his eyes off Sherry's ass, which jiggled and jostled inside the skimpy green fabric, as she pardon-me'd and excuse-me'd in front of him. Once out, however, it was clear sailing through the bar into the backgammon room, and Moe hooked one arm cozily around the curvaceous body as they walked, partly to give an impression of intimacy and partly to steady himself.

He was disappointed to see that Harry Norton's party was no longer in the dining room, and he had a sudden urge to forget the whole thing, to go home alone and go to bed. But he couldn't back down easily now, not without appearing foolish to Sherry.

Just inside the game room, Moe saw success. At the third table from the door sat Harry Norton, playing backgammon with the other girl, while Karen watched. As the hostess approached, Moe quickly gauged the best location to observe and to be observed by the Norton party.

"How about a table over against the wall?" He weaved slightly and tried to smile back at the smiling hostess.

"Certainly," she replied, and turned to lead the way.

Moe seated Sherry with her back to Harry and Karen so that he would be able to observe them. He signed the tab for the first game, ordered a Manhattan and a Bugs Bunny, and settled into explaining backgammon to Sherry, keeping one alcohol-blurred eye on the other table. His view was perfect; although

Karen's back was to him, he could see her face reflected in the mirror, so he knew she could see him.

After so much alcohol, it was a bit of a strain to keep the degree of alertness he needed to concentrate on two things at once, but Moe felt he could do it if anybody could. The blonde was dumb, anyway, and wouldn't know if he slipped up on his instructions; whatever mistakes he might make could be glossed over by charm and wit.

As the lesson progressed, Moe became aware of someone standing beside him. He looked up to see the girl with the mousy hair, the one who had approached him on the couch in the disco.

"Hello, tall-dark-and-handsome," she said flirting ineffectually. "If you were looking for someone who knows how to play games, you could've asked me. I already know the rules."

"Buzz off." Moe scowled. "I told you you aren't my type." With an irritable sigh, he returned to his explanation, aware that the pushy girl remained standing there for a while before moving on.

Glancing across the room, Moe thought for a moment that Karen and Harry were leaving, but it was simply that Karen and the other girl were exchanging places. Apparently, Harry had won the first game, and Karen was now playing the winner. It was easier to watch Karen this way, but it was also more uncomfortable for Moe, knowing that Karen could look directly into his face. Somehow he felt that the mirror would reveal less to her, while telling him all he needed to know.

But Karen did not look at him.

When Moe had explained to Sherry everything he could about the game of backgammon, he signed for a second game and ordered another round of drinks. Now they would really play in earnest, and now he could make a real show of enjoying himself with his gorgeous blonde partner.

It was virtually impossible to appear cozy and intimate across a backgammon table, but Moe exerted himself to make it seem as if he and Sherry were having a good time. If he caught her making a wrong move, he would touch her hand in a gentle caress and smile patiently.

Each time, he would glance up to see if Karen had caught the movement, but she seemed to be concentrating intensely on her own game. The more he tried without result, the more irritated he became, and the more irritated he became, the more drinks he ordered.

After a while the room began to grow unsteady, and he had trouble concentrating on his two objectives, both of which he found himself losing. Not only was Karen ignoring him, but the blonde beginner seemed to be winning the game. Instead of giving Sherry gentle little caresses on the hand, he now began to accuse her sullenly of cheating.

Women are all cheaters anyway. Look at Karen; she was cheating on him—with the man he had always considered his best friend. Shit, the whole world was fucked up, and everything Moe did to try to change it turned to work against him. But he would show them; just wait and see.

With childish delight, Sherry made one final move and won the game, shrieking happily, "I won, I won!"

By now Moe could hardly see the board. He protested slurringly, "Oh, no, you didn't."

"Yes, I did," she said, pointing gleefully. "I got all of my little things all the way around."

"You cheated," Moe exclaimed, sprawling back in his chair, flinging his arms aside. As his right arm swung out, it toppled the drinks resting on the side of the table, causing the mixtures to slosh onto the green felt of the backgammon board.

The blonde was making an ungodly racket. Moe couldn't figure out what all the fuss was about; all he'd done was spill a couple of drinks. As Sherry got to her feet, Moe vaguely noticed a trickle of orange liquid running down her green dress. "Aw, shit, it can be cleaned," he muttered. But his protests would not calm her; she had attracted the hostess and several of the other players in the room. What the hell was she trying to do, embarrass him, making such a fuss?

In a rage, Moe rose to his feet, intent upon stalking proudly out of the room. Instead, he knocked over his chair and took a nose dive over the table, turning a somersault and landing flat on his back on the soft carpet.

As he lay there, he was aware that a great crowd had surrounded him. He giggled, then tried to say smoothly, "Bet nobody else could do that," but nobody seemed to hear.

Suddenly, there was someone bending down to him, helping to lift him to his feet. He tried to focus on the face. From the feel of the body and the clothes, he thought it was a woman. Sherry? Could it possibly be Karen? His eyes kept wanting to close.

The familiar voice near his ear said softly, "I think we'd better get you home to bed." It was Karen; Moe was sure it was her voice.

"Whose home?" he gurgled. "Yours or mine?"

"In this condition," she answered wryly, "I hardly think it matters."

Moe was aware that there were others helping Karen lift him and assist him out the door. But he felt pleasantly passive and didn't protest. Waiting outside for the attendants to get his car, he leaned comfortably against his wife, with his head softly on her breast.

He opened his eyes once and saw a face peering at him mischievously. Did he recognize that face? Oh, yes, it was that girl who had been following him all evening, the one with the mousy hair. She grinned at him and said, "Hello, tall-dark-and-handsome, I see you've finally found your type—strong and motherly."

23 MIRIAM WEXLER

November 20, 1975, Fairfax Area

Her religion had very little provision for a woman
in Miriam's state of mind. Jewish men could attend
prayers to find relief in their anguish and their grief
during mourning, but Jewish women simply had to
endure. However, Miriam wasn't quite sure that there
had ever been a Jewish woman faced with the kind
of problems she was facing. She certainly hadn't expected any of them.

She had expected to be lonely, but she had not
expected her loneliness to feel quite this helpless. She
had been brought up to live a simple life, one that
required her to be a good woman who would serve
her man well, giving him equally good children and
keeping a good house.

Miriam did not know doctors who made mistakes in
judgment and children who sued doctors over those
mistakes. And she had never in her life expected
that she would have to play a decisive part in affairs
of importance, affairs that could mean life or death
and that might hang heavy upon the soul. Those
things in life were supposed to be set aside for men,
who were reared from childhood to cope with the terrible thoughts that were the consequences.

What Miriam was about to do was somewhat un-
orthodox; she was going alone to temple in hopes of
finding some answer in the sanctuary. There would be

no service or prayers at this time of day, but the
shamus would be there, and he might be persuaded
to let her inside to sit on a bench and think. But—she
was a little frightened—it was such an unusual request,
he might want to know why. And Miriam did not
quite know what she would say.

She tried the door, and it was unlocked. As soon
as she stepped inside, she felt the coolness of the
shadows, and that alone made her feel better. There
was no one about, so she quietly slipped inside and
sat down on the back bench in the most unobtrusive
corner.

Here, at least, there was order. And tradition. Here
she felt comfortably small and insignificant in her
own small lifetime. She looked up at the ark, at the
dark wine-red curtain with the gold threads that
formed the Star of David and a pattern of lions. Had
not King David himself brought his troubles here
and found some comfort?

She knew, of course, that he could not have come
to this specific sanctuary, but she knew that time and
distance did not alter the experience greatly.

What finally held her gaze and steadied it, so that
she might look inward, was the eternal light, hanging
suspended over the ark. That, she knew, had been
burning for centuries, and it would still be burning
after she and her small private agonies had been
forgotten. She wasn't sure what she expected to find
there; perhaps she expected to see what could not be
seen, the face of God. Perhaps she hoped to see the
beloved face of her own dear Hermie once again.

Hermie was gone. Would that thought continue to
occur to her over and over endlessly, each time aris-
ing as if it were a new realization? There was such a
finality in the fact that Hermie was no more that
Miriam found herself wondering, Did he ever really

exist? Is it possible that I merely imagined him in my mind? That I invented all the things that I thought had happened over all those years?

No, Miriam was confident she could not have imagined her life with Hermie. If she had, she would have made it far more beautiful than it had been. She would have made it the way she had expected it to be so many years ago, before she and Hermie had been married. She would have given her beloved husband all the luck in the world. She wouldn't have given him all those responsibilities and worries that just seemed to drag him down further and further, day by day.

That was the thing that weighed upon Miriam most—she realized she deserved every bit of pain and suffering she had known; she deserved every bit that was to come. Sure, Hermie and his drinking had been a great burden to her, but she knew she had given him all those troubles that had made him drink.

Oh, of course he had been a dreamer, but she should have let him try to make something of his dreams; she shouldn't have kept reminding him of his responsibilities. Sitting there in the sanctuary, gazing at the eternal light, Miriam could see how foolish her little cares had been. In all the centuries the light had been burning, how insignificant seemed her great preoccupation with how she and Hermie were going to find one month's rent, or whether little Sarah could make it one more season with that shabby coat.

If Miriam had only known at the time that her Hermie's life and happiness had hung in the balance, she might have said, "Write, if it means so much to you. We'll manage somehow, or I can get a part-time job." But she had not known. She had not under-

stood how precious a lifetime was, and how insignificant the needs of a single moment.

A number of times Hermie had said wistfully, "I
should really take off six months and take a writing
course at some college." But she had gotten angry at
him and said, "But you can't. Where will we get the
rent money? And Sarah needs a new coat, and . . ."
And, and, and—over the years, Miriam's list had been
endless. There had been eyeglasses for Robert, and
shoes for the both of them, and . . . And where were
all those things now, now that Hermie was dead?
They had been thrown into the garbage or passed on
to some other child long ago. Miriam and Robert
and Sarah had none of the possessions now. They
had no need for any of them, because their needs had
changed from day to day.

Miriam Wexler stared into the eternal light and
wept. She wept because she had in part destroyed her
husband, killed him without ever having given him
the chance for life. And there was no one who could
forgive her because she could not forgive herself. It
was now too late to change anything. Too late.

November 21, 1975, Beverly Hills

As soon as Robert had mentioned to Sarah that he had decorated a number of the offices for Pathfinder Insurance, Sarah had known that he would back down on the lawsuit. Now it was left entirely to her to pursue the matter, and it was with a certain amount of trepidation that she entered the elegant building in Beverly Hills to take the elevator up to Dick Darwin's offices.

Of course, Max was with her, and so was her lawyer, but she would have felt much more secure in approaching this meeting if she had had the rest of her family by her side. Michener had told her the case was as good as settled, and all that was left was this meeting of the parties involved to agree on the details. But Sarah wasn't so sure. Last night her mother had become almost violent, demanding that she call off the suit.

To calm her mother, Sarah had promised to talk to the lawyer about it today; but when she had mentioned the problem to Moe Michener, he had explained that it was too late, and he had told her of this meeting. Sarah had been unable to face her mother with this fact, so she had reported that the lawyer had not had time to speak to her when she had called. Sarah did not know how or when she would be able to tell her mother the truth. She was terrified that her mother might find out on her own. Against Sarah's orders, Miriam had already gone to see Dr. Norton once this week.

Visions of her mother running screaming into the room kept passing through Sarah's mind.

My God, Sarah thought, as she stepped off the elevator, how chichi can you get? At least her lawyer had a sensible, functional office. This regal splendor she found ludicrous for the transaction of hard-nosed business. But she acknowledged silently to herself, it just goes to show you what kind of a doctor this Norton is—doesn't even know what simple honesty is, can't even make a pretense of having normal human values, has to get himself a fancy dancer for a lawyer. Money is everything.

The representative of the insurance company was already in the waiting room. He was a thin, nervous man and got up immediately as soon as he saw Michener, who made too much of a show—Sarah thought—of performing the introductions. Sarah and Max and the insurance man sat down uncomfortably on the French furniture while Moe informed the tastelessly feminine receptionist of their business.

They could talk only so long about the weather, so—after waiting more than ten minutes—they all fell into silence. Sarah was sure the delay was deliberate; the god-damned lawyer was probably sitting at his desk filing his nails. He was probably waiting until fifteen minutes after the hour to call them into his office. She was almost right; it happened seventeen minutes after their appointed time. Sarah was no dope. She had often used the same technique in her own office.

As they entered the office, led by a bosomy secretary, Dick Darwin rose and approached them graciously, but Sarah noticed that Dr. Norton was seated in the far corner of the room, and he neither stood nor acknowledged their presence. Sarah suddenly felt butterflies inside, realizing that the settlement was not to be as easy and peaceful as Michener had tried to make her believe.

They seated themselves in a great semicircle facing Dick Darwin's impressive desk: the insurance man nearest Norton, with Moe Michener next. Sarah sat between her lawyer and her husband. Almost unnoticeable, in a corner, sat Darwin's secretary. Sitting in the small, stiff, uncomfortable French chairs, Sarah felt she was attending a princely court rather than a settlement meeting. It was a mistake, she began to suspect, to agree to settle out of court. Here, in this office, they were not bound by laws, and the outcome would depend entirely upon power and the ability to barter.

Despite the differences between Sarah and her parents, she was not so cold as to see them as objects to be traded upon. Her lawyer had planned to sue for one million dollars, but she knew that they were about to settle for much, much less. As for her, she could not place a monetary value on her father's life.

"Well," Dick Darwin began, smiling benignly, "since we all know why we're here, it simplifies matters."

If that, Sarah told herself, is Dick Darwin's idea of a clever opening, he's a bigger show-off than I thought.

"Before we begin"—Darwin's tones became more formal—"I want to remind you that my client and I are participating in these discussions under protest. We feel that a meeting of this sort at this time is outrageous, but, since Pathfinder Insurance seems to be intent upon a hasty course, we are willing to hear its opinions and its intentions. We must advise, however, that we may not necessarily go along with whatever decision is reached."

Sarah was puzzled. She did not understand legal double-talk, and this lawyer's words seemed to be more ambiguous than most. How could the insurance company settle and the doctor hold out? She knew it had been too much to hope that everything would be over and done with today.

"What is at stake here," Darwin continued, "is more than money; it is also Dr. Harry Norton's reputation and his livelihood. It is true that a man—a patient of Dr. Norton's—has lost his life, and that is a very serious matter. It might—I emphasize *might* —have been a case of malpractice. No one—not even my client—knows for sure. The cause of death is not as yet determined. But within three days of the demise of the patient, a lawsuit was filed; and now—less than a week having passed—the company that holds the insurance on my client wants to settle. Is eager to settle for a quarter of a million dollars. Why?"

The lawyer paused to stare around the room importantly. Sarah could see the point of his remarks, but she thought the drama he was trying to put into them was nothing more than silly. Who did he think he was talking to—a jury of plumbers, bus drivers, and housewives with a fifth-grade education?

Darwin leaned back in his chair, satisfied that he had asked an important question. "Doctors all over the state of California have made plans to go out on strike, in order to highlight what they see as a very serious problem brought on by the medical-malpractice insurance companies. Is it possible that Pathfinder Insurance is trying to use the case of Dr. Harry Norton as a way of saying to the public, 'Look, we're not at fault; it's doctors like this who make it necessary to charge such high fees!' "

"Mr. Darwin"—the insurance man, whose name, Sarah thought, was Charlie something, leaned forward in his chair—"you are entering into conjecture here. We have to remember that it is your client who is being sued, not Pathfinder Insurance."

"That is what I had thought, Mr. Rothweiler," Darwin responded with mock sincerity, "but this is the first time this week I have heard you admit that fact."

Sarah was growing more and more puzzled. Who was fighting whom here? It was all much more complex than she had thought it would be. To her, the important fact was her father's death, and an unnecessary operation that had brought about that death, but that seemed to have been forgotten. She might as well have stayed home.

Finally, Sarah's lawyer entered the discussion. "Mr. Darwin"—Michener's baritone resounded smoothly—"you seem to have ignored the fact that the preliminary autopsy report has acknowledged that the operation performed by Dr. Norton was an unnecessary one. Whatever the findings of the other tests being performed, there is already a clear case of malpractice here. And the doctors at Valley View Hospital—through their review board—have acknowledged that fact by suspending Dr. Norton."

"Only temporarily." Darwin smiled.

"You do realize, don't you," the insurance man interjected, "that there is the possibility that the final report may be even more damaging to Dr. Norton? Assuming we can agree on an amount, a quick settlement could be advantageous to your client and to my company. Right now all we have to settle for is an unnecessary operation. Next week we might have to settle for a cause of death."

Sarah bent forward eagerly. That's true, she tried to

indicate to Michener with her eyes. Why don't we wait?

"My client doesn't think so," Darwin said simply. "My client has confidence that he will be completely vindicated."

Dick Darwin detested bickering but he had become a lawyer anyway, mostly to please his parents, who thought he ought to do something useful with his life. When he had protested that he didn't really want to be a lawyer, they had asked him to tell them what he did want to be. Since he had never found the courage to admit he wanted to be a movie actor, and since he couldn't come up with any other alternatives, he just went along with their wishes.

Sometimes—like today—he wished he hadn't. Cases like this one could get so involved, with charges and countercharges, that they could exasperate a saint. And, Dick Darwin admitted proudly to himself, that was one thing he wasn't.

And the same was true of most "useful" people, like doctors and lawyers. The closest thing to a saint in the room, he suspected, was his secretary, Madge. Quiet and patient, with an innate ability to perceive the basics in a complicated situation.

In the movies Dick Darwin had seen as a kid, there were always good guys and bad guys, and it had been easy to tell the difference between them. That had been one of the reasons he had wanted a life in the movies; his path could always be clear and virtuous. Of course, as a lawyer, it hadn't been. As a lawyer, his course had always been muddled—a little bit of good, a little bit of bad, all mixed up together in each case he took on.

But this case—*Wexler* v. *Norton*—seemed more than

normally muddled. Dick liked his client, but he strongly suspected that the doctor was guilty of malpractice and ought to have to pay for it. The lawyer for the Wexler family was not really a bad sort; he came on a bit too strong and seemed to be impulsive, but much of what he said showed ideals and conviction, however muddled. And the Wexler daughter? Well, who can be too critical of how someone else behaves under this kind of stress?

The closest thing to a villain Dick Darwin could find was the insurance company. Not the counsel for the company, but the insurance company itself. Like most of the villains today, it did not carry a human face but hid behind an amorphous institutional facade, so that no one individual had to bear the responsibility of villainy.

Dick had tried to convince himself that he would win the case for Harry Norton, but he still did not believe he could. If Norton could have had the insurance company behind him instead of against him, he might have had a chance. But, as it was, both the power and the evidence were on the other side.

However, when Dick had stated to Charlie Rothweiler, "My client has confidence that he will be completely vindicated," Dick had been speaking the truth. His *client* had confidence; Dick Darwin did not. Harry Norton seemed to be living in some kind of dream world where eternal optimism was possible, and nothing Dick had said to him had swayed him from his belief that he had a chance to win the case.

Dick glanced at Madge, then at Moe Michener, and then at Charlie Rothweiler before speaking. "Of course, you realize what is of greatest concern to Dr. Norton is how any settlement might affect his career. If he should agree to Pathfinder Insurance making a settlement, would he in turn be given some assurance that he could continue to receive insurance coverage at the normal rates?"

Rothweiler started to answer, but Michener got the first word in. "This sort of concession would be entirely unacceptable to my client."

Darwin noticed a slightly puzzled expression on Sarah's face. This, he suspected, was more Michener's requirement than that of the Wexler family.

Charlie Rothweiler finally had his chance to speak, and he took it slowly and carefully. "This is something that will have to be left to my company's discretion. While Pathfinder is willing to consider continuing coverage of Dr. Norton, we simply cannot include a commitment one way or the other in any settlement agreement."

Moe Michener leaned forward to look at Rothweiler as if about to speak, but he changed his mind.

Dick Darwin began to fear that the meeting was going to go in an endless circle. "There is one other factor," he said, frowning, "and that is, who exactly is bringing this lawsuit? Mr. Michener has stated that he represents the Wexler family. However, the widow—Mrs. Herman Wexler—has denied any involvement in the suit."

Michener broke in testily. "My client is Mrs. Sarah Wexler Howard, who is bringing the lawsuit on behalf of the Wexler estate. Whatever Mrs. Wexler has to say about her own lack of participation should not influence any decision we make."

Darwin smiled. "But it should, because it could influence a judge and a jury. Especially when Mrs. Wexler is willing to testify on Dr. Norton's behalf."

Michener and Sarah glanced painfully at each other before Michener spoke. "Unfortunately, Mrs. Wexler has been extremely distraught since the death of her husband. She is not of sound mind, and there is the possibility that she may have to be put into a home for some psychiatric care." He hesitated before continuing. "We did not want to bring this matter up in these discussions, but since you have, I might point out that this would create more sympathy for the Wexler side than it would for Dr. Norton."

Dick Darwin felt a great sinking inside. There was no way he was going to be able to save his client.

Charlie Rothweiler knew exactly which points he could concede and which ones he could not, and he was sure the other lawyers in the room had a similar inventory. It was a little like playing poker. He wished he could see the hands of the other players. He had been given his instructions, and they had been pretty liberal. Too damned liberal to suit him, and he had given up very few of the concessions that he had been told he could. The less he gave away—still settling quickly and quietly—the more commission there would be for him.

He was aware that both of the other lawyers looked upon him as a sort of incompetent stooge—a fool. He didn't mind; he had always been able to use his simple, unpretentious manner to his own advantage. As long as no one could see what cards he held in his hands, it was unimportant to him what others thought of him.

But one thing bothered him; he had expected Dick Darwin to pursue the matter of Dr. Norton's insurance rates. It perplexed him that he didn't. If he had, the case might have been settled then and there. He did have a few concessions he could make in that regard. And, as far as Charlie could see, that was the only thing that really ought to matter to the doctor. Hell, he wasn't going to be out any money in this deal.

If he could get out of this jam with his job and credentials intact, why should he care about the money?

Charlie didn't like to take the lead in this kind of situation, but he had come to the conclusion that he would have to. "Mr. Darwin," he began slowly, "we don't seem to be getting anywhere. We could go on discussing this case for weeks at this rate. As you know, what Pathfinder Insurance is most concerned about is that we settle this quickly. And by 'quickly,' I mean today. In this meeting."

Darwin scowled down at the top of his desk. "I just don't think that's going to be possible."

It *was* getting late. Through the enormous window behind Darwin's desk, Charlie could see that the hills were turning a deep purple, and the sky above them a melancholy gray. He would have to give up one of his precious cards.

"I think if we were each to give up some of our demands, we might come up with a settlement that would satisfy all concerned. Now, as I understand it, your major concern is that Pathfinder Insurance be fair to Dr. Norton when it comes time to reconsider his malpractice coverage. While I can't guarantee terms or rates, I do think we can incorporate something that will satisfy him."

Moe Michener lurched forward in his chair, his long legs flopping. "I'm sorry, but we cannot permit—"

But Charlie Rothweiler firmly overrode him. "I realize this has been one of your stipulations, Mr. Michener; but, as I said, we each have to give up something, and this ought to be the least of your concerns. After all, you are seeking compensation for your client, not punishment for Dr. Norton."

"But still—" Moe blustered.

"Let me finish," Charlie insisted firmly. "Pathfinder

Insurance is willing to give your client a quarter of a million dollars—that's firm. And, I must add, that is as much if not more than many courts would award in such a case." He paused dramatically to look seriously, first at Michener and then at Darwin. "If each of you has the opportunity to confer privately with your clients, I think we can all walk out of here with the satisfaction that we have reached an amicable settlement that can be put onto paper sometime in the next few days. Considering the anxiety and the tension that these disputes carry with them, wouldn't it be worth a try?"

Darwin gave him a look that seemed almost grateful. "I think that's an excellent idea. If you don't mind waiting outside in the waiting room, Mr. Rothweiler, I think I would like to have the opportunity to confer with my client." He turned to look at Moe Michener. "And if you wish to have a private conference with Mrs. Howard, Mr. Michener, you are welcome to use the conference room just across the hall."

25 MOÉ MICHENER

Dick Darwin's conference room looked like a museum. Moe wondered how anybody could concentrate on business around this enormous inlaid table. He didn't know if the paintings on the wall were considered masterpieces or not (they were certainly importantly framed and hung), but he was sure that anybody sitting at the table would be unable to keep his eyes off them.

And obviously Max and Sarah Howard were thinking the same thing. They looked around the room, and then Sarah cast her eyes heavenward in mock disbelief. "My God," she exclaimed, "do you think this Darwin is in the habit of going to garage sales?"

They all laughed and sat down to try to concentrate on the offer that had been made to them.

Moe hoped Sarah would reject the offer. He did not really want to have to push her on that clause about denying Norton insurance, but he was still determined to get it in somehow.

"Well," he said, grinning jovially, "we seem to have them over a barrel." And he glanced at Sarah, looking for a similar reaction. But she had turned oddly serious.

"Would it be all right with you," she asked meekly, "if we took the offer and settled?"

Moe was baffled. "You know we could get more—

maybe everything we're asking for—if we pushed?"

Sarah nodded in acknowledgment. "Yes. But I think we might also be pushing our luck."

Moe had hardly ever heard Max Howard speak a word. Sarah's husband had always sat quietly and let Sarah do the talking. Now, however, he finally spoke up, and he had that sort of gentle but confident manner that Moe always found unsettling. "Mr. Rothweiler said something that made a great deal of sense to us. This past week has been a great strain on Sarah and on her family. I realize that we initiated this lawsuit, but none of us expected to have to face this much pressure this quickly. It would be worth it to us to accept the offer just to avoid any more mental anguish."

Moe conceded to himself that the settlement was a good one and that he would be getting a hell of a lot of money for one week's work—$125,000 of the total—but that was less important to him than the one clause that his clients were now urging him to give up. He searched desperately for a way to persuade them to hold out.

"I understand that"—he smiled reassuringly—"but I just hate to see this guy Norton get off so easily."

Sarah hesitated; she would not look at Moe. "We don't want to destroy the man. And, after all, he's already been suspended by the hospital."

"But that's only a temporary suspension." Moe's voice was becoming more strident. "If we let this go by, that fucking—excuse me—that corrupt medical establishment will close around him and protect him. And—in the end—he will have gotten off without any real punishment at all." He glared at Sarah and then looked at Max for some kind of affirmation. "They stick together, you know."

"But, the articles in the newspapers," said Sarah,

looking plaintively at Moe. "Won't people realize how irresponsible he is? Won't he find it difficult to get patients after this?"

Moe felt he was gaining. "People have short memories. They'll say, 'Oh, well, he made one little mistake.' The issue here is more than just the death of your father, although that's a pretty important matter. We have a responsibility here to change the system so that other unsuspecting people like your father don't have to suffer the way he did."

Sarah started to reply, but Max squeezed her arm gently and spoke first. "We realize that, Mr. Michener; we've understood it all along. But what we're saying now is we can't afford to give up any more of ourselves for the sake of the public good. We aren't crusaders; we aren't politicians; we don't have the emotional stamina. Mr. Wexler's death was a big loss to my wife's family. Now we're in danger of Mrs. Wexler losing her mind and spending the rest of her days in a mental institution. To us, that's a bigger responsibility than bucking the system." He paused for a moment and took a deep breath. "And if you aren't willing to go along with our decision, we'll just have to get ourselves another lawyer."

26 HARRY NORTON

November 21, 1975, Beverly Hills

It was settled. Harry felt an odd mixture of disappointment and relief: disappointment that he had not won a total victory; relief that it was over and that, in one way or another, he would be able to stay in practice. None of it was what Harry would ever have expected. But, when he thought about it, nothing that had occurred this week *could* have been expected.

As the group began to wander out of Dick Darwin's office, Harry stared at Moe Michener's back. The loss of his friend was still the greatest surprise of all, the one thing Harry still had difficulty adjusting to. But Moe's determination to destroy Harry's medical career had finally come through to him.

What Harry felt as he stared at his old friend's departing back was not so much anger as it was hurt— and a desire to hurt back. He wasn't sure what he was going to say, but he hurried to catch up with Moe and the others before they got to the elevators. It was an uncomfortably silent group that Harry approached.

He smiled broadly and extended a confident hand toward Moe. "Well, Michener, I guess you win a few, lose a few." He paused. "And a few get rained out."

Moe did not take the extended hand, nor did he smile. "I hate to tell you this, Norton, but this is California. Next time the sun's sure to be shining."

Harry withdrew his hand, but he kept his confident smile. "You know, Moe," he began slowly, "there was something they tried to teach us back in med school—I wonder if you remember it. They tried to teach us to cover our asses. You and I didn't believe them then. And I still didn't believe in that rule last week. But I believe in it now, and I don't think there'll be a next time."

As the elevator door opened and everyone crowded in, there was considerable embarrassment all around—except for Harry. He realized in this group he had the upper hand. His face was only a few inches away from Moe's now, and he stared straight into his eyes. "I had a nice long talk with your wife the other night"—he paused to smile—"and in case you're interested, she's doing fine."

Moe's response was quick and hostile. "I'm not interested."

But Harry continued. "She reminded me of something—back when you were kicked out of your residency at City Hospital. It was because you failed to cover your ass. Do you remember? And when you were working down in Florida, it was the same thing. But then, there are some things you can't cover up, aren't there? Not completely. Not from everybody."

There was a long silence, as everyone watched the descending red numbers over the elevator door, probably wishing the number one would hurry up. At number three, Harry spoke up again. "You know, that little rule can apply to the legal profession just as much as it can to medicine."

Moe's eyes were smoldering, but he held back until the elevator doors had opened and the others had anxiously moved on out through the lobby. Then he grabbed Harry by the arm, squeezing it tightly, and with his voice soft but vicious, he spat out, "Listen,

Norton, I'm warning you now—watch out for me, because I'm going to get you. If it's the last thing I do."

Harry smiled and pulled his arm free. "You know, you only got this far this time because it was a sneak attack. Next time—if there is a next time—you won't have that advantage. I'm on to you now. And I've got another advantage: I understand you and I know your weaknesses. So"—he grinned and slapped Moe on the back—"I wish you luck."

Harry was surprisingly happy as he walked alone out onto the dusky street to look for his car. And he grew even more happy as he thought of Ellen. Ellen will be glad that it's over, he thought, smiling quietly to himself.

She had been another big surprise to Harry. He was totally baffled by the importance she had begun to play in his life, as if his life had been miserably incomplete until she had come along. Anything that was important to him, he felt, was equally important to her. Now, he could not wait to tell her the results of the meeting that had taken place in Dick Darwin's office.

Harry knew Ellen would be at home, expecting him; they had made plans to have drinks and dinner together. (In fact, they had had dinner together every night since the mess had started.) Although it was only a short trip from Beverly Hills to Ellen's Brentwood apartment, Harry felt he couldn't move his little Mercedes fast enough.

When Ellen greeted him at her door, she looked beautifully domestic, with her falling softly around her face and with a brightly colored apron tied neatly around her waist.

Without stopping to think, he threw his arms around her and danced her excitedly into the living room, concluding the turns with a big ecstatic kiss. Still holding her after the kiss, but more quietly subdued and intimate, he announced, "It's all over, and I'm still *Dr*. Harry Norton. So if you've had your heart set on marrying a doctor, we're still in the ball park."

"You won?" she asked, grinning.

"Not exactly." Harry grinned back. "I lost to the tune of a quarter of a million, but I can still get malpractice coverage. The insurance company gave in. It'll probably cost me through the nose, but they'll still cover me."

Ellen suddenly turned very serious. "It's very important to you, isn't it? Being a doctor?"

Harry threw himself down onto the couch and looked up at her. "It's the only thing there is." He paused. "Well, not quite the only thing any more. There's you, and after that comes medicine."

Ellen sat down beside him, tucking her legs beneath her. "What about the hospital?"

Harry had almost forgotten that he was still under suspension at Valley View. He shrugged. "I don't know. There is the meeting next week, and I have no idea how the staff will vote. If I'm kicked out, I'll simply have to try another hospital. If I can't get accepted someplace else in the United States, there's always Canada or Europe or Asia or Africa. The world's a big place."

Ellen's hands clenched on the dishtowel she was holding. She did not look at him as she asked, "You expect to have a difficult time?"

Harry put his arm around her and gently pulled her head down to his shoulder. "I don't know what to expect right now, and I don't really want to think about it." He gave her a kiss on the forehead. "Right now, I still have a week of vacation. Do you know I've never had a real vacation? I want to take you away from all this. Where would you like to go?"

Ellen answered quietly, just above a whisper, "Oh, I don't know. Canada or Europe or Asia or Africa. I don't care. Whither thou goest."

"How about a week in Acapulco?" he asked. "Just you and me."

"That's the nicest proposition I ever got." Ellen nestled in his arms.

"It's not a proposition unless you want it to be," Harry said softly. "If you'd like, we can make it legal."

27 ROBERT WEXLER

November 22, 1975, Fairfax Area

When Sarah had called Robert to tell him that she
was worried about their mother, Robert had figured
his sister was just exaggerating things the way she
always had. But now he could see for himself, and
there *was* something terribly wrong with Miriam
Wexler. Sarah had asked Robert to go to see their
mother, because Sarah was no longer permitted inside
the house—since the case against Dr. Norton had been
settled.

Robert had driven out to Fairfax without calling
first, and he had found the house uncharacteristically
filthy. There were newspapers scattered all over the
living room. There was food left out in the kitchen,
with dirty dishes stacked carelessly in the sink. He
had found his mother sitting in her bedroom, looking out her window at the backyard. She wore a
soiled blue bathrobe that had belonged to his father,
and her hair was dirty and matted.

There were dark shadows under her eyes that suggested she had not slept in days. And from the hollows
in her cheeks, and the weak way she stood up to greet
him, he suspected she had lost at least ten pounds.

It may have been that she was embarrassed at being
surprised in this condition, but Miriam was very upset at seeing Robert. Her hands shook as she tried
to straighten her hair, and her eyes darted nervously

about the unkempt room. Robert could hardly hear the feeble words she muttered. "Oh, Robert, it's the middle of the afternoon. Shouldn't you be at work?"

Robert didn't bother to explain. "Mama, are you all right?"

"Of course," she protested. But it was obvious she didn't believe her own words. Suddenly she burst into tears, her frail body giving the impression it would break with the great sobs. "No," she half whispered, "no, darling, your mama's not all right."

Hearing his mother refer to herself in the third person made Robert shake his head. Fearfully, he took hold of her, putting his arm around her for support, and led her out of her room toward the kitchen. "Let me make you some coffee, or some tea," he soothed. "And we can sit down in the kitchen and have a good old-fashioned heart-to-heart. Just like we used to when I was little."

But, even after they sat sipping the hot liquid at the kitchen table, Robert could not determine exactly what was wrong with his mother. She still would not look at him; and, when he asked her questions, she would simply sigh or moan vaguely.

Finally, after they had sat silently for some time, she spoke. "Hermie's better off dead, isn't he?"

"Mama." Robert reached his hand out to his mother's. "It's not a matter of better or worse. He's dead, and you have to try to get over it. There's nothing you can do about it."

"Not now," she whispered huskily, "but there were things I could have done when he was still alive. I could have let him live. I didn't, you know. I never let him have his life. Not from the first day we were married." She tried to choke back a sob. "And not to the last."

Robert didn't know quite what to say, but he knew

he had to say something. "Mama," he tried, "you mustn't torture yourself this way. It's not good for you."

But his mother didn't seem to hear him. She had drifted away again, to whatever it was she saw in her mind. Robert decided to sit patiently and wait for her to return, to say whatever it was she was thinking.

Robert realized Sarah had been right; his mother seemed to be losing touch with reality. She needed help, and more help than he and Sarah could give. The best he could hope for was to try to get through to her with the truth. He tried again. "Mama, are you forgetting? Papa didn't have cancer. He had pains, but they weren't unbearable pains. Do you hear me? Papa wasn't like Uncle Sidney. He didn't die in such terrible pain."

28 MOE MICHENER

November 23, 1975, Los Angeles

Moe was beginning to get tired of living in the hotel. This morning, as he read the paper over breakfast, he decided to thumb through to the apartment section. He hadn't seen or talked to Karen since she had scraped him up off the floor at Pip's, and he figured she must have meant what she had said about a divorce. If she wasn't going to change her mind, he'd better get himself a more permanent place.

Moe generally didn't read the entire paper—usually just the news section and the sports section—but he would often thumb through every page, just to give himself the impression that he had looked at it from front to back.

That's what he did this morning, and that's how a small item in the society pages happened to catch his eye: MISS ELLEN HOPKINS MARRIES DR. HAROLD NORTON. And there, with the article, was a picture of the girl Moe had seen with Harry and Karen that night at Pip's. He quickly read the article. Yes, it had to be the same Harry Norton.

Nothing made sense. What about Karen? What about their affair? And who the hell was this Ellen Hopkins? Moe knew everything there was to know about Harry Norton, and he had never even heard him mention an Ellen Hopkins.

There must be some mistake.

November 25, 1975, Acapulco

Harry did not really want to leave Acapulco. When the telegram had arrived informing him that the M and M conference was to be held at Valley View on the day before Thanksgiving, Harry had thought, To hell with it! But Ellen had pushed and prodded, and finally she had persuaded him to fly back to Los Angeles early. If medicine was what he wanted, she had insisted, he had to go back and fight.

But Harry had never been so happy as he had been there with Ellen, and he wanted to prolong it as much as possible. It hadn't been just the time spent with her that had been good for him. He had spent some time walking and sitting alone on the beach, thinking. Straightening a great many things out in his mind.

Funny how it is, he mused, when you work so hard, you never have time to think.

But in the quiet of the Acapulco days and nights, Harry had found the time. He had thought a great deal about his work as a doctor, what he really wanted to do. He also had thought about Herman Wexler, and about his own father, and about himself, Harry Norton, as a person rather than as a doctor.

It was funny how the human mind could put completely different people into the same pigeonholes—this person is like that one, and that person like this—without ever really realizing it. Harry had really looked at Herman Wexler pretty much as he had looked at his own father. And in trying to save Wexler, Harry had really been trying to save his father—who *had* died of cancer, when Harry had been off in Sweden.

Of course, Harry had flown home for the funeral, but he had felt guilty at not having been there when his father had needed him. Felt guilty at having disappointed his father all the way along the line.

Sitting on the beach at Acapulco, Harry Norton thought about the irony that he didn't especially want to go back to private practice in Beverly Hills now—to his own office—to his medical building—to everything he had always worked for.

Harry remembered a conversation he had overheard between Dr. Gustafsen and Dr. Dagerman on the day before he left Sweden for City Hospital.

"God!" Gustafsen had cried. "I wish I were going back to the states with Norton—to private practice and fee-for-services medicine. That bastard is going to be rich! I'd give my right testicle to be in his shoes."

"I'd give both of mine," Dagerman had agreed, nodding wistfully.

Harry hadn't bothered to comment at the time. Neither Gustafsen nor Dagerman had been particularly friendly to him during his year in Sweden. He still remembered Nils Wenkert, the patient with the stomach ulcer and the odd-numbered birthday. He was glad the two doctors were unhappy in their "idealistic socialized state."

But what was happening to the practice of medicine in his own country now? Harry wondered. Was the Swedish system getting closer to America's shores? Were MediCal and Medicaid and Medicare just the beginning?

Harry found himself thinking a lot about Sweden

during his week in Acapulco. Maybe the Swedish medical system was the best. After all, no exorbitant malpractice insurance (maybe twenty-five dollars per year)—so lawsuits. Free medical care, cradle to the grave. No Moe Micheners, no Buxbaums or O'Haras to answer to, no hospital suspension—

Maybe . . . No!

Harry had learned long ago that the Swedish approach to medicine was not the answer. And Dr. Groton's Medicaid Factory was not the answer. And City Hospital wasn't, either. The answer had to lie somewhere in between.

Harry sat there on the beach with Ellen and remembered how many of his patients in Sweden had not been happy. At all. How many had taken their own lives— It was strange to sit there in the sunshine with someone he loved and think about patients who had died almost ten years ago, thousands of miles away. But that was what Harry found himself doing.

He closed his eyes. . . . He was back in Sweden now in the *akut intagning,* the emergency room. . . .

He remembered the ambulance unloading its passenger, and finding himself staring at one Swede who was not happy—a cold, glassy-eyed man, lying on a stretcher.

"We found him in an alley," the driver said.

Harry had seen two broken bones protruding through the skin above the ankle, a battered torso, and a partially collapsed skull. He had listened dully to the chest. No heartbeat. No pulse. Cold. "He's been dead for at least six hours. DOA. Label him dead on arrival."

The man's identification card was found, and a sobbing relative had told Harry one hour later of the unfortunate fellow's depressions. He had been threatening suicide for two months.

The suicide rate in Sweden was higher than in most countries. Harry had looked up the numbers out of curiosity in the hospital library. Sweden and Finland, with 21 suicides per 100,000 population, were fourth in the statistics, following West Germany, Czechoslovakia, and Austria. The United States, with 10.8 per 100,000, was farther down the list.

It was difficult to explain this fact. The standard of living in Sweden was second only to that in the United States, and the people were supposedly cared for by the government from the cradle to the grave. For some reason they seemed obsessed with the idea of taking their own lives.

And the method? Guns had little place in Sweden. Most suicides involved jumping off one of the many bridges that span the valleys, quarries, and lakes. Not many of these patients had reached the emergency room alive.

Some had. Elsa Linhamn still came to Harry's mind. She had been a twenty-five-year-old girl, quite pretty, who worked in sales for the Max Factor store in Malmö. She had a good income and had been living comfortably with her *pojke* (boy) for the past three years. They had a son and were planning to get married soon. But the *pojke* had met another *flicka* (girl), it seemed, and was in the process of moving out of her apartment when Elsa Linhamn jumped off the thirty-foot bridge at the end of the street.

The patient had very shallow respirations, and her blood pressure was barely palpable when they carried her in. Harry had worked on her for two hours, putting an endotracheal tube in her throat to assist her breathing, and filling her with intravenous fluids to support her heart and kidneys. He had gotten an x-ray of her neck, which showed a fracture at the fifth cervical vertebra. Elsa Linhamn died in the *akut intagning.*

Harry thought one reason for the high suicide rate in Sweden related to the peculiar style of life. In a country where the government took care of all problems, the citizens became accustomed to outside assistance. They were not used to settling their own problems. Thus, when something did come up, when they were faced with frustrations in their efforts to achieve their rather rigid goals and expectations, they simply could not handle it. It seemed overwhelming, and their first thoughts turned to self-destruction.

Harry thought the second factor was the weather. While it remained light for longer during the summer months, the opposite was true as winter approached. The sun rose at ten in the morning and set around three in the afternoon. People went to work in sub-zero cold and darkness and returned under similar conditions. Indeed, it was very possible for most workers not to see the sun at all for two or three months in a row. This must have driven them indoors mentally as well as physically, and contributed in no small part to their severe depressions.

Jumping off bridges wasn't the only method. Harry remembered Olaf Fischson. He earned his living writing poetry and short stories for several leading Swedish magazines. Some of his work had been translated and published abroad. He had a small cottage in the country, and he lived there alone, keeping mostly to himself.

One day Olaf Fischson ingested a bottle of sedatives and "downers." He was brought to the *akut intagning* in a coma six hours later. He was admitted to the intensive care unit and put on the SI (seriously ill) list. Harry had monitored his vital signs and fed him intravenously. His blood pressure and pulse were good. Harry had put a Foley catheter in his bladder and an NG (nasogastric) tube in his stomach. He had pushed the fluids and given him Lasix when his urine output lagged below thirty cubic centimeters per hour. He had given him intravenous Adrenalin and digitalis to strengthen his heart and keep it beating.

Olaf Fischson's blood pressure was ninety over sixty in the emergency room. One hour later it had disappeared for good. The patient's kidneys completely shut down. Harry had kept him going a little longer, but his pupils gradually dilated, and he had died without regaining consciousness.

Harry had had a certain sympathy for Olaf Fischson. He had felt that he knew him even though the patient had never spoken one word. In a sense, Harry and Olaf Fischson were both outsiders in Sweden—Harry as a foreigner, and the patient as a talented and creative writer. And Harry had watched him die.

Many people had noted the significance of *who* were committing suicide in Sweden rather than *how many*. Harry learned that over the past thirty years a large percentage of the country's leading poets, playwrights, and novelists had killed themselves.

Out-of-the-ordinary people, gifted individuals not cast in the Swedish mold, did not fit well into the state-designed pattern. They were different. They were outsiders and, as such, were stifled, and this, in the end, overwhelmed them.

Harry remembered thinking that his patient, Olaf Fischson, had felt that way. But Harry also knew he'd never know for sure.

Now, sitting on the beach in Acapulco, Harry's mind flowed back on them all—Elsa Linhamn and Olaf Fischson and the patient with no memorable name at all—just DOA, dead on arrival. He realized he had tried to play God much too often in his career. Maybe that was why he had wanted to be a doctor in the first place: he had felt inadequate at playing a man, so he had tried something better—playing God.

Harry was now beginning to realize that he had never been all that inadequate as a man. In fact, being a man didn't require being all that adequate in the first place. Just because Harry was too short to play basketball, his father should not have been so disappointed in him.

Harry knew he was a good person, with a lot to offer, just as a human being; Ellen was proving that to him. He could give pleasure and joy and love. And so much more, because he was also a doctor. A doctor who could help people in their illness and infirmity, not a doctor who could play God.

Harry wasn't exactly religious. Religion was for the Miriam Wexlers of this world, simple people who needed simple comfort. But he was finding a profound comfort in discovering how very small he was, surrounded by the vast expanse of sand, looking out at what seemed to be an endless ocean, and watching the spectacular displays the southern sunsets made.

How sad, he found himself thinking, it must be to be God, and to have nothing bigger than yourself to appreciate.

In Acapulco, being a doctor had become a very unimportant thing to Harry Norton. His honeymoon had convinced him that the very best thing in the world to be was a beach bum. Maybe do a little writing, the way Herman Wexler had wanted to. No worries about malpractice insurance, or lawyers and patients treading on your heels. Or about whether or not you were hardened enough to treat patients with the right kind of cold objectivity.

All those years in med school had been geared toward dehumanizing doctors and patients, so that the doctor could be a good machine, and the patient could be nothing more than an object to be treated—a gallbladder, a liver, a heart, an ulcer. Not Mrs. Goldstein or Mr. Murphy or Miss Johnson. Certainly not Myra or Tom or Laura.

The Dr. Harold Norton who had existed two weeks ago would not have had this problem. He would have been eager to get back to Valley View Hospital to fight—to toss the patients around as if they had never really existed as human beings. But Harry Norton, who had lost his objectivity and found a human being, simply did not know how to play the doctor game any more. He had given up his scorecard.

Ellen had tried her best to help him get through this problem, but she hadn't been able to understand it completely. She had told him that he was simply experiencing what it was like to fall off a horse, and he was resisting getting back on again. If he decided, after he got back to work, that he didn't want to continue working as a doctor, Ellen would go along with whatever he wanted to do. But he couldn't quit because of one mistake; he had to go back and try to prove to himself that that mistake had not made him afraid. He just couldn't quit out of fear.

But Ellen couldn't understand that it wasn't fear. He couldn't make her realize that he didn't want to give up his human feelings. He wasn't sure he could, even if he wanted to. Because of Herman Wexler, Harry would always be conscious that what he was cutting into was not an abstract textbook case but something infinitely more precious.

30 JOE GREGORIO

Joe Gregorio had mixed feelings as he hurried down the halls of Valley View Hospital toward the conference room. He was pleased that his suspicions about Herman Wexler had been confirmed, but he was annoyed that other doctors could not perform their duties with the same kind of precision and care that he did. When he had first emigrated to America, he had had a high regard for the American medical system, but that regard had dwindled in recent years.

He was not sure if the system had changed, or if he himself had altered his attitude toward it as he became more familiar with it. Perhaps his initial feelings had been simply a reaction to the freedom of medicine he found in the United States, after the terrible problems he had experienced in Nazi Austria.

He had never quite gotten over the dilemma he had faced back there so many years ago. In a way, it had been comfortable giving up his individual responsibility to the state, so that he would not have to feel guilty for any possible mistakes. But somehow Joe Gregorio had managed to feel guilty anyway. For, after a while, his mistakes had incresed in number and frequency; and eventually the great burden of so many mistakes had come to weigh heavily upon him.

By escaping to the United States he had tried to

nullify that burden. And it had also been to rid himself of that problem that he had decided to give up practicing medicine and to go into pathology. By the time he would see a patient, the serious mistakes would already have been made. And he would bear no grave responsibility.

But now he was no longer sure. Now he wondered if there was any medical system anywhere that was entirely satisfactory. He wondered if any such system was even possible, considering the odd nature of medicine.

He held his container of slides tightly under his arm, opened the door of the conference room, and hurried inside.

The meeting was already in process, so he tiptoed quietly to his place in the back of the room near the projector. "Better late than never," he heard someone —he thought it was O'Hara—mutter sardonically.

But it was Norton who seemed to have the floor. He was saying rather nervously, "It is easy to look back with hindsight, Dr. Buxbaum, and say I would have done this or that. But I was there at the table. I had to make the decision.".

As Gregorio sat down, O'Hara was interjecting, "You know what I think? I think one of the problems here is that the bastard had too many tests. Too many fucking preoperative tests. My God, angiogram, liver scans, gastroscopy—it's a wonder he didn't die from the tests alone."

Yes, Gregorio thought, O'Hara would think that about Norton. The pot calling the kettle. He wondered if O'Hara had ever considered the number of tests he'd run on each patient. O'Hara was so much like a child playing a game. All these doctors seemed like so many children to Joe.

Suddenly, Norton slammed his fist down on the

table and spoke so stridently it was almost a shout. "Goddamn it, I admit I made a mistake in the operation I performed on Herman Wexler. But every single doctor around this table has made mistakes just as serious as mine, and none of them have been kicked off the staff. Is there anyone in this room whom we can call a god or a saint? Anyone who hasn't made an honest mistake? Why, just two months ago, I recall a patient who died because he was given too big a swallow of barium for his x-ray!"

O'Hara blustered, "That wasn't my mistake! Can I help it if the damned x-ray department can't read?"

"I'm not accusing anyone, Dr. O'Hara, just making the point," Norton continued. "And what about another patient six months ago who got the wrong prescription for her heart condition?"

"Gentlemen!" Buxbaum pounded on the table. "Gentlemen, please. This kind of arguing is getting us nowhere. Since Dr. Gregorio is here, I think we'd better move on to his autopsy findings, so that we all know precisely what we're talking about before we make our final decision."

Grgeorio was somewhat disappointed that Buxbaum had intervened. He rather enjoyed watching the other doctors tear at each other so irrationally. It would make them all feel like such fools when he finally announced the cause of death. Let them all hang themselves.

And yet, they were all good doctors, most of them conscientious. It was just that they were all so tied to the apron strings of their system. As he got to his feet and turned to the slide projector, Gregorio felt that familiar ache inside—that yearning for the impossible ideal of his science—to be able to know as much about a living organism as one can learn about a dead one.

Gregorio understood. These were good men in the room sitting around the table. Useful. Well-trained to help society. But they were only people. Norton was right. They were not gods or saints—just people. They got pimples on their faces like everyone else—and they made mistakes.

Yet perhaps it was the fault of the patients themselves. Perhaps the patients contributed to this god-like aura—an aura the doctors tried and strained desperately to attain, but couldn't. The patients wanted them to be gods beyond reproach, beyond everything, but it could never be.

"Turn off the lights, please," he said simply.

The room went dark, and Gregorio turned on the machine, focusing the lens on the first slide. "Here is the heart," he confirmed to himself as well as to the others. "There was no gross evidence of acute infarction or damage in the past. And this is confirmed on microscopic. You can see the normal muscle cells there before you. Now, under high power"—he changed the slide—"the same. No evidence of infarction. But you will notice the small areas of bleeding just under the endocardium of the heart."

Gregorio looked around the darkened room at the faces, starkly highlighted by the beam from the projector. How much medicine did they really know? he wondered. Were they even paying attention, using any of their critical faculties, or just watching some abstract case history, like students in a class?

He switched to the next slide. "The kidneys were also swollen and pale. Now, under the microscope you can see the actual damage to the glomeruli and nephrons. And here it is under higher power."

Gregorio again glanced around the room, looking for reactions. Norton was frowning in concentration, leaning forward on the table as if trying desperately to understand. O'Hara was leaning back in his chair, carelessly straightening the crease in his trousers, not even looking at the screen. Buxbaum was furtively eyeing Karen Marshall's breasts.

Suddenly, Norton turned to Gregorio and said intensely, "Do you think these changes could be postmortem, Dr. Gregorio?"

Gregorio answered confidently, "No, I am positive they occurred prior to death." And he quickly changed the slide. "You see here the slides of the pancreas. Classic changes of chronic pancreatitis, the scarring and infiltration of inflammatory cells into the acini and the liver—the typical changes of a moderate cirrhosis, infiltration of fatty cells, and some fibrosis around the portal triads. There is no doubt the years of drinking had done damage to both his pancreas and his liver."

Gregorio waited for a reaction, but there was none.

"Would you care to show us the slides of Dr. Norton's biopsies taken at surgery?" Buxbaum asked. "Can we see those?"

Gregorio turned on the next slide. "As you gentlemen can see," he began, "the portion of pancreas I received for frozen section showed chronic inflammation and scarring, with a few suspicious areas. Now, under higher power, you can see the irregular nuclei, and heavily vacuolated cytoplasm in these cells—almost wild-growing, one might say. . . ."

"How much of that is artifact, Dr. Gregorio," Buxbaum questioned, "due to the frozen-section staining technique?"

"Unfortunately, it is difficult to tell. I can say, however, that what we were calling malignant really wasn't. All benign. But the slides did have a high suspicion for cancer. One can see where one might be tempted . . ."

"We're not interested in your clinical opinion," Buxbaum interrupted. "Or in your temptations. Only the facts and the slides."

Norton stood up and leaned against the table. "I felt that by taking out the cancer, I was doing what was best for my patient. I was being fair to him. I could have closed and waited. Or done a bypass. I could have played it safe. But I did what I thought was best for Herman Wexler. And he survived."

"We are not talking about one-week cures!" O'Hara blasted. "The patient is dead. The fact remains that you operated on him, he didn't have cancer, and now he is dead."

"And our department of surgery," Buxbaum added, "and our hospital are being held accountable."

Dr. Harold Norton sat down again. "Aren't we all being a little high and mighty here?" he asked. "We've all had our share of complications, of cases where things didn't work out—of cases we'd rather not discuss."

"At the moment that is irrelevant," Buxbaum put in. "We are discussing the case of Herman Wexler. And you are the responsible surgeon. We are trying to see if there is any basis for permanent punitive action here, whether it be a letter of reprimand, suspension, or—"

"Suspension?" Norton asked.

"Yes," Buxbaum said. "We all know the case has been settled legally. But the publicity, and our image to the rest of the medical community . . . something's got to be done."

"We can't risk the hospital's reputation," O'Hara added.

Norton rose again. "The hospital's reputation? Were we thinking of that, when one of us here operated on a lady with a normal gallbladder and no stones? The gallbladder that was removed was perfectly fine. It wasn't the first time—"

"Those are errors that cannot be helped," Buxbaum returned. "It was nonvisualizing on x-ray. Ninety percent of those are diseased. How was the doctor to know his patient hadn't taken her six pills the night before x-ray?"

"He could have asked her," Norton replied. "Or repeated her gallbladder x-ray with a second dose. The point is, it was a mistake. Who says a doctor can't make an honest mistake? Are we beyond that, gentlemen? Have our patients convinced us of our own infallibility? Have we convinced ourselves?"

"Bringing up these cases won't get you off this," O'Hara said. "Your time has come. Personally, I think it should have happened a long time ago. There was always something wrong with you. Like the guy whose lip you sewed up as a medical student. Remember the tetanus shot you forgot? And how you ran from his room like a damn coward when he dropped dead? Remember the doctor heart stat, and how fast you ran?"

"You bastard, O'Hara!" Norton lashed out. "You dirty—"

"Gentlemen! Gentlemen, please!" Gregorio turned on his machine again and flashed a final slide. "I suggest we all calm down. I suggest it very strongly. And listen to me. I have something very important to say. To all of you—"

Norton was beside himself. "Letter of reprimand! Suspension. Like hell!"

"We must think of the good of the hospital first," Buxbaum said. "We must protect ourselves!"

"Were we thinking of the good of the hospital," Norton asked, "when we gave a lady a pint of blood in transfusion before fixing her elective hernia?"

"That has nothing to do with the matter before us," Buxbaum repeated.

"That is *precisely* the point, Dr. Buxbaum. It was a mistake. An honest mistake. So her blood count was a little low before an elective hernia repair. So what? We could have given her iron pills and waited a few weeks to fix it. Strictly routine. But no, *you*, Dr. Buxbaum, *you* knew she was moving to the East Coast for a while. She wanted it fixed now. So you gave her a unit of blood in transfusion and did her the next morning."

"See here," Buxbaum stated, "I don't know what connection this has with . . ."

Norton continued in high gear now. "It has every connection, Dr. Buxbaum. It shows quite clearly that none of us is infallible. I'm sure Dr. Buxbaum would like to forget that he subjected Mrs. Wringle to the risk of a transfusion reaction and hepatitis with that pint of blood, just to get her into the operating room! Why didn't you wait a few weeks, Buxbaum? You made a judgment: the hernia neded to be fixed then. It might have incarcerated, or strangulated—whatever your reasons, you made an honest mistake."

"Why don't you shut up?" Buxbaum was getting upset.

Dr. Gregorio interrupted. "Gentlemen, please, if I might continue."

But Norton went on. 'And when she did come back with a fever of a hundred and three and bright yellow eyeballs three months later? Do you remember that? I was here that night. I'm sure Dr. Gregorio remembers the slide of the liver biopsy: 'Acute necrotizing hepatitis.' Each week, thousands of her liver cells dying, as she became sicker and sicker . . . and all because of that fucking unit of blood!"

"I refuse to listen to any more of this," Buxbaum said.

"And what did you tell her family on that last weekend in the intensive care unit?" asked Dr. Norton. " 'We've done everything we can!' you said. I heard you. I remember that you told the nurse, 'Call me, nurse, if the patient goes into coma.' She died the next morning, Buxbaum. A mistake is what killed her. And did anyone mention suspending you from the staff?"

"Why, you bastard. You dirty bastard!" Buxbaum roared. "I'll sue you for slander!"

"Don't be so sure I won't see my lawyer first!" Norton shot back angrily.

Dr. Gregorio banged for silence. "I must be heard. Gentlemen, I must be heard. There will be no lawsuit here, I can promise you that. Now please control yourself. There will be no lawsuit against anyone in this room!"

O'Hara said, "But why? How can you be so sure?"

"What do you mean?" asked Buxbaum.

"Now the returns are all in," said Dr. Gregorio. "Now we can put together all the findings, gentlemen. It took two weeks to get all the slides back from Derrington in San Francisco. I called him in on consultation, as you know. And we now have the chemistry reports from the lab. They arrived this morning. Remember, please, that there was no gross explanation for Herman Wexler's death. In other words, there was no abscess under the anastomosis; the stitches did not fall apart; there was no heart attack; there was no clot to the lung."

The pathologist went on. "The subendocardial hemorrhages, the swollen kidneys, the dark pigment under Mr. Wexler's nails, and the thickening of the skin of his palm immediately indicated some sort of poison."

"Yes, but—" Buxbaum said puzzledly.

Dr. Gregorio ignored the interruption.

"Further, when the area of this patient's Whipple operation was normal and intact . . . well, gentlemen, please. There will be no further action here!"

Gregorio paused for a moment and again surveyed the faces around the dim room.

"You can see from the final slide of Dr. Norton's operation that all anatomoses are intact. No evidence of leak. Here is the suture line between the pancreatic duct and the small bowel. Perfectly well healed . . ."

Gregorio stood up. "Lights, please," he said. When the lights were on and he had shut off the projector, Gregorio coughed importantly and very gently asked, "Dr. Norton. I wonder if you could tell me something? Was the patient's diet very carefully controlled? Was he eating only food from the hospital kitchen?"

Norton stared at him in puzzlement, then stammered, "I . . . the first few days he was eating a strict diet, but . . . but his wife complained about how undernourished he looked, so—when he appeared to be sufficiently recovered—I permitted her to bring him home-cooked food." The doctor looked frightened, confused. He continued to bluster. "However, I did . . . I mean, there were some restrictions placed on what she could offer him."

Gregorio realized he was carrying his little drama a bit too far. He did not want to torture Norton. So he finally interrupted, saying, "That confirms one of my suspicions. And you told Mrs. Wexler that you suspected her husband had cancer?"

"No," Norton blurted out, "as a matter of fact, I was very careful to remind her we had no definite signs of a malignancy, but . . ." He heaved a desperate sigh. "She was certain herself that it was cancer, a repetition of a malignancy from which her brother had died."

"Ahhh." Gregorio sighed in confirmation. "Do you recall, at the autopsy, I pointed out the dark pigment under Mr. Wexler's fingernails and the thickening of the skin of his palm?"

"Yes," Norton replied, nodding in puzzlement.

"I sent the scrapings from the nails along with tissue samples of the liver, kidney, hair, and blood to the lab for heavy-metal analysis. And I just received the report this morning. Gentlemen, the results confirm my suspicions that the cause of death had very little to do with the Whipple operation performed by Dr. Norton. While it *was* an unnecessary operation, the operation itself was not the cause of death."

Gregorio again looked around the room, this time knowing he had the attention of everyone seated about the table.

"Gentlemen. The normal concentration of arsenic in hair is measured at five hundredths of a milligram per hundred milligrams of hair. Anything above one tenth milligram per hundred milligrams of hair can kill a patient. Gentlemen, the arsenic level in Herman Wexler's hair was two tenths of a milligram, more than double the level necessary to indicate poisoning."

"Poison?" Buxbaum asked. "How did that get into the act?"

"What I don't want to do," Gregorio stated, "is try to establish how the poison got to Mr. Wexler. There could be several theories. Possibly Mrs. Wexler made a human error in her kitchen. Possibly it was deliberate—a sort of 'act of love' because she *assumed* her husband had cancer and did not want to see him suffer as her brother had. Nor can we totally rule out a mistake at our end. Mistakes in hospital kitchens are not too uncommon."

"But that's all so speculative," O'Hara pointed out.

"The poison part is *established*," Gregorio stressed flatly. "How the poison got to Wexler is conjecture. Only a thorough police investigation could establish the facts, but do we really want to pursue matters further?"

No one cared to offer a challenge.

EPILOGUE

December 1975, Philadelphia

Harry took Ellen to the American College of Surgeons meeting in Philadelphia the following week. It had been over fourteen years since he had heard the dean's opening-day speech.

The medical school looked much different to him now. Many of the older buildings were gone. The emergency room where he had sewn up Mr. Almond's lip was now replaced by a clean modern structure. The operating room where he had held retractors for Mrs. Marvin Goldstein after Moe's glasses fell into the wound was changed, too. And Moe's Moat was no longer part of the corridors.

There were several highlights of the meeting.

(1) Sims presented a paper on collagen fibers at the scientific session; it had something to do with the passage of sodium ions into membranes during wound healing.

Harry felt a little sorry for Sims, as the black surgeon stood up there and acknowledged the scattered applause. It was a good solid paper. Not a great one. Sims appeared older, with heavy lines etched into his face. He also appeared drained, as if his vitality had been sucked out of him during the past ten years; as if he had suffocated in the laboratory.

Sims, with the best pair of hands City Hospital had ever seen. The masterful surgeon. He was strictly research now. He had been turned into a lab rat. And the big plum, the promise of someday sitting in the Professor's chair, which had been dangled in front of him since his chief residency, was going to somebody else. A new man was being brought in from the outside.

Sims had become a victim of another type of vulture —worse than all the Dr. Grotons, and worse than anyone in private practice; the academic boys, the pompous theoreticians, who stood around with their thumbs up their asses and talked about collagen fibers and rats' bowels, had claimed him as their own. Harry knew that Sims would never recover from the lost ten years.

(2) Ellen went shopping every day, bought several dresses, and seemed to love every minute of it.

(3) Harry slept late and attended only a few of the conferences.

(4) A slightly drunk O'Hara confessed to Harry at the City Hospital cocktail party that he was frightened at turning forty. He had worked hard all his life, he said, and he was afraid a heart attack would claim him before he had "reaped his rewards."

Then he blustered at length about the upcoming malpractice crisis and the doctors' strike in California. "It's gonna cost me twenty-five grand just to take out a few fucking gallbladders, appys, and stomachs," he groaned. "We ought to go on a full-scale strike next month. And I mean *full*. Close every hospital, every emergency room in California. . . .

"Sure, there'll be a few casualties," O'Hara went on, "but this is war. Economic war. As doctors, we're fighting for our lives. We've got to show our strength to those bastards in the state capitol by closing everything. A few deaths because the doctors aren't available, and they'll listen. Believe me, those cocksuckers will listen. . . ."

(5) An equally drunk Buxbaum, who came to the convention alone, was seen with two curvaceous blondes in the lobby of the hotel. The next morning he called up his fourth wife, long-distance, and told her how much he loved and needed her.

(6) Harry ran into Karen Marshall. She was talking with a group of friends about the projected strike. Karen wasn't as adamant as O'Hara. She felt the doctors should stick together by striking, but that the emergency rooms should remain open. She felt a few deaths from ruptured appendices would not help public opinion for the doctors at all.

Karen kissed Harry politely on the cheek. No, she hadn't heard from Moe, but she had heard he was planning to open another office in Beverly Hills soon.

(7) And finally, Harry cornered the dean at the medical-school reunion bash. "I remember, sir," he began, "what you told me about a suit of white armor nearly fifteen years ago—"

"What's that, boy?" The dean looked up with red and weary eyes. "A suit of what, you say?" He took Harry by the arm. "Let me buy you a drink, son, and we'll discuss it at the bar. . . ."

They crossed the room, the dean and Harry, and had a few good ones for the years that had passed between the dean's speeches.

Miriam Wexler was found dead in bed on the week Harry returned from the college meeting in Philadelphia. Her daughter, Sarah, discovered the body. It was established that she died of an overdose of barbituates, and that she had been dead for about two or three days when Sarah found her.

There was no note or letter left anywhere in her room. The people from the coroner's office who picked up Mrs. Wexler's body found her house to be in perfect order and spotlessly clean.

AUTHOR'S NOTE

The doctors in southern California staged a strike in January 1976, following an enormous hike in malpractice premiums throughout the state.

No elective surgeries were performed in hospitals, and very few patients were seen in any doctor's office. The doctors did not remain united, however. They were unsure of their position. There were leaks. Most emergency rooms remained open. Patients were seen and treated by doctors (called "scabs" by their fellow physicians) who did not support the strike.

State committees were formed to look into the situation. Senators and local politicians promised to settle the matter quickly and decisively. The governor even proposed several plans.

As with the heal-in strike in which Harry Norton and Moe Michener had participated at City Hospital years before, nothing substantial was done for the doctors' cause. After approximately six weeks, the doctors, already anxious about their loss of income, went back to work. Most paid the high malpractice premiums, which have since gone even higher and are expected to rise again. Other doctors joined one of several alternative plans which cropped up. They cost less money, but all had loopholes in terms of coverage. Still other physicians "went bare," practicing medicine without any insurance at all and putting all their worldly possessions in the name of their wives or some other "untouchable corporation."

In theory, committees are still working on the problem at the local, state, and national level. In theory, the doctors' malpractice crisis is still being given top priority today.

Meanwhile, the doctor game in the United States goes on at all levels. The number of well-trained applicants for medical-school positions has increased with each passing year. Straight-A students now have a difficult time competing for acceptance. Living conditions for the students, interns, and residents in training at the city, county, and university hospitals have gradually improved.

In the arena of private practice, much more than a single isolated battle is going on. It is a war, a revolution. It is much more than just a matter of medical malpractice premiums now. It is a tightening of the purse strings by Medicaid, MediCal, and Medicare and by private insurance companies. It is a team of state workers invading hospitals and doctors' offices to scrutinize and regulate their practices and their fees. It is an administration committed to national health insurance within the next four years.

And it is, above all, the ominous shadow of increased government intervention, as the system of socialized medicine practiced in England, Sweden, and many of the countries of the world today creeps closer to our shores.